The

Recuperating

Prophet

By

Susan Davis Sandberg

ISBN-13 (Print): 978-1-939577-07-8
ISBN-13 (Kindle): 978-1-939577-08-5
ISBN-13 (ePub): 978-1-939577-09-2

Cover design by John Sandberg
Cover photograph © Vertyr, Shutterstock.com

To my dear sister Peggy

Chapter 1

Robert Locke, while a partner in the firm of Praetzel, Locke and Praetzel, knew it was Stanley's firm even as Aleta did. Both deferred to his wishes at the office.

The question uppermost in Stanley Praetzel's mind that bright summer morning was why couldn't Aleta defer to his wishes at home?

Jamara entered the bedroom as soon as she finished nursing Gerard and handed him to Bertha to change and put in his infant seat in the kitchen. Both women kept the baby with them most of the day.

Jamara closed the door to the master bedroom.

The huge picture window overlooked the orchard, the path to the newly renovated barn, the field beyond and the woods that separated the Praetzel farm from the estate of the senior Praetzels. Its one-way glass gave the occupants privacy and a view simultaneously.

"I don't want a bath," Stanley announced. "I do need the dressing changed."

"We'll do both," Jamara stated firmly.

"We'll do what I say," Stanley proclaimed.

"We'll do what your wife says and what you need."

"I haven't been anywhere. I'm not really dirty."

"You've been lying in bed. Your skin needs a washing."

"My legs only. I can wash the rest of me."

"Your wife was specific."

"Specific?" Stanley asked. "What do you mean specific?"

"Lay down and relax," Jamara said. "I've done this lots."

"She was specific," he murmured, as Jamara went into the bathroom to fill the basin. "I hope it's not what I think it is."

He laid back and stared at the ceiling as Jamara exposed his body in sections, carefully covering each after finishing. It isn't too bad he thought until she neared the end. Just before she did his second leg, he found out what Aleta meant by specific.

The change of dressings came last.

Thoroughly embarrassed, Stanley found himself being dressed as well. He had to admit Jamara knew how to do it without hurting him.

"How'd the injury look?" he asked as she neared the end.

"Quite well, considering," Jamara said.

"She told you, didn't she?"

"She was concerned."

"When Bertha first came, Aleta was worried that Bertha would guess when we had sex and now she describes it?" Stanley asked.

"It was necessary," Jamara said matter-of-factly. "She wanted me to call the doctor if she'd damaged you."

"I told her she hadn't," Stanley said.

"She wanted a second opinion," Jamara replied. "There, we're done."

"Thank you, Jamara. You did a splendid job."

"Mrs. Praetzel told me to tell you to expect another bath tomorrow," Jamara said.

"With the specifics, I assume."

"Yes, Sir."

"She has no idea how private a man I am."

"Yes, Sir. She does. She also knows what you need," Jamara said, handing him his crutches. "Emerita needs an hour in here. You can go watch the workmen."

"Workmen? What workmen?"

"The ones building you a new patio."

"A patio?"

"Your wife said not to worry. If you don't like it, she'll remove it after the construction of the new wing is done."

"What construction?"

"It's starting on Monday," Jamara said. "Didn't you know?"

"I go to the hospital for five days and she rearranges my world," Stanley grumbled.

Paul Locke called from the kitchen when Stanley hobbled into the living room, "Stanley, are you ready to go over the plans with me. I want to walk you through the changes before they're set in stone, so to speak."

"I thought the patio was temporary."

"It is, but you're going to have to live with it for several months so let's make it as inoffensive as possible."

"Aleta's been talking to you too," Stanley mumbled.

"Aleta talks to everybody," Paul said.

"Pay no attention to me. I'm grumpy."

"She said you didn't want a bath," Paul said. "I think I'd enjoy being bathed.

"Show me what's going to happen. There's no use wasting my grumpy mood."

"Come on, man, cheer up. You're alive. Aleta's alive. Mother's alive. In fact, we're all alive. Jocelyn's back home. My family will be here in a week. And we have no guards!"

"Now you've done it!" Stanley exclaimed. "You've killed my bad mood. Now I'll like everything you've done."

"Did you give Aleta any instructions?"

"I told her only wills and contracts for three weeks. How can she get in trouble doing those?"

"Will she do what you ask?"

"Unless God has other plans."

"Does He interfere much?" Aleta's Uncle Paul asked.

"Her last three clients He chose."

"So we may have only today to bask in the sunshine of ordinary life, right?"

"Let's go bask," Stanley said, heading for the front door.

Chapter 2

Aleta strolled down the pleasant, tree-shaded renovated main street in downtown Willow Glen. Stanley owned the property on both sides of the street and had invested heavily in renovating the shops, leasing them to entrepreneurs catering to the wealthy patrons living on the farm-sized estates on the outskirts of Willow Glen.

Above the shops were various offices. The firm of Praetzel, Locke and Praetzel now took half of one side of the street.

Aleta took the elevator to the second floor. It was a tiny five-person elevator tucked in one corner of the lobby behind the open winding staircase.

She greeted Stanley's secretary, Alice and walked into his office on both sides of which were huge aquariums filled with Koi, all of which were named for people in his life. His clients, all of whom were children, were fascinated by his huge walls of swimming of fish.

Aleta searched the tank for the one small lively fantailed goldfish he'd named after her. She had worried that the little one would not survive in a tank full of big fish, but it had.

She left Stanley's office and walked into her own office, now housing their two new associates–Andrew Jackson, a black man as tall and presupposing a figure as her father and Roland Chin, a smaller Chinese man who bought his suits second hand and had a tailor alter them to fit him. It was Aleta's suggestion. Jackson now did the same. .

Roland Chin looked up as she entered.

"Mrs. Praetzel's," he exclaimed. "How are you feeling? How is your husband?"

His voice drew Andrew from the law library.

"How may we help you?" Andrew asked.

"I'm fine, Stanley's fine and I want to sue Mrs. Amend on Stanley's behalf. She had no business having him shot."

The two men smiled. That was an interesting way to put it.

"Have either of you two ever been shot?" she asked.

Both shook their heads.

"Well, it's no picnic," she said,

Both nodded.

"We have a line coming up the stairs," Aleta said. "I'm going to make our library a temporary waiting room. We'll spend the first hour making appointments. We'll interview our prospective clients in Stanley's office."

The two young lawyers donned their coats and straightened their ties. Aleta walked to Alice's desk and gave her instructions.

Aleta went to the door and announced that those in line would be seen in order. She also said that the firm did not handle divorce cases. Two people left immediately.

The people in line were heartened by this change in procedure. They'd heard stories about groups being turned away without a chance to be heard.

The first was a distinguished looking man with streaks of gray in his hair. He held out his hand to Jackson first.

"Tobin Conrad," he said. "Thank you for seeing me." He then shook hands with Chin and finally with Aleta who bade him be seated.

"In ten words or less, give us the gist of your problem," she said.

"Age discrimination, but it must be handled delicately. I don't want to be out on the streets."

"How many words was that?" Aleta asked Mr. Tobin. The two associates stared at her.

"Eight in the first sentence. Sorry about the nine additional."

"We'll take your case, Mr. Conrad," Aleta said. "Mr. Chin will see you at one o'clock this afternoon. Can you leave work at that time?"

"I can take a late lunch," Conrad said. "Thank you."

"Next," Aleta said into the intercom.

The gentleman was old and walked with a cane.

Andrew Jackson shook his hand, as did Roland Chin.

"Thomas Graves," he said. "It's about my wife."

"Mr. Graves, Mr. Chin will see you at 9:30 this morning. You will be his first priority. Will that be satisfactory?"

The old man pulled out a pocket watch.

"That's a long wait," he said.

"Alice, please come in here," Aleta said.

In a moment Alice appeared. "When you finish with Mr. Conrad, have Mr. Graves sign fee schedule 100. Then have him wait in our lounge. He's been up all night with his wife. He needs to rest. His appointment is at 9:30 with Mr. Chin. Block off the entire morning for this case."

Chin didn't know how she knew what Mr. Graves needed. He assumed that she had talked to him earlier. He refused to consider the alternate explanation—that this slender auburn-haired beauty was a prophet of God. He had chosen to work here because she was an outstanding trial lawyer.

Aleta accepted three cases and rejected four after asking only a question or two of each one. The two men with her liked the cases she took on and silently bet that the young man who entered the office next wouldn't be rejected. They liked his pleasant smile.

"How old are you?" Aleta asked.

"Twenty-one," the young man replied.

"Prove it," Aleta said.

Aleta barely glanced at the driver's license he offered. "You would walk into a lawyer's office and produce a fake ID? Dumb move."

"It ain't fake."

"Then it's not yours," Aleta said. "I don't represent liars. Now why are you so intent on lying about your age? You don't smoke or drink."

"How do you know?"

"You aren't old enough."

"I am so. I got the birth certificate to prove it."

"Show me," Aleta said.

He produced a birth certificate.

"Sit down. Before I prove this isn't yours, will you level with me?"

"I'm telling the truth."

Aleta picked up the phone and punched in a number. "Ed are you in your office... Good...David Roach, 221 Walnut Street... Yes, that's right... I'll wait..."

The young man fidgeted as he waited.

Finally, Aleta thanked Ed and hung up.

She smiled at the young man. "David Roach is indeed twenty-one, and he has a younger brother, Tyler and two sisters."

"That's right," the boy said.

"Don't you have an uncle or aunt or grandparent to take care of your younger sisters?"

"I'm their legal guardian," the boy said.

"So what kind of problem is facing a twenty-one-year-old guardian of two young girls?"

"There was this auto accident. The guy rammed into my car and Molly was hurt and he don't have no insurance and he just says, 'get yourself a lawyer kid and sue me.'"

"Stanley will handle your case. He comes back on Monday. By then you better have hold of the truth, Tyler, and be ready to trust a man who can help you not only take care of Molly but stay together as a family. You have an appointment for... You're upset..."

The boy's head bobbed.

"This is an emergency?"

Aleta picked up the phone and dialed a number. "Stanley are you out in the yard staring at the men digging?"

"How did you know?"

"I have an emergency. It's right up your alley, but I think he thinks child advocates are wimps."

"He's passing as an adult?"

"Right."

"I don't want him!" Stanley said.

"Stanley!" Aleta gasped.

She held out the phone. "He won't take you because you lied."

"Can he really do what you said?" the boy asked.

"Yes."

"Is he expensive?"

"He costs less than me."

"How come?" the boy asked, intrigued.

"Because children get half rate," Aleta said. "I know you're Tyler. As a court officer I have to report that fact. Now do you want help or not?

The boy looked desperate, "Can you get him to take me?"

"No. I can't. But maybe you can."

She handed him the phone.

He cleared his throat. "Mr. Praetzel. It's Tyler Roach— no relation to the bug... Sorry about that. That's how my brother used to... I need a lawyer. My kid sister was hurt in a car crash this morning and the hospital won't keep her because I ain't got insurance and I need someone now. The guy wasn't insured."

"What's your sister's name?"

"Molly. She's twelve."

"Give Mrs. Praetzel the phone."

"Ship him over. I'll call Wayne."

Aleta handed Tyler the form. "Correct your name on this form. Alice will give you directions to our home office. Mr. Praetzel will be the man on crutches. He's already seeing that you sister receives the care she needs."

Aleta put her hand on his. "Tell him about your father. He can help."

"How did you know?" Tyler asked.

"My private investigator told me," Aleta said. "Did you think I was psychic?"

"Sorta," he confessed. "You knew I wasn't David."

"Easy. You took off your school ring," Aleta said. "You've got tan marks around where it was."

Roland Chin breathed a sigh of relief. There must be a logical explanation to her knowing about Graves. He didn't mind the fact that she sometimes predicted death. He just didn't want to discover that she could read minds.

The woman who entered next was a well-dressed matronly woman who dismissed him with a glance. He fervently wished that Mrs. Praetzel would reject her.

"Mrs. Lanning, is it?" Aleta said. "Your case doesn't interest me."

"But, you're a lawyer. You represent people," she argued.

"Mr. Chin is a lawyer," Aleta said, turning to Roland. "He's been wanting to try a criminal case."

"I'm not a criminal!" the woman shot back.

Aleta then smiled at the man seated on the other side of her.

"Mr. Jackson is also interested in dealing with criminals"

"Shoplifting is a sickness," the woman protested.

"One easily cured," Aleta said coldly. "Stay out of stores."

"I want you to represent me," Mrs. Lanning insisted.

The two men rose as one. Mrs. Lanning refused to get up.

"I insist. I won't be turned away."

"I am not available," Aleta said. "Good day, Mrs. Lanning."

"What if I refuse to go?"

"I will call the police and charge you with trespassing."

"You wouldn't dare."

Aleta picked up the phone.

"Chief, I need a police officer at my office to arrest a trespasser."

"You're bluffing," Mrs. Lanning smirked.

"Mrs. Praetzel doesn't bluff," Roland stated flatly.

"I don't believe you," Mrs. Lanning said folding her arms.

"Mr. Chin, see who else is waiting. Bring anyone who will not mind discussing his or her case with us while we're waiting for the police."

Roland Chin came back with a man hunched over with age gripping a gold-headed black cane with a gnarled hand.

"Dr. Schwartzman wants to execute a durable power of attorney," Roland said.

"Dr. Schwartzman, have a seat," Aleta said. "I will be with you in a minute. Please ignore Mrs. Lanning. The police will be removing her in a moment."

She looked at Chin and asked, "How many more are there?"

"A couple dozen," Chin relied.

"A durable power of attorney will take a while and it must be done immediately. This is the case I came in for today."

"He said Mrs. Cook sent him," Roland said.

"You two take care of the rest," Aleta instructed. "Reject any person you don't like. You may each take on one criminal case that intrigues you. Turn away the rest."

The two associates left the office where Mrs. Lanning was still sitting. Dr. Schwartzman sat down in a chair nearer the desk.

"We need to speak discreetly," Aleta advised the doctor. "Do you want a medical or financial or both?"

"Both."

"Write the names of your banks on this paper."

Dr. Schwartzman wrote down two names.

Aleta called Alice on the intercom. "Alice, I need the bank power of attorney forms for two banks. Please come and get the names."

Alice entered the room. "Mrs. Lanning's presence prevents us from speaking. How quickly can you get the forms?"

"We have a copy of the forms required for every bank in the Tri-City area."

Aleta smiled. "Leave it to Stanley. He plans for every contingency."

Alice left at once.

Dr. Schwartzman nodded happily and relaxed. Martha was right. This was a good place.

"Now," Aleta said, "Why do you want a durable power of attorney and why do you want it to go into effect immediately when you are obviously capable of handling your own financial and medical decisions?"

Alice walked in with three forms. Aleta glanced at the bank forms and then at the generic medical form. She handed the medical form back to Alice.

"Dr. Schwartzman has prepared a form. We need it typed up, signed and notarized before he leaves today."

Herve Schwartzman reached into his inner coat pocket and withdrew an envelope. Mrs. Lanning stared at the envelope that the old hand held out shakily. Aleta took it, withdrew the papers inside and read them.

She handed the sheaf to Alice. "Don't change a word. All the necessary information is on it."

"Why not use my original?" Dr. Schwartzman asked.

"You believe we are in for a court battle. You wouldn't be here otherwise. It is best if the document is whole. You have added notes in the margin which could be subjected to censure."

The old man nodded.

"Now Dr. Schwartzman, do I have your permission to name my two partners and our two associates as backups?"

"Why so many?" Schwartzman asked.

"My husband has a private plane. My father is learning to fly. Neither of our associates leaves the ground regularly."

The old man smiled a crooked smiled. He enjoyed the playfulness of the response. He nodded.

Alice left.

Two Willow Glen police officers entered the office and arrested Mrs. Lanning, stood her up, handcuffed her, Mirandized her and led her away.

Aleta returned to Schwartzman, apologized for the interruption. She smiled when she realized Dr. Schwartzman had thoroughly enjoyed the drama.

"Now why are we executing a durable power of attorney today?"

"My sons have scheduled a meeting with me to go over my financial affairs again," Herve Schwartzman said. "I've been having a series of small strokes. They seem to correlate with arguments with my children over financial decisions. I have struggled back from a couple of these strokes. If I'm not to have a massive stroke, I must get rid of the causes. I also want to change doctors. Martha said you could help me with that."

"Why are you changing doctors?" Aleta asked.

"Because Dr. Trattner is strictly a medicine man."

"A 'medicine man'?" Aleta queried puzzled.

"Only deals with drugs. No clue as to the role of stress," Schwartzman replied. "He nods at my supposition but doesn't even put a note on his pad. Of course, he doesn't have a pad anymore. He has a computer gizmo. Maybe it doesn't have a space for 'stress' on it."

"You hold a doctorate in psychology?"

"Clinical psychology," Schwartzman replied. "I'm also a psychiatrist. I need to know more than my students. You'd think one doctor would appreciate the expertise of another, but Dr. Trattner doesn't."

Aleta nodded. "I will see you are transferred to Dr. Hughes' care immediately. You do not need that kind of stress right now. Do not give it another thought."

Aleta pressed the intercom button.

"Alice, make an appointment with Dr. Hughes for Dr. Schwartzman for ten this morning. Tell the receptionist that Martha Cook and Aleta Praetzel consider this an emergency. Have a cab here at nine forty-five to transport him."

"I have a car," Dr. Schwartzman objected.

"Dr. Schwartzman, believe me, we are walking on thin ice here. I know that what we are doing will relieve you of considerable pressure and that this is the time to do this."

"I feel okay."

"I do not want you driving. That also stresses you out. Please take my advice."

"Yes. Yes. I will take your advice," he agreed taking out his handkerchief and wiping his brow.

"Dr. Schwartzman, you have the right to cancel the power of attorney at any time. I will, however, not let you be pressured into it. Now, while we wait for Alice, see if you can guess which fish is named Martha Cook while I check on my associates.

The old man smiled, his smile slightly more crooked. "Does Martha know?"

"She loves her fish," Aleta said. "Our next baby, if it's a girl, will be named after her. Did you know she and my grandmother cooked up a scheme to get Stanley and I together?"

"Are you happy with Martha's choice of husband for you?"

"Ecstatic!" Aleta said. "This is his office. Those are his fish. I will be back shortly."

Aleta dropped in on Jackson and Chin, again between interviews. She approved of both criminal cases that the two had taken on and told Chin he was to handle the Ronda Lunt case."

"Who is that?"

"Her daughter is in line."

"Is there a special case for me?" Andrew asked.

"Tobin is yours," Aleta said. "It's a class action suit. I thought you knew that. He shook hands with you first."

"I missed that," Andrew admitted abashed.

"He likes you."

"But I think he is expecting to see you this afternoon."

"For some reason, I won't be back," Aleta said.

Roland's world was rocked again. How could she know that?

When Aleta returned to Stanley office, Dr. Herve Schwartzman observed casually, "Your husband specializes in representing children. Does he plan to move up?"

Aleta laughed. "Stanley has said a thousand times, 'I'm a child advocate, Aleta. That's what I am. That's all I ever want to be!' So, Dr. Schwartzman, he doesn't plan to 'move up' as you put it. Once in a while, I drag him into a new area so he can stretch his legal wings. He's a brilliant attorney."

"Better than you?" Schwartzman asked slyly.

"I think so," Aleta said. "He disagrees, so I had to promise not to get involved in his arena. That leaves me a lot of law to dabble in."

"Interesting," Herve Schwartzman murmured.

"Have you figured out which Koi is named Martha?"

"That one," the old man said. "The one with the pretty tail. And you're that little fan-tailed goldfish flitting about."

"How'd you know?"

"I looked for the most special looking Koi in the tank, for Martha and I figured your husband would pick a unique fish for you."

"Clever analysis," Aleta remarked. "Where did you teach?"

"University of Chicago."

"Do you know any good psychologists in the Tri-City area?"

"Several," he replied letting Aleta lead him.

"Do you know anything about the Rape Crisis Center?"

"Yes."

"I need a name," Aleta said.

"Reggie Barre."

"Thank you."

"How long ago?"

Aleta thought for a moment then said, "Over a week, less than two."

"Was the man caught?"

"Both were," Aleta said. "It happened in a hospital."

"The serial rapists," Schwartzman commented. "I read about the case. Didn't they think you were a retarded deaf mute?"

"Yes," Aleta said. "At the time I was under orders not to speak."

"Whose orders?"

"Stanley's," Aleta said. "It's complicated."

"We're whiling away the time, so tell me."

"Simply put I vowed to obey him on our wedding day. When he evokes that promise, I do what he asks."

"That's a dangerous power to give a person."

"Stanley has never misused it. He has saved my life more than once. This time he gave the order when he saw that talking was sapping my strength. I was suffering from severe anemia at the time. Then as I was being driven home, I was involved in an auto accident and I had no identification."

"Surely he would expect you to speak and identify yourself."

"Actually, I knew he wouldn't."

"Your obedience is that absolute?"

"It must be. To pick and choose is not to obey at all."

"Did he order you to go to the Rape Crisis Center?"

"He was going to. I asked him not to, so he didn't. He said he would appreciate it if I would walk in the door. If I got a bad vibe, I could walk out and he'd never mention it again."

"Why did you ask me for a name when you have an out?"

"Because I want to honor his request."

"Interesting," Schwartzman murmured. "He is a very self- assured man to keep such a power under control."

"I guess he is."

"I'm surprised he'd send you to a counselor."

"He says only another woman can truly understand what I went through."

"He is probably correct."

Alice arrived with documents, which Herve Schwartzman read and signed. Alice notarized them. A copy was given to Dr. Schwartzman to hand Dr. Hughes when he visited him.

"From now on you can't sign any authorizations. Dr. Hughes's office will have to fax everything to me," Aleta said. She turned. "Alice I need an authorization to transfer the medical records from Dr. Trattner to Dr. Hughes."

"Are any of your bank accounts joint accounts?" Aleta asked.

"No. My kids made an appointment at both banks today."

"What time?"

"One thirty–after lunch–at First National," Herve said.

"Have they filed for a competency hearing?"

"Not yet."

"Alice, check on that, will you?"

"Yes, Mrs. Praetzel," Alice said and left.

"Is your will in order, Dr. Schwartzman?"

"Yes."

"Do all your beneficiary forms match the terms of your will?"

"Yes."

"Good.   I will deal with your children.   You concentrate on remembering that I have taken over."

"My children will raise a fuss."

"Tell them to call me. It is my job to deal with them now with regard to any medical or financial decisions."

"They aren't going to like this."

"Now I want all your cards," Aleta said. "I will be canceling all of them. I am assuming some of your children have use of those accounts. I will tell them I've cancelled them."

"How do I get money?"

"How much do you need a week?"

"Three hundred?"

"We can start there," Aleta said. "Tomorrow I will send a bookkeeper to your house to review your finances. She will arrange for automatic payments where necessary. We won't let anything go unchecked. I am available to take your call anytime I'm not in court. Your children will not have that privilege after the first call."

"Your bill?"

"I am expensive," Aleta said.

"Martha said you would be," Herve Schwartzman said.

"Three hundred an hour," Aleta said forthrightly, setting the contract in front of her client. The old man looked it over carefully.

"Any senior discount?" he asked wryly.

"That is the senior discount," Aleta smiled.

He signed the contract.

Alice reentered the room with the authorization to switch doctors. Both signed.

"No competency hearing is scheduled," Alice reported.

"Good," Aleta remarked.

"The cab's here," Alice announced.

Aleta's father entered her office and was introduced to Dr. Schwartzman. When the doctor left, Aleta fell into her father's arms and cried.

"Rape is assault," her father declared. "You were beaten."

"Dad, he ejaculated inside of me!" Aleta whispered infuriated. "That's more..."

Her father gathered her into his arms.

"I know. I know," he said softly, his fury barely contained. "He violated you."

Tears sprang into his eyes.

"Oh, Dad, I feel so ashamed," Aleta murmured, burying her head in her father's shoulder.

Alice entered.

"Are you... excuse me."

Aleta pulled away and wiped her eyes on the handkerchief her father held out. "It's okay, Alice. Just give me a couple minutes, then send in the last person."

"I can take you to the center before lunch," her father said.

"Maybe I should," Aleta pondered. "I do have a name. Reggie Barre. But, she might not have..."

"I'll call. Just tell the last client, Stanley will take him," Robert said.

"It's a woman," Alice said.

"Show her in," Aleta decided. "I'll do it your way, Dad."

Kim Witherspoon was ushered into Stanley's office. A woman the same age as Aleta, she gasped delightedly when she saw the fish. "Oh Kitty would love to see this! Would it be possible? I know this is an office, but it's so nice in here. And she can't do much anymore."

"Yes, you can bring her to see the fish," Aleta said. "How old is Kitty?"

"Not quite five," Kim Witherspoon said as Aleta glanced at the form Kim handed her. Kim walked closer to the tank. "Do they have names?"

"Yes, they do," Aleta said. "Which brings me to something I must tell you."

The plump blonde woman turned, her eyes filling with tears. "You're my last hope."

"I was merely going to have you speak with my husband, Stanley. This is his office. He named the fish. You could bring your daughter. He'll be back on Monday."

The woman's face fell. "I don't really know what I was expecting, but maybe just seeing the fish will be enough. Monday is fine."

"Stanley is a very fine lawyer."

"It's just I heard you were here today and accepting clients. I tried calling others but if they didn't reject me outright, they offered appointment weeks from now. There isn't that much time."

"Are you facing eviction?" Aleta asked.

The smile was wan. "I guess you could put it that way. Kitty is dying of cancer."

Aleta blanched.

"Your child is dying?" she managed to whisper.

"That's why I'm here," she said. "There's a local charity that grants wishes to dying children. When I found out she'd be first on Mrs. Fraza's list, I didn't submit her name anywhere else."

"What's the name of the group?"

"Tri-City Wishes for Kids," Kim said reaching into her purse and pulling out a flyer. "That's Kitty. It was taken last year."

"What is Kitty's wish?"

"To go to Disney World."

"Bring Kitty here at one thirty to see the fish. I will see that Stanley is here to talk with you. Can you do that?"

"Yes, I can."

"My husband is a child advocate. He's just recovering from surgery so he's free to devote time to your problem."

"One thirty. We'll be here. All three of us," Kim said enthusiastically.

Aleta walked her to Alice's desk. "Witherspoon. One thirty. Mr. Praetzel."

"At your home office?"

"No, here. Kitty wants to see the fish," Aleta said. "Please call Stanley and tell him."

Robert appeared. "The doctor will see you in ten minutes. Are you ready?"

"The hospital faxed over this form. I filled in the data. It needs your signature."

"Dr. Schwartzman?" Aleta asked.

"Yes."

Aleta signed the form and then said to Alice, "You know where I'll be."

Chapter 3

Fifteen minutes later, Robert Locke was in the men's room at the Rape Crisis Center talking to Stanley on his cell.

"I'm sorry, Stanley," he said. "I was trying to slow her down, stop her actually. I never saw anyone in a law office move that fast through a waiting room full of people. It was wild. One woman wouldn't leave. She had her arrested and saw another client while waiting for the police. Andrew and Roland are ecstatic. They have real cases."

"So is Aleta talking to a counselor now?" Stanley asked.

"I told the woman running the center it was an emergency. She said she'd see Aleta herself."

"So how come you're not in there?"

"Aleta shook Dr. Barre's hand and then told me to leave. Aleta said she was supposed to be there."

"She had a premonition," Stanley exclaimed. "She doesn't need this now. Dad, stay close. Don't let them put her in a hospital."

"Trust me. I'll park outside the door."

"Call the police if you have to."

"I have a better idea. I'll call Dr. Chesney and ask him what to do."

Inside the room, Aleta sat down opposite Dr. Reggie Barre, a woman of considerable girth with round cheeks and dark brown eyes. Her dark brown curly hair framed her face giving it a softness that made her an easy person for people to confide in.

"When you were raped, was that the last time you prayed?" Aleta asked pointedly.

"We're here to talk about you," Dr. Barre said surprised but not shocked. Women frequently tried to steer the conversation away from their own trauma.

"That's what I came here to do," Aleta said. "So let's get that out of the way. I was raped twice while strapped to a hospital bed. It may have been more comfortable than the hard concrete of an alley in the pouring rain, but rape is rape. Now tell me why are you so angry with God? He didn't rape you."

"He allowed it to happen. He just stood by and watched."

"He was answering your prayer," Aleta said firmly.

Dr. Barre's face reddened as the words reached deep into her soul where her anger lay like a stone.

"I was told you needed to see me right away," she accused heatedly. "I'm in no mood for a lecture."

"When my father called, I'd broken down. I was in tears. Dad is having trouble with what happened to me and my sister."

"Your sister was raped too?"

"Molested would be the layman's term," Aleta replied evenly. "Legally she was raped. It was ugly."

"Rape is always ugly," Dr. Barre agreed, slowly reining in her fury. "But let's concentrate on you."

"God wants you to know that I prayed too."

"And did He stop your rape?" Dr. Barre asked. The words slipped out past her usual safeguards against getting personal.

"No."

"So your prayer wasn't answered either."

"I can't say that."

"A man raped you. Did he complete the act or did he stop midway?"

"Both men completed the act. The second was worse than the first. He was more violent. I didn't know I could stand that much pain without screaming."

"Why didn't you?"

"I'll give you the short version. I was in California on a case, my sister's case to be exact. I was severely anemic and the case took all the stuffing out of me. My husband said that talking was making me weak so he ordered me not to speak. Then there was an auto accident. I didn't have identification on me. I couldn't tell the doctor who I was or that I was pregnant. The doctor found out I was anemic and ordered an iron pill. The dose was too high for me in my condition. I fought taking the pill that evening. The nurse thought I'd eject it by vomiting so she strapped me down for the night. The orderly with her was one of the rapists. She told him I was a retarded deaf-mute."

"That's why you weren't killed."

"It's also why I was raped. The two rapists only went after young women who were comatose or unable to speak," Aleta explained.

"Why do you say your prayer was heard?"

"Because it was," Aleta proclaimed.

"I think the first thing you need to do is accept the reality that God didn't answer your prayer."

"Jesus was crucified," Aleta said abruptly. "God heard him too and didn't stop that either."

"So what use is prayer?" Dr. Barre asked irritably.

"Prayer is not about what God can do for you but so you know you aren't alone."

"Bullshit!" Reggie exploded. "You won't ever heal buried under that garbage."

"Are you telling me you're healed?"

"I've learned to live with what happened."

"Bullshit!" Aleta retorted. "I don't intend to live with it."

"You can't erase it," Dr. Barre said. "Such a serious trauma leaves a deep scar that never quite heals."

"So you're saying the best I can hope for is to shove it down so deep, it surfaces rarely and go on as if it never happened."

"Think of it as a rough rock with multiple sharp edges. Therapy dulls the sharpness of the edges so that the rock isn't constantly irritating one's psyche."

"How's the rock in your soul? Smoothed over yet?"

"Pretty much."

"Then why are you planning to kill yourself?"

"I'm not planning to kill myself," Dr. Barre said calmly.

"You prayed two prayers that day. God has answered the first with a yes, but all you remember is the no."

"The no was the important one."

"When I was praying and the rape was happening I felt all that you felt. I wasn't in some ethereal world and thus floating above the experience. I felt every jab, despaired every second that it would never end. When the first man was done, I hoped with every fiber of my being that the second man wouldn't take his turn. I couldn't believe I was going to have to go through the horror a second time. And then it turned out to be worse. He was bigger, stronger, and angrier. The rape went on forever. I think that he was a man who needed the woman to fight to reach sexual satisfaction. I begged God to shorten my agony. It didn't happen.

"But, He was there with me. I didn't feel it at the time. I felt abandoned. Bereft. Forsaken. That was the hardest part. Pain is a singular phenomenon. One can share the experience later, but one endures it alone.

"Afterward, because I couldn't tell anyone, my isolation was complete. Finally, a nurse gave me a pen. She didn't unstrap my hands. I was afraid she'd take away the chart so I only dared write two words. I wrote 'rape' and 'pregnant'.

"They misunderstood my message. They examined me. I had been raped. I was torn up pretty badly. They assumed I was worried about a pregnancy, so they scheduled me for a D&C.

"I couldn't believe God wanted my baby aborted. Still, I couldn't speak. My husband had been hunting for me all night. He didn't make it to my side in time. I have never known such despair. My tears just kept coming. No one would ask me a question or give me a pen. They were so sure of their decision. I can't say I blame them. I was obviously a nursing mother. They assumed I couldn't be pregnant. Even understanding why didn't help."

"Did you pray?" Dr. Barre asked, captivated by the story.

"With my whole heart."

"And?"

"The doctor paused at the last second and asked me if I was pregnant and I nodded and he stopped, and Stanley came and took me home."

"This not talking makes no sense," Dr. Barre remarked.

"It was my wedding gift to my husband. If he gives me an order, I obey it."

"But surely he expected you to break your silence when you found yourself in the hospital especially when your unborn child's life was at stake."

"No, he didn't. To obey when it's convenient is not to obey at all," Aleta said.

She stopped suddenly.

"My cell is vibrating," she said as she pulled her cell from her pocket and glanced at the caller's name. "Do you have a fax number?"

"Work can wait," Dr. Barre said. "What we're doing here is more important."

"Dr. Barre, you are so wrong. This call is more important."

She opened her cell. "Yes, Dr. Hughes... Yes I will authorize it. Fax the form to the Rape Crisis Center. That's where I am. I'll wait for it, but please go ahead with the treatment."

Dr. Barre stammered out the number and Aleta repeated it.

Aleta Praetzel was still in Dr. Barre's office when a second call came before she could explain the first.

"Sorry," she said. "This can't wait either, but please Dr. Barre, be aware that I am in crisis... Hello, Dr. Trattner, Aleta Praetzel here... Yes, I did that... It was my client's choice... The recommendation came from another source. The fact that Dr. Hughes is my neurologist is coincidental... My office did that...? No, I wasn't aware, however, I will look into it... No, do not ignore it... My associates were acting hastily because the situation called for it. And yes, I will take you to court... As for Dr. Schwartzman, if you attempt to approach him at this time, I will nail your hide to the barn door. Am I clear...? No, I never bluff... Yes, do that. Getting legal advice would be a good idea. Goodbye, Sir."

"Now, Dr. Barre, my recitation of the event may have seemed unemotional to you because, frankly, it was. I'm not interested in reliving the nightmare on any level. I am only willing to deal with the feelings I have as they pop to the surface. Right now I'm grieving over my loss of...of sexual purity. Until this happened the only man I knew was my husband. I feel... er... contaminated. There seems to be no end to the guilt. I'm a prophet. Why can't I handle this better?"

"A prophet?" Dr. Barre said. "Perhaps we should start with that fantasy."

"Excuse me, Dr. Barre, that is not a fantasy."

Aleta looked at her cell phone. "I have to take this."

"If you don't turn that thing off, you will have to find yourself a new therapist."

Aleta looked into Dr. Barre's brown eyes. "You need me. Come to my house for supper at six... Hello, Aleta Praetzel here... Yes, Mr. Schwartzman. Your father executed a durable power of attorney this morning and I am in charge of all medical and financial decisions... Yes I changed his neurologist at his request... No, I will not let Dr. Trattner near him. He upsets him... I am not concerned with your friendship. My first concern is my client... Dr. Hughes is right. Dr. Schwartzman should not be bothered at this time... Yes, I will meet with the family and answer your questions. Two o'clock...? Yes, I will come to the hospital... Goodbye."

"Dr. Barre, please excuse these interruptions. Please come for supper. We can talk in my office afterward. I believe I can help you."

Startled, Dr. Barre protested. "I'm the therapist."

"Yes, you are. And when I'm your patient, we will meet here. But tonight we will talk about you. Tonight there will be no interruption."

Dr. Barre shook her head in disbelief. "Why do I believe you?"

"If you come tonight, I promise that the next time we meet, my cell phone will be left in my car. I have a great cook."

Dr. Barre smiled. "How can I refuse such an offer?"

The two shook hands and Aleta smiled. "I'm having a big barbecue tomorrow night to celebrate Stanley not being killed. You are invited. Don't worry. It's strictly social. Most of my doctors will be there so you'll find yourself surrounded by familiar faces, which reminds me I should invite Dr. Hughes."

Aleta breezed out of the office and her father paused to ask Dr. Barre how the session went.

"I'm not sure," Dr. Barre said. "She invited me to supper. She said she had a great cook."

"Bertha is that," Robert grinned. "That's one of the reasons I married her. See you at six."

"A family meal?" Dr. Barre said. "I'm not sure..."

"Don't worry. We don't bite. Hubbs will be there. He's their groomsman. Paul is living with them until the rest of his family gets here. His daughter came back from California with my youngest daughter and somehow it seemed reasonable to eat together until Paul's family gets here. My mother and her new husband will be there. If you're going to help Aleta... but wait, this isn't about Aleta. She wants to help you, doesn't she?"

"I'm sorry," Dr. Barre said. "Give her my regrets."

"You've got to be kidding!" Robert said. "Didn't you learn anything about Aleta in the last hour?"

"I learned she's used to getting her own way."

"Doesn't fit with the rape, does it?"

Dr. Barre thought for a moment. "No, it doesn't."

"As I said, we don't bite. One meal with us will jump start your work with Aleta. I think that's where you're heading. She needs you. Please don't let her down."

"I'll be there," Dr. Barre agreed.

Chapter 4

Stanley had just finished lunch when Robert delivered Aleta to the house. She headed straight for the bedroom. Bertha fixed up a milk shake and followed. She emerged with the empty glass and the message that Aleta had an appointment with the Schwartzman clan at the hospital at two. The men at the table frowned.

"That gives her barely two hours for a nap," Stanley protested.

"I'll drive her," Bertha said. "I'll wait and drive her home."

"She invited a guest for supper," Robert said, "the head of the Rape Crisis Center, Dr. Barre."

"I'll make the dessert now," Bertha said. "Boy, it's a good thing she hired Jamara."

As if on cue, Gerard started to cry.

"Bring him in here," Bertha said.

"He needs to be fed," Jamara said.

"Robert won't mind," Bertha said. "And Paul will probably sketch you."

Jamara glanced over at Paul, "Really?"

"I would love to," Paul said. "Is it alright with you?"

"I'll get the baby," Jamara said.

Kitty Witherspoon was wheeled into Stanley Praetzel's office at precisely one thirty. Her eyes grew wide as she saw the huge aquariums that covered both walls. She was entranced with the flirty little fan-tailed goldfish. Before long she discovered a small Koi swimming around along the bottom of the tank.

"Does the little one have a name?" the child asked.

"Her name's Kitty."

The child looked up. "That's my name."

"She's new. I just met her today. So I named her after you."

"Mommy, she's got my name!" Kitty squealed delightedly.

"Watch her for me for a few minutes while I fetch my partner, okay?"

The child adjusted her hat.

"You can take off your hat in here," Stanley said. "There's no sun to give you a sunburn."

He hobbled to the other room quickly. He told Alice he'd be in with Robert. After a brief consultation and one phone call, Stanley was back in his office. Robert Locke was with him.

Stanley introduced the Witherspoon family to his law partner and showed them the fish named after his mother, Judge Davis, and then announced, "Mr. Locke has arranged for private airplane transportation to Florida. His stepfather, Professor Luther owns a plane. Mr. Locke will be the co-pilot. You leave Saturday morning. Meanwhile, I will work or your case."

"Mrs. Fraza won't give you any money," Kim interjected. "Especially if someone else takes us."

"I'm going to force her hand," Stanley declared. "You just get ready for the trip."

"Suppose she doesn't come through?" Kyle, Kitty's father, asked. "Will the trip be cancelled?"

"No," Robert said. "Your half is being underwritten by a private party who wants to remain anonymous. I'm paying half the cost because I'd planned this trip a while ago. It's my honeymoon. My daughter's been promised this trip. She was told she could bring a friend. Her cousin will be coming. Both girls are sixteen."

The two parents stood dumbfounded.

Kitty was the first to speak. "When's Saturday?"

"In two days," her mother replied absently. "Your honeymoon?"

"It'll be my fourth honeymoon since I got married," Robert said with a broad smile. "This is the one I planned. My daughter insisted on coming on this one."

"I am going to hold Doris Fraza accountable," Stanley said. "However, I want your daughter to get her wish. First, there'll be the plane ride. We will have a mattress in the plane. Kitty can use it for part of the trip. You'll get to stay in the Disney Hotel and visit the park and buy a stuffed Tigger. Robert's wife Bertha is a practical nurse. She will help you care for Kitty."

By the time Aleta left for the hospital, she knew what Stanley had arranged for Kitty Witherspoon. Bertha spent the drive reassuring Aleta that she'd be fine when her father and she left for their Disney World honeymoon.

"Your Uncle Paul is eager to get a couple more work days. Hubbs will be here. Jamara will come and nurse Gerard. She can change Stanley's dressings. There are still meals in the freezer, and there will be lots of leftovers from the barbecue"

As she talked, Aleta began to relax. "You're right."

"If you'd feel better, I can ask Lauren and Lyle to come over."

"No, that's not necessary. I'm feeling tired, but I'm not working this weekend, so I'll have plenty of time to rest."

"Are you going to be able to handle this meeting with Dr. Schwartzman's family?"

"I believe so. I just have to remember that I don't need their approval. Dr. Schwartzman made the decision, not me. I don't even need to defend it, merely to uphold it."

"Remember, if his family had been easy to deal with he wouldn't have taken the route he did. Treat them like a cantankerous opponent. They may love their father, but they have no reason to love you."

"Thanks Bertha. That's good advice."

When they arrived at the hospital, Aleta breezed past the group waiting for her in the waiting room and headed for the nurse's station. Bertha, who was following her, saw a couple of men rise from their seats in the waiting area. She hesitated. A thin-faced, clean-shaven man with sharp features, spotting Bertha, asked if the woman passing by was Mrs. Praetzel.

Bertha acknowledged that she was. The man, his eyes narrowing and a deep frown appearing between his brows, asked Bertha where Mrs. Praetzel was going.

"To check on her client's condition," Bertha replied.

"I need to know that too," the small man decided.

A second man, a twin of the first except for his beard, jumped up. "We should both go."

"What you should do," Bertha said stepping in their path, "is sit down and wait."

"We want to know how he is," the bearded man insisted trying to step around her.

"They will stop talking if you show up," Bertha warned.

"Who are you anyway?" one of the women asked.

"I'm Mrs. Praetzel's nurse."

A second woman, the shortest of the group, whose plumpness rounded her face and softened her features, rose. "She has a two o'clock appointment with us."

Bertha glanced at her watch. "She will be on time."

"George," the bearded man said, addressing a third man, "can't we get her removed? This is ridiculous. We are intelligent adults. We can make decisions for our father. We don't need some stranger messing in our affairs."

"David, the nurse is right. Let us all sit down and wait," George Pritiken said. "She is acting appropriately."

"Well, I don't like it," the bearded man said. "She walked right by us."

"I'm not waiting!" the thin-faced man declared.

"Jacob, where are you going?" His brother asked.

"To find her!" Jacob said.

David trotted after him.

"Where'd she go?"

"That room down the hall."

"Can we just barge in?" David asked, hurrying after his brother. "Suppose it's someone's room?"

Jacob put his hand on the door as it opened.

"Excuse me," Aleta said, brushing past the two men and hurrying back toward the waiting room. Jacob and David found themselves rushing to catch up.

Aleta entered the waiting room at exactly two o'clock, introduced herself to the two women and had just turned toward the two gentlemen with them when Jacob and David entered.

She turned, "I'm sorry this is a private meeting."

"With us," Jacob said. "I'm Dr. Schwartzman's son, Jacob. This is David."

Aleta offered her hand and she was then introduced to Dr. Nils Trattner and George Pritiken, their attorney.

"Dr. Trattner, it is inappropriate for you to be here," Aleta said. "I must admit I'm surprised at your presence."

"I'm a close friend of the family," he said stiffly.

"Mr. Pritiken, you may stay," Aleta said. Her tone was decisive, authoritative.

"She's not a family member," David blustered, pointing at Bertha. "What do you need a nurse for anyway? We have the right to know."

"No, Mr. Schwartzman, you do not have that right," Aleta said coldly. Bertha quickly withdrew.

Aleta looked at Dr. Trattner and waited.

"Er... maybe this should be for the family only," he said. "I have a patient to check on."

"Why did you fire him?" Deborah asked before the doctor was out of earshot.

"I didn't," Aleta said. "Your father chose another doctor."

"Recommended by you?" the lawyer asked.

"Mr. Pritiken, I am not on the witness stand. I am here as a courtesy to Dr. Schwartzman's family. Innuendos are unwelcome. I received specific instructions from Dr. Schwartzman."

"I'm his lawyer."

"You were his lawyer," Aleta proclaimed. She handed him a folder. He began to study the documents. He had to admit that the woman had crossed every 't'. This women knew contracts.

"Well?" Jacob pressed. "Is everything in order?"

"Yes it is. She has power of attorney in both medical and financial matters. She is your father's new attorney."

"But she's sick," David protested weakly. "Suppose..."

George Pritiken replied before the query was fully framed. "If anything happens to Mrs. Praetzel, there are back-ups in place. Mrs. Praetzel, I assume these are all members of your law firm."

"That's correct," Aleta said.

"Why didn't he come to me?" George Pritiken felt suddenly compelled to ask, his ego pressing for an answer. He knew the question was uppermost in the minds of the family. This was an important group to keep as clients.

"Dr. Schwartzman considers you an able attorney but he wanted a personal attorney."

"Conflict of interest," George Pritiken concluded turning to the brothers. "While I don't think there is any, obviously your father thought there was."

"We can't afford two attorneys," David bitched.

Aleta eyed him coolly. "You, Mr. Schwartzman, are not paying me."

"I mean the family," David blustered.

"I am not working for the family. I am exclusively Dr. Schwartzman's attorney. This meeting is a courtesy rendered by me to aid all of you with the transition of power."

"You can't direct my father's financial affairs!" David declared.

"Yes, I can," Aleta said. "And let's be clear on this, Gentlemen and Ladies, he cannot tell me what to do. He gave me full authority to act on his behalf. He can't even advise me. That means to approach him with a financial venture will be a waste of time. I will not be consulting him or you. And I will listen to none of your suggestions as per his directions. Am I clear?"

"He told you not to listen to us?" Deborah asked.

Aleta gazed into the brown eyes of the woman whose chubbiness made her appear friendlier. "Yes, he did."

"But why?" she wailed.

"He loves you all. Each of you is independent and has a firm mindset. He was being torn apart by trying to please all of you. I, on the other hand, have the option of not listening to any of you."

Jacob interrupted.

"Why his medical decisions? He had one of the best neurologists in the area."

"He now has a doctor more suited to his personality."

"That's not a prime consideration!" Jacob asserted. "We'll go to court and fight you on that one."

"You won't win," Aleta stated with certainty. "I did not recommend Dr. Hughes. Your father made the choice on the basis of a personal recommendation by a person he regards highly."

Aleta softened her tone and explained. "Your father may be old, but he is a man of learning. He has been a respected professor in clinical psychology in one of the country's finest universities. He is used to having his opinion valued. Dr. Trattner dismissed his ideas and..."

"He's not a neurologist!" David interjected.

"He's a psychiatrist as well as a clinical psychologist," Aleta retorted. "Strokes are exacerbated, if not actually caused, by stress. That, Mr. Schwartzman, is your father's area of expertise. He took it upon himself to reduce the stress in his life. The decision itself was stressful, which is why he is here."

"So you caused his stroke," David concluded.

"As to your father's medical condition," Aleta continued, ignoring the accusation. "I have talked with Dr. Hughes and he recommends only one visitor today. I will be that visitor. Tomorrow he may have two visitors other than me, one in the morning, one in the afternoon. That will be the pattern for his entire stay. One means one. Not a pair. Children only. If any of you upsets him, I will see that visiting privileges are withdrawn."

"You can't do that!" David said. "You can't keep us from our father!"

"We'll take you to court," Jacob said. "You can't decide..."

He stopped when Aleta gazed at him with a smile on her face. "Mr. Schwartzman, I am very expensive. And I love the courtroom."

Jacob turned to Pritiken and silently asked him to step in. George Pritiken merely shook his head.

"Why not?" David blustered, upset with the non-verbal response.

"Her actions are not inappropriate. She is not denying you access. She is merely limiting it."

"There must be something we can do," David exclaimed.

"You can figure out which of you sees your father first," Aleta said.

She signaled Bertha who approached.

"Ready?" Bertha asked.

"I need to make one stop first. Dr. Hughes has a patient he wants me to see."

"Jacob, follow her," David hissed. "She's going to see Dad."

Aleta heard him. "No, I'm not. Please don't follow me. I will have you arrested if you enter a patient's private room unbidden."

Jacob stepped back. He turned to his lawyer. "Can she do that?"

"If it's not your father's room, she can."

Aleta walked to the end of the hall and entered the elevator.

"You disgust me!" David snarled. "I'll go."

Half an hour later, Aleta returned to Dr. Schwartzman's room.

"Dr. Schwartzman, Bertha has me on the clock. Bertha's my nurse. She's also my mother. I can argue with my mother. I can't argue with my nurse. She's also my cook and housekeeper and that's why she has the power. It's hard to find a great cook."

Dr. Schwartzman smiled. "My kids were assholes, weren't they?"

"That's a bit harsh."

"But true."

"Yes, that's true. But they didn't make a dent. I'm still in charge. You're not to be bothered with any decisions, medical or financial. I told them I wouldn't listen to your suggestions or theirs. That should take the pressure off you completely. Oh, and I put David in jail."

"He probably deserved it."

"Yes, he did."

"He has a wicked temper."

"Don't worry about it," Aleta said. "He's probably being released right now. I sent the others home until tomorrow."

Aleta saw the old man relax visibly.

"What a relief."

"You'll be able to have visitors tomorrow."

"I'm not sure I'll be up to facing the group tomorrow."

"They won't be allowed to visit as a group. Only one at a time. Only two per day. Do you want me to limit the visiting time?"

"Could you?"

"That I can do," Aleta said.

"That's not me making a decision?"

"No, that's you transmitting a need and me making a decision based on that need."

"Boy, Martha was sure right about you."

Aleta smiled then said, "Fifteen minutes I think. If it goes well, we can increase it."

"They won't like it," the old man said, tensing up.

"I'm sure you're right. But that's not something you need to concern yourself about because it's out of your hands."

"Suppose they stay longer?"

"I'm going to take measures to see that doesn't happen. Trust me."

"I do trust you," Dr. Schwartzman said, relaxing once again.

"I'll see you tomorrow," Aleta said.

Chapter 5

At six that evening, Dr. Reggie Barre approached the front door to the Praetzel house. The number of new expensive vehicles scattered around the end of the driveway told her that, as unprepossessing as the house appeared, it was the home of a wealthy man.

The bark of several dogs heralded her approach, but a command from someone inside sent them away from the front door. The door opened and a chunky woman greeted her warmly.

"Dr. Barre, please come in. I'm Bertha Locke, Aleta's mother. Stanley is waking Aleta now. We're eating in the kitchen because Paul's made a mess of the family room. Show her Paul."

Reggie followed the tall man through the kitchen into the family room. She heard the dogs scratching at the closed laundry room door. Paul opened the gate across the family room door and Reggie entered an artist's studio. Sketches were everywhere.

Several were of Aleta nursing a baby. She found them alive with love, but when she came face to face with the huge oil of Aleta with her baby nursing at her breast, the bed sheet gathered around her lions, lifting her face to receive the goodbye kiss of her husband obviously dressed for work, Reggie Barre gasped. While all that was visible was the curve of Aleta's back, one nonetheless felt one was witnessing an intimate scene.

"Stanley's already purchased that one," Paul said. "An appraiser is coming tomorrow."

"It should be hanging in the Art Institute," Reggie breathed. "It's breathtaking."

"You know, Paul," his brother said, "that's not a bad idea... I don't mean the Art Institute, but seeing if Stanley will let a gallery display it. It could mean commissions for you."

"Are you selling your sketches?" Reggie asked.

"They're working sketches. I plan to render most of them in oil," Paul replied.

"Have you done any of Aleta lately?" Reggie inquired dropping her voice level significantly.

"One," Aleta said from the doorway. "It's a sad one. Paul, take it into the den. I'll show it to her later. Right now it's time to eat."

The front door opened and three big Chessies rushed in followed by a seventy-year-old woman as lithe as Aleta, as tall as Aleta but with gray hair, cut almost as short as Aleta's. Behind her was a big bear of a man, but it was her voice, rough and cracked that called the dogs to heel before they even reached Dr. Barre. It was her voice that led them to various spots in the living room and commanded them to lie down and to stay.

Reggie watched them to see if when the old woman walked away they would rise and follow her. Instead all three laid their heads down on their paws and watched her move toward the kitchen and food without them.

The supper was lively. The two teenagers had just been told Grandpa Claude was flying to Disney World on Saturday.

"Uncle Paul," Jocelyn said brightly halfway through dinner. "Why don't you come?"

Paul couldn't think of an answer right away. Finally he said, "I'm going to be watching the dogs."

"If you want to go," Stanley said. "Aleta and I can take care of the dogs. We've both taken the weekend off... Aleta, why are you shaking your head?"

"We will be busy," she replied. "But Paul can go. We'll be working at home."

"I'll leave your liver shake in the refrigerator," Bertha said.

"Why am I drinking one of those?" Aleta asked, distraught.

"Because you're working and not resting."

"I don't think I'm anemic anymore," Aleta declared.

"Stop acting like a child," Bertha scolded. "You know you can't take as much iron as you need in pill form. In fact, Stanley, I'm going to teach you how to make them. If she works, she drinks."

"I have to work!" Aleta cried.

"Am I going to get shot?"

"That's all you've talked about for the last week," Aleta complained.

"And what happened a week ago?"

"You got shot."

"So, isn't my concern reasonable?"

"It happened a week ago."

"So what? My leg is still sending me pain signals."

"That's because you're not resting it."

"And whose fault is that?"

"Yours."

Stanley's look of surprise was genuine. "You sent Tyler Roach to the house and you set up the appointment with the Witherspoons."

"You named the fish."

"How is that a cause?"

"Kim asked me if the fish had names. Was I supposed to lie?"

"No, but you can name most of them."

"You can name all of them," Aleta said with a finality that told all those listening that she believed she had won the argument.

Robert and Paul laughed.

"She's all yours, Stanley," Robert commented.

Stanley gazed at his wife and said softly, "Now, Aleta?"

She nodded. "Yes, please."

She rose quickly and wordlessly walked toward their bedroom. Stanley struggled to his feet. Claude handed him his crutches.

As he was positioning them under each arm, he said, "Paul, Robert needs you to go to Disneyworld with them to watch the girls at night."

Both brothers were taken aback by the implication, but Jocelyn jumped in. "You can have your own room!"

"Please say yes, Dad," Lettie begged.

Once in the bedroom, Stanley locked the door.

"You are upset," he said.

"You don't want to get shot," she said.

"Aleta, where did your brain go? Of course, I don't want to get shot!"

Aleta began to cry.

Stanley embraced her and murmured, "You're pregnant. Your emotions are taking over your reason. Just because I don't want to get shot doesn't mean I don't want you to be a lawyer or that I've stopped loving you."

"I can't handle how I feel," Aleta sobbed. "I don't deserve you."

"That's true," Stanley said. "Do you want to look around for a new and better husband?"

Aleta began to bawl.

Stanley sat her down on the bed and took off her jacket. Carefully he hung it up, fetching a hand towel from the bathroom for her to cry in. Next he carefully unbuttoned

her blouse and slipped it from her shoulders and then hung it
up.

"We can't have sex," she whispered.   "We have
company."

"We can't have sex because my leg's not working,"
Stanley said. "The company is irrelevant."

Stanley continued to talk to her quietly as he removed
her clothes, folded them and put them in the laundry pile.

His habit was strangely soothing.

He pulled back the covers and led her to her half of the
bed and had her lay down.

He bent over and kissed her gently.

"Stanley, I'm undressed but you're not."

"That's because you need to rest. I will make love to
you later. Your job is to stay there and wait for me to join
you. That, my dear Aleta, is an order."

"But Dr. Barre? I must help her."

"You're not in any condition to help her," Stanley
declared.

"I think she's planning to kill herself," Aleta blurted
out.

"There are two prophets eating at the table with her,"
Stanley said. "God can use one of them. You've been taken
out of the game."

"You promised you'd never interfere with anything
God asked me to do," Aleta said obviously distressed.

"He asked you to invite her for supper," Stanley said.
"You did that. Let God take over now."

"But I..." she began.

Stanley leaned over and kissed her. "Close your eyes
for ten minutes. If God wants you to handle this, He'll wake
you. And I'll allow that."

Aleta relaxed. "I can do that."

Gazing at her in the dim light, he whispered, "You are
as beautiful a woman as God ever created."

He put one hand on her breast and kissed her tenderly. She could feel the warmth of his love. Slowly, she let her eyes close.

"Ten minutes," she murmured.

Stanley waited until she was asleep before he went back to the family.

Bertha and Harriet were clearing the table when he returned. Bertha set down a plate with a slice of homemade apple pie on it.

"Is this on my diet?" he asked.

Bertha smiled. "We had it ala mode. This is a diet portion."

Stanley dug in immediately before anyone changed his or her mind.

Harriet set a cup of coffee in front of him. "Is Aleta sleeping?"

"Yes," Stanley said. "I put her to bed. She's exhausted."

"Dr. Barre was expecting to talk with her."

Stanley looked around.

"Jocelyn took her to the study to see the sketch Paul drew of Aleta," Harriet said. "I think they're talking, so enjoy your pie."

In the study, Jocelyn untied the string holding the paper wrapping around the sketch. "Uncle Paul can't bring himself to destroy it, but he's not happy with it."

She held it up and Reggie Barre stared at it.

"My God!" she exclaimed. "What sorrow! He's captured it in her eyes, in her whole face. When she came to my office earlier, she seemed so removed from any emotion."

"Aleta cries mostly in front of Stanley," Jocelyn said. "She thinks she let him down. She's so dumb about how he feels sometimes."

"Explain that."

"He loves her. He doesn't love her any less because she was raped."

"Some men do."

"Is that what happened to you?"

For some reason Dr. Barre decided to reply honestly. "Yes, it did."

"That's too bad," Jocelyn said. "That must've hurt a lot."

"Yes, it did."

"Aleta says some hurts last forever. Do you believe that?"

"I hope death ends the pain," Dr. Barre said.

"Is that why you plan to die tonight?"

Instantly incensed, Dr. Barre stepped back and shut the study door.

"Aleta had no business telling anyone about her so-called prophecy," she declared indignantly. "Especially a person as young as you."

"Aleta didn't tell me. She never shares her prophecies except with the people involved."

"They why would you say such a thing?"

"Didn't Aleta tell you that Grams and I are prophets too?"

"She said something like that, but you all joked about it at dinner."

"We're teasing Lettie. She wants to be a prophet too," Jocelyn said. "She has no idea what it means."

"And you do?"

"I mostly know when something bad is going to happen to an animal. I don't really want to see what Aleta sees. She has terrible nightmares."

"Why does she have nightmares?"

"Because...well...for example, she saw a man burned alive. She saved him, but she still sees it in her dreams. It's buried in her memory as if it really happened."

"But it didn't."

"But her memory remembers it as if it did."

"So do you see me dead?"

"God spared me that. All I saw was the note you left."

"There is no note," Dr. Barre protested.

"Yes, there is. You're already written it. It's in your desk drawer."

"You can't know that."

"You're right. I can't," Jocelyn said. "You know I'm not experienced at this prophet stuff. You don't have to explain to horses. All you have to do is save them. I don't want to move on to people. They only think you're crazy."

"You really believe this prophet stuff?"

"Yes. I guess I do. It keeps happening. It's hard not to believe in reality."

A soft knock on the door caused Jocelyn to open it.

"Stanley, come in. Help me, please."

Stanley stepped in and closed the door. He spotted the sketch.

"Paul never showed this to me," he murmured. "My poor Aleta... Those bastards ripped her apart inside. No wonder she made Chesney sew up every tear."

Jocelyn went over and turned the sketch around. "It makes me sad too."

Stanley shook himself back to Jocelyn's plea when he entered. "How can I help you, Princess?"

"Dr. Barre plans to go home and kill herself. I can't say the right thing to stop her."

"Jocelyn, I'm not sure anyone can say the right thing."

"Aleta could," Jocelyn said. "Aleta is really smart."

"Aleta's asleep," Stanley said. "She was worried, but I told her she'd done her job. She brought Dr. Barre here."

"Aleta told you of her weird prediction?" Reggie Barre said accusingly.

"She wouldn't have if I hadn't ordered her to stay in bed."

"You ordered her? Like you ordered her to be silent at the hospital."

Jocelyn butted in. "Stanley takes care of Aleta. He loves her."

"By bossing her?" Dr. Barre scoffed.

"She doesn't have to obey him," Jocelyn argued. "He wouldn't hurt her. It's weird, but Aleta says it's okay."

"Your sister is wrong," Dr. Barre protested. "It is not okay!"

"Aleta was exhausted," Stanley explained. "I told her if God woke her up in ten minutes, she was released from the order."

"If God woke her... If God woke her... You know the early minutes of sleep are the deepest... God has nothing to do with this. He wasn't there for her when she needed Him most," Dr. Barre spat out. "She'll never heal in this world of fantasy."

"Is that true, Stanley?" Jocelyn asked. "Won't she get better?"

"She's already better," Stanley responded.

Dr. Barre eyed him suspiciously. "You think because you've ordered her to have intercourse with you that she's healed, but what you did was exacerbated her problem."

"Did you have sex with her?" Jocelyn asked.

Stanley gazed at the child. Aleta had told him to be honest with Jocelyn, so he said simply, "We had sex."

"Did she want to?" Jocelyn asked.

"Yes, she did," Stanley replied, remembering Aleta's admonition.

"She had stitches. Didn't it hurt?"

"Not her, but my leg wasn't too happy," Stanley said.

"Why'd you do it with a sore leg?"

Stanley saw the amusement on Dr. Barre's face, but Jocelyn's expression was one of open curiosity.

"There'll come a time when you'll understand that sometimes the woman initiates sexual relations."

"Like mother?" Jocelyn asked.

"Not like that at all," Stanley said. "There you were told what to do. In our case, Aleta wanted to see if she could... I'm not sure I'm the best one to explain this Jocelyn..."

"Could what?" Jocelyn pressed.

"Could enjoy having intercourse again," Stanley said.

"And did she?"

Dr. Barre interrupted, "Don't lie to the child. You enjoyed it and your wife lied to you because she was afraid of losing you."

"Was she?" Jocelyn asked.

"No, she wasn't," Stanley replied. "In the morning you can ask her."

"No," Jocelyn stormed. "You answer. If she didn't have sex would she have lost you?"

"Not a chance!" Stanley said.

"That's a lie!" Dr. Barre spat out.

Stanley looked at Jocelyn. "I'm not lying to you. Your sister and I married for life. Even if she never wanted to have sex again, I would have stayed happily married to her until the day I died."

"And live a celibate life?" Dr. Barre scoffed.

"That was my offer," Stanley responded evenly. The certainty in his voice told Dr. Barre that he was stating a fact.

Stanley turned to his wife's younger sister who wore a puzzled frown.

"Jocelyn, your sister wanted to see what she could still do after what happened. I was pretty immobile because my leg wasn't yet healed. I think it was healing for her to be in control. The situation was reversed, you see."

Suddenly, Jocelyn's face lit up. "Yes, I do see. She raped you!"

Stanley laughed.

"Not exactly. I wasn't raped by her just because she was in control. I was willing, even eager. No, I wasn't raped at all."

"It wasn't just sexual feelings made you want it," Jocelyn surmised.

"It was love that made me want it."

"But Aleta's still not well. Why didn't that help?"

"It did help," Stanley said, "but Aleta is suffering a double trauma just like you."

Dr. Barre remained quiet. Her experience told her the man was telling the truth. He was not talking down to the child. She, a psychiatrist, had taken her despair out on the child. She had battered the child emotionally in his presence and instead of going after her, Aleta's husband had turned his attention to the young girl.

"Double trauma? I didn't...there weren't two..." Jocelyn corrected.

"No, I don't mean the rape, I'm talking about what the two of you did to your mother."

"You don't think we should have?"

Suddenly, Stanley said, "Of course. Why didn't I see that? How could I have been so blind?"

Jocelyn was startled and confused.

"See what?"

"You know what to tell Dr. Barre," Stanley said. "Ten days ago you were thinking what she's thinking now. Do you remember?"

Jocelyn grew thoughtful. Then she said, "But Aleta and the rest of you guys came and saved me. Who's coming to save her?"

"I guess that's why Aleta brought her here," Stanley said. "Go ahead and tell her why you wanted to stop living."

"Perhaps you should leave," Dr. Barre suggested.

Stanley reached for his crutches.

Jocelyn objected. "No don't go. You won't let me get into trouble, right?"

"Jocelyn, you're a child. You were molested. The law considers you an innocent."

"Please stay," Jocelyn begged, her lip quivering.

"Okay. I'll stay," Stanley assured her.

Jocelyn told her story with remarkable brevity. "My dad had custody, but Mother took my horse and then when we went to court to keep him, she tried to get custody. The judge told me I had to spend the summer with her. That was because I was so hateful toward her in court. I sure learned not to do that again. Mother decided to brainwash me into choosing to live with her."

She looked at Stanley. "Can you tell her the rest?"

Stanley nodded and then picked up the story.

"Jocelyn's mother locked her in a bare room, denied her bathroom privileges, food, water and light. The windows were boarded over. Jocelyn's salvation was the trap door that led to under the house. Jocelyn bargained with her mother for a bucket to urinate in."

"So her mother talked to her?"

"Briefly at first," Stanley explained. "She didn't know what she was doing. She was following Jayline's instructions. Jayline, Jocelyn's sister, had taken a political science course and considered herself an expert."

"What did she bargain with?" Dr. Barre asked, guessing that this was when the molestation started.

"Her meals. She gave up three days of meals for the bucket and a lot more for a blanket. She was allowed a lunch when the social welfare workers visited. She also had her first bath in ten days. Her mother made a great impression and the social service worker assured the two of them that Jocelyn's visit would be extended. Her mother was scheduled for cosmetic surgery and would be gone a week. The night before she was to leave, she seduced Jocelyn who was panicky over being left for another week without food. During her entire visit, Jocelyn's mother had cooked for hours and then thrown everything down the garbage disposal. Not only was the house full of the smell of freshly baked biscuits and sizzling bacon, the television set was set to the cooking channel all day long. I'm only tell you this so you'll understand why Jocelyn was so quickly tempted to earn food by doing what her mother asked. The first steps were easy ones. When what her mother asked became abhorrent, her horse's life was put on the line. Jocelyn gave in.

Stanley pause and then said, "Now, Jocelyn, tell Dr. Barre what you did the day your mother left you to get a facelift."

Jocelyn took a deep breath and relaxed. Stanley had talked about the hard stuff. She started right in.

"I went down under the house and rescued my clothes from the garbage can where Mother had me throw them. They were filthy so I washed them in the pool. The house was all locked up. There was an alarm system. I found a tank suit in the pool house so I wore it while my clothes dried. That's when I realized Mother would find out about the trapdoor if I wore the clothes after she'd made me throw them away. She might even give me more days of fasting."

"More days?"

"I had ten days left only I wasn't sure Mother wouldn't say the week she was gone didn't count because I had food."

"How much food?"

"Five oranges, two apples, half a hunk of cheese and two partial loaves of bread," Jocelyn said. "It was enough for a week only I decided to eat it all up and then die."

"Why didn't you run away?"

"Mother said they'd only return me to her. Either that or put me in jail. And if I lasted the two months then I'd be able to live with Dad forever. But after the social worker came and said that she would see to it Mother got to keep me for longer, maybe forever, I knew I couldn't stay there for a whole year, so I decided that I'd eat up my food and then die. That's when the judge visited. We shared my food and talked. It was fun. I didn't tell her what I was planning just like you don't want to tell us. But she stayed with me until my family came. Then Aleta talked to me and told me I wouldn't ever have to live with Mother again. So, Dr. Barre what about your life can't you stand anymore?"

"My job," Dr. Barre said. "It reminds me of what I want to forget."

"Change it," Jocelyn said.

"I can't just walk away."

"Isn't that what dying is–walking away?"

"Yes, I guess it is, but at least dead I don't have to explain."

"That's what I didn't want to do either," Jocelyn said. "I didn't want to explain."

"My situation is different," Dr. Barre insisted.

"You made Stanley explain," Jocelyn said. "You were mean to him. Is that what you don't want to explain–that you're mean to people?"

"Pressing for the truth is not being mean," Dr. Barre insisted.

"But you did it sarcastically."

"Maybe so. I thought..."

Jocelyn interrupted. "You thought he was like that man that dumped you."

"Yes, I did."

"You need to get out of the business you're in," Jocelyn declared.

"And do what?"

"Do you like cutting people open? Lots of doctors do that?"

"I majored in psychiatry," Dr. Barre said. "Besides I have people to answer to."

"Who?"

"Well, Martha Cook for one," Dr. Barre said, knowing how unavailable Martha Cook was to any kind of approach.

"She's my friend. She's the one who got Aleta to fall in love with Stanley. She and Grams. She's Bertha's friend too."

Jocelyn turned to Stanley, "Can't Martha help Dr. Barre find another job?"

"Does Mrs. Cook know you and Aleta claim to be prophets?" Dr. Barre asked abruptly.

"Sure. She's one too, she and Grams," Jocelyn said. "She's coming to our barbecue tomorrow night. You could talk to her then."

Dr. Barre rose. "I think I'll go home now."

Jocelyn turned to Stanley. "She can't be alone tonight."

"You're sure?" Stanley asked.

Jocelyn nodded.

"Dr. Barre, follow me," Stanley said.

He led the way to the kitchen. Since it was also the path to the front door, Dr. Barre followed him.

Bertha and Harriet turned.

"We'll see you tomorrow night?" Bertha asked.

Dr. Barre nodded her head.

"Jocelyn says we can't let her spend the night without supervision," Stanley said.

"You can't hold me," Dr. Barre said.

"The police will hold you on our say-so," Stanley said. "They will put you on a suicide watch."

"There's no proof I plan to do anything. I haven't said a word to anyone."

"There's a note in her desk drawer," Jocelyn interjected. "It says 'To Whom It May Concern as if it concerns anyone...'"

"That's enough for me," Stanley said.

"You can't touch me," Dr. Barre declared vehemently. "I'll be gone before the police get here."

Stanley smiled. "They're already here."

Dr. Barre looked around panic-stricken. "Where?"

"One of them is standing right in front of you," he replied.

"And I'm another," Harriet said. "And Claude's another."

"Next you're going to tell me Robert and Paul and Bertha are cops," Dr. Barre scoffed.

"They aren't," Stanley said pulling out his badge.

Dr. Barre stared at it and collapsed into a nearby chair. "I can't go to jail on a suicide watch."

"We have an alternative," Stanley said. "You stay here and we take turns guarding you against yourself."

"Claude and I will take the first eight hours," Harriet offered immediately.

"Wake me at four," Stanley said, turning and heading for his bedroom.

"Don't I get a bed?" Dr. Barre asked.

"No," Stanley said. "You can lay down on the couch if you're tired, but we want you visible."

"I need to use the bathroom," Dr. Barre said.

Stanley nodded at Bertha who led the way and locked the door as soon as Reggie Barre was inside.   Bertha, however, was also inside.

"I can do this alone," Reggie protested.

"I'm a nurse," Bertha said. "And you're on a suicide watch."

"What makes you think I won't go home tomorrow and commit suicide if I'm intent on it?" Reggie asked.

"We're only giving you a chance to rethink your decision, that's all," Bertha said.

"I'm not going to get out of here, am I?"

"I wouldn't try it.   Stanley, Harriet and Claude are terrific marksmen.   They'll shoot you.   Then you'll be in the hospital on a suicide watch and have a sore leg to boot."

"You're kidding, aren't you?"

"No," Bertha said. "They're acting as deputies now. They take that duty seriously."

Stanley entered his bedroom and whispered in Aleta's ear. "Dr. Barre is safe.   We have her here under a suicide watch.   Jocelyn talked to her.   You can sleep until morning unless you want me to make love to you."

"Rest your leg," Aleta murmured.

Stanley undressed and climbed into bed beside his wife. He ran his fingers down her body. She turned over on her back and took his hand and kissed it.

"Tomorrow," she whispered. Her hand came over and found it's favorite location and Stanley laid back and closed his eyes. He was going to be in trouble come 4 AM, but right now her touch soothed him.

He closed his eyes and slept.

Chapter 6

At eight o'clock that night, Roland Chin appeared on the doorstep of Stanley Praetzel's house asking to talk with Aleta.

"She and Stanley are both asleep," Harriet said. "Is this an emergency?"

"My client's wife is in extreme pain and I need help," Roland Chin said.

Harriet invited him in and called Robert on his cell. He and Bertha were out walking the dogs she told Chin.

"Tell me a bit about what's happening medically," Dr. Barre said.

"My client's wife, Gloria Graves, is dying of ovarian cancer," Chin said. "She's on morphine, but it's not a high enough dose. Her pain is terrible. I couldn't stand staying with her for very long. Her husband is beside himself."

"Do you have any figures," the doctor asked. "I'm a doctor."

"Tell me, doctor, do you pay any attention to the experience of other doctors, experts in the field who discovered that a patient requires more and more morphine to overcome the patient's increased tolerance of the drug which means it is less and less effective in pain management."

"All doctors know that?" Dr. Barre returned.

"And all doctors know that too much morphine depresses respiration and caused death," Chin added.

"That's the dilemma," Dr. Barre asserted.

"But the dichotomy is that for patients who have been introduced to morphine over time, an increase does not affect the respiration at all. It just reduces the pain."

"Can you cite any studies?"

Roland Chin said opened his briefcase and pulled out several articles. "And I have studies that show that patients that received stunningly high doses of opiates died no sooner than those taking lower doses. Some even lived longer."

Dr. Barre took the reports and read them quickly. She studied the charts.

By the time she finished Robert was sitting beside Chin received an update on his legal maneuverings.

"Who is Gloria Graves' doctor?" Robert Locke asked.

"Dr. Nils Trattner."

"The neurologist?"

"The nursing home director won't up the morphine without the doctor's okay," Chin reported. "Trattner won't give it. The court won't overrule a doctor's decision without a trial. We need another doctor to oppose him, but no one will."

"Did you find anyone willing to take over Gloria Graves' case and increase her pain meds?"

"I tried," Chin said. "I'm coming up dry. Dr. Matsuki's arrest scared a lot of them."

"I'll do it," Dr. Barre said. "Nobody can touch me."

"What does she mean?" Chin asked Robert.

"She has a special temporary immunity," Robert said.

"Let's go," Dr. Barre said.

Chin got up.

Robert stopped her. "You can't go."

"Why can't she?" Chin asked.

"Dr. Barre is under house arrest," Harriet said. "I'll accompany her."

"Are you a legal doctor?" Chin asked Reggie.

"The arrest has nothing to do with that," Harriet responded, taking her badge from her purse and pinning it on her shirt. "Let's go, Doctor."

"Are you going to tell everyone I'm under arrest?"

"Not unless you try to run."

"How are you going to stop me?" Reggie challenged. "You haven't a gun."

"You are going to make me wear a gun?"

"Yes. I dare you."

"Claude get me Stanley's gun and holster," Harriet said. "Don't wake them."

Claude tiptoed into the bedroom and went to the cabinet where Stanley kept his gun. He grabbed the shells as well. He glanced at the two sleeping figures in the bed and smiled. He was going to have a suggestion for Harriet if ever they got to bed.

Harriet put on the shoulder holster, checked the gun and then loaded it. She slipped the loaded gun into the holster while Reggie Barre watched her open-mouthed.

She felt a twinge of apprehension. She was being taken seriously.

It was July when even the nights were hot in Illinois. Harriet didn't don a suit jacket, but wore the holster as openly as the badge.

Reggie Barre figured that if she promised not to run, Harriet would probably be persuaded to take off the gun and holster. She decided to try it.

"What if I promise not to escape?" Reggie asked. "Would you leave that gun in the car?"

"No. I can't do that. I'd lose my badge," Harriet said.

"What's so important about being a deputy?"

"I get to shoot people."

"You shot anyone?"

"I've killed several."

"Several?"

"More than several, but I'm not proud of killing people," Harriet said.

"So you will shoot me if I try to escape."

"If you don't stop when I order you to, I will. But I'm an excellent shot. I know exactly how to bring you down without permanent damage."

"Well, I'm glad everything's clear," Dr. Barre said.

"Is that a hint of humor peeking through?" Harriet queried.

"You'll have to admit this is a ludicrous situation."

"I don't admit that at all. It isn't foolish to alleviate pain of any kind."

The nurse on duty woke the nursing home director. She allowed them to proceed to the room without waiting for the arrival of the director because a police officer was accompanying them.

Chin had a directive for a change of doctor in hand. His explanation was brief. Thomas Graves signed it immediately and his wife managed a scrawling semblance of a signature.

After changing the orders on the chart, Dr. Barre, with Harriet accompanying her, sought out the nurse and called for the medication to be begun immediately.

By the time the director arrived, the first shot had been administered. Dr. Barre had started with a high initial dose.

Gloria Graves felt some relief immediately. She smiled at her husband and squeezed his hand.

Dr. Barre explained what she was doing and that new research had shown this to be effective in a situation where the patient had already been introduced to morphine.

"Otherwise this much would be dangerous," she finished.

Thomas Graves left the room and returned with an old woman who asked if the doctor could treat her husband as well.

"I will sign the paper," she said. "Please!"

She handed Dr. Barre his chart.

Dr. Barre read the diagnosis and the notations.

"At least it's a different doctor," she quipped. "Mr. Chin, do you have another form? Dr. Nokes is about to lose a patient."

Chin and Dr. Barre followed Lorraine Babroff to her husband Otis' room. He looked up hopefully.

Dr. Barre explained her method of treatment. "This doesn't work except on people who've had a lot of morphine therapy. The body has already adjusted to the morphine and having complications are no longer an issue.

It wasn't until after she'd taken care of Otis Babroff that Dr. Barre noticed that Harriet wasn't around.

The night orderly rushed in. "The policewoman needs you in Room 115. Follow me!"

Dr. Barre found Harriet on the bed, pumping the chest of a large man. The nurse arrived a few seconds after the doctor. Dr. Barre, seeing her, began barking out orders. The orderly meanwhile called for an ambulance.

Harriet rode with Dr. Barre to the hospital. Chin was told to assure both the Graves and the Babroffs that their new doctor would return as soon as the heart attack victim had been taken over by the emergency staff. Roland Chin was happy to deliver that message.

When the time came for the second injections, he monitored them being given. Both couples were brightened by the presence of the young Chinese lawyer. He spent time in both rooms. Roland Chin liked older people. They had wisdom to impart. He listened respectfully as they talked.

As he was passing between rooms, the orderly stopped him and asked him to stop in and talk to a lonely patient.

"He's awake. The nights are long. He's in a lot of pain. His daughter has a baby and a toddler at home. She can't be here day and night."

Chin followed the orderly.

Ivan Smitrovich was the man's name. He was dying of pancreatic cancer. He was in pain. The orderly liked the man. So did Chin.

Chin had to be careful what he said. "

"Is there nothing that can be done?"

"Nothing," Ivan said sadly. "I'm at the end of my run."

"You admitted yourself," Chin said. "Why?"

"Kids are smart. They sense stuff. They'd get scared without knowing why."

Suddenly, Roland Chin had an idea. He shared it with Ivan.

"It's okay to show it to others, but no before and after stuff."

"Just the good stuff so they have a live video of you playing with them. They'll watch it because they're in it."

"Do it."

Thus Dr. Barre acquired a third patient that night. She stayed at the nursing home to monitor the effectiveness of the morphine levels well into the night, promising to return in the morning.

At two, Chin headed home. A short time later, Dr. Barre and Harriet headed for the Praetzel house.

Harriet woke Claude and took his place on the bed in the baby's room.

Dr. Barre went to sleep on the couch. Claude made himself a pot of coffee and sat staring at his charge wondering why a woman in the prime of life would choose to end it. He didn't wake Stanley at four, figuring he should at least put in four hours.

Aleta woke at six and discovered she'd kept Stanley prisoner again.

She glanced over at him. His face was turned toward hers. He was smiling.

"Why do you let me do that to you?"

"I have such pleasant dreams when you do."

She looked both surprised and delighted. "Really?"

"Can we make love?" she asked abruptly.

"Yes," he said, his heart singing.

"Let me shower first."

"I'll join you."

"Your leg?"

"This man is not having another bed bath."

"You're the boss."

"Finally!"

"When haven't you been?" Aleta challenged.

"When you are," he replied calmly leaning over and kissing her. "But I don't mind."

They rolled out of bed together. Stanley tried not to limp.

"I hope Gerard doesn't wake up," Aleta said turning on the shower.

"The house is full of people. Someone will take care of him," Stanley said.

"What people?"

"Friendly people," Stanley hedged. "If we can concentrate on our goal here..."

"What aren't you telling me?"

"Get in the shower and I'll tell you," he said.

As the water cascaded down on them both, she whispered, "Can it wait?"

"Yes," he said slowly beginning to wash her. "It can wait."

At seven thirty they both emerged, fully dressed and cheerful. Stanley was on crutches still but today there was a shoe on his foot instead of a slipper. He felt the extra weight and decided he was asking too much of his leg. He went back and exchanged the shoe for the slipper. His leg had been stressed enough.

"What this area needs is a palliative care facility for patients with end stage cancers and the like," Dr. Barre was telling the group at the table.

"What's that?" Jocelyn asked.

"A place where relieving pain is the main focus."

"You mean for people like the ones you helped last night?" Jocelyn questioned.

"Yes," came the reply.

Aleta went straight to Bertha, put her arms around her as she was standing at the grill and kissed her.

"Thanks, Mom," she said. "That liver shake did the trick."

Bertha turned. "Are you alright?"

Aleta smiled. "That doesn't mean I ever want another one. Keep that in your memory banks. What's for breakfast? I'm starving."

"Liver," she replied straight-faced.

Aleta gasped.

Bertha laughed. "That's for threatening to fire me. Now we're even.

"Bacon, eggs, pancakes, biscuits and hash browns. And you can have it all."

"I'm guessing I can't," Stanley said.

"Just look at Robert's plate. That's what you get."

"How come Claude gets to eat everything?" Stanley complained.

"Because Harriet hasn't put him on a diet."

Claude glared at Stanley. "If you want to remain my favorite grandson, you better not say one word about this in front of Harriet."

"I'm your only grandson. Where is your wife?"

"She spent the whole night as a deputy guarding me at the nursing home," Dr. Barre said. "And I assume I can go home and change. I have patients to check on this morning."

"It's your call, Jocelyn," Stanley said. "Is she free to go?"

"Not until after she sees Otis," Jocelyn said.

"Who's Otis, Dr. Barre?" Stanley asked. "Your cat?"

"He's a patient at the nursing home," Dr. Barre said. "I was planning to go there this morning, but I have to go home and freshen up."

"No," Stanley said.

"You can shower here. I can steam press your suit and blouse," Bertha said. "Jamara, Dr. Barre is on a suicide watch. You will need to watch her in the bathroom."

"Oh for God's sake!" Reggie Barre exclaimed angrily. "I don't need to be watched!"

"Jocelyn says you do," Stanley said.

"She's a child!" Dr. Barre spat out, incensed.

"That doesn't mean she should be ignored," Stanley returned. "The question is which one of us should go with Dr. Barre to the home."

"I'll go," Claude said. "I want Harriet to sleep."

He felt his wife's hands on his shoulders. He looked up and she kissed him.

"You stay here and finish the prep for the party tonight," she said. "I'll come fetch you when I'm done and we'll go home and nap."

"Are you going to wear that gun again?" Dr. Barre asked, obviously peeved by her imprisonment, casual as it was.

"I don't trust you," Harriet said.

"I want Claude," Dr. Barre said.

"Claude has to set things up for the party," Harriet said. "You've got me. This is not open for negotiation."

"I bet you think I'm a hard-headed bitch, don't you?" Dr. Barre asked Harriet as they walked toward the entrance to the nursing home. "Probably even think I'm not worth all this trouble."

"The decision's not mine to make," Harriet said coolly.

"Hey, where's the warm expression of love?"

"I'm cranky when I don't get enough sleep," Harriet said. "The truth is you are hard-headed."

"So why are you here?"

"God ordered me."

"Jocelyn is sixteen years old! She's not God."

"She's a prophet. In our family we respect God's direction no matter who gives it."

"You'd feel guilty if I died."

"No, I wouldn't. Sorry, maybe, but not guilty. I wouldn't have been responsible."

"But if you could have prevented it?"

"The point is that watching a suicide-prone individual is pointless. Unless his attitude changes, he will succeed."

"Then why do it?"

"Because God has a plan. All I know is that we're to watch you right now."

"And tomorrow?"

"After you see Otis, the watch is over."

"After that I can kill myself?"

"If you want to."

"And you won't stop me?"

"No."

Thomas Graves met them in the hall. "I was watching for you. I think she needs a higher dose."

Dr. Barre followed him to Gloria's room.

"How is the pain?" she asked.

"So much better," Gloria said.

"Well, let's up the amount a bit and see if we can make you even more comfortable."

She picked up the chart and wrote new orders.

Ivan Smitrovich was the next patient. He told her about the upcoming video he was going to have done that morning.

"How's the pain?"

"Tolerable," he replied. "I can hide it from my grandkids."

"Let's see if we can make it so you don't need to hide it," Dr. Barre said writing new orders on the chart. "I'll check back in an hour."

Before she got to Otis' room, an older woman approached her. "Are you Dr. Barre?"

"Yes, I am."

"My name is Germaine Kurtzman. My daughter is dying of cancer."

"Where's your daughter?" Dr. Barre said. The woman led the way to her daughter's room. It was in the opposite direction from Otis Babroff's room.

Dr. Barre almost smiled. It served Harriet right. She knew Harriet hated wearing the gun. She decided she'd spend a bit of time with this patient.

After Dr. Barre tracked down the nurse, gave her verbal orders and told her the first injection was to be done immediately, she went back to Dawn's room and began chatting with her newest patient.

A short time later, Dr. Barre went back to Gloria Graves' room and found her smiling.

"Better?"

"Much."

She visited Ivan Smitrovich and the report was not as good.

"About the same," he said.

She increased the dosage again.

Harriet patiently trotted after her. Not once did she press her to see Otis Babroff.

Finally Dr. Barre headed for Otis' room.

His wife greeted her. "I told him you were in the house. I said he had to wait his turn."

Dr. Barre immediately regretted her petulance over being guarded by Harriet.

"I'm so sorry. I gather the dosage isn't high enough."

"It helped a lot," Otis said. "I didn't know if I dared ask for more."

"He had such a hard time waiting," his wife said. "He kept saying that God should have answered both his prayers, not just one."

Dr. Barre started.

"You prayed for two things?" she asked. "And He only gave you one?"

"Can you do anymore?" Otis asked.

Dr. Barre picked up his chart.

"I can do quite a bit more," she said making a new note. "Let me get the nurse."

When she left the room, Harriet followed her.

She whipped around. "Are you still here?"

"God will tell me when to leave," Harriet said.

"You're never going to leave, are you?" Reggie snapped. "You're a permanent fixture, attached to me like a tail on a dog."

"Maybe."

"Damn you! Damn Aleta! Damn your whole family! I wish I'd never gone to her house last night!"

"Take care of business," Harriet said coldly. "Don't punish Otis anymore for my presence."

"Then, go away."

"I will when God tells me to."

"I don't believe in God."

"That's your right."

"He doesn't exist."

"I know He does."

"How do you know? He doesn't answer prayers."

"He answers mine."

"And you're going to tell me that when your requests are ignored, He's saying no!" Dr. Barre scoffed. "That's hogwash!"

"Take care of Otis, please," Harriet said. "He's in pain. You can castigate me afterward if you like."

Dr. Barre continued down the hall, found the nurse and told her what she wanted. The nurse came back with the doctor and gave Otis his injection.

"That's better," Otis murmured. "Thank you God. Please no more long waits. I never prayed for patience."

"Long waits?" Dr. Barre asked.

"He answers in His time not ours," Otis said. "Never been able to figure that out. If He wants us to know He's up there, all He has to do is answer every prayer right away. But He don't."

"Some He doesn't answer at all," Dr. Barre said.

"Oh, you think no is no answer?"

"Put that together with delayed answering," Dr. Barre argued, "and what you have is happenstance, an event that occurs naturally and you tag it as an answer to a prayer."

Harriet wanted to speak, but Lorraine put her hand on Harriet's arm and Harriet followed her outside.

"I saw you fretting," Lorraine said. "Don't think Otis can't out argue her. He can."

Harriet smiled. "Then let's watch the show."

"I give you that God likes stuff to be as natural as possible. Otherwise we'd be too scared to make a choice to believe or disbelieve. Just think how hard it would be to argue with Him if we were scared shitless."

"Aleta says she argues with God," Dr. Barre remarked.

"Who's Aleta?"

"I forgot. It's Ivan that knows her. Or thinks he does. She's one of the prophets," Dr. Barre responded.

"You know one of the prophets?"

"So she says."

"I asked God to let me meet one," Otis said. "That was the prayer He didn't answer."

"What was your other prayer?"

"To take away my pain. I thought maybe the prophet could help me, but God sent you. And, you know, His choice was better."

"How do you figure that?" Dr. Barre asked, shocked.

"You're a doctor. It's natural that a doctor should use a drug we all know about. Don't you agree? God likes natural. I was praying for a prophet because Dr. Nokes has got this attitude that some deaths are painful. Shit! We all know that."

"What did you expect the prophet to do?"

"Just tell me that God cares about me. My doctor sure don't."

Dr. Barre turned to Harriet.

"Mr. Babroff, may I introduce Aleta's grandmother, one of the prophets you wanted to meet."

Harriet stepped forward and took Otis' hand. "My name's Harriet Locke. And God does love you."

"Why hasn't He removed my pain before now?"

"You'll get to see Him before I will. You ask Him."

"I know what He'll say."

"What?"

"That just because He loves us doesn't mean we're exempt from the worst experiences common on earth. Jesus wasn't exempt and He loved him most of all."

"My granddaughter, Aleta, was raped two weeks ago while in a hospital with a concussion. Two men. She said that God was with her the whole time. She said she asked Him to stop it, but He didn't. She said she felt forsaken and alone even though she knew God was there. It was a strange dichotomy she still hasn't been able to reconcile, but she doesn't deny the existence of both her feeling of being abandoned by God and yet knowing that He was allowing her to suffer and was with her."

"I've felt like that a lot," Otis said. "I thought I shouldn't have both feelings. I'm a Christian, so how could I?"

"Jesus felt that way on the cross," Harriet said.

"I guess I never thought of that. I just assumed that.... I never thought of that. That means God understands, doesn't it?"

"He knows our hearts," Harriet said.

"Your granddaughter. How is she?"

"She seemed good when I got up this morning," Harriet said.

Dr. Barre stepped up. "Actually, before you got up, she told us God healed her."

"Overnight?" Harriet said shocked. "Yesterday she was in terrible shape."

"She kissed Bertha and thanked her for the liver shake."

"She hates liver. Why did she say that?"

"She never explained only she did say that she never wanted to be served another one."

"What do you think?"

"She was a changed woman. Her happiness was real and her husband shared it. I think he must have said and done all the right things during the night."

"Claude said they were both sound asleep when he went in to get the gun at eight," Harriet said.

"Yes, why do you have a gun?" Otis asked.

"I'm on duty."

"But you've been with Dr. Barre all the time," Otis observed.

"Is she in danger?" Lorraine asked.

"Yes, she is," Harriet said, then looked at the doctor. "That is she was. I do think Mr. Babroff that you just saved her life."

"Is that so? I thought I was past being a use to anyone."

"Time for me to go," Harriet said.

"You don't know what I'll do," Dr. Barre said.

"You have your answer. It's what your heart was praying for. You can choose freely now."

"You're just going to leave?"

"I'll see you tonight at the barbecue. Meanwhile tell Otis about the three prophets you have personally wrestled with. Otis, remember how Jacob wrestled with the angel?"

"Oh, Doctor, do you have time," Lorraine said.

"I can tell you about one between each round. I guess I'll start with Aleta since she's the first one I met."

"You actually talked with her?"

"I was her doctor for about thirty minutes, then she became mine."

"How'd she do that?" Otis asked.

"Very cleverly."

Chapter 7

Earlier, before Dr. Barre and Harriett left for the nursing home that morning, Stanley called a partnership meeting in his study.

"With Robert leaving tomorrow and me not fully functional," Stanley said, "we need to figure out what our priorities should be today."

"I have two hospital visits," Aleta said. "One is to our new client, Dr. Schwartzman, the other, as a favor to Dr. Hughes, I'm translating for a stroke victim. I need to take care of certain financial matters for Schwartzman and to outline his needs. We have his medical and financial powers of attorney."

"I asked Ed to look up Tyler Roach's father," Stanley said. "Social services let me place Tyler and Paige overnight with friends but..."

"What friends?"

"Beatrice and Ed Ornstein," Stanley said. "I promised them it was only for one night. The youngest, Molly, is still in the hospital, but she'll be out today. Slight concussion. Broken arm. I need time to find out why Tyler didn't go to his father for help."

"Why not send them on the Witherspoon trip?" Aleta suggested. "There are seven responsible adults for six kids. Social Services will accept that ratio."

"I'm going to need another honeymoon," Robert commented wryly.

"Oh, Dad, you had that one, remember?"

"Stanley, put this girl back and give me the morose one who would have said, 'Oh Dad we can't do that to you. We'll think of something else.'"

"Why would I do that? I think it's a great idea."

"We can ask Bertha," Aleta suggested.

"Never! She'll have us adopting the whole bunch."

"What a great idea, Dad!" exclaimed.

"We have a baby coming," her dad insisted.

"That'll only give you a family of two. Your house is big enough for five."

"The answer is no," Robert said. "I will let them share my honeymoon, but that's all."

Stanley sighed happily.

"That's a relief. I know I can get Social Services to okay that. I'll have Beatrice bring them to the barbecue tonight. They can go home with you."

Bertha knocked on the door. "Alice called. Are any of you going to the office?"

"We all are eventually," Stanley said.

"Ed has some reports to deliver."

"Where is he?"

"In his car."

"Tell Alice to have him come here," Stanley said. "We're having a partnership meeting."

A short time later, Ed arrived. He nodded at everyone and started right in.

""The Roach kids," Ed said, "that's not their real name. Their father is Kurt Van Horne."

"The Van Horne's on Chicago's north side?"

"Winnetka. Yep."

"So there's money there," Stanley said. "Why did Tyler panic over Molly's hospital bill? All he had to do was tell Dr. Brice who his father was."

"I told him you'd gotten Dr. Cook to take care of his sister. I told him Cook ran the free clinic. That was okay with him," Ed said.

"What did you find out about Van Horne?"

"There's no record anywhere. He's remarried. Some rich dame. Lots of society stuff. Divorced his first wife when the kids were two, six, seven and eleven. She got custody. No custody battle. He still pays child support. Even after his wife died. The oldest brother was nineteen. And get this. He got custody of the others. The father paid the child support to him."

"So why is Tyler so panicky?" Aleta asked.

"Money is gonna stop now," Ed replied.

"Does the father get custody?" Stanley asked.

"Tyler says yeh. Their grandmother died last year."

"What is wrong with the father?" Robert asked.

"Tyler don't have a clue. He says David knew and promised he'd tell him someday. He never did."

"It had to be more than hearsay," Aleta put in. "The father paid child support to his eldest son."

"David worked as a data processor," Ed said. "He told Tyler that he was gonna have to go to a junior college because their dad weren't gonna fork over college money without David turning over custody."

"So, David had clout," Stanley surmised.

"But Tyler doesn't," Aleta added. "The secret went to the grave with David."

"Not necessarily," Stanley said. "Ed, get Tyler to take you over to his mother's house and help you search it."

"Is Social Services gonna come for the kids?"

"Robert is taking them to Disney World tomorrow. They'll stay with him tonight," Stanley said. "I'll tell Social Services."

Aleta spoke up. "Ed, tell Beatrice I'll get Dr. Cook to release Molly to her."

While Ed called his wife, Aleta called Dr. Cook.

Robert rose. "I'll get Claude to reserve another room at the hotel and I'll tell Bertha we're going to have company tonight. I'll be back."

Stanley dialed Social Services and briefly told the person in charge that the children were going to stay in the custody of the law firm representing them until the truth was uncovered.

When the woman protested, Stanley said simply, "Work with me. The children are being well cared for."

"They will be placed in a foster home today," the social worker said. "We do things by the book in this office."

"I'm calling the police. I'm insisting the children be put under protective custody."

"Then they can't go on a trip," she announced smugly.

"Two police deputies will accompany them," Stanley said. "You can check with Chief West."

Stanley's signal told Aleta to get Lyle on the phone immediately. She punched his private cell phone number.

"Lyle," Aleta said, "Stanley has an emergency request."

"Anyone hurt?"

"Not yet."

"Put him on."

"Hi Lyle, don't answer another call until I finish," Stanley said and he outlined his request.

"You're pushing my friendship."

"Van Horne has done something. I'm guessing it might be child molestation, but I don't know. His wife knew. His eldest son knew. He paid child support without ever visiting his children. Tyler is scared of his father, but I don't know why."

"And you think a trip to Disney World is the answer?"

"No, of course not," Stanley said. "But I need time to investigate. And the kids need a break. They're lost their mother, grandmother and brother all in the last two years."

"I understand Harriet has been sporting her badge and gun at the nursing home."

"You were called?"

"Of course, I was called. I told them it was legitimate. I expected an explanation, but you guys never called me."

"Sorry about that. We were trying to prevent a suicide. We arrested her and then watched her."

"Dr. Barre?"

"Oh, hell, Lyle, do you know everything?"

"Is the crisis past?"

"Yes."

"I want a report on my desk today."

"For your eyes only?"

"Yes."

"And you want a written request to put the children under police protection too, don't you?" Stanley asked.

"You got it."

"You put us under protective custody at the drop of a hat. Do you and Tom always file a report?"

"Always," Lyle said.

"You shall have it," Stanley said. "Ed wants to search the house with Tyler."

"When's Beatrice picking up Molly?"

"This morning."

"Tell her to expect a police guard."

Later that morning in the office of editor of the Tri City Register, with the young black reporter Justin Conway on one extension and his editor on the other, Stanley Praetzel called Doris Fraza at her home in Arborville.

He started out, "Mrs. Fraza I have a client who wishes to donate however much money you need to make Kitty Witherspoon's wish come true immediately."

"Who are you?" the voice was smooth and even.

"My name is Stanley Praetzel. I dialed the number on your flyer and you said you only needed a little more to make Kitty's dream come true. My client has a few questions."

"Have her call me," came the response.

"This is a wealthy lady. She doesn't make phone calls. I do that," Stanley replied crisply. "She would like to know how much of what she donates will go directly to making Kitty's wish come true."

"All of it."

"You don't take out anything for expenses?"

"I volunteer my time," Doris Fraza said.

"What about the flyers and other small expenses?"

"I may take a little out for them, but it's less than five percent."

"95% will go to Kitty's trip expenses?"

"Maybe even more," Doris replied.

"Good!" Stanley said. "How much do you need to get Kitty in the air?"

"I haven't the exact figures," Doris said slowly.

"A rough guess will do. Five hundred? A thousand? Two?"

"Close to a thousand," Doris replied, cleverly not reaching for the highest number.

"I will call you back in ten minutes," Stanley said.

After he hung up, Justin asked, "Why did you hang up?"

"I couldn't tell her about Martha arranging for a plane in that phone call."

"I don't see why not?"

"Trust me," Stanley said leaning back.

Fifteen minutes later, Stanley picked up the phone. The other two men picked up their extensions.

"Mrs. Fraza, Stanley Praetzel again. "I have good news for you. My client has arranged for the Witherspoon family to share a charter flight to Orlando. The charter is leaving at nine tomorrow morning from the Willow Glen Airport."

"Why that's er...wonderful!" the woman stuttered.

"She also arranged for TV coverage of Kitty leaving the airport."

"TV coverage?"

"Why yes," Stanley said. "Of you and the Witherspoons. I assume you will want to hand them their expense money personally."

"Er...you've caught me off guard," Doris said.

"I know this is sudden," Stanley returned, "but you do know Kitty has only a couple weeks left, don't you?"

"No, I didn't."

"That's why my client is coming up with a large donation at this time. That's why she arranged and paid for the charter. She wants this girl to have her wish."

Doris Fraza finally found her voice.

"I certainly understand her wanting to hurry things along, but I'm not comfortable with rushing into expenses before I have the money to pay for them."

"You said you only needed a thousand. My client is personally underwriting Kitty's share of the charter. There will be a bed on board for Kitty to use during the flight if she tires as well as a nurse to help care for her. Don't you think that this is better than a commercial flight?"

"Well, yes it would seem so," Doris stammered. "Still I need time to plan the details of the trip. I'm sorry but this is too fast."

"What details?"

"I like to make special deals so the money will go farther," Doris said. "I won't be party to a haphazard arrangement."

"Are you refusing to even underwrite the cost of the hotel room and tickets to Disney World with the money given specifically to fund this trip for Kitty?"

"I don't know you. I'm not handing over any money to you."

"I don't want any money," Stanley said coolly. "I am going to present you with a check, but not unless I see evidence of good faith."

"I need to keep track of expenses," Doris argued.

"If you're afraid that the Witherspoons will overspend, just hand him the funds collected. Her father will see that Kitty has a good time and your foundation will get the credit," Stanley said evenly. "We will see you at the Willow Glen airport at eight thirty to do the TV taping. The plane leaves at nine sharp."

Stanley hung up and looked at the two newsmen.

"Want to bet she's a no-show?" the editor queried. "Greedy people won't give up a cent, even to get more."

"You know," Justin said, "I can't help but think about little Kitty. Lots of people contributed to helping her get her wish. They need to know she got it. She needs to know she has lots of well-wishers."

"What do you propose?" Stanley asked.

"That we make this about Kitty," Justin replied. "We give her a happy send off. I'm assuming that the people on the plane are willing to absorb her costs if need be."

"They are, but I want the Witherspoons to be able to claim the money donated for Kitty's trip," Stanley said.

"Give Kyle Witherspoon a credit card. When he gets back, he can ask the foundation for reimbursement," Justin said.

"We have blank cards," the editor said.

"We need to get Doris Fraza to take credit for the trip somehow," Stanley said. "She can argue that she was planning on a trip for Kitty and we want ahead without her."

"Can we run an announcement in today's paper about the departure?" Justin asked his editor. "That'll bring out some contributors. Then Doris Fraza will have to publicly answer to them."

"We need to get her there," Stanley said.

"I'll take care of that," Justin said.

Stanley went back to the office and called Chief Lyle West about the Witherspoon trip and what he suspected.

"Can you be there?"

"You're a deputy. You can make the arrest."

"Lyle, why are you giving me a hard time?"

"Because you're using me."

"Of course I'm using you. "You're the chief of police and have an astute legal mind-set. You will keep me from getting into trouble. On top of that you're a friend."

"I guess those are good enough reasons."

"You want more?" Stanley inquired.

"Do you have more?" Lyle asked. Stanley knew he was being challenged.

"I can give you eight hours of deputy time anytime you want so you can boss me around."

"I'll take that," Lyle said. Stanley knew he was smiling.

"You're going to wring that eight hours out of me aren't you?"

"You can count on it," Lyle said. "You've put three children in protective custody on nothing more than a hunch. You owe me big time."

"Has Beatrice picked up Molly from the hospital yet?"

"She's late which means you're up to something?"

"Ed is searching the house with Tyler for clues as to what the father did that made him so scared of his wife and son."

"I have men that could do that."

"The kid hired me, so I get to do it."

"And my men get to stand around twiddling their thumbs and watching a couple kids no one is after?"

"Okay, you win. Send your best man to the house to help Ed," Stanley said. "I'll have Beatrice pick up Molly immediately."

"Now you're getting the picture," Lyle said.

"So who'll I tell Ed is coming?"

"I'll tell him when I get there," Lyle said.

"I can see I'm going to get a really nasty assignment on my eight hours."

"You can count on it."

When Aleta came in, she went straight to her office. Stanley assumed she didn't know he was there, so he flicked on the intercom to ask her to come to his office. He heard her on the phone with whom he could only assume was Schwartzman's broker. She was placing a sell order. As far as he knew she hadn't even received a copy of Schwartzman's holdings.

He clicked off the intercom. He wanted to see her. He wanted to complain. No, he thought, not complain, blame. He was still scowling when she breezed into his office, came over and kissed him on the forehead.

"Why are you pouting?" she asked.

"Lyle extracted a promise from me to give him an eight hour shift free."

"Were you disrespectful?"

"He thought so," Stanley admitted grudgingly.

"Then accept the consequences."

"He's going to give me a nasty assignment. He even said so."

"Swallow your medicine and remember to give him his due."

"It's all your fault, you know. You took cases with aspects bordering on the criminal. I needed his help on both."

"Why didn't you call Chief Milani?"

"Because Lyle is..."

"...A personal friend?" Aleta finished.

"Yes. And personal friends don't punish personal friends," Stanley pontificated.

"Did he think up the eight hours or did you?"

"Me, but he accepted."

"He doesn't want you to feel guilty. Guilt interferes with friendship."

"He could have just told me not to feel guilty."

"He knows you better than that."

Stanley sighed.

"Did you sell stock without reviewing the whole portfolio?"

"Called Grams. She said if he was holding any Shearing Corp stock to sell it, so I did."

"I'm sorry."

"You thought I was doing what?"

"I said I was sorry."

"You are really pissed about this deputy thing, aren't you?"

"I'll get over it," Stanley said. "Lyle won't ask me to do anything as long as I'm on crutches, so the weekend is still ours."

Robert strolled into the office.

"Lyle's on the phone. He had a question about the Witherspoon case and I told him you were here."

"You're working," Lyle stated flatly. "At the office."

"Yes," Stanley admitted. "But I'm sitting down."

"Then, I'm going to have you do your eight hours tonight."

"Aleta has the party."

"I mean tonight–eleven to seven," Lyle said. "You're going to guard the Roach kids at your father-in-law's place. Ordinarily I'd put two men on, but since you have a dog..."

"You mean Scooby?"

"He'll tell you if anyone is sneaking up on you. Besides he's chocolate. He'll be hard to spot in the dark."

"But he's a pup," Stanley protested.

"Be good training for him and he'll help you stay awake. Outside guard duty is lonely, boring and sleep-inducing. You'll check in every thirty minutes."

"You're determined to make me pay, aren't you?

"You offered. And I'm short handed," Lyle said. "And I'm not convinced the children are in any real danger."

Suddenly, Stanley knew what this was all about.

"Can I have a chair?" he asked meekly.

"Yes," Lyle said, satisfied that finally Stanley had gotten the message.

"Scooby and I will be there," Stanley agreed equably.

When Aleta and Robert arrived home for lunch, they were surprised when Bertha told them Stanley was in bed.

"He's working the eleven to seven shift tonight as a deputy," she announced.

"With his leg?" Aleta questioned.

"He says that was considered in his assignment," Bertha replied. "He also said you were to wake him for lunch."

Aleta entered the bedroom. "What's this deputy-thing all about? You're not well enough!"

"I'll handle it," Stanley said rising.

He limped into the bathroom. Aleta followed him, protesting. He turned and kissed her and his kiss told her he was not upset with the assignment. This was a turn around and she was puzzled by it.

"What's different?" she asked.

"They came up empty at the house," Stanley said. "Not a clue as to what happened that spooked the mother and brother."

"Who searched?" Aleta asked.

"Ed, Lyle and French." Stanley responded.

"Not Hawk?"

"There was no crime committed," Stanley said.

"Do we still have permission to search?" Aleta said.

"Of course. Tyler is still in protective custody. Our investigation is ongoing with Lyle's blessing, but he's done."

"Will he give me Hawk in exchange for you?"

"Me?"

"Sure. He gave you an easy assignment. Guard duty on a warm July night with Scooby and a chair. Pretty comfortable, if you ask me. You can sleep the night away. Scooby will tell you if anyone approaches."

"Right. And he'll check in every thirty minutes."

"You didn't tell me about that," Aleta said. "But it doesn't change anything. I have a couple hours. Dean is checking out some stuff. He doesn't need me pacing behind him all afternoon, so I may as well see what I can find at the Roach house."

"It's been searched!"

"Not by a woman."

"Why do you need Hawk?"

"Fresh eyes," Aleta replied. "And he picks up stuff others miss."

"Lyle may not agree to the exchange."

"Ask respectfully," Aleta coached, then added, "Be your usual persuasive self."

"I don't want to do this," Stanley said grumpily.

"You will," Aleta predicted as she locked the door and unbuttoned her blouse.

He found her powers of persuasion exceeded his. It always surprised him a bit that she could turn him around so completely and not feel the least bit guilty about doing it. She knew she was manipulating him. He knew she was manipulating him. And yet it worked. It was one of the mysteries of their marriage that his brain still puzzled over.

One part of him didn't mind at all.

Hawk met Aleta at the Roach house.

Unknown to them, they were being watched.

"I was told two hours," the lanky man with long, straight blonde hair said smiling. "I've never been limited before. What's up?"

"Stanley's paying Lyle with deputy duty," Aleta said. "I guess you're worth four times what Stanley is."

"Well, I'm not cheap," Hawk said. "Why didn't your husband offer to pay for my services?"

"I guess because it's an exchange of favors."

"And if it takes us longer?"

"Stanley will have to do another shift," Aleta said so matter-of-factly that Hawk suspected he didn't have to be concerned.

"Fill me in," he said.

Aleta briefed him, then said,

"Let's start in her room."

While Aleta looked thorough the drawers, Hawk measured every drawer to see if there were any hidden compartments.

When Aleta sorted through the jewelry drawer, she came across four lovely gold lockets each with a photo of a baby and a small lock of hair. On the cover of each the child's initials were engraved.

Aleta picked up the lockets one by one. When she looked at David's face she thought of his untimely death and wondered briefly what he had grown up to look like. Such a serious face.

She smiled when she looked at Tyler's. He was born mischievous she felt. He had in impish grin.

Paige was a lovely baby with bright eyes and the same seriousness as her eldest brother.

Molly was a feminine Tyler with freckles and curly hair.

Lovely children, Aleta mused. She put all four in the box they were stored in and an indentation in the velvet told her that once there had been five lockets.

She called to Hawk. "What do you make of this?"

"We're looking for a fifth locket, I guess," he said.

"She wouldn't have hidden it in any temporary location," Aleta said.

"You're a woman," Hawk said. "We'll start with where you might hide something. I only have two hours, remember."

"You have as long as it takes," Aleta responded.

"How clever do you think she was?" Aleta said.

"Phi Beta Kappa from Northwestern."

"What was her major?"

"Sociology."

"She'd probably read The Purloined Letter," Aleta remarked. "She'd hide it in plain sight."

"That brings us back to her jewelry drawer," Hawk said.

"I looked at every piece of jewelry in that drawer," Aleta said.

"If she kept the locket," Hawk posed, "her ex-husband must have been frantic when she died."

"David managed somehow to allay his fears," Aleta returned, "because the checks kept coming and David only needed a part-time job to stay in college even though he was over eighteen and from his comment to Tyler over the age where his father's support would continue."

Hawk went into David's bedroom while Aleta entered the room the two girls shared.

On Molly's bed sat five stuffed animals. Among them were Pooh Bear and Pluto.

Molly's going to love Disney World, Aleta thought. She glanced around the spacious room with pale yellow walls and colorful quilts. Molly's depicted cartoon characters, mostly animals. Paige's spread matched her sister's in color only. The figures in the larger squares were of dogs, cats and horses. The two quilts were hand stitched by someone who knew the girls.

On Paige's bed were furry zoo animals. There was a lion, a tiger, a hippo and a walrus. In the center was a girl doll, neatly dressed in a partly torn straw hat with a sunflower, a well-washed yellow dress with a still white slip and a frilly white apron all of which were knee length. Below were white silk stockings and black ankle-high, button shoes with scuffed toes.

On a gold chain, hanging around the dolls' neck was a gold locket identical to those in the case. This one, however, carried Paige's initials.

Aleta pondered over the second locket. She picked up the doll and opened the locket. A lock of hair was encased under plastic on one side. On the other was a baby picture. The child looked like Paige except for the eyes. They were smaller and slightly almond-shaped.

She took the doll with her and sought out Hawk. Hawk was seated at one of the desks in the boys' room staring at the computer menu. He turned as she entered.

She handed him the doll.

"So there was another child," Hawk said. "And there is no record of her birth."

"She could possibly have been a child with Down's Syndrome," Aleta intimated.

"Where'd you find the doll?"

"On Paige's bed."

"Isn't she too old for dolls?"

"I'm guessing it was her grandmother's. It's an old doll, nothing that I ever saw when I was young," Aleta said. "It probably sat on the mother's bed. When she died, Paige took the doll. Or her mother gave it to her for safekeeping."

"Do you think she knows something," Aleta said. "She would have opened the locket. Did you find anything?"

"David was majoring in computer science. If he hid anything, it would be in one of those CD's or on a flash drive. It'll take me time to discover if the CD's might contain the information we want. I haven't been able to find a flash drive."

"His brother doesn't know what the secret is," Aleta posed. "So if it's here, it's on a CD Tyler wouldn't touch."

"Thanks," Hawk said.

"His mother would have used a book," Aleta said. "I'll search the bookcase."

"Paige could have been given a diary to keep," Hawk said. "We could ask her."

"I believe David was his mother's only confidant which is why Tyler is so panicked. David was eleven when the divorce took place. Tyler was seven; Paige, six; Molly, only two."

"You're right. Tyler and Paige were too young to be brought into the circle of secrets," Hawk agreed.

"Let's look until we run out of ideas," Aleta said.

"Not time?"

"I told you before. Time is not a consideration," Aleta said. "Stanley will go along with a thorough search now that we've found something concrete."

"Lyle may forgive him extra duty," Hawk put forth.

"Not a chance," Aleta said. "Lyle enjoys bossing Stanley around."

"Does everyone boss Stanley around?"

"Actually, no one does," Aleta stated. "I have to persuade him and bribe him both. And I can only boss him around in little things, like what he can eat."

"That's not little," Hawk chuckled. "What about Lyle?"

"I haven't figured out what his leverage is, but it's a good one."

"Friendship?"

"No one who isn't his friend can get Stanley to do anything he doesn't want," Aleta said, "but it's more."

"Lyle better watch out or he'll lose a friend."

"Stanley won't let that happen," Aleta stated. "He's loyal as hell!"

"Sounds like a good man to have as a friend."

"And as a husband. I can't believe other women didn't know what a jewel he was."

"Maybe they just weren't his equals."

"What a really nice thing to say," Aleta rejoined. "We're having a barbecue tonight at our house. All the police chiefs and their wives will be there, plus some doctors, lawyers, artists and professors. You should fit right in."

Hawk guffawed. "Me? I don't ever fit in."

"Exactly," Aleta smiled. "That's why you'll fit right in. Most of the people there don't feel as if they belong.

After a few parties, while they still feel that way, they don't mind it much."

"I'm not married.

"Well, if it doesn't bother you, it doesn't bother me."

"No, it doesn't bother me," Hawk said quickly, then after a brief hesitation, added, "Well, yes, sometimes it does."

"Ambivalence. Good. I like that. Dress is casual. We'll be outside all evening. Claude is manning the grill. Several ladies bring side dishes. You are not expected to do more than come."

"What time?"

"Six."

"So I guess there is a time limit on this investigation after all."

"The kids are going to Disney World for the weekend. You can come back tomorrow if you think of anything."

"Stanley will be working for Lyle forever at this rate."

"I guess I better stop chatting and let you get back to work if I ever hope to see my husband again."

For the next hour, Aleta took one book after another off the shelves and paged through them. No notes or photos slipped out. When Hawk joined her, she shrugged her shoulders and admitted defeat.

"Pick out the five books you would choose," he ordered. "I'll take them with me and check out the bindings and look for any other... Those?"

"Yes," Aleta said. "They are grouped together on a shelf too high for a toddler. I'll bet the children were told not to touch them because they are old. Even I didn't touch them. I thought they'd fall apart in my hands."

"Let's look over the rest of the house," Hawk said, "together. It will be a thinking exploration."

"You want me verbal?" Aleta asked.

"I want to know why you wouldn't use certain places and why you might consider others," Hawk said. "It's the best use of your mind right now."

"Me think. You work. I like that idea."

"When do you have to get back to prepare for your party?"

"Lauren directs everything. She just uses my house and my people except for me. I provide the guests. She gets to throw as many parties as she wants. We celebrate everything."

"People get shot at."

"I forgot you had to investigate those."

"Do I need a password?"

"Not this time. Nobody's gunning for us tonight."

Chapter 8

When Aleta arrived home, she found a limousine parked next to the house. She parked her car in the garage around back and ran out to meet Paul Junior. His father explained that when Lettie emailed her brother about going to Disney World, he begged his mother to let him go too. Andrea told her husband that Paul Junior did twice as much work in one day as he had in the last four days so she wouldn't change her mind.

Jocelyn was there to greet Paul and announced that Gramps had said Tiffany could come too. It seems she had promised her the trip before she'd gone to California.

"Will the plane hold all of you?" Aleta asked.

"Gramps says since Molly and Kitty are half size and Lettie and I are three-quarters size; it's okay."

Aleta walked over to the barbecue grill where Claude was setting up.

"Claude, did you tell Jocelyn that she could add Tiffany?"

"She made a promise. Tiffany is near the top of the list, not the bottom."

Aleta frowned. "That's a total of fifteen."

"Eight are young and lightweight," Claude said, "and one is old and light as a feather."

"You only have twelve seats," Aleta pointed out.

"Fourteen. Robert and I sit when we pilot."

Claude gazed at Aleta's worried face and assured her the plane could carry the weight.

"I am never foolish in such matters," Claude assured her. "Harriet will sit in the jump seat in back until Kitty decides to use the mattress."

Aleta became apologetic immediately, but Claude assured her that her concern was reasonable. "I should be able to answer such queries. Actually, I'm glad you asked. Gave me a chance to show off a bit."

"On another note, when did Jocelyn decide to call you Gramps?"

"I think it was when I told her Tiffany could come," Claude said. "She says it matches Harriet's name."

"Do you like it?"

Claude smiled broadly. "What do you think?"

"Okay," Aleta said. "Gramps it is. Are we all set for tonight's barbecue?"

"Yes. I have a steak for everyone."

"I invited a couple more men."

"I guess you and Stanley will go meatless."

"I can't. I need the iron."

"Stanley can't give up two steaks since I only allotted him one," Claude said.

"Some people have two?"

"You have three. You need the iron."

"Three? I can't eat three!"

"Aleta, you are so easy," Claude joshed. "I know you."

"I invited Dr. Hughes and Hawk–you know, the forensic genius. Oh, yes, and Dr. Barre," Aleta said.

"Matchmaking, are we?"

Aleta gasped. "Martha and Grams would kill me!"

"Relax, Aleta," Claude said. "Lauren has the party under control as usual. And Harriet has me in tow. Was your afternoon successful?"

"Enough so Stanley won't mind doing another shift."

Claude eyed her askance. "You do realize that there's something wrong with this picture. Lyle extracts his pint of blood, but from Stanley, not you."

"Stanley gets it replaced by me."

"No wonder he's been smiling all afternoon," Claude commented.

"He didn't go to work?"

"He came home early to take a nap. He means to guard those kids."

"He never takes being a deputy lightly."

"I offered to spell him, but he said Lyle wouldn't like it if he did that," Claude said. "I told him if he got suspicious to fire his gun in the air and Harriet and I would be there within minutes."

"Thanks, Gramps."

The guests with side dishes arrived early and the party started then. Lauren, as usual, mixed the tables and Dr. Hughes relaxed when the only single lady at his table was Bessie Dobbins. Obviously, he wasn't being matched with anyone.

The teenagers were relieved that Lauren didn't mess with them other than to assign them a brand new redwood picnic table that had four curved benches, each seating two. The talk was about the next day's flight to Florida and the trip to Disney World.

Hawk found himself tabled with Martha Cook, Evelyn Chesney, Dr. Barre, Professor Burrows, Hubert Praetzel and Ed Ornstein. He only knew Ed by reputation. Martha Cook he knew because she was Arborville's leading citizen and Lyle and Tom jumped every time she coughed. Ill at ease, Hawk hunched over even further letting his long hair cover his eyes when Professor Burrows spoke directly to him.

"I had a young man in class who used to sit just as you are doing now," he said. "I didn't think there could possibly be another. Brilliant man as I recall."

"I wasn't ever in your class," Hawk said raising his head slightly.

"But you fit the brilliant part, don't you?" the professor said.

"I was only replying to your main query," Hawk replied stiffly.

"I don't bite, you know," Professor Burrows said.

"Dr. Hughes said that's what Aleta told him."

"Who are you most afraid of at this table?" Reggie Barre asked.

"Leave it to a psychiatrist to treat this like a psychiatric interview," Hubert said. "Relax Reggie. Somehow you impressed Aleta. That makes you a quality person."

"What impresses Aleta?" Hawk asked.

"Well, she liked me right off because of Emma," Ed put forth.

"Your wife?"

"My dog. Beatrice is my wife. Scooby is Emma's son."

"You have Labs."

"I have two Labs, Emma and her daughter Minx. Beatrice breeds Scotties. She has four."

"Well, she liked me right off," Hubert said, "because I looked like my son."

"She liked me," Evelyn Chesney said, "because she likes people who love dogs. I have three Goldens."

Martha Cook chuckled as she spoke, "I have friends in high places."

Everyone looked at her quizzically.

"Her grandmother is at the top of Aleta's list of people she likes. I came in on her coat tails."

Everyone laughed.

Reggie Barre said. "She turned the tables on me. I was supposed to be her doctor. Instead I became her patient."

"That I believe," Hubert commented. "She's a more powerful woman than she realizes."

"That's part of her charm," Martha said. "She's the equal of every person here, yet she considers them all superior to her."

"Equal to you?" Reggie asked, surprised.

"Oh yes," Martha replied. "Of us prophets, she is the one God uses the most."

"Does everyone here believe she can prophesy?" Reggie asked unable not to pursue the topic in the light of her own experience.

"I witnessed one," Professor Burrows said. "It was the darnedest thing. Here she was in the middle of an interview with the committee, her ability to practice law hanging by a thread and she makes a phone call to Hubbs over there and tells him to take two horses out of the barn and walk them to the house."

"That sounds crazy," Reggie popped out.

"The kids who stole the horses knocked out the guard she'd hired to guard them," the professor continued. "If they'd have knocked Hubbs on the head, he probably wouldn't be standing there waiting for his steak."

"Stanley knows her best of all," his father said. "And he believes in her ability one hundred percent. Everyone who works here is told to do exactly what she says when she gives an order which is why Hubbs took the two horses from the barn to the house even though it made no sense to him. And to add a bit to the story, both of those horses were injured and if they had been ridden it would have been catastrophic for both the horse and rider."

"Mr. Monroe," Reggie said directing her query to Hawk, "You're a man of science. What's your take on this?"

"Call me Hawk," he said. "Everybody does. You want my take? Why?"

"Just curiosity," Reggie shot back casually.

"Well, for one, the lady's got a mind to be reckoned with. I'd hate to be a criminal trying to put one over on her."

"You're hedging."

"Even the seemingly inexplicable occurrences frequently have an explanation," Hawk said. "While I absolutely would take her advice, I'd reserve judgment on whether she was receiving a prophecy from God or the combination of a finely honed sensibility coupled with a brilliant analytical ability was the underlying cause."

"So you don't believe yet?" Ed said.

"You could translate that gobbledygook?" Louis Burrows chuckled. "You would have aced my class."

"I think Ed wants people to think he's a simpleton," Martha Cook put in. "So, Reggie, is Hawk's view one you can live with?"

Reggie blushed. She didn't want her opinion known. And she especially didn't want Martha Cook to realize that she didn't accept her claim either.

"It's okay. Aleta doesn't insist we all be like-minded," Martha said.

"What does she want?"

"For you to hold your judgment in abeyance and be open to the possibility that she is who she says she is and I am who I say I am."

"Aren't you going to add Jocelyn and Harriet to those I'm supposed to believe in?"

"My," Martha breathed. "You did have an experience, didn't you?"

"Yes," Reggie said tartly. "And I'd rather not talk about it."

"Those Roach youngsters," Evelyn interjected, "they seemed really nice."

"The middle one is troubled," Reggie said, happy to be on a new topic.

"Tyler has good reason to be," Evelyn responded. "He's suddenly in charge. He not only has to deal with being head of the family but with the death of his brother. I think they had barely recovered from their mother's death."

"They're all scared," Reggie said, "but Paige has a face to her fear. The other two are just scared."

"Really?" Hawk asked. "How can you tell?"

"Molly is worried most about being separated from her siblings," Reggie said. "Tyler is worried mostly about letting down his brother, but Paige actually is more afraid of being returned to her father than being separated from the others."

"How long did you talk with them?" Hawk asked.

"I didn't talk with them at all," Reggie replied. "I just listened."

"You listen well," Hawk remarked.

Reggie decided to switch the subject. She didn't want people thinking she spent her time evaluating their emotional state. A child was an open book. It only took a bit of listening to find out what was bothering him. Her overhearing the conversation had been accidental.

"Is this really Robert and Bertha's fourth honeymoon?" Reggie asked.

Hubert laughed. "I think Robert just uses that as an excuse to get more time off, but considering the fact that they got it right the first time..."

"Got it right?" Reggie asked.

"You weren't present at the wedding were you?" Evelyn said. "They had two ceremonies, a civil one first because Robert wanted a private honeymoon. They'd promised Jocelyn she could come with them on their planned honeymoon. Bertha got pregnant on the first one."

"They're expecting?" Reggie gasped, obviously shocked at the idea.

"Same time as Aleta and Stanley. Paul and his wife are too," Evelyn said. "We didn't catch the bug."

Martha patted Evelyn's hand. "Neither did we, my dear. Neither did we."

"I think I always dreamed someday I'd have a family," Evelyn said. "It's a blow to realize you're too old."

"Did you know the Roach girls are interested in animals?" Ed Ornstein put in.

"Teenage girls usually are," Reggie said.

"Paige asked Beatrice if it was hard to show dogs," Ed added.

Evelyn looked over at the group of teens. The Pug was sitting in Paige's lap. Scooby was sitting next to Molly who was feeding him tidbits from the table.

Martha leaned over, "Don't worry, Evelyn, Aleta is trying to get her father to take them in."

Evelyn reared back.

"But that's all wrong! Robert and Bertha are expecting a baby. And Jocelyn is still at home. And both of them work. These kids need a stay-at-home mom."

"I agree," Reggie said, "but teenagers are difficult to place. And three? It won't happen."

"Aren't you and Bernard ever going to take a honeymoon?" Martha asked Evelyn. "Look at Robert and Bertha, two of theirs were only a couple days long."

"It's hard for a doctor to get away for a long period," Evelyn explained.

"I was in Florida earlier this years," Ed said. "It's a nice place to honeymoon, especially Orlando."

"Claude's plane is full," Evelyn said.

"Stanley's plane only needs one pilot. And it holds four," Hubert said. "Lydia and I could use another second honeymoon."

"Suppose Stanley needs his plane," Evelyn posed.

"Stanley can't fly for another week," Hubert said. "Not with that leg."

"It would be fun to go to Disney World with a group," Evelyn said.

"We could help with the kids," Hubert said. "There are eight of them and only seven adults."

"They're teenagers," Evelyn said.

"Exactly my point," Hubert said. "None of them will want to go in the same direction and Kitty's parents will be focused on her."

"It could be fun," Evelyn said a bit timidly.

"It will be fun!" Hubert emphasized. "You game?"

Evelyn smiled and nodded.

Hubert leaned back and spoke to the next table.

"Hey Lydia, Evelyn and I are flying to Orlando for a fun weekend. Do you and Bernard want to come along?"

Both spouses laughed.

"Whose plane?" Lydia asked. "Ours needs a co-pilot."

"Stanley's. Lean over and ask him."

Lydia leaned over toward the next table.

"Stanley, can we borrow your plane? We want to go to Disney World this weekend."

"You too?"

"Us and the Chesneys," Lydia said. "Why are you even hesitating? You can't fly."

"Sorry, Mother. Of course you may borrow it."

Hawk leaned over and whispered to Ed, "I need to talk with you when we're finished."

"I'm done," Ed said. "Excuse us for about five minutes, Folks."

He promptly got up and Hawk followed him. They were an odd pair, Ed's rotundness accentuated by Hawk's lanky frame. Hawk, as usual, walked hunched over and so their height differential appeared less.

"Give," Ed said.

"You still on the Roach case?"

"That's privileged."

"Sorry," Hawk said. "Stop me if you aren't. We found something and I need help."

"Go on," Ed urged.

"There are five lockets."

"Yeh, I know."

"Five children," Hawk surmised.

"Paige's initials on two," Ed countered.

"Two children with the same initials," Hawk returned.

"I missed that," Ed said.

"Aleta was with me," Hawk said. "I had an advantage."

"Lyle better not hear you say that," Ed quipped.

"Speaking of whom," Hawk said, "we come to my dilemma. Stanley is paying for my services."

"So?"

"I'm too expensive."

"Hey, Man, I ain't cheap."

"You only charge money," Hawk went on. "Stanley is paying Lyle in hours as a deputy for my services."

"So?"

"Evidently, Stanley works eight hours for my two."

"Whoa!" Ed breathed. "I thought they was friends."

"The thing is, I've got too much to process," Hawk went on. "I've got a handful of CD's that David probably used to back up stuff on his hard drive. Aleta thinks the mother might have put some sort of explanation along with proof in a book. I have eight Aleta selected for detailed examination."

"The old set of books."

"Right."

"Really dusty buggers," Ed remarked.

"They could be valuable," Hawk said. "I have to move slowly."

"So you plan to hand me the CD's."

"Yes," Hawk said. "They're in my car."

"Okay. After," Ed said. "We gotta go back. Beatrice made chocolate cake."

As they turned Scooby ran up to Ed. He turned to Paige who was with him. "I got his mom. I kept his sister too. He can smell them on me."

"You belong to that lady, don't you?"

"Yep," Ed agreed grinning. "I sure do."

"You've got lots of dogs."

"I like animals. I got a pet store only someone else runs it. It's got snakes and lizards and parrots and fish and guinea pigs, but they aren't for sale except to people I like."

Paige's eyes widened. "You own a pet store full of animals that are yours?"

"They like visitors, so come visit."

"And I can play with them, except for the snakes."

"I got a boa. She'd like you."

"To eat?" Paige giggled.

"To hug," Ed replied. "You're too big to eat."

"I'd like to see her," Paige said eagerly.

"Say, my friend Hawk's got a question," Ed said.

Paige looked at Hawk inquisitively.

"It's my nose," Hawk said. "Some people think it looks like a beak, hence the name Hawk."

"It's nice," Paige replied with candor. "It goes with your face."

"When you're older, I'm going to marry you," Hawk said impulsively, smiling at the young girl.

"I don't like people to break promises," Paige shot back abruptly. "You got a ring?"

Taken aback, Hawk replied nonetheless.

"Yes, my college ring."

She held out her hand and Hawk, who couldn't resist the openness of her request, took it off and gave it to her.

"Now, we're engaged," Paige said. "I'll marry you when I grow up."

Ed poked the tall man, "Ask your question."

"Um...er..." Hawk stuttered. "You don't know me."

"I like you. You bend over all the time so people don't have to look up to you. You have a nice face. Mom always said that if a man looks like a good person that's the man to marry."

"You're only sixteen," Hawk exclaimed. "You should think about dating and stuff, not marriage."

"I'm nearly seventeen and I plan to finish school," Paige said. "Mom said a family deserves a mother who's educated."

"Your mother was wise," Hawk remarked.

"If you find someone else, I will give you back your ring."

"What about you? Don't you want to date?" Hawk asked.

"No."

"Not even me?"

"When I'm eighteen we can date. Then you won't get in trouble," Paige said judiciously.

"I want you to have fun," Hawk stammered, surprised at her prudence.

Ed nudged Hawk again. He got a glare in response.

Paige smiled. "I'm already having fun. Doesn't being engaged feel good to you?"

Hawk nodded numbly. Engaged to this child-woman felt surprisingly satisfying.

"I'm a serious person. I scare boys away. Am I scaring you or exciting you?"

"Exciting," Hawk managed. "But, our age difference is too great. You're a child."

"Mom told me there are places where children are engaged at three. The men have to wait. Being engaged means that the girl has a future. I think it's a good idea."

Hawk took Paige's hand and closed it around his ring. "I can wait. You have a future with me if you want it."

"When I'm eighteen, we can kiss," Paige said.

Ed's mouth by now was permanently agape. Hawk, seeing it, realized how bizarre this whole exchange must seem to anyone looking on.

"My question was: did the baby that died have a name?"

Paige paled. Her hand trembled. Hawk squeezed it lightly. "You were only six. What happened wasn't your fault."

"Penny," came the answer in a whisper, then the fear-coated question. "How do you know?"

Hawk kept hold of her hand as he spoke softly, "We are both criminal investigators. It's what we do for a living.

We work for the police. We found your sister's locket on your doll."

Paige found her voice in her need to explain. She didn't know if what she had done was wrong or not. She explained it as if she were fearful it was.

"I took it when Mom died. I was afraid Dad would find it and take it. Mom wore it a lot. Molly thinks I took it because it was Mom's. Tyler thinks that's why too. They don't know. Just David and Mom and me."

"Does your dad know you know?" Hawk asked.

"No," Paige said. "David told him that he saw him. He didn't. I did."

"Saw him do what?" Hawk asked gently while Ed held his breath.

"Will you tell my father?" she asked, obviously scared.

Hawk felt her tremble. He picked up her other hand and held it gently.

"No," he promised.

"He will kill me if you do," Paige said, her voice shaking.

"I won't let him," Hawk said. "I plan to marry you."

Ed watched this statement wipe away Paige's fear. The response was unfathomable to him. Her voice interrupted his reaction and brought his mind abruptly to the present.

"He put a pillow over Penny's face to stop her from crying. She kicked but he didn't take it away. I was scared so I ran back to my room."

"Where was your mother?" Ed asked.

"I don't know. I think she was in her room. A few minutes later I heard yelling. They were both screaming at each other. I buried my head under my pillow. I was so scared."

Hawk drew the young girl into his arms and she started to cry. Ed patted her on the back.

"Don't be scared, kid," Ed murmured kindly. "We ain't gonna hurt you."

He nodded at Hawk who followed him into the barn. Hawk sat down on a bale of hay and brought Paige down beside him. Ed pulled over another bale and plopped on it.

"You gotta tell us all you know," Ed said. "We can help."

"My father will know I told."

"We won't tell him," Ed reiterated.

"My father's very smart," Paige said. "He'll find out the minute he sees me that I know."

"Did you choose to become engaged so you'd have a protector?" Hawk asked abruptly.

"Hawk!" Ed blurted out. "Don't get personal."

Hawk squeezed Paige's shoulder. "I will protect you whether we're engaged or not."

"You want your ring back?" Paige asked, quivering.

"No, I don't," Hawk said firmly. "Believe me, I will not think you are bad because you didn't yell out. I'm not sure you could have saved your sister."

"I didn't try."

"You were only six," Hawk responded. "You weren't sure what he was doing was wrong, but you knew he'd be angry if you yelled so you got scared and you ran."

"I'm a coward," Paige said with determination.

"You were a child. Children can't be cowards."

"What?" Paige asked bewildered and intrigued both.

"Children are instinctively programmed to save themselves from harm," Hawk explained. "You acted on instinct. Animal instinct. It's what a deer would do. Deer aren't cowards. It's what a cat would do. Cats aren't cowards. It's what a bird would do. Birds aren't cowards."

"Are you still going to marry me?"

"Yes, Paige. When you are eighteen, I will kiss you and give you a diamond ring and ask you to marry me all over again."

"Can you do that?" Paige asked.

"The Praetzels seem to have cornered the market on marrying the same person more than once, so I guess we can have the corner on getting engaged more than once."

"Promise you won't hate me if I tell you the rest?"

"I already know most of it," Hawk said. "I promise I not only won't hate you, but that we will still be engaged."

Ed realized at once that Hawk had not chosen a personal path, but had chosen a way to assure Paige that she could be absolutely honest.

"Mom saw me outside the door, I guess. Even with my head buried in the pillow, I heard Daddy yell, 'Who saw me?'"

"I shook and shook. I thought he'd come into the room any second. After a while Mom came in along with David. I told them what I saw. Mom said she told Daddy that David was outside the door."

"We're going to divorce Dad," David told me.

"I wet my bed every night afterward. I was too scared to go to the bathroom. Mom changed my sheets before Daddy got up, so he wouldn't guess about the lie."

"It's okay, Paige," Hawk said. "You were too young to cope."

"I never told anyone it was me," Paige confessed. "I didn't tell Tyler I knew."

"He is probably safer because he doesn't know."

"You mean Daddy killed David?"

Ed and Hawk exchanged glances. Neither had considered that possibility. Both began thinking about running an investigation into David's accident when Paige began to cry anew.

"Daddy killed him," she murmured. "I know it. I let David take the blame and Daddy killed him. David said he'd found out how Daddy got away with doing what he did. I miss him. He was such a good brother."

"I can be your big brother, Paige," Hawk offered. "I can watch out for you. We don't have to be engaged. You don't have to..."

Paige lifted her head. "I have a brother. Tyler is my brother. I want you to be my husband when I'm old enough."

"Paige, do you know what a husband is?" Hawk asked. Ed stayed silent, this time knowing that Hawk was somehow tuned in to this girl's needs.

"Sure, I so. Boyfriends you kiss and go on dates with and maybe even love for a while. Husbands are men you chose to spend your whole life with because you want to be with them forever. That's what Mom said."

"The person you choose at sixteen won't be the one you will want at thirty," Hawk pointed out. "Did your mother tell you that?"

"She told me about crushes," Paige said. "And she told me to pick a man I could see all the faults right away and if I liked him anyway, he was a good choice. If he had no faults, he was a bad choice. You are a good choice."

"What faults do you see?" Hawk asked, not so much to test her theory, as to find out a bit of truth about himself.

"Mom said never to tell the man I chose what his faults are. She said telling him would hurt him," Paige said.

"But maybe I could fix them so people would like me more."

"But I don't want you fixed," Paige said. "You're interesting and kind and smart and you like me. People like you already."

"People think I'm weird," Hawk shot out.

"Your friends don't think you're weird, do they?"

"I don't have a lot of friends," Hawk said.

"Then I'll be your wife and your friend," Paige said. "And you can be mine. And Ed will be a friend to both of us, so now we each have two friends."

"You didn't ask Ed," Hawk protested for some reason he couldn't pinpoint.

"Ed has been backing you up from the time we met. That's what friends do," Paige said. "And he offered to share his boa with me, and even though I don't like snakes, he does and he likes her especially and that was the kind of offer a friend would make. And I want to be friends with a man who owns a pet store that doesn't sell pets and that's weird, but it's a really great kind of weird."

"You take my breath away," Hawk explained.

"So we are still engaged?"

"Yes," Hawk replied softly. We are. And I'm happy about it."

"Me too," Paige said opening her hand. "Will you put the ring on my finger?"

"It will be too big," Hawk said. "It will slide off."

"Some girl's tape boy's rings so they fit," Paige said. "There's a first aid box on the wall."

Working together, the ring was fixed. Paige beamed when Hawk slipped it on her finger. Just seeing her so happy made him resolve to take her to the jeweler and have it cut to fit her finger.

"I like having a future," she said looking at it. "Don't you?"

"I do," Hawk said. They both smiled.

"Practice makes perfect," she quipped.

He liked that touch of humor. There was little about this child-woman he didn't like.

"We gotta know more about Penny," Ed said abruptly.

"I asked Mom about her more than once. Her reply was that Lindsman held the answers to my questions.

"Who is Lindsman?"

"I don't know," Paige said. "We should go back now. Ed will you announce our engagement. I don't have a mother to do it."

Shocked, Ed looked at Hawk.

Hawk nodded. "You are our first best friend."

"I don't speak too good," Ed said. "It won't come out as nice as it should."

"Just tell them I plan to court Paige not date her. We will have a chaperone whenever we're together," Hawk said.

"Tell them he's the man my mom picked out when she told me what to look for," Paige said.

"We could tell Stanley and he'd make it pretty," Ed offered.

"We want you," Hawk said.

Ed led the way back to the group still seated around the tables, desserts half eaten, and walking over to Claude had him ring the dinner bell. The groups grew silent.

"I gotta speech," Ed said. "You all gotta be quiet until I finish."

There was a titter from the table of teens. Ed glared at them and warned them that if there was one peep from them he'd see they never sat together again. He was rewarded with instant silence.

"These parties we come to always got a surprise in the package. I think this time we thought the surprise was not getting shot at."

The group laughed. That was what they thought.

"The new guys don't know about how things were, so let me tell them a little bit. Here was where we found out Claude and Harriet snuck off and got married on us. Harriet went south to shoot ducks. And here's where Alan Peets found out Eloise was gonna have a baby same time we did. He ain't never forgot that night. Then Evelyn and Bernard surprised us with being engaged. We was gonna be told about Martha and Michael that time. Then Lauren gave us the biggest surprise. She popped her fourth during dessert. It surprised everybody by being a boy. At one party Robert proposed to Bertha and surprised Aleta, which is always the most fun. Anyways, we got a special surprise for everybody again."

Ed stopped and the group waited silently.

"And you gotta let me finish before you react."

The group sat silent and motionless.

"I need head nods," Ed said.

He got them so he continued.

"As Paige Roach's stand-in mother," Ed said, "I'm announcing that Hawk asked her to marry him when she grows up and she said yes and he gave her his ring and they are engaged. Now this ain't no big joke and it ain't bad neither. This is real. Paige says her mom told her what kind of man to marry. She says Hawk is that man. Hawk says she is too young."

Ed paused. "Yeh, most of you agree. A lot more was said which is confidential, but I heard it all. This is real, Guys. It ain't love-at-first sight. It's choice. It ain't going steady. These two is engaged. Can't last? Well, I ain't a prophet so I don't know that, but I think it's got a better chance than most marriages do. One more thing. A lot of us see the uglier side of life a lot. This ain't that. Hawk plans to court Paige with a chaperone along on every meeting. He will kiss Paige for the first time on her eighteenth birthday. Yeh, that's right. They got engaged with no kissing. Paige thinks marriages planned by parents are best. She says her mom would have picked Hawk for her. She is right. That's all I gotta say."

The group was silent for a long moment.

Then Claude spoke up. "Hawk, you're welcome to come to Disney World with us. There's room in the plane for you. Just gotta put back those two seats I took out."

He winked at Aleta.

"You can bunk with us guys," Paul added. "Welcome to the trip!"

"I have work..." Hawk began.

Molly interrupted him. "You gotta come! Then I won't have to go on rides with grown-ups 'cause you'll go with Paige...Please!"

Hawk looked at Paige. "I want you to have the most fun you can. I do have a lot of work..."

"Please come," she said. "I'll have more fun if you come."

"Then, yes, I'll come," Hawk said. "I've always wanted to go to Disney World."

It was Martha who spoke next.

"Come, Paige, sit at our table."

Paige and Hawk moved toward Martha.

"You couldn't have picked a better man," Martha said graciously. "But I'm surprised you acted so quickly."

Paige looked straight into the sparkling blue eyes of the old woman and smiled. "Have you seen the competition?"

"Who?" Martha queried.

Paige nodded toward Dr. Reggie Barre. "My competition is any woman with brains and there are several of them here tonight. And a lady doesn't slough off a gentleman's proposal lightly. She doesn't play games with his feelings. A lady lets a gentleman know if she's interested. Hawk masked his feelings as he usually does, but they are real. He makes me feel warm and protected."

Evelyn could contain herself no longer.

"You want a brother to replace the one you lost," she charged and then blushed.

"Don't be upset," Paige said. "Hawk made that same suggestion."

"He said he'd be a big brother?" Evelyn queried.

"I told him I had a brother. Tyler isn't David, but he's a good brother too," Paige said. "If you knew him, you'd know that."

"You're too young to be making such a choice," Evelyn said, encouraged by the lack of censorship from those at the table.

"But Hawk isn't."

Evelyn turned her focus to Hawk. "She's a child!"

"Yes, she is–partly," Hawk said. "But she's the most enthralling person I've ever met. If two years or two months from now Paige decided not to marry me, I will still be richer for having known her. And I would appreciate it if you would all remember what I just said and remind me of that if I lose her."

Paige looked at the tall man whose hair covered half his face and said, "I'm so glad you've been wearing your hair so long so no woman has gotten a clear view of those eyes... Don't blush... Please... I'm sorry."

"I see the same miracle Ed saw," Martha announced.

"You think God approves?" Evelyn breathed.

Martha nodded.

"They have both made a choice that has resulted in joy. I consider this happening to be an extremely unlikely event."

"Well, Paige is less troubled," Dr. Barre noted.

"I told you I feel warm and protected," Paige repeated.

"Hawk," Martha said in her high-pitched crackly voice, "you've won yourself the grand prize. Congratulations!"

"And me?" Paige asked.

"You have made a great choice. Your mother would be so pleased."

Paige leaned back against Hawk's arm. "I told you."

"Yes, you did," he said softly. Whatever was going to happen, he decided, he was in for the duration. He wasn't an unlucky man so there was no reason to feel this detour into an unlikely romance was doomed. He was enjoying being with Paige. He'd never been so comfortable with a woman before. He couldn't help but think of her as a woman. She was almost as tall as Aleta. Her face had lost the roundness of childhood. Her waist curved in. Her body was no longer undefined. It was the body of a woman. Jocelyn looked younger although she was the same age.

Paige was his emotional match. He had no experience in love. Nor had she, but she knew how to be kind. He liked that. It was the one trait he wanted in a wife. So, she was perfect.

Too bad I'm not, he thought abruptly. In little over a year, she would be able to pick and choose. A dozen handsome men would be vying for her favor.

"What do you like best about Hawk?" Martha asked with childlike curiosity.

Paige thought for a moment.

"His looks, I guess," she said finally. "His face has character."

Hawk's surprise was so real that Martha and Hubert laughed.

"That's what Aleta said about Stanley," Hubert shared, still grinning. "It's a good omen, Hawk."

"Does my face have character?" Paige asked Hawk suddenly.

Those at the table held their breath. It was a tough question for a man unused to the traps women set.

Hawk, however, answered straightforwardly, "Your face has a special beauty, a beauty that comes from within as well as without."

"You impress me more each time you speak," Paige remarked. "You are a poet-philosopher I think."

"I'm a forensic scientist," Hawk clarified.

"That's your brain," Paige said. "I'm talking about your heart."

"I think you're met your match, Hawk," Hubert said. "Congratulations!"

The three police chiefs, who were approaching the table where the two sat, heard the exchange. They quickly added their congratulations to Hubert's. Others gathered around the couple immediately.

Much later, with Paige in tow, Hawk sought out Ed.

"You did a great job," he said.

"What a kick!" Ed remarked. "All them lawyers and doctors listening to me. Wow!"

"I think we underestimated Paige's mother," Hawk said. "I don't think we're looking for hard copies. I'm guessing she gave them all to her husband. He would never have let her leave otherwise."

"Mom said Lindsman would answer all my questions," Paige put in. "You need to find him."

"That's my next job," Ed said. "I'll hit the house first thing tomorrow."

"I guess the books and CD's can stay in my trunk until I get back," Hawk commented casually.

"Gimme the CD's," Ed decided.

Hawk led the way to his car still holding Paige's hand. She peered inside the trunk when Hawk opened it.

"You have the old books," she said. "Why?"

"Aleta thought that's where your mother might have hidden information."

"How?"

"Between the pages."

"You will be careful," Paige worried. "Especially with big Man book."

"That's why I took them from the house," Hawk replied. "So I could open them under ideal conditions."

Ed picked up the few CD's and closed the trunk. He turned to Paige and asked bluntly, "Do you know Penny's birthday?"

"No," Paige replied.

"When she died, was it snowing outside?" Hawk asked.

"It was warm."

"Why were you out of bed?" Hawk asked.

"Penny was crying. The firecrackers scared her," Paige said. "I was going to close her window so she couldn't hear them. Daddy always got mad when she cried."

Suddenly Paige began to cry. "She was so little. She didn't know not to cry. She was just scared."

Hawk put his arm around Paige and she turned and buried her face in his shoulder.

"You can stop remembering now," Hawk said. "Ed and I have enough information to start our investigation. So you start thinking of the fun we're going to have."

"Will you hold my hand in the airplane?" Paige asked.

"If you want me to," Hawk responded.

"I really am a coward," she confessed. "I'm afraid of airplanes and Ferris wheels and roller coasters and lots of stuff. I'm afraid to drive, so I don't have a license."

"We don't have to go on any rides that scare you."

"I don't want to ruin your fun."

"Sitting on the bench will be fun for me if you're there," Hawk said. "I won't push you to ride any ride you don't want to."

"Tyler will tease me. He always does."

"I'll take care of it," Hawk promised, then added so quietly he thought no one heard, "Somehow."

Paige giggled. "Somehow?"

"My mind's working on it," Hawk said defensively.

"Tyler thinks if he pushes me, I'll get over being scared," Paige said. "He's not trying to be mean."

"Thanks," Hawk said. "Now I know what to do."

"I helped?" Paige queried surprised.

"Yes."

Impulsively, she kissed him on the cheek. "Thanks!"

Flustered, Hawk said, "We better find Robert and Bertha and let them know you're okay."

"You are so funny," Paige quipped.

Hawk scowled. Paige saw it in the dim moonlight.

"I love that about you," she added and watched the scowl fade.

Chapter 9

The man parked on the road packed up his long range listening equipment and pulled away as the first cars left the party. He hadn't heard what went on in the barn. The fact that they went in a building blocked their conversation. Their lowered voices when they were near the barn hid the rest. Ed's announcement, however, came through loud and clear as did the conversation at the car.

Tully Machi was pleased with his night's work. He decided that it wasn't too late to make his report immediately. Kurt Van Horne seemed the impatient type.

The tall blonde thin-faced Dutchman greeted him coolly. Tully wondered if he ever greeted anyone warmly.

"I've got a lot of information. Some of it won't keep," Tully announced. Van Horne led him into his study and closed the door.

Tully told him about the engagement announcement.

Van Horne's first query was whether he thought Paige was pregnant.

"They just met."

"Then why?"

"She's a great looking chick. Why not?"

"You said he promised to keep his hands off," Van Horne said. "Will he?"

"Not a snowball's chance in hell."

"Good," Van Horne commented.   "I can use that. What else?"

Tully told him that they went into the barn and he couldn't hear or see them.

"Good! Good!" he exclaimed.

"Good?" Tully reacted.   "Good that I couldn't see them?"

"I can use it," Van Horne said.   "What else?"

Tully told him about the Disney World trip and the fact that Ed was going to go back to the house to look for some clue as to who Lindsman was. According to Paige he has all the answers."

"I want you to hit the house tonight," Van Horne said. "Get David's computer and any of my former wife's address books. Take the jewelry. I want the lockets. You can keep the rest. Make it look like a robbery."

"I don't do illegal stuff," Tully said.

"Then find someone who does," Van Horne ordered.

"Don't do that neither."

"How much?"

"I said I don't do that."

"How much?"

"Ten grand."

"Done," Van Horne declared turning around and opening the safe on the wall behind him. He handed Tully a small packet of bills. "Half now. Half when I get the computer, the address book, and the lockets."

Tully took the money.

"When you leave," Van Horne said casually, "torch the place."

Tully handed Van Horne back the money. "No."

"I want the kids to have no place to go when they come back from their trip."

"I'm no arsonist."

Van Horne added a second packet to the first. "Half now. Half later."

Tully looked at the money.

The slender Dutchman turned back to the safe and took out two more packets then closed the safe. He added both packets to the pile.

Twenty grand, Tully thought, with twenty more when he delivered. It was too tempting.

He reached for the money. Van Horne put his hand on top of Tully's. "I want half the house completely gutted."

"Gotcha," Tully said.

Van Horne's hand was withdrawn. Tully gathered up the four packets.

"No one is going to be at the Roach house, right?" Van Horne asked.

"The kids are staying with Robert Locke. He's got a big house over on the lake in that new subdivision on the western edge of Willow Glen."

"I want you to be sure the kids are in Willow Glen before you do anything," Van Horne said.

"You got it!"

Chapter 10

Stanley took Lyle aside as the guests were leaving. "Who do I report to?"

"You're still under me," Lyle replied. "You're guarding Arborville residents. I know Tontine Lake is in Willow Glen, but the Roach kids live on Walnut Street in Arborville."

"How are negotiations going for a joint force?"

"Oakwood is holding back. They don't want to pay for what they call their "crime-ridden" sister towns," Lyle said. "If you could get Aleta to accept a few Oakwood residents, the council might change its mind."

"Robert and I are considering not letting her accept any more clients ever."

"That works for me," Lyle quipped. "By the way, Hawk tells me you owe me one more shift at least."

"He's not charging for the time he spends with Paige, is he?"

"Shouldn't he?"

"No. He's mixing business with pleasure."

"As I recall, you did that too."

"Hell, Lyle!" Stanley exclaimed, exasperated. "You work it out. I owe whatever you say I owe."

Lyle nodded, accepting his grudging acquiescence.

"According to Ed, Paige is afraid. Even if nothing happens, your guarding her will help her sleep."

"But I'm still doing it alone," Stanley grumbled.

"I gave you Scooby," Lyle noted.

"I'll be chasing down nocturnal animals all night long," Stanley griped.

"It'll keep you awake."

"Yeh. It'll do that," Stanley groused. "That's the only thing that'll keep me awake."

"You called for police protection for those kids," Lyle said. "Are you saying it was merely a legal maneuver?"

"You had to remind me."

"I want you to start taking my men seriously."

"I take them seriously," Stanley protested.

"No, you don't. But a few more night shifts and you will," Lyle pronounced. "I understand Hawk took eight books to examine. That'll cost you at least four shifts."

"An hour a book?" Stanley asked, dismayed.

"Hawk is a careful researcher. He doesn't miss much."

"I have a day job, you know," Stanley reminded him.

"That's why I'm only using you evenings, nights and weekends."

"And I have a bum leg," Stanley went on.

"Which is why I'll give you the really dull assignments, the ones where it won't matter that you can't run."

"You're enjoying this."

"You bet!"

"Shit!"

Lyle drove Stanley and Scooby to their post. They entered the area ahead of the dinner guests departing from the Praetzel house. Stanley noticed that three officers left various locations when Lyle drove through the gate.

"You had three men on?"

"I didn't want bombs planted while we were partying. It would have been an ideal time to plant one."

"Did I ever tell you you're one hellava police chief?"

"Finally. Some recognition."

"I am honored to be a member of your force."

"You still have to stand guard."

"Have a good night, Chief," Stanley said as he got out of the car, hopping on one leg until he retrieved his crutches. Scooby pranced around him as soon as he was released from the car.

The kids piled out of Claude and Robert's cars.

"They gave us a police guard on crutches," Tyler said. "What's with that?"

"Because next to the chief, he's the best shot on the force," Claude said.

"Cool!" Tyler exclaimed.

"It's Scooby!" Molly squealed. "He's a guard dog!"

"Guard dog-in-training," Robert said.

"Can we watch him guard?" Molly asked.

"He doesn't go on duty until you go into the house," Robert said.

"Can I watch him from the window?" Molly persisted.

"Sure," Robert said. "Stanley, do your rounds with Scooby so Molly can watch."

"Scooby, heel!" Stanley ordered. To his amazement Scooby ran to his left side and trotted beside him down the road. Stanley moved at an uneven pace, but Scooby adjusted. When he passed the Luther's house, he paused to ask Claude where their dogs were.

"Guarding your wife," Claude said. "Harriet's idea."

"Thanks."

"King's there too," Claude added. "Scooby is our sole protector this evening."

"I don't expect trouble," Stanley predicted.

"Neither, obviously, does Arborville's finest. They've left you to fend for yourself."

"Lyle considers Scooby the real guard. I think I'm just window dressing."

One by one the lights in the houses went out.

Stanley found he liked the absence of the light better. His eyes quickly adjusted to the dim light of the half moon and he found himself more comfortable shrouded in darkness. He and Scooby walked around the houses every half hour and then reported in.

At one thirty, a car came through the gates without lights. Scooby bristled at its approach and Stanley rose from his chair. The car moved slowly down the road that circled the lake. Stanley called for backup.

When the car stopped at the corner of Claude's house, Scooby barked in protest. A flashlight caught Scooby and Stanley in its beam.

Stanley, who had been told by Aleta, to have his gun drawn whenever he patrolled using his crutches, had it in his hand with the safety off. He instantly shouted an order.

"Police! Come out of the car with your hands up."

The man shoved the gear into reverse and gunned the engine. Stanley shot a round into the driver's side door as the car leaped backward.

Instantly, the lights came on in the house he was standing in front of.

The car continued to move down the road. Its headlights were suddenly flicked on. Stanley moved his head slightly and again shouted at the driver to stop. The car kept moving. Stanley aimed and fired. His second round hit the car's right headlight. Lights came on in all the occupied houses.

A police siren could be heard in the distance.

Stanley took another shot and the other headlight was shattered.

He saw the gate open and the car back through it. It sat motionless alongside the road leading to the subdivision gate. The patrol car flew past it.

Stanley radioed that he'd shot out both headlights and the car was heading north.

The police car turned around and took off.

A second car arrived and turned around as well.

Using his flashlight, Stanley directed the gathering of the headlight fragments by Claude and Harriet. At the same time, he calmed the rest of the residents and sent them back to their houses.

Strangely, the road between Willow Glen and Arborville was missed in the police search. Tully Machi cursed all the way between the towns. What had possessed that cop to start shooting? And what was he doing on crutches? But most of all, why was there a police guard on the house where the kids were?

One thing that told him. Those kids were going nowhere. Their house in Arborville would be empty. He only hoped it would also be unguarded.

He pulled into the driveway of the Walnut Street house and bumped into the garage door. Swearing, he set the brake and leaped out.

He broke the glass in the back door and let himself in. He started in the mother's room. He opened the box holding the lockets. Four. One for each child. He grabbed a handful of jewelry and went over to her desk.

He found two old address books and stuck them into the backpack. He grabbed the personal correspondence he found in the second side drawer and added it.

He stopped in the boys' room. He found a stash of unmarked CD's and decided they could be either the mother's files or back-up files. How could the searchers have missed them? It didn't matter. He put them in the backpack. He searched both desk drawers and dumped out the pencil holder, hunted through the model airplanes on the shelf. No flash drives, no I Pod's, no PDA's.

He tucked the laptop under his arm and went into the girls' room. He was surprised Paige didn't have a computer of her own. He searched for hand-held devices and came up with nothing. That was reasonable. If they had any, they would have them with them.

As he left the girls' room he shut the door. He did it without thinking. He set the backpack and laptop next to the back door and picked up the gas can. He walked through the house splashing gasoline on the most flammable items in each room. By the time he reached the girls' room, the can was empty.

He carried it back into the kitchen thinking that if he left it, it might be traceable. He carried everything out to the car and put it all in the trunk. He looked around. Every house on the street was dark. No cars were even traveling on the cross street. It was truly the dead of night.

He ran to the back door and opened it. He struck a match and tossed it on some of the gasoline spill. He watched the flames sprout up and travel along the rope of gasoline that led through the two bedrooms into the living room.

He backed out and ran to his car. He drove down a few blocks, turned off his engine and waited in the darkness under a huge oak tree.

He watched the numbers on his digital watch count off the minutes. Five minutes passed before he heard the sirens.

He waited until the firefight was at its zenith.

While the fire fighters fought to save the house and the police kept people out of their way, Tully Machi eased his car down the street. Slowly and cautiously he slipped out of town without lights.

Stanley heard the radio calls and recognized the address. He stepped up his patrols and varied his route each time. He was behind the houses on the lakeside when the two Willow Glen patrol units entered the grounds.

Both cars parked and Stanley and Scooby hurried to meet them.

"So it's true," one of Milani's men said. "You're working on crutches."

"It was suppose to be an uneventful night," Stanley said.

"We heard you shot up a car," the other man commented.

"I don't like to be disobeyed," Stanley quipped.

The man from the second car said, "Chief West wants you at the arson site."

"Me? Why?"

"Chief Milani didn't tell me. He just dispatched me to fetch you."

"And these two stay here, right?" Stanley asked.

"Which house?" one of the other officers asked.

Stanley pointed to Robert's house, holstered his gun and headed for the patrol car. Scooby followed him.

"Milani didn't say anything about a dog," the driver objected.

"He lays at my feet," Stanley said.

"Then he does it in back."

"Fair enough," Stanley said agreeably. He realized he could use the extra room for his leg.

The firemen were finishing up when Stanley arrived at the scene. Stanley saw Hawk talking to Lyle. He joined the two.

"I hope you're not backing out of the trip," Stanley said to Hawk. "Paige won't understand."

"I've got him until eight," Lyle said.

"I'll make sure they hold the flight," Stanley promised. "Tyler told Paul Junior he'd never seen Paige smile so much."

"Or cry, I'll bet," Hawk added. "Her emotions were on a roller coaster."

"We didn't see her crying," Stanley mentioned. "That was reserved for you."

"Remember, she's young," Lyle cautioned.

"You think she's using me?" Hawk asked.

"People who don't need each other don't get married," Lyle responded. "Stanley is there any chance you remember what the guy you shot at looked like?"

"Yes."

"Do you remember exactly where you shot out the headlights?" Hawk asked.

"Pretty much."

"I can probably find fragments then," Hawk told Lyle.

"No need," Stanley said. "I picked them up, bagged them and Harriet took charge of them."

"She's a deputy," Lyle said.

"Did you find any fragments here?" Stanley asked.

"Some up near the garage door. I'm guessing that driving without lights, he banged into the door," Hawk said. "There weren't enough fragments for him to have broken his headlight there, besides the bumper would have hit the door first, so the pieces were jarred loose from a headlight that was already smashed."

"So you think it was the same man?" Stanley asked Lyle.

"I'm thinking I owe you," Lyle said.

"How much is your gratitude worth?" Stanley inquired. "Do I get to go home and crawl into bed?"

"As soon as you give me the man's description, you're free to go."

"My leg thanks you," Stanley said.

"You still owe me another couple of shifts," Lyle said.

"I still owe you?" Stanley asked, staggered.

"I'll wait until your leg is better," was Lyle's response.

"How many shifts?"

"Three."

"That isn't a couple!" Stanley protested.

"Four."

"That's even less of a couple."

"Do you want to go for five?"

"Whose court have you been visiting?" Stanley said. "Now that I know better than to argue with you..."

"Only when you're working under me," Lyle explained.

"Okay, now that I understand that, can we go back to three?"

"You're stuck with four."

"Yes, Sir," Stanley said respectfully. This man didn't command his men's respect because he was bigger or stronger physically. Lyle was barely average height, lightweight and without apparent muscular strength. Stanley was taller, heavier, although not by much, and more muscular. Lyle was the best marksman on the force and his intellect matched Stanley's. Both men were leaders but Lyle expected even leaders working under him to acknowledge that he was in charge of all police matters. The lines had been blurred by their friendship. Stanley realized that Lyle needed him to be as compliant as his other officers when he was wearing a deputy's badge. He realized that he could argue with him when he wasn't.

"Four," Lyle repeated.

"Whatever you say, Chief. As I said before, it's your call," Stanley replied evenly. "Thank you for the time off."

"Let's do the sketch now," Lyle said.

Stanley stayed in place while Lyle fetched his pad. He remembered that Lyle hadn't come rushing over when he'd shot up the car. Lyle had assumed Stanley had acted appropriately. Stanley appreciated that level of trust.

When Lyle returned, Stanley asked, "May I do my report on the shooting tomorrow morning?"

Lyle shook his head. "Sorry. I need it tonight."

"Then I'll do it as soon as we finish," Stanley said plowing immediately into the description. "The man had a large head with a square face. He was older and heavy-set. By older I mean late forties, maybe early fifties."

As Stanley recalled what his eyes had seen, Lyle sketched. Afterward, Stanley was driven to the station where he completed his report about the shooting. Then he was driven to Harriet's where he picked up the two marked packets of headlight fragments and gave them to the driver to deliver to Hawk. He was dropped off at his house at five thirty.

"An hour and a half," he murmured. "Lyle, you are a taskmaster."

For some reason he respected him even more because he was.

He awakened two hours later when he felt Aleta unbuckling his belt. He didn't remember falling asleep fully dressed.

"Hard night?" she asked.

"I shot up a car."

"What did it do?" she asked concentrating on removing his trousers without hurting his leg.

"It wouldn't stop when I told it to," Stanley went on. "I had to write a report. Do you know how hard it is to justify shooting a car?"

"But it got away," she said pulling his trousers off.

"Yes. It went over and burned up the Roach house," he replied, wondering where his shoes and socks were.

"How bad?" she asked folding his trousers just as he would have done.

"From what I could see, there was almost nothing left."

"Do the kids know?" she said, laying down his trousers and coming back toward him.

"I told Harriet. She and Claude are going to tell them when they wake up."

"Does Hawk know?" she asked taking hold of his briefs and easing them down his leg.

"He was on the scene," Stanley replied, unbuttoning his shirt.

"Is he still going to Disney World with Paige?"

"Yes, he is. I'm going to hold the plane if I have to."

"Good. Now you have to get up and get ready to close the trap on Doris Fraza," Aleta said stepping back. "I won't be able to go. Jamara called. Her son is sick. We have a spare bottle in the refrigerator. She'll drop off two more bottles at eleven."

"I need you, Aleta," Stanley said. "Can't we take Gerard with us?"

"I can't get three of us ready."

Stanley stiffened at the implication.

"I can take care of myself."

She took his shirt and began to fold it. "You can't, but don't worry. I'll figure it out."

Aleta bandaged his wound. It was nearly healed. The bandage was mostly for protection. The leg was still stiff. He started therapy on Monday.

After Aleta had helped him dress, he noticed there was little time left for her to dress let alone eat. He walked into the kitchen and found Paul feeding Gerard.

"I can't be late," Stanley stated flatly.

"I can finish feeding Gerard on the way," Paul said, rising. "The bags are in the car."

They made it to the airfield with ten minutes to spare. All the travelers except for Hawk were there.

The TV cameraman was set up and taking photos of the group as they boarded the plane. Paul handed Aleta the baby and hurried to join the group. Paige looked worried and Stanley assured her Hawk was coming. "He and I worked last night, but the chief promised Hawk would be done in time to leave."

"He is intense," Paige said. "He could just get so involved that he'd forget time."

"You know him well," Stanley said. "But I need you to wait for him inside the plane. It will not take off without him."

"Promise?"

"That's a promise," Stanley said.

Paige withdrew into the interior of the plane and took a window seat.

Paige stared at the empty airfield on the opposite side of the plane. It was so empty. Tears sprang into her eyes. She couldn't believe how often she was crying since meeting Hawk. It was as if by sharing her secret she'd opened the floodgates to her emotions. She could finally feel once again. She didn't know if she was happy or sad.

Even though her mother and brother knew her secret it was never discussed. Whenever she'd attempted to broach the topic, her mother had said that the answers were in Lindsman.

She had needed to talk, to have questions answered, to hopefully be absolved of her feelings of guilt over her inaction. Hawk had somehow recognized that part of her wounded emotions and had spoken the words she longed to hear. But she had needed to hear them from her mother, her mother whose child Penny was. She needed her mother's forgiveness. She was so confused as to why she alone was home schooled until she reached junior high.

She remembered how great her fear of starting school was. Her mother had agreed to teach her at home. The bed-wetting had stopped as soon as the family minus the father had settled in the comfortable old house on a tree-lined street in Arborville.

Their mother had chosen the neighborhood carefully. David, Tyler and Molly had fit in well. Only Paige didn't fit in. The neighborhood children didn't understand why she didn't go to school with everyone else. Also she didn't come out to play very often, electing instead to stay inside and read.

Then Hawk broke through her reserve with that single comment. Paige had been schooled enough by her mother to recognize that the lightly offered comment sprang from a need matching her own.

Now she wondered if she had been mistaken. It had seemed so right last night. Had a night of working brought reality raining like cold water on his head? Was she just a flight of fancy in his mind's eye?

Had he met with derision over his quick engagement? He was a man of great sensitivity. Scorn would crush him. Last night his new friends, who included men he worked with, had showered him with approbation. Had it been enough?

She leaned against the window and let her tears flow. She feared the worst.

The hand that touched her shoulder was gentle. She quickly wiped her eyes and looked up.

"Hawk!" she exclaimed, choking back her sobs. "You're here."

He slipped into the seat beside her and put his arm around her and held her. She buried her head in his shoulder and cried quietly, clinging to him fiercely.

He kissed her hair and let her cry. As Stanley had said, her crying was reserved for him. He liked being special.

He knew the crying wasn't anything he had done. It was still the result of the memories that had been stirred up yesterday. The fire had given validity to her story.

The computer was gone as were the lockets. While he'd taken some CD's, he noticed that more were missing. The desk was a charred mess, but he saw that the drawers had been opened. All this he pointed out to Chief West.

He'd gone into the girl's room and noted that while water damaged, the quilts and stuffed animals were intact. He'd worried aloud that someone might figure they were ruined and toss them.

Lyle had gathered them up. He had stashed them in his trunk telling Hawk that if Lauren couldn't restore them, no one could.

"I owe you," Hawk had said.

Lyle had smiled. "Never say that to me. I collect."

"So Aleta told me," Hawk had admitted. "I'll pay."

Now as he held Paige he realized he'd done the right thing. This child didn't need to lose everything she valued.

Bertha came over. "Can I help?" she offered quietly.

Hawk shook his head. "She's just glad I'm here."

Paige's head, despite being buried in Hawk's shoulder, nodded in agreement.

"Well, as long as you're happy," Bertha said, "I'll leave you be."

Hawk was glad everyone's attention was focused on the other side of the plane. He would feel Paige settling down. Another fifteen minutes and she'd be able to pull herself together. He hoped it would take that long for Stanley to take care of business.

Outside the plane, Stanley, using a portable mike, was thanking the supporters for their contributions. He then presented Kitty's father with a credit card to pay for room, tickets, meals, souvenirs and whatever else Kitty wanted. The crowd clapped.

Stanley noticed Justin Conway's car approaching. Justin was not alone. Stanley pointed to the car and announced, "It looks as if Mrs. Doris Fraza is going to make a rare public appearance.

The crowd turned and clapped as Justin pulled up and opened the door. A small, fat woman with tight curls hugging her head struggled to get out of the car. Justin offered her his hand, but she brushed it away.

The TV cameraman moved in and the fat woman smiled. The crowd parted and she had no choice but to walk toward Stanley.

When she was only a few feet away, Stanley said, "Mrs. Fraza, your group of supporters is here to thank you for making this trip possible for Kitty Witherspoon."

Stanley handed her the mike and she turned and smiled at the crowd. She thanked them for their support of her fledgling group.

"Support," she said, "which has made this trip possible."

Stanley realized, at once, that this woman was going to say nothing incriminating. He announced that Kitty needed rest for the trip. People shouted their well wishes and Kitty waved at them. Her parents, having been prepped in advance by Stanley, carried her to the bed in the back of the plane and bade her rest until the plane was ready to take off.

Stanley nodded at Justin who asked his first question, "Exactly how much money were you able to raise for this child's wish?"

"I don't want to discuss figures at this juncture. The trip will cost what it will cost."

"But your foundation is underwriting this venture?"

"We will cover the expenses within our budget," Doris said smoothly.

"How much does your budget allow for this trip?"

"The child's portion," Doris responded. "We are paying all the child's expenses but we are not paying for the parents'."

"Children Kitty's age stay free at the hotel," Justin commented.

"There are many other expenses," Doris said.

Aleta saw Doris slipping past Justin's questions. She caught her husband's eye and her raised brow was answered with an almost imperceptible nod.

Baby cuddled against her shoulder, Aleta took a step forward and said, "You take your responsibility in this venture seriously, don't you?"

"Yes, I do."

"And you intend to pay for all Kitty's expenses this trip, correct?"

"Yes."

Doris eyed the young mother suspiciously. Her sixth sense told her there was a trap about to be sprung.

Aleta smiled. "According to my calculations, Tri-City Wishes for Kids will write a check for $2,287.13."

"That's too much money," Doris faltered. "I need to consider each expense."

"Did you make a reservation at the Disney Hotel for Kitty?"

"No, I was planning to do that."

"You were told about the trip yesterday. The room rate is standard. Why didn't you make the phone call to order the room and the tickets to Disneyland?"

"I needed time to plan."

"Plan what?" Aleta said. "The transportation has been taken care of. All that was left was the room reservation and Disneyland tickets."

"Little extras to make the trip more fun."

"Like balloons and stuffed animals to greet her in her room and a limousine ride from the airport?"

"Yes, like that," Doris said.

"I called the hotel this morning and arranged for that as well as for the tickets to the Magic Kingdom and the Animal Kingdom. I also ordered unlimited room service and transportation to the theme parks. That's why I know how much is due."

Stanley stared at his wife. When had she done all this?

"Who are you?" Doris said. "How dare you act so presumptuously? You have no right to spend the Foundation's money."

"We are Kitty Witherspoon's attorneys," Aleta said.

A cheer went up from the crowd.

"We are here to see that Kitty gets her wish and that you turn over the money collected for that purpose."

"I won't! You can't!"

"Are you publicly going to refuse to fund Kitty's wish with the monies you collected for that purpose?"

"Yes," Doris said. "I'm in charge. And I will grant her wish in my time, not yours."

"The time was dictated by Kitty's health," Aleta said. "Chief West, she's all yours."

To Doris Fraza's shock she was arrested for fraud while the TV cameras recorded every minute.

The crowd cheered as she was led away.

Kitty and her parents appeared in the doorway and the crowd's cheering increased in volume. Kitty smiled and waved and the crowd waved back and shouted at her to have fun.

The plane's door was closed and Claude and Robert took their seats and did their final pre-flight check. It was exactly nine o'clock.

"That was anti-climactic," Stanley commented as he and Aleta drove home. "We didn't get the money."

"She's in jail," Aleta said quietly.

"I couldn't believe she refused outright."

"That will make the news," Aleta rejoined. "Her Foundation won't recover."

"The money's already gone."

"We put Doris Fraza out of business."

"She'll just go elsewhere."

"You don't think she'll be convicted," Aleta asked.

"I think she'll squeeze out because you called the hotel and set things up," Stanley said. "She'll accuse you of taking over."

"I messed up?" Aleta asked, woebegone.

"Yes."

"I thought I was helping."

"I had a plan."

"Would your plan have worked?"

"No better than yours actually," Stanley admitted. "I feel like we both failed."

"We're not used to that, are we?" Aleta said.

"I fail enough so I'm used to that," Stanley said. "But I'm not used to you failing."

"It's not a total loss," Aleta said. "Kitty got her wish."

"And she's going to enjoy sharing her experience with a bunch of kids," Stanley added. "Disney World is always more fun with a group."

Before the plane took off, Hawk fastened Paige's seat belt and his and then put his arms around her again.

Tyler looked over.

"She's scared of everything!" he sneered.

"Actually, she's not," Hawk said coolly. "She's a very brave person."

"She shouldn't be scared of riding in a plane," Tyler declared.

"Fear isn't a rational behavior. It just happens. She's actually being brave right now because she's doing something she's afraid to do. That's what bravery is–facing what you're afraid of."

"She's not brave. Soldiers are brave. Those guys face real danger," Tyler shot back. "She's a baby."

"You hurt her when you call her names," Hawk said.

"She needs to grow up."

"She's working at it," Hawk said. "How about you? When are you going to be adult enough not to call your sister names? David never did it, did he?"

"How do you know?"

"I just do," Hawk said. "Tell you what. Every time you want to call her a name and you don't, I'll give you a buck."

"How'll you know I won't cheat?"

"Because you're too grown-up to cheat," Hawk said. "And if you slip up, you owe me two bucks each time."

"I won't slip up," Tyler stated. "You're gonna be broke."

Hawk smiled. "I'm betting you can't do it."

"You'd be surprised what I can do," Tyler bragged.

"We'll see."

He looked down at Paige who was pushing herself back into her seat. The plane began to taxi to the runway. Instantly, she was back burying her head in his shoulder.

Hawk looked at Tyler who held up a finger.

"One nothing," the boy said.

Hawk nodded. The plane bumped along the runway and Paige gripped Hawk's shirt. He tightened his embrace slightly as the plane sped up. It left the ground smoothly. Hawk leaned over and told Paige they were in the air.

"We just missed the rabbit hole. I was sure we were going to wind up in China instead of Florida."

Paige said nothing but stayed attached to his shirt.

"You can cling to me the whole trip if you want," Hawk said, "but if you lean back a bit I can hear your answers."

Paige mumbled, "What answers?"

"To what kind of wedding you want," Hawk said. "We are, after all, engaged. We can talk about that. Weddings take a lot of planning."

Paige lifted her head slightly.

"You'd be beautiful in white," Hawk commented.

She wiped her eyes on his shirt. Suddenly she realized what she'd done. She drew back and apologized for her action.

"No harm done," Hawk said.

"Do you want children?" Paige asked abruptly.

"If you do."

"I want to know what you want."

"I'll leave it up to you. You're the one who has to be pregnant."

"Mom said her pregnancies were easy," Paige said. "It's inherited you know."

"Pregnancies?" Hawk joked.

"No, that we have to do," Paige said soberly. "Carrying the baby. Mom said that part was easy."

"How many children do you want?"

"Four."

"That's a nice number," Hawk said. "Four boys. I'd like that."

"Half and half," Paige said.

"How do you make babies that are half boys half girls?"

Paige sat back and scowled, "Two boys. Two girls."

"And you know how to do this?" Hawk asked.

"Yes," Paige said. "Early part of the cycle you get boys, later part you get girls...or the other way around. I forget, but we can experiment on the first one."

"So the first one can be either?"

"So can the second," Paige said.

"And if we get one of each, we don't have to worry about the third one either," Hawk added.

"Let's do it that way," Paige said.

"What do we do if we have three boys in a row?"

"Then we have five instead of four."

"And four boys in a row?"

"Then we adopt two girls," Paige said, a twinkle in her eye. "I have my limits you know."

"Evidently."

"We need to wait until I'm finished with school," she said.

"High school or college?"

"We aren't even getting married until I'm finished with high school," Paige said. "I'm young. I'll still be in my twenties. And men's sperm stays good forever."

Hawk laughed. "I'm glad to know that. Here I thought there was an expiration date stamped somewhere."

"Aren't you glad I'm the one that's younger?"

Hawk smiled. "Yes, I am."

"You do know I can cook, don't you?"

"No. I didn't."

"Mom taught me. She started when she got cancer. Seriously, that is. She thought I'd have to cook for the rest. And after she died, I did."

"What else can you do?"

"Laundry."

"My, you are a prize!" Hawk said.

"I'm a good shopper too," Paige said. "It's an art, you know.   Sometimes it's smart to pay more for quality. Sometimes generic is as good."

"I'm good at my job and that's about it."

"You're good at making me feel good," Paige said. "That's important to me."

"You do have your priorities in order," Hawk said. "You make me feel good too. You make me feel special."

"I cry all over you all the time."

"Yes, you do," Hawk said. "But you need to cry right now.   You've saved those tears for so long you almost drowned in them."

"This morning I was scared you weren't coming," Paige said. "I didn't know how much it mattered until then," Paige said tremulously. "If I tell you I need you, will that scare you?"

"No, it won't," Hawk replied evenly.

"It's not normal," Paige said. "I know that, but I can't help it."

"You are going through an extremely trying time, Paige. But the woman I see, fear and all, I've fallen in love with."

The words were spoken so quietly that Paige almost didn't hear them. That she did didn't help. She was certain she hadn't heard Hawk correctly. He couldn't have said that.

"What did you just say?" Paige asked.

"That you've been through too many losses. Last night's fire was one too many."

"After that," Paige urged.

"I said that I've fallen in love with you," Hawk reiterated. "Does that frighten you?"

"No, it's like you've just filled all the holes in my heart," she murmured, snuggling closer. "Do you want to kiss me?"

"More than anything, but I'm not going to."

"Even if I said it was okay?"

"Even then."

"Not until I'm eighteen, right?" Paige posed. "Suppose we were married, would you do it then?"

"Yes, but I'm not marrying you early."

"Not even if my life depended on it?"

"Not even then."

"My father is going to kill me," Paige stated flatly. "I'm not being scared of nothing. And you know it. Somehow he knows that I know."

"You're free to find someone else to marry if you believe that is your only way out," Hawk said.

"No. I'm not," Paige said.

"Of course you are. I won't hold you back."

"I know you won't," Paige said. "But I'm not free to marry anyone else."

"Why not?"

"Because I love you," Paige said quietly. "I want to be your wife."

"But I won't marry you before you're an adult," Hawk explained. "I won't marry a child, even if she is more woman than child."

"I'll just have to wait then," Paige said somberly. "Life without you won't be any good at all."

"You're willing to wait?" Hawk asked, pleased that that question was answered.

"Yes, I am," Paige said, laying her head on Hawk's shoulder. "And I've decided that I'm not letting you go no matter what."

As she lay in his embrace, Hawk wondered if he could last until she was eighteen.

Chapter 11

Back at the Praetzel farm in Willow Glen, Ed Ornstein entered the front door without knocking. Emma was at his side as usual.

Scooby was ecstatic. He loved his mother and now that he was maturing, he had a new reason for his effusive greeting. He told Stoney, Harriet's big male Chesapeake Bay Retriever, that Emma was his property.

One whiff told Stoney she wasn't in season. Ed felt Emma's warning rumble against his leg. No sound accompanied the tremble as far as Ed could tell, but Stoney got the message and backed off.

"I was going to ask you to wait until I put Stoney up, but I guess Emma took care of things," Aleta said. "So, Ed, what's up?"

"I got a report," he said as he went into the kitchen and lifted the cake cover. "Bertha left us homemade rolls. You got any coffee?"

Stanley took the pot off the warmer. "Enough for you and me. Aleta, you get milk."

Aleta settled Gerard in his infant seat and took the pot from Stanley.

She waited on the two men while Ed talked.

"I got a visitor at my place this morning," Ed said. "He were put off big time."

"He didn't see the real layout, did he?"

"Just the front office. He figured me to be a real loser."

Aleta sat down. "It's hard sometimes when you're successful at your subterfuge to be successful."

"Aleta, you're talking double talk," Stanley said.

"No, I'm not. Ed put on the front of being an inept private eye barely eking out a living. Only a few people know he's one of the sharpest men in the business. He puts people off with his talk, manner and office. But when a stranger accepts his cover, it sometimes hurts."

"She's right," Ed agreed. "I got an ego and Van Horne is one arrogant ass. I wanted to knock him off his pegs."

"Thanks for not doing it," Aleta said. "We appreciate your keeping a low profile."

"That's why I come in person. I needed a cup of coffee and one of Bertha's sweet rolls."

"And the respect of two people you respect," Aleta stated openly.

"Yeh, that too," he agreed.

"So what did Van Horne want?" Stanley asked.

"To tell me that Paige was crazy. That her mother coddled her. That when he got his kids back he'd see she got proper psychiatric help."

"What does he mean?" Aleta asked in a whisper.

"A nut house," Ed said. "Only he called it a fancy name."

"What did you say?" Stanley asked.

"That she seemed okay to me."

"Go on," Aleta urged.

"Then he give me a bill from a home for retards. He claims Penny lives there. He tells me I can check, as if I need his highness's permission. He and his late wife fought over 'burying Penny'. Them's the words she used."

"Did you believe him?" Aleta asked.

"I checked. There's a Penny Van Horne living there. Been there for ten years."

"So Paige is delusional?" Aleta queried.

"Would seem so," Ed said. "Only I believe her."

"Will a judge?" Stanley asked.

"No way," Ed said. "The man convinced me and I know he was lying."

"Know?" Aleta questioned. "You know? How?"

"He burned the kids outta their home."

"There's no proof," Stanley said.

"Hawk called me. The lockets and the computer was taken. Jewelry too. Only Hawk figures that was to make the fire look like a cover up on the theft."

"And you don't think it was a cover up?"

"Oh, it were that alright. Only it were a cover up for something else. He took the CD's, the ones I was going for this morning. Who the hell steals CD's?"

"Lots of people," Stanley offered.

"These weren't music CD's. All them was fried in the fire. He took the computer CD's."

"It's thin," Stanley said. "I trust your judgment, but it won't hold up in court. I need more."

"That's why I'm here," Ed said. "It'll take a lotta digging."

"Anything on the CD's you got?"

"Not so far. Dean's on them."

"Keep going. Everyone will be back on Tuesday," Stanley said. "I have to turn the kids over to Social Services then."

"Anyway you can keep them like they is?"

"If you can get any evidence that can keep the investigation open, then we maybe keep them in protective custody. I'm going to owe Lyle the next year of my life on this one unless you can give him an argument he can use to support his using his force this way."

"You get the night shift, huh?" Ed asked.

"Oh, I'm counting on it," Stanley sighed. "I'm cheap labor."

"You're actually free," Aleta put in.

"Don't you dare smile!" Stanley warned. "It's not funny."

"You can always quit," Aleta retorted.

"No, I can't and you know it. I can't quit because I don't like the assignment or the hours."

"You do have a firm to run," she pointed out.

"I want those kids protected," Stanley declared. "It's worth my time."

Aleta became silent. He said it. Now he would believe it. And it would make things easier.

Aleta's mind made a quantum leap.

"Can those computers that do age-progression to picture lost children reverse the process?"

"I dunno," Ed said. "Nobody wants to go the other way."

"We have a picture of Penny as a baby," Aleta said. "It is in the fifth locket. Hawk still has it hasn't he?"

"You want an age-progression on that?" Ed asked.

"Yes, I do," Aleta said, "but I want an age-regression done on Penny Van Horne in the home."

"It's not proof," Stanley said.

"We need to keep the investigation open," Aleta said. "If it looks like it's possible that there are two kids involved, we can ask for a footprint of the Penny Van Horne in the home and compare it to the one on the birth record. If the experts say that the Penny in the home is not Van Horne's Penny then the police can start an investigation."

"Hawk is gonna stay in touch," Ed said. "How much do I tell him?"

"Just that you're working on it," Stanley said. "We absolutely must keep our suspicions between us until we have enough for the police to investigate," Stanley said. "If we even hint that we believe Paige, she will be in danger."

"He will want to assure Paige," Aleta said.

"He can't," Stanley said. "What we don't want is to raise her hopes and then watch the judge give her father custody."

"You think Van Horne is going to get them kids back?"

"That's what I think," Stanley said. "Our problem with the age-progression or regression is that kids with Down's look a lot alike. The syndrome, which is genetic, alters their appearance. It changes not only the look around the eyes but other facial characteristics as well."

"So whatcha want me to do?"

"Go ahead with the plan," Stanley said.

After Ed left, Aleta kissed her husband and said, "Go lay down."

"Will you join me?"

"I've some things to do," Aleta said. "One of them is to take care of your son."

"I want to finish what we started."

"After Jamara delivers us the milk."

"Promise."

"I feel sorry for Hawk," Aleta said. "Do you remember what it was like?"

"Remember? It hasn't even been a year. My memory is fine."

"But, we're seasoned."

"Seasoned? We're seasoned?" Stanley breathed.

"Yes, as in experienced, practiced..."

Stanley cut in. "As in hardened, 'veteran', battle-scarred?"

"Oh, must you men always think in terms of battle," Aleta retorted. "Seasoned as in practical, skillful, accomplished, competent, sophisticated..."

"Sophisticated? You?"

"Be careful. You're near the edge of the ice."

"It's summer. There is no ice."

"Go to bed," Aleta said. "I'll join you when the coast is clear."

"You'll wake me?"

"I'll wake you. We're going on a picnic, remember."

"Oh, Aleta," Stanley groaned. "I can't do that. My leg won't take a horseback ride."

"I'll tell Hubbs."

"Finish dressing first," Stanley said.

"You noticed."

"Look, teasing me is one thing, but teasing Hubbs is wrong."

"I thought no one would notice," she blushed.

Stanley was abashed. "No one did. I just guessed because you got dressed so fast."

"I don't want to embarrass Hubbs," she said, pulling off her blouse as she walked toward the bedroom.

"Aleta!" Stanley shouted limping after her.

By the time he entered the bedroom, she was stark naked, her clothes draped casually on the chairs in the room. She was rummaging through the dresser drawers.

"Stop!" he called.

Aleta turned.

"My God, you're beautiful," he murmured. "You still take my breath away. We don't have to remember how it was. It still is the way it was."

"Really?" Aleta queried softly.

"Come here so we can pick up from where we left off this morning."

"Jamara might come."

"Lock the door," Stanley said. "She knows where the refrigerator is."

"I have things to do," she protested mildly.

"Yes, you do, beginning with helping me. I'm still a cripple, you know."

"That's true," Aleta said. "I'll dress and then I'll help you."

"Reverse that order," Stanley said, sitting on the edge of the bed. "I need to be rewarded right now. I just practically volunteered for permanent duty as a night watchman."

"You're going to milk that noble sacrifice for all it's worth."

"I'll use any ploy available."

Aleta came over and sat beside him and kissed him. It was a passionate kiss and Stanley found himself weak-kneed even though he was sitting.

"You have no idea how attractive you are to me, do you?" Aleta said as she sat down beside him.

She kissed him again before he could respond and then she helped him undress. Again she folded every item of clothing just as he would have done.

He reached for her repeatedly and he could feel her respond to his touch each time, still she kept on with her task.

"How can you keep going?" he finally asked.

"Aren't you enjoying it?"

"I can hardly stand it," he whispered.

"So you'll be ready soon?"

"I'm ready now."

"Today we're going to do it like the first time."

"But we haven't done that since..."

He hesitated. His mouth found the taste of the word 'rape' bitter.

"I know," she whispered, folding his last piece of clothing. "Can you do it?"

"I..." he hesitated.

His leg ached. What she was asking would be painful. Bouncing his sore leg would send shock waves of pain through his system. He'd learned not to even put his toe on the ground.

She didn't know how painful his injury was. He hadn't wanted her to know. Now she was asking for something he didn't think he could do.

He remembered how desperately he had wanted to erase the memory of the rape from her mind. She had first begun to heal when he came home from the hospital. She had done everything she could. This was her last request he knew.

He could say no. But if he did, would she ever ask again? For some reason, her mind and body had chosen this moment. It might never come again.

He'd often wished he could have taken her place and taken the attack for her.

"...I can do it," he finished. "I'm a bit stiff..."

He laughed and she joined him.

"We couldn't do it otherwise," she said. "Are you sure?"

"A little bit of discomfort, maybe," he said bravely as she lay down beside him.

He rolled over and thought he'd hit a nerve when he rose on his knees. The lightning bolt of pain almost made him faint. He gritted his teeth and lowered himself.

The injured muscle screamed at him and he wondered briefly if he would be able to function. Each thrust sent waves of pain throughout his body.

How could one wound hurt everywhere, he mused.

His brain screamed at him to stop, but he overrode it. He had to finish. He shut his eyes to keep back the tears, but he kept on. It never occurred to him to stop short of finishing, to lie and say he was done, to offer an excuse, to suggest they vary the position.

The pain didn't become more bearable. He had hoped it would, but it didn't.

Then suddenly, inexplicably, he ejaculated. So surprised was he, he stopped cold. He collapsed on top of his wife and she hugged him.

"I love you so much," she whispered.

The throbbing of his leg didn't disappear.

Then he felt a warmth slowly infuse his body.

He had walked through fire for his beloved wife, and even thought she didn't know it, he knew the sacrifice had been worth it. She was back. Deep inside, he recognized the restorative power of his act.

"It hurt didn't it?" she whispered.

"A little," he admitted.

"Someday we will both be more honest about what just happened, but not now."

"Not now," Stanley murmured. "Not now."

Chapter 12

An hour into the flight, Robert Locke gave his co-pilot seat over to his daughter, Jocelyn.

Tyler and Paul Junior hung over her shoulder as Claude explained a few flying basics. The boys asked a multitude of questions and Claude could tell he had three fledgling pilots on his hands.

Robert bent over and asked Hawk how Paige was doing.

"You're a lawyer, right?" Hawk stated.

"And you need to know what?" Robert smiled, sitting on the arm of the seat in front of them.

"About how early we can get married?"

"Eighteen."

"Not before?"

"Sixteen with parental consent from both parents, and they actually have to appear in person, prove they're the parents and then give their consent."

"Biological parents?" Paige asked.

"Yes, or guardians or a Judge," Robert said. "Illinois has its laws clearly spelled out."

"What if we got married somewhere where the law isn't so strict?" Paige asked.

"The laws are similar in most states, but where there's a little wiggle room there's usually a caveat that you must be a resident to be married there."

"Oh," Paige said in a small voice.

"If you did marry elsewhere, the Illinois court might rule the marriage invalid and put Hawk in jail for cohabiting with a minor," Robert said. "States don't like people trying to get around their laws that way."

"When would a judge allow it?" Hawk asked.

"That depends on the judge. But I'll tell you one thing. Pregnancy isn't considered a valid reason for underage marriage."

"That was never an option," Hawk declared.

"Good!"

"What can a judge do?"

"Waive the consent requirement."

"Do they ever do it?"

"Rarely," Robert responded. "Paige, is Hawk considering marrying you before your eighteenth birthday?"

Instead of answering, Paige began to cry. Hawk gathered her to him and smiled at Robert.

"She's having trouble with her emotions lately," Hawk said. "I think she's happy."

Robert nodded. "That sounds about right."

He left the couple and went to talk with his wife.

"So they're serious," Bertha said. "Pretty fast."

Harriet butted in. "Claude and I were just as fast."

"But you were both experienced. You knew what you wanted," Bertha proclaimed unequivocally.

"I'll bet Hawk knows what he wants in a wife," Harriet commented. "Still, she's pretty young."

"I may have spoken too soon," Bertha put in. "She's been the mother in that house since her mother died–cleaning, cooking, shopping. She's more adult than most her age."

"So she knows the less attractive side of being a homemaker," Harriet said. "She has two...er had two brothers. Maybe she knows what she wants in a husband too."

Hawk heard most of the conversation on the other side of the aisle. He was pleased that it only involved speculation and no criticism, just some questions.

He had questions too. What he hadn't thought about before was that Paige had stepped in when her mother died. She'd still be doing that if David hadn't died. He guessed that David took care of Tyler and left Molly to Paige. But now Paige was left with Tyler who wanted to change her.

Paige couldn't help herself. She knew her fears were unreasonable but she couldn't conquer them. They were displaced portions of the giant fear underneath that her father would kill her if he knew her secret.

The investigation into the family must have told the father that one of the three remaining children knew something. Tyler didn't approach him as David did. That told his father he didn't know the secret David and his mother shared. Molly had only been two when the incident occurred. That only left Paige.

He would have thought that if she didn't know, she would have approached her father. She had taken over for her mother. Tyler might be the second oldest, but Paige had been the second in command.

Yes, Hawk mused, Kurt Van Horne knew that Paige was the final person who knew what he'd done that Fourth of July a decade ago. And he took the most reasonable steps. First he removed everything in the house that he thought might contain information. And then he burned the house to destroy anything he might have overlooked. Very thorough.

Paige would be next on his list.

Perhaps that was the only reason she was marrying him. Even if it was, it was a good reason. But he sensed that she seemed to genuinely like being with him. She had seemed more mature than her age would indicate. Now he knew why. She had actually run a household for two years.

She wouldn't be walking into marriage with the naiveté of a normal love-struck sixteen year old.

She was grounded in reality.

She was sensitive.

And she was kind.

But most of all, she was an adult. She'd jumped from childhood to adulthood with almost no transition years. He wouldn't count the years her mother tutored her in the finer points of shopping, laundry, cleaning and cooking in preparation for the unthinkable–her own mother's death. What a terrible burden that must have been. No, Paige hadn't had an adolescence. She'd jumped from childhood straight into adulthood.

She was past dating teenage boys. There was no going back for her. She could only go ahead.

"Paige," Hawk whispered. "I owe you an apology."

She looked at him quizzically.

"I've been calling you a child. You aren't a child. You are an adult. You make adult decisions continually."

Paige looked at him. "Are we still engaged?"

"I want to marry you before you turn eighteen," Hawk said.

"We can't," Paige whispered. "And we can't even kiss. I don't want anyone to be able to accuse you of anything."

"We can find a state that will let us get married and move there," Hawk said.

"Molly needs me here," Paige said sadly. "I almost forgot about her."

"Remember the Chesneys from the party?"

"I'm not sure," she murmured.

"They are going to join us in Disney World. They are interested in having you three live with them."

Paige sat up.

"Did they say so?"

"Sshh," Hawk said drawing her back to him. "Evelyn objected when someone else was mentioned as possible foster parents. She said Molly needed a stay-at-home mom."

"She does," Paige whispered.

"Evelyn is a shy woman," Hawk said. "I'm guessing she's afraid you three might not like her, so she's joining us hoping you might come to like her."

"She sounds nice."

"She thought you were too young to be engaged. She has dogs. Three big ones and a puppy. She knows you like animals."

"So does Molly."

"She wants to teach you how to show dogs."

"Really? That would be fun."

"I wanted you to know, you might come into a family when we get back."

"And we'd stay engaged even if Mrs. Chesney doesn't think it's right?"

"We will stay engaged no matter who thinks what," Hawk whispered. "I love you. I want to marry you. And even though I want to marry you now, I understand about Molly. I will wait for you."

Paige leaned close and whispered,

"Hawk, I don't want to wait. I want to be your wife. But Molly has lost too many important people in her life. And now our home is gone. I can't leave her now."

"I agree with you."

"You are the most wonderful man in the world. I love you more every hour," she whispered snuggling close to him.

When the plane was in its final approach, Hawk fastened Paige's seat belt. He tried to do it gently, but he woke her.

"What is it?" she cried, frightened.

"We're landing," Hawk said. "It's probably going to be smooth, but if you want us to do a couple somersaults, now's the time to ask. You're all strapped in."

"Are we going to crash?" she asked.

Hawk saw her face whiten and a tremor capturing her hands.

"Odds are against it," he said taking her cold hands into his warm one.

"You're sure."

"As sure as I am that while I'm in Florida, you're somewhere in Alaska."

Paige looked outside.

"There are palm trees."

"Funny, I never knew there were palm trees in Alaska."

"There aren't."

"Then I guess you're here with me," Hawk said lightly. "I'm not going to crash, so I guess if you're here, you aren't either."

The wheels hit the ground. It was the last bump they felt.

"I guess we're flying again," Hawk said.

Paige looked outside. "We're slowing down."

"That can't be good."

"That's very good," Paige announced. "We're here!"

"Tyler and Paul Junior were talking about a ride that soars above the park. I thought we'd try that."

"No way!" Paige said.

"You get to pick the first ride them."

"Pirates of the Caribbean," Paige said. "Tyler said it's sailing on a smooth water in a tunnel."

"He didn't tell you about the waterfall?"

"What waterfall?"

"The one that gets your heart racing so you'll enjoy the ride more."

"Can we ask for a boat that goes around?"

Hawk laughed. He leaned over and whispered, "If you chance it, I'll give you a kiss at the bottom."

"You can't."

"I said I'd kiss you for the first time on your eighteenth birthday. My reason was that on that day you were officially an adult. Do you understand what I'm saying?"

"That today is my eighteenth birthday?"

"Today I am recognizing that you are an adult. That's why I can kiss you now. While I'm literally breaking the promise, I'm figuratively fulfilling it."

"You will get in trouble," she whispered, tears springing into her eyes.

"I won't do it unless you understand."

The tears washed down her cheeks, "I do understand. You are the first person to acknowledge that. I've been resenting being forced to be an adult but not be recognized as one."

"It's very dark in that tunnel. We will sit in the back of the boat."

"Can we do that?"

"Yes, we can do that."

Everyone crammed into two limousines. Paige invited Evelyn and Bernard Chesney to share their limousine. Evelyn smiled happily at the warm gesture.

"Molly," Paige said, "Mrs. Chesney is thinking that we could all bunk with her when we go back home. She has a big house close to where we've been staying. She has four dogs. One of them is a puppy. Maybe he could sleep in your room with you."

Molly turned to Evelyn. "Oh, could he?"

"He would like that," Evelyn said. "His name's Tyler."

Everyone laughed.

"Guess he needs a new name," Evelyn said. "His father is Topaz."

"How about 'Sonny'?" Molly said.

"She wants a name that starts with a 'T'," Tyler said.

Molly grew thoughtful.

"Trooper," she offered.

"That's a good name," Evelyn said. "Trooper it is."

"You want us for longer than a couple nights, don't you?" Tyler asked.

"We'd like to be your permanent foster parents," Dr. Chesney said. "That's the reason we came along on this trip."

"All of us?"

"Yes," came his response.

"Paige is engaged," Tyler said. "She thinks she's a grown-up."

"She's been handling grown-up responsibilities for a couple of years," Dr. Chesney said.

"So you think it's okay?"

"I guess I'd have to say yes," the doctor said. "Evelyn has a different view."

"So will you get a divorce?" Molly asked.

"No, we won't," Dr. Chesney said. "We won't even fight about it. Paige seems to have a good head on her shoulders. I trust her judgment."

"Paige is a..." Tyler started and then stopped. "That's four you owe me."

Hawk pulled out his wallet and handed Tyler a five. "One in advance. Paige and I are going on the Pirates of the Caribbean ride first. I told her about the waterfall."

"She'll..." Tyler started.

"The five is yours," Hawk said.

"What's going on?" Dr. Chesney asked.

"Tell you later," Hawk said.

"Molly," Paige said, "we're all going to the Magic Kingdom first, and then if you want to go to the Animal Kingdom, I'm sure you can count on Mrs. Chesney to take you there. I know others will want to go too, but you need someone you can count on that wants to go with you."

"Dr. Chesney," Tyler said, "Paul and his father are going to Epcot Center tomorrow and they're going to let me tag along. You want to be my partner? It has some boss rides."

"How about trying out Space Mountain today? I could use a partner. There's no way I'm getting Evelyn on that ride!"

"We could do Splash Mountain too," Tyler said excitedly.

"Animal Kingdom has that brand new ride," Dr. Chesney said.

"Everest Expedition," Tyler said. "It just opened up. I hear it's scary as hell. You practically hang off the side of the mountain."

"That's the one!"

"You got yourself a partner, Doc," Tyler said.

"Paige, what about you?" Molly said. "What'll you do when Hawk wants to go on the scary rides?"

Paige laughed. "I guess I'll have to go with him."

Tyler stared at his sister his brows arched in surprise. "That I gotta see."

"No, you don't," Hawk said. "You can watch us exit and if Paige isn't smiling, I owe you five."

"Man, am I gonna be rich!"

It was a jocular group that left that limousine. Hubert and Lydia had been in the group, but neither had said a word. The dynamics of the small family of three interacting with these comparative strangers had fascinated them.

Lydia was impressed with Paige's leadership in overcoming the awkwardness that naturally occurs when strangers meet. Paige had known exactly what would warm Molly's heart the quickest and she seemed completely unselfish in her desire to foster a relationship between her sister and the woman who would take her place in Molly's life.

Hawk had already established some sort of repoire with Tyler, which seemed to let Tyler know he could be a kid again. Tyler's eagerness to go on rides with Bernard

Chesney stemmed, Lydia knew, from his own desire for a father like his friend Paul had.

Then there was Paige herself, exhibiting a new confidence. That she had been fearful of amusement park rides had been made obvious by Molly's concern. That she was planning to go on any ride had actually shocked her brother. Hawk seemed to be working wonders with her. They reminded her of Stanley and Aleta when they first met.

Early afternoon found the entire group entering the Magic Kingdom Theme Park. Lettie had complained that her brother got to ride the big rides with her father. Claude offered his services. Hubert stepped up to be Tiffany's partner and Robert kissed Bertha who told him their honeymoon had to take a back seat to the pregnancy that dictated that she not go on the jolting rides. She was taking no chances. Lydia and Harriet decided to go on the ride together.

Bertha joined the Witherspoons and enjoyed the perks of being part of the small group with Kitty who bypassed the long lines on every ride by passing through the handicapped entrance with a special pass. The fact that Bertha was with the Witherspoons meant she could be found easily because Kitty had told everyone what rides she was going on and in what order, so the rest of the group checked in with Bertha regularly, leaving messages for one another. She was happy to be in a position to ride only the gentlest of rides since her stomach seemed sensitive to too much irregular movement.

Hawk and Paige were the only ones of the group to elect Pirates of the Caribbean as their first ride. As they waited in line, Hawk whispered into Paige's ear that he wanted their first kiss to be one she would remember all her life.

He whispered what she could expect. It sounded like what was going to happen going over the waterfall. He repeated the sensations she would feel several times. Eventually, she became excited over a kiss that could produce those sensations.

The line moved slowly and Hawk had her repeat the sensations and then he put a meaning to each. Paige was fascinated by his labeling. First came eagerness, then depth and finally completion.

Hawk wrangled the two back seats by waiting patiently until he was allowed to seat Paige in the last seat.

Once seated, he put his arm around her.

"You remember my instruction?"

"I'm getting really scared," Paige confided as the boat began to move into the cavern.

Hawk embraced her, tilted her head up and lowered his lips to hers. She felt the boat rise as their lips touched. Her eagerness to kiss captured her focus as the boat seemed to rise in the water. As his passion grew, the boat fell and she felt her stomach rise into her throat. It felt as if his kiss went right into her very soul. The sensation thrilled her unexpectedly. She felt the excitement race through her body like an electrical charge. The boat splashed as it hit the bottom, Hawk drew back, and suddenly it was over. Completion.

Paige was breathless. And speechless. Hawk gathered her to him. As the boat traveled its designated path she began to delight in the panoramic scenes of lifelike figures of pirates capturing, looting and burning a town. Finally, they sailed past the pirate ship and cannonballs splashed in the water around their vessel as it sailed along.

When the ride was over, Paige asked, "Can we go again?"

"Only if you smile. Tyler has Bertha recording our exit."

Paige laughed. "He wants that five bucks but not more than he wants to ride Space Mountain.

"Do I get another ride like that one?" Paige asked.

"Yes."

"Did you enjoy the ride?" Bertha asked.

"What a thrill that waterfall was!" Paige said.

"It takes your breath away," Bertha commented.

"That's just what it does," Paige agreed, smiling. "We're going again."

Paige couldn't believe that the second kiss was as thrilling as the first. Again she was left with breath and voice suspended, heart beating rapidly, mind agog at the discovery that this man could affect her to such an extent.

"Are we never going on another ride?" Hawk asked after their fourth time.

"If I go on Splash Mountain with you, can we do Pirates two times afterward?"

"Yes, but you do understand I can't kiss you on that ride."

"I understand. I want to try."

"Once we climb in the boat, there's no turning back."

"I understand. And no matter how scared I get, you won't kiss me. Promise. I don't want you to get into trouble."

"I promise," Hawk said. "But, you know, we could try a less scary ride first."

"I feel like I'm up for that ride right now."

"We'll go with your feeling," Hawk said.

"And if I cry, you won't kiss me."

"No, I won't. I promise."

"Let's go have an adventure," Paige said gaily.

As they stood in line, Hawk said, "Everyone's in the line up ahead."

As he spoke, Tyler looked around. Hawk's tallness made him readily visible and his blonde hair that hung over his eyes was his trademark. Tyler nudged Paul Junior and pointed back. Hawk waved.

Hawk pointed out Tyler to Paige and she laughed when she saw her brother's expression.

"He's so surprised," she said delighted at her own action.

"He has reason to be. This is a giant leap."

"It's just a multiple of the ride we did four times."

"It's more than that," Hawk cautioned.

"I know."

Paige thought she was going to throw up when it came time to step into the simulated hollowed out log. She felt Hawk's hand on her arm guiding her. She knew she could still turn around. When she hesitated, he leaned over.

"I've got a secret for you."

She sat down in the boat and waved at Tyler and Molly who were in the middle of the group that had stayed in the area to watch her.

She turned to Hawk, "I can't smile."

"You're doing fine. You waved."

"Molly looks scared," Paige said.

"She's being empathetic. She knows how she'd feel."

"She won't try to imitate me, will she?"

"With Evelyn as her partner?"

Paige smiled. "You're right."

Their conversation stopped when the boat began to twist and turn as it moved along the waterways in the back before ascending multiple stories to the top.

It was here that Paige began to quiver.

"What's the secret?" Paige asked desperate to learn how to survive the fear that was beginning to overwhelm her.

"I can't give you a kiss going down," Hawk whispered, "but I can give you one going up."

Hawk took her face in his hands as the boat began to ascend. Paige found this one as astonishingly sweet as the ones before had been. She felt herself succumbing to the waves of pleasure it brought with it. Hawk gently disengaged as they reached the top of the ride.

She felt the slight bump as the boat was moved into position on the rollers. Still dazed by the kiss, Paige nevertheless came awake. Her eyes opened as the realization of the height hit her. Hawk tightened his embrace.

"You made it," he exclaimed. "It's all downhill from here."

"That's the problem!" she shouted as the boat approached the edge. "It's all downhill!"

"Take a deep breath and scream!" Hawk advised. "It's more fun that way."

Paige found his instructions easy. She took a deep breath just as the boat started down.

She screamed as it began to fall.

Hawk's shout matched her scream.

When they hit bottom, the water splashed into the boat. Hawk shook his head like a wet dog. Paige's scream turned into laughter. Hawk squeezed her shoulder.

"You did great!" he exclaimed. "Two rides on Pirates coming up."

"Can we go on this again?" Paige asked.

"Are you sure? You were pretty scared up there."

"Once more," Paige said.

"Hey, I'm game. This is one of my favorite rides."

The group waiting off to the side were surprised when Hawk and Paige merely waved at them happily and got back in line.

"How'd he do that?" Tyler wondered aloud. "She screamed all the way down."

"Girls do that," Dr. Chesney said, "but if she hadn't liked it she would have said, 'once is enough'."

"She won't even sign up for driver's training," Tyler said. "I have to do all the driving."

"So she's gaining confidence?"

"Yeh. Now she'll really be bossy."

"Women are always bossy," Chesney said. "Older sisters are the worst."

"I'm older!"

"Not in her eyes."

"That's the trouble. She thinks she's my age."

"She will be in a month," Chesney noted.

"Worse month of the year," Tyler grumbled.

"I want to go on that ride," Molly said. "Doc, will you take me?"

"Sure, I will," Chesney replied. "If you're sure."

Lydia saw Tyler's disgruntled expression and came up with, "Tyler, how about you taking Tiffany, so I can go with Hubert?"

Tyler looked at the pretty blonde sixteen-year-old and smiled. "Okay, Tiffany?"

She nodded and he said, "If we hurry, we can get in the same boat as Paige."

The two hurried to the line and settled in two couples away from Paige and Hawk.

"Tyler's behind us," Paige whispered in Hawk's ear.

"Does that bother you?"

"You have no idea what a good... er... job you do."

Hawk smiled. "That's nice to hear."

"Come on," Paige said.

"Where?"

"Back by Molly," Paige said smiling at Tyler as they passed him.

"I knew it!" he said watching her. His grin faded when she slipped in behind Molly and in front of the Praetzels. She wasn't leaving. In fact, she'd axed all chance of being alone in a boat.

"After this ride," she asked Molly, "where are you going?"

"The Haunted House," Molly said. "Wanna come?"

"Sounds like fun," Paige said cheerfully. "Sure, we'll come."

"Maybe we'll be in the same boat," Molly said.

"Maybe," Paige agreed. "Hawk told me it's more fun if you scream on the way down."

"So that's why you screamed."

"That and the fact that I was scared."

"But you're going again?" Molly asked puzzled.

"Sometimes being scared is exciting," Paige said, squeezing Hawk's hand. "Hawk taught me that."

"So are you going on Everest tomorrow?"

"No way! I don't think I'd like being that scared."

"Me neither," Molly agreed.

Paige turned to Hawk. "You can ride the Everest ride tomorrow if you want to. I'll be okay watching."

Hawk shook his head. "No thanks."

Molly eyed him curiously. "Are you scared to go on it?"

"Yep," Hawk grinned. "That's why I'm with Paige. She'd never go on it, so I'm safe."

"Never?" Paige questioned, chewing on the word.

"Never," Hawk stated flatly.

"Would you go on it if I did?" Paige asked.

"I guess I would," Hawk said. "But I'm not challenging you."

"Oh, yes, you are," Paige said. "And I accept. Tomorrow we're going on Everest."

"Not unless you ride every ride in the park," Hawk announced flatly.

"Every ride?"

"Every ride I pick."

"Okay," Paige agreed.

"You trust me that much?"

"You aren't Tyler. You'll pick rides that'll get me ready."

"I'm not sure any rides will get you ready," Hawk cautioned.

"After today, we'll know, won't we?" Paige asked, a gay lilt in her voice. She was getting excited about training for tomorrow's ride. Hawk would make it fun. Of this she was sure. He wouldn't trick her or try to get her to fail. She knew his caution stemmed from concern.

Hawk and Paige wound up in the last seat in the log boat.

She leaned over and whispered in Hawk's ear. "We can't, can we?"

He knew to what she was referring.

"Probably not," he responded regretfully. She wasn't the only one who liked those kisses.

"Let's not take a chance," Paige whispered, "even though that was the best part of the ride."

He held her as the boat wound through the channels of water through the Brer Rabbit adventure until they came to the section where the boat ascended to the top of the ride.

She tightened her hold on his arm and Hawk felt her fear rising.

Without warning, he leaned over and kissed her.

Surprised, she melted into responding and found herself again amazed by how completely she was captivated. She knew the risk he was taking to calm her but she couldn't push him away. No part of her being wanted him to stop.

In the brief few seconds their lips were joined, Paige realized how a girl could be swept away by a kiss. She'd never understood it before. But now she understood. She wanted it to go on and on.

When Hawk drew back, she wanted to tell him not to, but her voice failed her. The boat stopped ascending and moved onto the rollers leading to the five-story drop.

He'd done it again. She couldn't believe that he could continue to astound her. Her mother had told her it might happen, but the words had had no meaning until this moment. Her heart soared as the boat tipped over the crest and began its downward plunge. This time her scream was one of joy as much as fear.

When the boat crashed into the pool at the base of the ride, Paige's shout turned into laughter.

Impulsively, she reached over and kissed his cheek.

"Thank you!" she murmured.

"Careful," he cautioned.

Paige leaned forward and put her hand on Molly's shoulder. "How'd you like it?"

Molly simply nodded.

Paige sat back. "My sentiments exactly."

She turned to Hawk. "I'm having such a great time. You are amazing."

He leaned over and whispered in her ear, "That was the last kiss."

"It'll last me the rest of the day," Paige rejoined.

"It'll have to last longer than that."

"The therapy is over?"

"Yes."

"Thanks for curing me."

"You're welcome."

Later, to Hawk's surprise, Paige agreed readily to trying Big Thunder Mountain Railroad. Until then they'd gone on only the gentlest rides.

"This is a roller coaster type of ride," he cautioned.

"I want to try it," she said.

"It could be too much too early," he said. Already he could sense her tension mounting.

"I won't be able to kiss you at all," he said. "And we'll be jostled a bit."

"It feels right," Paige said. "It's something I need to do. I've got to stop being afraid of pseudo-dangers."

"Where on earth did you get your vocabulary?"

"Mother. I told you I was home-schooled, didn't I? Well, Mom was a sociologist and they have a lingo. I picked up a lot of terms."

Their conversation ended as their group was let through the rope and chose seats on the train. Paige chose the first seats in the second car.

The safety bar snapped into place and Hawk put his arm around her shoulder. This was a mild ride compared to the Everest ride, but he had no intention of withdrawing support to test her. He wanted her to have fun.

"You can hang onto the bar or onto me," he said as the cars began to move. Paige grabbed his hand.

"We're going to be thrown around a bit," he warned as the cars began to move.

Her other hand grabbed the bar.

The first turn was sharp and threw them to the left.

"Oh, boy!" she groaned. "I'm not sure I can do this."

"Do you want me to stop the train?" Hawk asked.

"You can do that?" Paige asked skeptically.

"Only figuratively, not literally."

Paige knew at once what Hawk was offering to do. It was dangerous. While the people on the train were strangers, they might make a comment. Or worse yet, someone they knew might see.

"No, don't do that," she said. "We're halfway, aren't we?"

"Just about."

"No sense turning back," she decided. "Let's go forward."

Hawk smiled. He loved the fact that she decided as if she had a choice.

When the ride was over, she told him she wanted to go again.

"I was too scared to see anything last time," she explained.

They went three more times.

"Is four your magic number?" he asked when she told him she was ready to try another ride.

"Maybe," she said. "Maybe later, we can try Splash Mountain again, but without the kissing."

"It's up to you," Hawk said.

They went from ride to ride, skipping the shows. Paige was on a mission. She was preparing for the next day and her big ride on Everest. Hawk found her single-mindedness gratifying. Several rides earned a repeat.

Toward dinnertime, Hawk said, "If you can learn to handle Splash Mountain you'll be ready enough."

"Okay," Paige agreed.

She made him take her a fifth time before she was ready to say, "I've conquered it."

Hawk agreed.

Everyone met back at the hotel to freshen up for dinner. Hawk took time to call Ed Ornstein.

"Where are we in the investigation?"

"Aleta is working on a couple ideas that she and Stanley cooked up."

"Don't hold out on me," Hawk enjoined him.

"Been asked not to tell you," Ed replied.

"Why?"

"They don't want to hoist no false hope."

"What made things worse?"

"Oh hell!" Ed exploded, and then stopped.

Hawk waited for him to make up his mind to tell him. Somehow he knew he would. He was right.

"I got a visit from Van Horne. What a prick!"

"At your office?"

"He didn't see nothing. He thinks I'm a third-rate geezer, but he give me the word anyways. Penny Van Horne is alive."

"That can't be!" Hawk gasped, shocked.

"She's in a home for retards. Been there for ten years."

Hawk knew he'd checked. All he could think to say was, "Paige is sure she died."

"Do you trust Paige?"

"Yes."

"So, do I," Ed said staunchly. "That house didn't burn itself down."

"So what's being done?"

"We're working on trying to figure out who the kid is."

"So the Praetzels believe Paige too."

"Yeh, but Stanley says we ain't got enough to win the custody fight," Ed said. "Say how are the Chesney's and the kids getting on?"

"Molly's latched onto Evelyn. Tyler and Doc are a twosome on the big rides."

"Do the kids know about the Chesneys wanting to be foster parents?"

"Paige told them in the limo going to the hotel with the Chesneys right there. Is Van Horne going to seek custody?"

"He's already got Paige signed up in one of them fancy lock-ups rich guys put their kids in to get them off drugs. He says the doc will take care of that delusion of hers."

"Oh, my God! That'll ruin her!" Hawk said.

"I'm telling you this so you can maybe figure something out."

"Like what?"

"You got a couple sharp lawyers and a judge with you. Use them for God's sake."

"Van Horne doesn't care about the kids," Hawk said. "He only wants to cover his tracks."

"Yeh, so?"

"So maybe he's got plans for the other two a judge wouldn't like," Hawk suggested. "He doesn't strike me as the father type."

"It ain't much, but I'll see what I can dig up."

Chapter 13

Back at the hotel after dinner, Robert gave Jocelyn over to her grandmother and entered the Hubert Praetzel suite where Hawk and Paige were waiting. As soon as he was seated comfortably, Hawk started by explaining that while Aleta and Stanley were working with Ed on the custody case, he needed advice on another matter and it couldn't wait.

"Paige and I don't want to do anything illegal, but we want to get married right away," Hawk started. "I've asked Paige to tell you why she believes her father gave her mother full custody of all four children and, after the mother's death, allowed her older brother David to continue as guardian. Tyler tried to take over when David died, but Mr. Van Horne cut off the child support."

Hawk nodded and Paige told the tale of how she'd watched her father smother her baby sister.

When she finished Lydia asked, "What kind of pajamas was your father wearing?"

Paige closed her eyes for a minute.

"Red striped ones," she replied finally. "Only just the bottom part."

Paige turned to Hawk. "When we get married, don't wear striped pajamas."

"If he does, what will happen?" Lydia asked.

Paige looked at Hawk. "I won't enjoy the kissing as much."

"As much?" Lydia questioned. "So he's kissed you?"

Paige paled.

Hawk had urged her earlier not to be afraid.

"But she's a judge," Paige had protested.

"That's why you tell the truth," Hawk had told her.

Paige looked at the floor and whispered her reply. "Yes, he kissed me."

"He swore he wouldn't," Lydia said. "Did you, in fact, kiss him?"

"He surprised me, but it's not like you think!"

"Tell me how it was."

"It wasn't a sex thing," Paige said lifting her head. "It was a therapeutic thing."

"Your words or his?"

"Mine, but it was his idea. How do you think he got me to go on those rides? I won't even sign up for driver's training."

"How did he get you to even go on the ride?"

"He promised to kiss me because I wasn't a child," Paige wrinkled her brow, her distress obvious. "This is coming out wrong."

"Just let it out," Lydia said. "You aren't under judgment."

"But Hawk is and he's done nothing but make me feel good about myself. He is the first person to tell me that I was really grown-up. My mother spent two years teaching me how to take her place. She used to say, 'You're going to be the adult woman in the family.' But even though I did all the things she did, all anyone ever saw was my age. It didn't count because I was only fifteen. After a year when I turned sixteen it was the same. I'm almost seventeen and I'm still being told I'll be an adult when I'm eighteen. That's bogus. I'm an adult now. Anyway, Hawk made that promise when he considered me a child, then on the plane his mind started to think about things. Our engagement happened pretty fast for him. It happened too fast for me too, but it felt so good I went with my feelings.

"Anyway on the plane, Hawk told me he'd been wrong calling me a child. So he released himself from his promise and promised me a kiss if I would go on the Pirates of the Caribbean and chance the waterfall. He said he'd kiss me at the bottom. I said I'd do it, but as the boat started I got panicky. I think I was even considering jumping out of the boat when he kissed me right through the whole waterfall. We did it four times and I figured I was ready for Splash Mountain. He surprised me by kissing me on the way up to the top. He did that only twice. The second time he said it was the end. We never kissed again on any rides even when I got scared."

"Are you telling me the kisses weren't sexual?"

"Oh, no! They were full of sex. At least I think that's what it was. I don't think I would have gotten over being afraid if they weren't. Those were pretty powerful kisses. They took my mind off how scared I was. Right now I would do just about anything for another one, which is why I'm glad, Hawk is as strong as he is. Our decision to get married was a choice we made before we kissed. Now it's stronger than ever."

"So now you will find it harder to be celibate?"

"Oh, yes," Paige exclaimed. "But I will do it because I don't want to get Hawk in trouble which I guess I've already done, but he was only trying to help me, not seduce me."

"He didn't touch you inappropriately?"

"No."

"And when he thought you were no longer afraid, he stopped?"

"Not quite."

"Oh?"

"I still got scared, but now I can handle it on my own."

"Why do you think he wants to marry you?"

"He loves me."

"Do you love him?"

"Oh yes!"

"Do you have plans?"

"Oh, yes. Hawk's going to make it so I can be what I want to be."

"Which is?"

"A writer."

"And how is he going to do that?"

"By keeping me in school and giving me a room to study and to write in. I haven't ever had that."

"What about children?"

"We're going to have four," Paige said matter-of-factly. "But later. I'm still young. School first. Then children."

"Okay, Hawk, tell me what is scaring you so?" Judge Davis prompted.

"I'm afraid that Paige's father may be granted custody. He plans to put her in a mental institution. He told Ed this. He said they'd get rid of her delusion about him killing his daughter. He said his daughter, Penny, is in an institution."

"Is she?"

"Someone with that name is."

"Maybe Paige is mistaken about what she saw," Lydia suggested.

"No, she's not," Hawk said. "She was six. If she were ten, you'd believe her. Well, I think mentally she's as smart as a ten-year-old. Her fear is deep and it's real. All I did today is nibble away at the outer edges of that fear. I only pushed it back a bit. It was beginning to paralyze her."

"She should tell her story to the judge," Lydia said.

"She can't," Hawk declared. "If she does that, her brother and sister will find out what she thinks their father has done. They will start trying to find out if it's true. Their search will put them in danger too. If she doesn't tell her story, their father will get custody."

Paige spoke up.

"The Chesneys would be good foster parents for Tyler and Molly. Two parents would be good for them, especially Molly. She hasn't gotten over Mom's death."

"Your father has remarried," Lydia pointed out.

"I know," Paige said, suddenly becoming angry. "Somehow love must count. My father doesn't love us. If he did, he would never have burned up all our things. He didn't even think that we'd want pictures of our mother and each other growing up, that we each had stuff we valued. Tyler had sports trophies. Molly had a collection of photographs she'd taken since she got her first camera when she was five. He robbed her of that. She doesn't realize what she's lost yet. We haven't seen the house. In our mind's eye it's still standing."

"That he had a hand in the fire hasn't been proven," Lydia stated.

"But shouldn't awarding him custody be delayed so the police have time to investigate?"

"I agree it should," Lydia said. "You realize I don't have the case. If I did I'd have to recuse myself."

"We need advice," Hawk said smoothly. "We can't make a mistake."

"First," Lydia said, "you need to see that Paige is examined by two psychologists that will testify that she shouldn't be institutionalized. Stanley will know who."

"What else?"

"As soon as we get back, get the blood tests done and an examination to verify that Paige is a virgin. Dr. Chesney will do that."

"Why?"

"You don't want Mr. Van Horne to accuse you of any sexual misconduct, Hawk. You could wind up in jail if he does."

"What about the kissing?" Paige asked.

"That interlude need not leave this room."

"You aren't going to put Hawk in jail?"

"For instituting a therapy that worked?" Lydia chuckled. "No, Paige, I'm not. However, there's to be no more therapy. And you don't mention it to anyone again."

"Anything else?" Hawk asked.

"You need a copy of Paige's birth certificate and one other document showing her age. I understand she doesn't have a driver's license, so we have to hope that some documentation survived the fire. Also the custody agreement executed at the time of the divorce. You need the death certificates for her mother, her grandmother and her brother as well. This is important to show that her father was never put into the line of custody. The implication should hit any judge in the face."

"Where did your mother keep her documents?" Hawk asked Paige.

"I don't know," came the response.

"Did she have a safety deposit box?" Hawk asked. "When Tyler needed his birth certificate for his driver's license, where did he get it?"

"I don't know."

"We'll ask Tyler," Hawk said.

"Stanley and Aleta may already be gathering some of these documents for the custody hearing," Lydia said.

"We'll check."

Aleta woke Stanley with a kiss and an announcement.

"They want to get married!"

Stanley attempted to move but his leg stopped him. He grimaced in pain.

Aleta caught it. "You're in real pain."

Still half asleep Stanley murmured an assent.

"Before, when I asked you to...it must've been very painful. Why did you do it?"

Stanley realized he'd messed up. He swiftly changed the subject, "Who wants to get married?"

"Hawk and Paige," Aleta replied. "They want to do it right away. Isn't that great!"

"She's sixteen!" Stanley demurred.

"Almost seventeen," Aleta responded. "We have to help."

"Help? How?"

"They talked to your mother. She gave them a list."

"My mother did that?" he asked still a bit groggy.

"She told them to call us."

"Oh, Mother, why?"

"Because we're their lawyers."

"Not Hawk's," Stanley said. "We're blurring lines here."

"Your mother outlined a strategy for us."

"You handle it," Stanley said. "Let me sleep."

Aleta felt Stanley's forehead. "You're burning up. Oh, dear Lord, what did I do?"

Stanley smiled weakly. "As I remember it, I did it."

Aleta kissed him lightly on the forehead. "I'm taking your temperature and calling Dr. Cook."

She not only took his temperature, she took his blood pressure and removed the bandage from the wound and lightly felt the area around it. It was hard and hot.

"It's infected," she announced.

She left and went into the kitchen where Stanley couldn't hear. She picked up the wall phone and punched in Wayne Cook's number.

"Stanley's got a 104 fever and his leg's infected. It looks bad."

"Are you alone?"

"Jamara's boy is sick," Aleta reported, "so, yes, I'm alone."

"Call the paramedics. I'll meet Stanley at the hospital. You stay there. The hospital is no place for a baby."

Aleta called the paramedics and then called Lauren who said she and Lyle would be right over. She added that

Lyle's parents had come for supper and would stay with the children.

Aleta hurried back into the bedroom and pulled out a hospital gown from the bureau. It was one she'd worn home months ago. Stanley eyed her drowsily and asked her what she was doing.

"Your leg is too sore for pants," she explained. "You don't want to go to the hospital naked."

"I'm not going anywhere."

"It's all arranged," Aleta said. "Now put your arms into the holes."

"It's the gown you wore!"

"Hospital gowns are unisex."

"Bertha ironed it."

"Bertha irons everything."

"I can't wear a hospital gown that's been ironed!"

"Why not?"

"I'll stand out."

"Nobody will notice," Aleta stated. "Put your arms in the arm holes or you go naked. I hear the siren."

Stanley held out his arms and she slipped the gown on.

"It's too short," Stanley complained once it was on.

"They are all too short," Aleta said. "Just stay there. I have to put the dogs away."

"I can't move," Stanley quipped. "Exactly where would I go?"

"Stay!" Aleta ordered rushing out. "Come on guys, kennel!"

The dogs each ran to their kennels and Aleta locked them in. Even the Pug went into his pen, sat in his round bed and waited for the opening to be clipped shut. Only Stoney wasn't closed in. He lay in an open crate as usual.

Lyle's chief's car roared in right behind the ambulance. He followed the paramedics into the bedroom. Lauren stayed behind and put her arms around Aleta.

"If you want to go to the hospital, I'll watch Gerard. Lyle can take you."

Hubbs came into the house. "Can I help, Ma'am?"

"Stanley's leg is worse," Aleta said. "Lauren is going to watch the baby. Can you see to the dogs in an hour?"

"Don't worry none. Even the little one minds real good," he said and then left.

The paramedics rolled Stanley out on a gurney. Lyle followed.

"First time we've had one dressed for the hospital," one of the paramedics said.

"He says the gown's too short," Aleta put in.

"Everybody says that," came the response.

Chapter 14

Chief Lyle West stood beside Aleta as Dr. Cook talked to the two about Stanley's condition.

"I think I did this to him," Aleta confessed.

"Nobody did this to him," Dr. Cook rejoined. "Infections aren't the result of any action."

"I made him work a full shift," Lyle said. "I feel responsible."

"I made him..." Aleta began.

Stanley intervened. "Nobody...and I mean, nobody, made me do anything."

"I'm keeping him here for a couple of days," Dr. Cook said.

"I'm putting a man on his door and one on Aleta," Lyle said. "I'm not happy with what's going on."

"Can you keep the Van Horne kids under police protection?" Aleta asked knowing that's what Stanley wanted.

"Can you get the group to stay in Florida another couple of days? They have two deputies with them."

"Harriet, Claude and the kids, yes. Paul and his kids, probably. But not Dr. Chesney or Stanley's parents," Aleta replied. "And don't we need Hawk?"

"Tell him to stay," Lyle said. "We always need him, but right now with the way things are falling into place, Paige needs one on one protection."

"How come you changed your mind?" Aleta asked, puzzled. "We haven't proven that the Penny in the home isn't Penny Van Horne."

"If the divorce resulted from the father putting Penny in the institution, why didn't her mother get her out later? Or visit her? Or tell Paige her sister hadn't died?" Lyle said. "Hawk will protect her because he believes she's in danger."

"I can get the paper work together," Aleta said. "I need to go back to the house."

"My man will go with you," Lyle said. He turned to the man in the bed. "Sorry, old man, I didn't mean to cause this."

"So you'll erase the time I owe you?" Stanley asked.

"Don't be ridiculous. Free help is hard to come by," Lyle returned. "But I won't assign you any shifts as long as you're on crutches."

"I'm not still racking up hours though, right?"

"Depends on whether I have to pay Hawk or he takes this as vacation time."

"Lyle!" Aleta exploded. "This police protection is warranted. You can't charge Stanley.

"Hush, Aleta," Stanley interjected. "This is between us. But don't worry. I'm thinking I'm really going to like being on crutches. I can go to the office every day and go to bed every night. Yes, crutches are the ticket."

"You'll pay me my due," Lyle predicted. "I'm a patient man. I suggest you do it before winter."

The phone on the bedside table rang. Lyle picked it up.

"Yes, he's fine," Lyle said, "well as fine as one can be when one is worrying about one's leg being chopped off."

Aleta's mouth dropped open.

Lyle hung up.

Aleta's expression caused him to blurt out, "Didn't Dr. Cook tell you? Stanley could still lose his leg."

Aleta paled and Lyle pushed a chair behind her.

"I've got to go get Lauren," Lyle said.

Aleta nodded numbly.

"You didn't tell me," she murmured to Stanley when Lyle left.

"I didn't know either. Dr. Cook just said it was serious."

"He told Lyle and not you?"

"Lyle made an educated guess," Stanley said. "I didn't dare think about it."

Aleta moved closer so the guards couldn't hear. "Stanley, I'm so sorry."

"I'm not."

"But it must've been agony."

"Pretty much like what you went through."

"Is that why I felt so good? I inflicted pain on a man in retribution?"

"Aleta, don't even think about it. What happened was good for both of us. It wrecked my leg but it restored my soul."

"I don't want you to lose your leg."

"That we're in agreement about," Stanley said. "Now go search the Roach house before Van Horne thinks about it."

"You want me to leave you?" Aleta asked, ruffled.

"I need a good night's rest. Jamara has a sick boy and there's no one to watch Gerard but you. And you have phone calls to make," he said. "Go. Let me sleep."

"You're more important than any of those things," Aleta declared.

"If you think that, go take care of my case for me," he shot back. He knew Aleta needed to be busy so she wouldn't sink into despair at her view of her own contribution to his state. He would have to repeat his assurances again, but he knew a good night's sleep coupled with the antibiotics Dr.

Cook had poured into his system would save his leg if it was possible.

If Aleta were here, every time a nurse came to check on him, her worries would rise up to haunt her again. At home she would envision him sleeping peacefully. The night was going to be a long one for him. He didn't need her to experience his anxiety with him.

He was more worried than he let on about his leg. Lyle had seen right through him. He was glad Lyle hadn't excused him from deputy duty. Lyle's treating this hospitalizing as a minor bump in the road helped. However, Lyle's comment to his father told Stanley he knew what was going on.

Aleta left, reluctantly. She headed for the Roach house and began to search through the mother's bedroom. There was nothing left except for a few bits of twisted pieces of jewelry and a wrapped metal box tucked in a back corner on the closet shelf under what was left of an old cowboy hat.

Aleta opened the box hopefully. The contents were intact: insurance policies on each child and one on the mother, house mortgage papers, and birth certificates for the four children who lived in the house.

She looked for the custody papers or any papers relating to the divorce but found none. Could they have been taken or were they hidden somewhere? The information about the deceased baby was also missing.

She searched the desk drawer for a safety deposit box key. She went into the other rooms. The officer with her helped her search.

They gathered every key they could find. After an hour, Aleta called Hawk as he and Paige were in line for their fifth Splash Mountain ride.

"I found Paige's birth certificate but I can't find the divorce papers. Ask Paige if she has any other suggestions.

Hawk reported back. "David had some boxes in the garage but she doesn't know what is in them. Paige says her mother told her that Lindsman holds a copy of everything important.   She thinks her mother told David where everything was."

"Lyle says to stay there a couple extra days," Aleta said, adding, "Too much is going on right now. The chiefs want the kids safe."

"Don't some of our group need to return home?"

"The Praetzels and the Chesneys," Aleta replied. "Tell the Witherspoons there's plenty of money to cover their expenses."

"Am I on vacation or am I being paid?" Hawk asked.

"If you take an unpaid leave," Aleta said, "we'll personally take care of your expenses down there."

"But Lyle wants me to watch Paige. That seems to me to be a paid assignment."

Aleta's voice toughened. "Do you want me to ever see my husband again?"

"He can't charge Stanley!" Hawk protested.

"Lyle's is putting the children under police protection on your gut feeling and his. He needs time for Ed to turn something up. He's in the middle of touchy negotiations right now with the Oakwood Council. He needs to use his volunteer deputies to keep his expenses down. Claude and Harriet are officially deputies assigned to protect the Van Horne children."

"You'll pay all my expenses?" Hawk said.

"You can even pick out wedding rings on us," Aleta said.

"I can buy those," Hawk snapped. "I'm talking about room, meals and tickets."

"Think of the rings as a gift," Aleta said. "Don't turn down gifts that represent support."

Hawk softened his stance.

"Well, if you put it that way," Hawk said. "Then, thank you."

He turned to Paige. "She's giving us wedding bands as a wedding gift. She says we should pick them out."

"And how is she going to pay for them from Illinois?"

"I don't think she thought of that," Hawk replied. "But it's still a nice gesture of support, isn't it?"

"It is nice."

"We won't mention it, okay?"

"Okay."

Aleta called her father and told him that they all had to stay for the protection of the Roach children.

"Dad," Aleta said. "I want you and Bertha to take Paige and Hawk shopping for wedding rings. I'm paying."

Late that night she called Claude and Harriet.

"Grams, I'm not asking what you're doing," she said. "But it was you or Dad, and it is his honeymoon."

"Aleta, what's wrong?" Harriet asked.

Claude scowled at his wife and hissed, "Can you call her back when we're finished?"

"She's crying."

"Why did you have your phone next to the bed anyway?"

"Robert told me things weren't going well, and she might call."

"What do you want me to do?"

"Just go to sleep. I'll wake you when I'm done talking."

"I'm not sure it's possible."

"Sshh. Close your eyes and relax."

"Grams, so much has happened," Aleta said, regaining her composure. "Stanley's not here. He sent me away. I want to be with him."

"Are you asking my permission?"

"What is it?" Claude asked.

Harriet cupped her hand over the phone. "She wants to spend the night with Stanley. He told her to go home."

"Tell her not to listen to him. He's trying to be brave. He needs her. Tell her to bundle the baby up and take it to

Beatrice's house and go to the hospital and hold Stanley's... er...what she always holds."

Harriet repeated Claude's words exactly and added, "Stop blushing. It's allowed."

"Thanks, Grams," Aleta said. "Oh, before I forget. I called to tell you I'm sending a Dr. Miles Greenwood down to interview Paige. He's a friend of Stanley's. Leave a note at the desk telling him where you'll all be."

Harriet kissed Claude when she hung up. "Did you save our place?"

"No need," he answered. "I never closed the book."

"Then let's finish."

Less than an hour later, back in Illinois, Aleta entered Stanley's room on the fourth floor of Tri-City hospital. She found her husband sleeping. She pulled up a chair and sat down. It felt good being here. It calmed her. She had been so unhappy at home. She had told Beatrice that she was ashamed of her lack of ability to cope and Beatrice had taken her hand and said that the choice was okay.

"You love them both, but Stanley is sicker."

"Gerard is fussy. He's not used to waiting for his feeding. Jamara nursed him personally and that helped some, but his stomach wasn't ready to settle."

"Don't worry. It'll be fun for us," Beatrice said. "He's so tiny. Babies are so precious at this age."

Now sitting beside Stanley comforted her. She laid her head on the bed and closed her eyes. She had slipped her hand under the sheet and placed it gently on his good thigh.

Stanley was not unaware of her presence. Even though exhausted, he could have responded. He chose not to. She needed her rest.

He put his hand on hers and gently moved it to its usual spot. Her fingers curled around his penis. She would sleep better now. So would he.

The nurse came in to take his pulse and temperature. Stanley asked her not to wake his wife.

He realized she probably saw where his wife's hand was. His look, however, told her to say nothing.

Aleta slept through three more of the nurse's visits. Usually the nurse chatted with her patients, but talk seemed inappropriate somehow.

At midnight Dr. Cook visited Stanley. He dismissed the nurse and told Stanley that it looked as if the antibiotics had taken hold. His temperature was dropping.

"Can the nurse visit less?" Stanley asked.

"You could remove Aleta's hand," Dr. Cook suggested.

"I put it there," Stanley said. "I don't want to wake her."

"Every two hours," Cook said, "unless your temperature goes up."

"Thanks."

"Your attitude about this little habit has changed," Dr. Cook said. "I'm curious as to why."

"She was raped," Stanley explained. "She didn't want to touch me at all for a long time afterward. Slowly she began to come back. Then earlier she took a big step back to normal. When my leg happened, she blamed herself. This is the only way I know to tell her I love her and trust her."

"I'll give you three hours, between nurse visits," Dr. Cook said. "I don't think your temp's going anywhere but down."

"Am I going to lose the leg?"

"Not if you do everything I tell you too."

"For real?"

"There are other bugs in your system waiting to rush in and take over if you take chances. The first onslaught is always the easiest to fight. People don't understand that. Please say you do."

"Will believing you know what you're talking about substitute for not fully comprehending?"

"Yes, it will."

"Whatever you tell me to do, I'll do it."

"Have a good night."

Aleta stirred twice, but didn't wake up until the sun lightened the sky. As the nurse came in for her second check on Stanley, her soft bustling around the bed woke Aleta. She finished and left as Aleta raised her head.

Her mind fuzzy, Aleta didn't realize she'd slept the night away.

"What time is it?"

"Morning," Stanley replied. "The sun's coming up."

"What time does the sun come up?"

"I don't know. I usually sleep past that."

"Where's your watch?"

"At home with every stitch of clothing I own."

"You don't need clothes," Aleta said. "How's your leg?"

"Dr. Cook says if I do everything he tells me to, it's going to be okay."

Aleta sat up and pulled her hand out from under the sheet and stretched.

"When are you coming home? I am miserable without you."

"I know. I miss you too."

Aleta's mind suddenly registered where her hand had been. "You didn't miss me at all!"

"I would have if I hadn't adjusted your hand."

"You did that!" she accused, her voice rising.

"It helps you sleep," he said quietly. "And me too."

"But there were nurses in and out all night, weren't there?"

"Quite a few. And Dr. Cook too."

"I'm so embarrassed," Aleta murmured.

"He already knows you do that."

"But he saw me."

"You were planning to deny it?"

"I was thinking about it."

Stanley chuckled. "Okay, now that we've had our morning repartee, did you take care of my case for me?"

"I sent Miles Greenwood down to interview Paige. I'll have his report Monday morning."

"We need more than one."

"He said he'd find someone the court would accept. I got a no from everyone else on your list. They all said they'd be glad to squeeze her in when she returned."

"That's reasonable."

"I have a feeling we don't have the time," Aleta said.

"Judge Jacobi is a reasonable judge," Stanley put forth.

"She's going to see the vacation we sent the children on as a ploy to delay the case and that's going to make her angry," Aleta said. "And you remember how she ruled in Jocelyn's case."

"You don't think she learned from that case?"

"She's going to see this case as entirely different," Aleta went on. "Van Horne's attorney is going to argue that Van Horne didn't fight for custody of the children because he thought they should be with their mother."

"And after she died?" Stanley posed.

"He was put off by the animosity of his eldest son."

"How do you know this?"

"Because those are the arguments I would use," Aleta said. "She'll plead that the father should be given a chance to reconcile with his children."

"You know something, don't you?" Stanley said. "You said 'she'."

"I don't know why I said that. And I didn't get a vision. Ideas just popped in my head and I went with them."

"If any other ideas pop in your head, go with them."

"I had one more, but it's crazy."

"Shoot."

"Your mother said that Dr. Chesney should verify that Paige is a virgin."

"For heaven's sake, Aleta. They're at Disney World."

"I told you it was crazy."

Stanley grew thoughtful. "Mother is never crazy. She's been on the bench for over a decade. Tell him to do it."

"You ask him."

"Me?"

"You've got a phone in here. You're the attorney of record."

"That's thin, Aleta, and you know it," Stanley protested.

"We need the report, so Hawk isn't arrested on suspicion of anything," Aleta argued.

"Get me the number."

The Chesneys were still in bed when Stanley called. After a brief conversation, Dr. Chesney agreed to find a place and examine Paige. He added that he'd suggest blood tests even though they weren't required after Stanley said that Aleta was going to try to get a judge to rule that parental consent was not required in this case.

When Stanley hung up, Aleta asked him what Dr. Chesney's reaction had been.

"He said Hawk is working miracles with Paige," Stanley reported. "He thinks they were made for each other."

"And Evelyn?"

"She wants Paige to wait," Stanley replied.

"Do you remember how difficult it was for us?"

"You had to have a kitchen," Stanley recalled.

"I wasn't moving into a house without one."

"You never use it."

"I do to," Aleta said. "I sit down at the kitchen table and eat what Bertha cooks."

"How long can you stay?"

"Ed and Beatrice have Gerard. Hubbs is taking care of the dogs. I can stay as long as you need me."

"That would be forever."

"I have to leave at nine."

"You have the shortest forevers on record."

Hawk had three phone calls that morning. Dr. Chesney told him about Stanley's request. Robert told him that he and Bertha were taking he and Paige shopping for wedding rings. Harriet told him that Paige would be interviewed by a psychologist named Dr. Greenwood some time that day.

Hawk told Harriet he wouldn't tell Paige about the psychologist until time for the interview and Harriet agreed not to say anything at breakfast. He asked Robert not to mention the shopping trip either and he agreed. The more he thought about it, the more he realized that it would be better if Paige were not told about the exam either.

The evening before Harriet had made breakfast reservations for the entire group at the Rainforest Cafe near the main entrance. At breakfast Harriet told everyone that Tyler was Claude's charge, Molly was hers and Paige was Hawk's. An elephant trumpeted and the group laughed.

"They're glued together," Tyler quipped.

Paige didn't react to the tease. Hawk squeezed her hand lightly and she smiled at him.

Two people arrived as the group was finishing. Everyone recognized Dr. Reggie Barre and welcomed her. She introduced her colleague Dr. Miles Greenwood.

Dr. Greenwood noticed recognition in only two faces. He was pleased. He wanted to observe the children casually. He also wanted them to be familiar with him. What no one but Dr. Barre knew was that he was to evaluate all three children. She had been given the same instructions. They were to take the whole day. They had agreed in advance to separate. But to the delight of both doctors the entire group elected to go watch Paige ride the Everest ride.

They all headed into Asia area. There was a raft ride all of them wanted to try and the Maharajah Jungle Trek was on everyone's list as well. Once the boys had been told that

Epcot Center would be on the next day's agenda, they settled down to enjoy the Animal Kingdom Park in full.

"Why is Paige's going on the big ride something to watch?" Dr. Greenwood asked the two boys in the group.

"Because until yesterday, you couldn't even get Paige on a merry-go-round," Tyler said. "And she rode down Splash Mountain five times."

"Splash Mountain?"

"You go down a waterfall five stories high."

"Whoa!"

"Yeh. She went on practically every other ride too," Tyler said.

"Maybe she's not afraid of amusement park rides."

"Mom took us lots of times. She couldn't ever get Paige on a single ride. Not one!" Tyler said. "You should've seen her coming out here in the plane. She was a basket case."

"So what happened?"

"Hawk did something," Tyler said. "Only none of us can figure out what."

"Hawk? Who's he?"

Tyler pointed. "That guy. They're engaged."

"Your sister looks young."

"She's younger than me. She's sixteen."

"That's too young."

"Yeh, that's what I thought, but if he gets Paige to do this, he's got my vote."

"Why is this important to you?"

"She won't learn to drive," Tyler spat out his vexation at her decision rising to the fore. "I've got to do all the driving–to the store, picking up the kids, everything."

"So, you're hoping this'll turn her around?"

"I guess that's kinda dumb. I keep forgetting. It doesn't matter much anymore," Tyler recounted sadly. "When we go back we got no home to go back to."

"I read about the fire," Greenwood said. "That's tough."

"All our stuff's gone too," Tyler said. "It's hard to lose your stuff."

"Yes, it is."

"So are you here to see if Paige is old enough to get married?"

"Something like that."

"She's been taking care of all of us since Mom died. She's a good cook. She knows how not to ruin sweaters and stuff when she washes them. Mom taught her all that stuff before she died."

"Your mother's death must've been hard for all of you."

"Yeh. She and David kept us going."

"Sorry about your brother."

"Yeh, me too," Tyler returned.

Seeing how uncomfortable the talk of the two deaths made the young boy, Dr. Greenwood changed the subject. "Do you think she'll do it?"

"Naw, it's too scary. Yesterday she was on some kind of high."

"Drugs?"

"No. Paige doesn't do drugs," Tyler stated flatly. "But why don't you ask her? She won't tell me."

"I don't think..." Greenwood began.

Tyler called to his sister, "Dr. Greenwood wants to know your secret."

Paige turned and grinned at her brother. "Hawk."

When Paige spotted the huge mountain with rails twisting in and out, she gasped, "Hawk, it's so high."

"It's your choice Paige," Hawk said gently.

Dr. Greenwood positioned himself behind the couple and found himself in line for the ride. He planned to step out near the gate.

"Wanna partner?" Tyler asked. "Doc finked out."

"Doc?"

"Dr. Chesney," Tyler explained. "He said he wants to keep his stomach right where it is. Something about not wanting to re-taste his breakfast."

"And you're not afraid you might throw up. You ate a big breakfast."

"Me? Naw. I can hold it in," Tyler bragged, "So are you going on?"

"Sure," Dr. Greenwood said. "I'm game."

Miles Greenwood was a small man, a bit young to be balding. He wore his light wavy hair long and pulled back into a ponytail.

"You might lose your glasses," Tyler said loudly enough so Paige could hear. "Some of the turns look wicked."

Paige leaned over. "Hawk, what if I throw up."

"We can go later," Hawk said gently. "Or not at all. I do have a great surprise for you however."

"Tyler's right behind us."

"It won't hurt if he hears," Hawk said.

"So you're not giving me the same surprise as yesterday?"

"No," came the simple answer.

Dr. Greenwood made a mental note to ask her about it. He saw Paige lean over and whisper in the tall man's ear. Hawk turned and whispered in hers as he drew her closer.

"It's really high, Hawk," she commented.

Greenwood heard the quiver in her voice.

"You can turn around until the safety bar is in place," Hawk said. "And I won't think any less of you."

"I have to do this," Paige said. "You will hold my hand?"

"Only if you sit on my left."

"Why?"

"Because I may want to write with my right hand sometime next week."

Paige looked askance at the man beside her. "Show me."

Hawk raised his hand slowly and let it hang as if it were broken.

Paige took it and turned it over. "It's black and blue. Did I do that?"

Hawk stared down. "It is not."

"I thought so," Paige charge gaily. "You're teasing me."

"Maybe a little," he admitted. "I still can't hear out of my right ear though."

She leaned up and whispered something very softly.

"I can't say that!" Hawk protested.

"Your ear is fine," Paige announced.

"It recovered in time to hear what you said."

"It hears everything I say," Paige said. "Besides you're the one who told me to scream."

"Guilty as charged."

"So don't complain when I do as you ask."

This repartee brought them to the front of the line.

"Are you ready?" Hawk asked.

"You didn't give me any time to get scared," she said. "So I don't know."

"I'll be getting in first," Hawk said.

"You want me on the scariest side," Paige accused him unexpectedly.

"I will switch if you like."

"Never mind. I'll take the worst side," she snapped.

Hawk took her in his arms and whispered. "The secret is that today we are buying our wedding rings. I want you to hold the hand you're going to put mine on someday soon."

Paige's face registered her pleasure, and her nod told him she agreed that sitting on his left had meaning. It wasn't a profound meaning. It was actually superficial. It was a fun reason.

"I'll try not to make your hand swell," she said as they walked toward the cars.

Hawk stepped into the front pair of seats first and Paige took his hand and let him help her into the seat beside him.

"The backs on the seats are so high," she commented.

"Oh, didn't you know," Hawk said. "This ride goes frontward and backwards."

"Backwards?"

The bar was lowered.

"It's too late to get off, isn't it?"

"Take a deep breath," Hawk said. "You're about to have the ride of your life."

"Hawk, I can't," Paige said as the car began to move.

"Just hang on to me," he said loudly. "I won't let you fall."

The car shook. Paige felt Hawk's hold on her grow stronger. He wasn't afraid, she realized.

Her stomach rose and her heart raced as the car jostled her from side to side at every turn. Every few moments, the car seemed to level off and she hoped briefly that the ride was over. And just when she thought she was going to make it, the car stopped suddenly and she found herself riding backwards.

Her screeches filled her eardrums. She couldn't stop. She fought the jostling, clinging to the bar and to Hawk's hand. There were monsters that popped out at her unexpectedly. Her grip on Hawk's hand tightened at each new scare.

This is going to last forever, she thought. I can't last. I'm going to die.

And suddenly, it was over. The car rolled to a stop. She swallowed her last scream and let Hawk help her out. Her legs were wobbly beneath her and there were tears in her eyes. As they went down the ramp, Hawk kept his firm hold on her.

"I didn't do it," she cried.

Hawk laughed. "We started over there. We ended up over here. In between you screamed a lot. Oh, you did it!"

"But I was scared to death!" she argued.

"People usually are."

"You weren't."

"You were too busy being scared to notice."

"I noticed," she demurred. "You weren't."

"I'm sorry I can't kiss you. You do deserve it."

"I thought I was going to do this so well."

"I thought you handled it surprisingly well."

"How can you say that?"

"Because you're okay now."

"I'm not going on that ride again," Paige stated flatly.

"Lydia Praetzel said those same words yesterday after Space Mountain," Hawk reminded her. "Let's go on the Jungle Trek. Walking will steady your legs. You'll feel normal soon."

"I'm still shaking," Paige said.

"Give yourself a break," Hawk urged her. "It was a rough adventure and you made it on your own."

Paige pictured them trying to kiss and giggled, "If we had kissed, we'd both have broken teeth."

Dr. Greenwood caught up to them in time to hear that and see Hawk give her a squeeze. "You are an amazing woman."

"So are we still engaged?"

"What?" Hawk said cupping his hand behind one ear. "What's that you say? Some woman was screaming in my ear. I can't hear so good."

Paige asked sternly, "Are we?"

"Are we what?"

"You know."

"So do you," Hawk said. "I can't wait to get married so you won't ask me that question again."

"I'll have a new question," Paige assured him.

Hawk laughed. "Yes, we are still engaged. Are you ever going to trust me?"

"I trusted you enough to go on the scariest ride in the park with you."

"You did that," Hawk agreed. "Okay, if it helps any, ask me that question anytime, but you know I don't expect you to be perfect."

"But I want to be."

"I can't love you any more than I do right now, even though I'm deaf in my right ear.

Paige giggled. "Be grateful I didn't kiss you."

Dr. Barre joined Dr. Greenwood on the Jungle Trek.

"How was it?" she asked.

"I should get hazard pay."

"That bad?"

"I wasn't planning to go on at all, then Tyler asked me to," Miles confided. "I thought it'd be a good time to get some real insight into the boy's thinking."

"And did you?"

"I was too busy being scared out of my wits."

"Men don't usually admit that."

"If I didn't, you'd psychoanalyze me," Miles quipped. "I know I'm still shaking."

"So what about our girl?"

"She was ashamed of being scared. She's got a real fear problem, but Hawk seems to know all the right things to say."

"But you were scared on the ride."

"But she thinks that her fear is so bad that Hawk won't want to marry her because of it."

"So you think it's a problem."

"Yes, but she's learning how to cope," Miles concluded.

"By going on rides?" Reggie scoffed.

"We all have to start somewhere."

Up ahead on the walk, Paige kept her voice low as she asked Hawk, "We are really going to get our wedding bands today?"

"Aleta told her dad to take us shopping for them."

"She did mean it."

"That's not all," Hawk said as they walked along the forested path simulating the Anandapour Royal Forest of Southeast Asia, replete with replicas of wild animals around the bends in the pathway.

The appearance of a tiger startled Paige who jumped back. Hawk put his arm around her.

"I need you to do something for me, for us."

"Anything."

"I want you to have a pre-marital exam and take a blood test."

"With a needle?"

"You don't like needles?"

"I hate needles," Paige said. "Is it necessary?"

"No, it's not, but we need to know if either of us has a STD."

"How could we?"

"I don't know, but if you don't want to, I won't insist. I will get one though so you'll know I'm clean."

"And you'll just trust me?"

"Yes."

"Will you hold my hand?"

"They'll give you a rubber ball to squeeze."

"And you'll ask them if you can keep it to hand me whenever I want to hold your hand?"

"Okay, you can squeeze my hand."

"I'll use the ball."

"I can't be with you during the exam," Hawk said. "Stanley told Dr. Chesney do it this afternoon. He needs the results tomorrow."

"Why?"

"Aleta thinks your father is going to fight a motion for a continuation of the custody hearing. She thinks she may not win that one."

"Shouldn't we go home?"

"If we do, you three will be put into foster homes."

"The Chesney's, right?"

"They aren't approved yet."

"You said homes. Will we be split up?"

Hawk nodded.

"Oh no!" Paige exclaimed.

"Aleta wants us to stay down here."

"I should do what she says, right?"

"Trust her," Hawk said. "She and Stanley have great reputations."

The two were so engrossed that they didn't notice that Dr. Barre and Dr. Greenwood had moved within earshot of them.

"Do they always win?"

"Not always," Hawk said. "So far your father has buried proof of his deed deep. It will take time to uncover the truth."

"Sometimes discovering the truth takes years, doesn't it?"

"Let's hope this isn't one of those times."

"You'll wait for me, won't you?"

"You're predicting failure?"

"It's hard for me not to."

"I guess I have reason to predict success."

"Let's move on your wavelength then," Paige decided.

"So you're ready for another ride before lunch?"

"On the Everest?"

"I thought you'd like to ride the rapids. I hear it's fun."

"I'm riding on your wavelength now," Paige said. "I like it better than mine."

They walked on hand in hand still oblivious to their shadows.

"I like the water rides best," Paige mentioned.

"You want to go to one of the water parks tomorrow??"

"I don't have a swimsuit."

"We can buy one after we get our rings," Hawk suggested. "You can get a bikini."

"A bikini?"

"Why not?"

"Mother would be upset."

"No she wouldn't. If you got one at fourteen she might be, but you're almost seventeen. You're allowed."

"You're sure?"

Hawk grinned. "Absolutely."

"You just want an eyeful."

"Absolutely!"

The two doctors following exchanged knowing glances. Then Paige said something unexpected.

"We can't go alone. You promised."

"I'll talk someone into it. Maybe Robert and Bertha," Hawk said. "Harriet and Claude have to watch Molly and Tyler."

"They might want to come," Paige said. "Can we buy them swimsuits too?"

"Sure. Do you know their sizes?"

"Who do you think buys everyone's underwear? Boys never buy that," Paige said. "When Tyler outgrew boys sizes, he complained that they didn't fit and I bought the next size up and David had to tell me Tyler wasn't in boy's sizes anymore. I never knew there was a difference in the cut. Mom never explained that. She left a lot of holes in my education."

"You are way ahead of other girls your age."

"Do I really know enough to be a wife?"

"I suggest you ask some woman that's married about the sexual part."

"Why do you think I want to know about that?" There was an edge in her tone.

"Because it's the only area you're lacking experience in."

"Oh," she said in a soft voice.

After the raft ride, Dr. Greenwood asked Hawk if he could talk with Paige privately. Paige looked surprised and Hawk explained that Aleta sent him.

"Just be honest and don't worry," Hawk said. "You aren't crazy or delusional."

"Why am I being interviewed?" Paige asked Dr. Greenwood.

"The court may need to make certain decisions about your future."

"Shouldn't I have a lawyer or something?"

"You have a lawyer. She sent me, remember," Dr. Greenwood said, a bit stiffly.

"Don't get testy," Paige quipped. "You need to be a passive listener to get a good clear view of the workings of my mind."

Dr. Greenwood masked his surprise, but Hawk laughed.

"Her mother was a sociologist. She taught her a lot," Hawk explained to the doctor, and then turning to Paige, he said, "Stop hiding. Just be honest. Be yourself. Aleta can work with that."

Paige dropped her head, "Sorry, Dr. Greenwood. Ask your questions."

"You like this man?" Dr. Greenwood began his voice even.

"I love him."

"Have you loved anyone before?"

"My mother, David, Molly, Tyler. But this is different."

"How is it different?"

"It just is."

"He's your first boyfriend, isn't he?"

"Yes."

"How did you meet?"

"At a barbecue. I was walking a couple of dogs and he was introduced to me and he make a joke about his name and

I responded and he said, 'when you grow up, I'm going to ask you to marry me.'"

"Those were his exact words?"

"Yes."

"So what was your response?"

"I told him I didn't like people who break promises and I asked him if he had a ring and I held out my hand and he gave it to me and we became engaged."

"Just like that?"

"Yes."

"Did he kiss you?"

"No, we talked, and I told him he was the kind of man my mother told me to marry."

"And you kept the ring?"

"He put the tape around it so it would fit my finger," Paige said. "Then Ed told everyone we were engaged to be married after I turned eighteen."

"So now you're going steady and dating?" Miles said, putting a spin of normalcy on it.

"No. We aren't going steady. That's for boyfriends. That's what kids in high school do."

"You're in high school."

"Yes, I am."

"So you're trying to get a jump on everyone and be the first girl to be engaged?" he prodded. This wasn't a therapy session. This was an analytical session.

"No. We're engaged because Hawk asked me to marry him and I accepted."

"Lots of kids that go steady talk about marriage as a prelude to sexual relations. Isn't that the case here?"

"Hawk is going to be sure we are never alone together. We will always have a chaperone. I'm underage. He could get in trouble."

"So you're friends?" Miles proposed.

"No, we're engaged," Paige insisted, "That's more."

Suddenly, Miles switched course.

"How did Hawk get you on your first ride?"

"Judge Davis said I wasn't to talk about that."

"I think I'm an exception to that suggestion."

"It wasn't a suggestion. It was an order."

"But I'm a psychologist. Anything you say to me is confidential."

"No, it's not. You're here to investigate me. You will make a report to the court."

"If you've done nothing illegal, why won't you tell me?"

"Because Judge Davis told me not to."

"Judge Davis doesn't hold your future in her hands," Miles remonstrated. "I do."

"But Judge Davis is a judge. Judges should be obeyed, shouldn't they?"

"Do you understand what I'm saying? Judge Davis may have given you good advice under ordinary circumstances, but you're fighting for your life here, for your freedom."

"I understand that my father plans to put me in a mental institution and the doctors there will torture me to get me to forget my father killed my sister. I'm not a brave person, so they will succeed. But my father won't believe them. He doesn't trust anyone. So he'll make them keep me."

"Won't Hawk come and take you out when you're eighteen?"

"My father will make sure that never happens."

"You think he will kill you?"

"He killed my sister and she was only a baby."

"But when you testify in court, he won't dare kill you."

"But I'm not going to testify."

"Why not?"

"I can't prove what I know to be true. In court you can't accuse someone without proof. Aleta told me that."

"But you could say what you think."

"No, I can't."

"Are you afraid to?"

"If I did, Tyler and Molly would know my secret. Their lives would be in danger then. I won't do that to them."

"Are you saying that to impress me?"

"You aren't impressed, are you?" Paige said. "So I guess I'm not."

Miles responded, a bit shaken by her acuity. He went on the offensive. "I have a different take on your refusal. "I think you're too scared to take a stand."

"Murderers can be prosecuted any time."

"What does that mean?"

"It means that if I were to testify when there is no proof it would be a waste. Right now there is no proof. My testimony isn't enough. It can only hurt my brother and sister."

"And if there was proof?"

"Then I would tell what I saw."

Miles Greenwood had one more series of questions to ask before he would be satisfied that his investigation was complete.

"Do you think it's fair to use Hawk the way you are?"

"Yes."

"Do you understand the question?"

"Yes."

"How can you justify using him?"

"I don't," Paige responded. "My brothers used me all the time to cook and clean for them and to take care of Molly. They never justified it. Families do that. Hawk and I are going to be a family."

"You're abandoning your sister when she needs you most."

"I'm not abandoning her. She's being taken from me. Tyler and I wanted to keep going, but the law won't allow that. And then Dad burned down our house," she choked, paused, and then suddenly her face contorted in rage. "Burning down our home was a mean despicable, hateful act.

My father is an abominable excuse for a human being. He is without a minimum of sympathy or love or compassion. He is self-centered and self-serving, a classic sociopath completely lacking in even a rudimentary conscience. I would call him an animal only he is lower than any animal on earth."

"But you're going to allow him to take Molly and Tyler rather than speak out. I suggest you're afraid."

"I want them to live, Dr. Greenwood," Paige said rising. "My outburst was in poor taste, and I apologize. May I go?"

"Yes. You may go. Thank you."

Paige ran to Hawk and made him take her away from Greenwood. She was close to tears so he walked her back to the Jungle Trek again.

"I messed up, Hawk," Paige said. "He was so...so derisive."

"He was probably testing you."

"I know he was and I failed."

"You got angry?"

"Yes."

"Argumentative?"

"Yes."

"Dishonest?"

"No."

"You told him everything?"

"Except what Judge Davis said I wasn't to mention again."

"Paige, you are a wonder," Hawk said, giving her arm a squeeze. "Again, I wish I could kiss you."

"I'm counting them, you know."

"Counting what?"

"The kisses you owe me."

"When do you plan to collect?"

"After we're married, when you're upset with me."

"So I owe you how many?"

"Somewhere between three and eight."

"Make it eight," Hawk said. "That sounds closer to right. I'm sure I've wanted to kiss you at least eight times."

Paige giggled. "So I read you right all those times you held back."

"Are you sure you read Dr. Greenwood right?"

"He didn't like me," Paige said.

"You scared him," Hawk said. "He doesn't know how to handle a woman like you."

"And you do?"

"I don't want to handle you at all," Hawk said.

"How did I overcome being afraid of rides?"

"You did that. I only helped."

Paige looked at him with amazement.

"That's the difference," she said.

"What difference?"

"Between you and Tyler. He always tried to handle me, push me, direct me, challenge me. All my energy was spent pushing back. You just supported me. More than that, you would have supported me no matter what choice I made."

"We're going to get through this," Hawk said. "Psychologists are just people with opinions."

"Can we tell Aleta to ship down another one? I'll try to be friendlier."

Hawk smiled. "It just so happens she did."

"Not Dr. Barre!" Paige gasped.

"You wanted a second chance."

"Yeh, with a stranger," Paige grumped.

"How many interviews do you want to have?"

"As many as it takes."

"Then you best get this one out of the way."

"She's waiting for me, isn't she?"

"Yes," Hawk replied.

The interview with Dr. Barre went about the same as the one with Dr. Greenwood. Paige came out disgruntled.

"I think it's me. I don't relate well to psychologists," she said. "And don't tell me she doesn't know how to handle women. She handles nothing but women and a lot of them are my age."

"Okay, I won't say she might find you disconcerting."

"Why would she do that?"

"You aren't the typical sixteen-year-old, Paige, which is why I want to marry you. What you know, you really know. What you don't know, you really don't know. The problem is you were schooled by a sociologist. Sociologists and psychologists don't think quite the same."

"We aren't aliens!" Paige protested.

Hawk laughed. "Let's go have lunch. If we're late Harriet will be upset. Now there's someone you don't want to upset, my little alien princess."

Paige laughed lightly. "Let's eat. We aliens have big appetites."

Chapter 15

Before she left the hospital, Aleta had stopped in to see Dr. Schwartzman and found him sitting up in bed with Dr. Hughes by his side.

"So, how is he?" Aleta asked.

"Another couple of days and I think he can go home," Dr. Hughes said.

Dr. Schwartzman looked distressed.

"He's not up to a full dose of family yet," Aleta said. "Let's talk about alternatives. Is he well enough to travel?"

"Not just yet," Dr. Hughes said.

"What about a nurse attendant full time?" Aleta asked. "To limit his visitors."

"A live-in aide?" Dr. Schwartzman asked. "I've heard horror stories about them. So have my kids."

"But you only have access to a couple hundred dollars a week," Aleta said. "They can't steal much."

"My house is full of valuables," Dr. Schwartzman put in.

"Forget I even suggested it," Aleta said. "I can't have you stressing out over your help. Let's chat for a while about other stuff. Your mind will come up with something when you least expect it. And you'll wonder why you didn't think of it earlier."

Dr. Hughes left and Herve Schwartzman asked Aleta about Tyler Roach.

"You know him?"

"I knew his mother Mary. She was one of my favorite students. Insisted on mastering in Sociology, but she took a tutorial from me. One on one. She picked an odd subject: 'The First Five Minutes in a Psychiatric Interview.'"

"That was odd," Aleta said. "Why did she want to study that subject?"

"Probably because I said they were the most important five minutes in therapy."

"Really?" Aleta said. "That's a frightening thought."

"Frightening? Why?"

"Because when I saw Dr. Barre, I did all the talking. I think I laid out my whole experience in five minutes."

"Why does that frighten you?"

"I don't want her to know me."

"Why not?"

"Are you interviewing me?"

"I guess I'm doing it, but I didn't mean to frighten you. It's just habitual like your question asking."

"You ask questions," Aleta charged. "How is my doing it different?"

"I'm probing to help a person to recognize the truth that his psyche has buried. You do it to expose the truth that a person is deliberately hiding."

"That sounds right."

"You don't trust Dr. Barre, do you?"

"No."

"So you overloaded her with facts without emotion so she couldn't know you."

"But I revealed myself, didn't I?"

"I'm afraid so."

"I took her home for supper."

"You did what?" Herve Schwartzman gasped.

"She was planning to commit suicide. I had to stop her."

"But you didn't trust her so you couldn't help her," Dr. Schwartzman said. "She'd sense that."

"Jocelyn took over."

"Who's Jocelyn?"

"My younger sister."

"Is she a psychologist?"

"She's sixteen," Aleta said, "but she's a prophet too. Then my grandmother watched her. She's a prophet too and a deputy. Claude took over around four in the morning. We couldn't let her go home. Then she went to a nursing home and Grams went along. She did some doctoring, helped some people and then decided to quit the Crisis Center. That's why she was going to kill herself. She wanted out."

"It was a bad match for Reggie from the start," Herve Schwartzman said. "You know who else made a bad choice? Mary Roach. She was wasted on Van Horne, a true sociopath, in my estimation."

"What else do you know about Van Horne?"

"Nothing much. Mary came to see me after their last baby was born. It was a Down's baby. She wanted to know how to persuade her husband to let her raise the child. She said she had the cutest dimple in one cheek."

"Do you know what happened to the child?"

"I heard it had been placed in an institution. I couldn't believe Mary had agreed to that, but then she divorced him. What happened to the baby?"

"We don't know," Aleta said.

"Is that why Tyler came to see you?"

"You know I can't discuss a case," Aleta said, "but anything he told you might be helpful."

"This is going to be one-sided, isn't it?"

"Yes, it is."

"Tyler didn't tell me anything. But Mary asked me some questions that were more legal than psychological and I told her she needed a lawyer. She got a divorce, so I assume she got one."

"What kinds of questions?"

"That's privileged, Counselor," Schwartzman retorted.

"Dr. Schwartzman, Mary is dead," Aleta returned.

"Privilege remains intact."

"Kurt Van Horne is fighting for custody of his children."

"Mary would have taken care of that somehow. Did you search for her papers?"

"Yes. We can't find them."

"Her mother would know where they are."

"Her mother died two years ago."

"What about David?"

"He died a couple weeks ago," Aleta said. "All Paige can tell us is that someone named Lindsman has all the papers. Do you know him? Was he a classmate of Mary's?"

"Lindsman? That sounds familiar," Dr. Schwartzman said.

Aleta waited quietly as the old man closed his eyes to let his mind try to recall the memory of the person.

After a few minutes, Dr. Schwartzman opened his eyes. "The memory's gone. Only I don't think Lindsman is a person."

"What else could it be?"

"I don't know. I just have this bit of memory that tells me I referred to it in my lectures."

""Do you have any copies?"

"I suppose I do. In my study."

"May I have permission to look?"

"Of course," Herve Schwartzman said. "I wish I could remember though."

"I may have to take those files with me."

"I'm not going to use them again," Schwartzman said sadly.

"Ever thought of doing tutorials?"

Schwartzman shook his head. "I'm afraid I'm not interested in teaching remedial students."

"I'm talking graduate level tutorials. Classes for one or two students only. Aren't you a professor emeritus at the university?"

"Yes, but..."

"Arrange it," Aleta said. "Post it. Offer credit. All you need is one person to sign up for each offering."

"The university won't want to pay for that."

"Oh, for heaven's sake, tell them you don't need payment. It'll mess up your retirement. What do they charge–several hundred dollars a unit? They'll love the idea."

"I'll be offering my services for free," he stated unhappily.

"Not really," Aleta said. "In exchange you'll be busy with students who will act as a buffer between you and your children."

Dr. Schwartzman grew thoughtful.

"It would be nice to deal with students like Mary again," he mused aloud.

"I'll check back with you tomorrow. I have a court date at two. I'll come here afterward."

"Good. That'll give me a chance to make some calls. Thanks, Aleta."

Jeff Roper, the Arborville officer assigned to guard Aleta drove her to Dr. Herve Schwartzman's house. When Aleta saw two cars parked in the driveway, her heart sank. At least two of his children were there.

As she got out of the car, the front door opened and the small, thin, balding replica of his father stood in the doorway smiling at her.

"Dad called," he said. "He ordered us to get our butts over here and help you find some lecture notes."

Aleta returned his smile. "I appreciate the help."

"Deborah's found a couple of files with lecture notes. Dad has a great many research files."

Deborah looked up when the two entered.

"I've only found two folders. I'm sure there are more. If we each take a cabinet, we should get through them in short order."

As they worked, Aleta asked the two how their visits with their father were going.

"It's nice being alone with him," Deborah said. "I wish I had a little more time, but I like the welcoming look on his face when I come in. It's as if he's been waiting for my visit."

"He gives me the same look," Jacob remarked.

"He loves you," Aleta said. "It's the bickering that stresses him out."

"He's handled us all this life," Jacob stated. "His mind's as sharp as ever."

"You need to listen to what I'm saying."

"Which is?"

"That the way your family interacts stresses out your father. Such stress caused his stroke."

"I don't like what you're implying," Jacob retorted.

"I'm not implying anything," Aleta said. "I'm stating the facts as clearly as I can."

"That I'm responsible..."

"Whoa!" Aleta interjected. "You are not responsible. Deborah is not responsible. As far as I can tell neither are your younger siblings. It is your way of interacting that's responsible. That's not something I can fix. All I can do is protect your father from the group."

"You mean we can never see him again together?" Jacob asked.

"It looks that way," Aleta said. "We're exploring after care choices now."

Jacob scowled, as did Deborah.

"Without our input?" Jacob grumbled.

"He could live with me," Deborah offered. "I have plenty of room."

"So have we," Jacob said.

"He won't be living with anyone in the family," Aleta interjected. "Not yet anyway."

"Where will he go?" Deborah asked.

"Home."

"I guess I can arrange to spend most of my day here," Deborah started.

Again Aleta spoke, "If you do, I'll move him to a nursing home with the same visiting restrictions as the hospital."

"You can't do that!" Deborah said. "You aren't in charge of where he lives or who takes care of him."

"Yes, I am. It would be a medical decision."

"Jacob, tell her we'll fight her in court."

"You won't win," Aleta said coolly. "Are we finished here?"

"What do you want with these old lecture notes? Dad's stuff is so outdated," Deborah rejoined, closing the box with the file folders.

"I see he gets all the latest psychological journals," Aleta said. "They look like they've been read."

"He devours them," Jacob said. "I told you his mind was sharp."

"What if he decided to teach again?" Aleta posed.

"I wouldn't allow it," Jacob responded heatedly.

"He's too old to work," Deborah added. "He should be enjoying life."

"I see," Aleta said. She picked up the box and left.

Chapter 16

Meanwhile, in Florida, at two o'clock, Robert drove his wife, Dr. Chesney, Hawk and Paige into the OBGYN clinic parking lot. Dr. Chesney was greeted by a fellow obstetrician who'd attended the same medical school he had.

"I told you to call me if you ever visited and to plan to have dinner with us, but this is an odd request, to say the least," Dr. Camp said.

"Cliff, relax. A judge ordered this. I'm not privy to all the details," Dr. Chesney responded. "Which room?"

Dr. Camp led the way.

Bertha remained in the room with Paige as she undressed and answered her questions. Her presence calmed Paige.

"Have you had this done?" Paige asked as she handed Bertha her blouse and bra.

"Yes, I have," Bertha replied, helping her slip into a gown.

"Does it hurt?" she asked as she took off her shorts.

"No," Bertha said. "But it may bother you. Many women find this embarrassing."

Bertha helped her sit on the edge of the table and lay down.

"Will I ever need to go through this again?"

"Yes," Bertha said covering her with a sheet and pulling up the stirrups. "But the doctors don't think of this as anymore sexual than looking down your throat to see if your tonsils are swollen."

Bertha told Dr. Chesney she was ready.

He came in, washed his hands and donned a pair of gloves. The examination was done quickly; however, he had Dr. Camp come in and repeat the procedure.

Bertha knew this wasn't normal, but she said nothing.

"When she's dressed, Nurse," Dr. Camp said, "Bring her to my office."

"Yes, Doctor," Bertha said.

Both doctors were in the office when Bertha and Paige arrived. Bertha excused herself and went back to the waiting room to wait with Robert.

"Something's wrong," Bertha said.

"Do you know what?"

"No idea."

In the room, Paige sat in the chair next to Hawk. He took her hand and then looked at her. She was pale.

"What's wrong?" he asked.

"I was examined twice," she said. "It's what the doctors do when they suspect cancer. My mother died of uterine cancer."

Both doctors looked startled.

"We didn't find cancer, Paige," Dr. Chesney said quickly. "I wasn't sure that my verification might not be thrown out of court since Evelyn and I have applied to be foster parents for the three of you, so I asked Dr. Camp to examine you too."

"Is that all?" Paige breathed. The color returned to her face. "I am okay, aren't I?"

"Tell me, do you experience a lot of cramping when you menstruate?"

"Yes. Mother said she did too. She said hers went away after David was born."

The two doctors exchanged glances.

"Sounds right," Dr. Chesney said. "Paige you have a tipped uterus. It's tipped over so far that it's unlikely you will be able to become pregnant until it is surgically repaired."

Dr. Camp added his take.

"Pregnancy sometimes brings the uterus back to a more normal position; however, in your case, I don't think pregnancy is possible without surgery."

"I measured you for a diaphragm, Paige," Dr. Chesney said. "Considering your family history, I'd rather you didn't use birth control pills. I'd like to examine you yearly."

"Why?"

"There are polyps that occur in many women and it is recommended that these be removed in someone with your family history."

"But I can have children?"

"Yes. Getting pregnant may be a problem," Dr. Chesney said, "but, as far as bearing children, we see no problem."

"One more thing," Dr. Camp said. "Intercourse may prove uncomfortable, even painful, with your uterus tipped as it is."

"Should she have the surgery first?" Hawk asked.

"No, Hawk," Paige begged. "No surgery. Please."

Dr. Chesney stepped in. "See how it goes first. See me if it isn't pleasant, Paige. I'll explain the surgery then. You may not need it until you decide to start a family."

"Hawk," Paige began.

Hawk interrupted her. "Yes, we are still engaged."

Both doctors looked at the tall man, surprise raising all four brows.

"Paige doesn't think she's perfect enough," Hawk explained.

"It's not only that," Paige said. "Hawk, please, I need to talk to you."

"Use my office," Dr. Camp said.

When the doctors left, Paige plunged in.

"I don't want you to be distressed on your wedding night."

"We won't get distressed. Now that we know, we won't feel guilty or frightened or even terribly worried. Knowing is a good thing."

"Let's get blood tests then," Paige said.

Their blood was drawn and the tests were run before Hawk and Paige left to shop for rings and swimsuits.

The shopping went fairly quickly. Paige spotted the ring she liked immediately. It fit. There was a matching one for Hawk that also fit.

Paige chuckled. "At least we have normal sized fingers."

The rings were purchased.

Paige tried on the first bikini Hawk picked out and said it was perfect. She bought a swimsuit for Molly in a matching violet and blue design.

"She likes it when we dress like sisters."

Paige picked out navy blue trunks for Tyler and Hawk bought a matching pair in his size.

"Brothers?"

"I like blue," Hawk replied.

"Well, we will look like a family," Paige remarked. "Molly will like that."

While Paige and Hawk were away, Miles Greenwood was sitting on a bench outside the Jungle Trek telling Judge Davis that Paige had withheld an important bit of information from him.

"She said you told her not to talk about it," he said.

"I did advise her," Lydia responded. "And the matter's not open for discussion."

"But I need to know," Miles insisted. "You know me. You know Stanley trusts me."

"I'm sorry," Lydia said. "It's privileged."

"You aren't a lawyer. You're a judge."

"Don't play games with me, Miles," Lydia said icily. "All you need to know is that Paige was telling the truth."

"Did it involve Hawk? Did he do something illegal?" Miles pressed. "Are you covering for him?"

"What bothers you the most," Lydia asked, "the fact that Paige is smarter than you–hell, she's smarter than me–or the fact that she doesn't need your help?"

"Oh, she needs help. She needs lots of help. And I'm going to see she gets it," Miles declared, vexed.

"Where does she need help?" Lydia asked.

"Her attitude," Miles declared. "She was scornful."

"Interesting," Lydia said. "You're going to give her a bad mark because she didn't like you."

Miles reined in his emotions.

"No. I'm more professional than that."

"Good," Lydia said.

"But she needs professional help."

"What she needs is for bad things to stop happening to her," Lydia declared. "What she needs is a break."

"People have to move on with their lives after a tragedy."

"It hasn't even been a month since her brother was killed," Lydia pointed out. "And it was only two days ago her home was destroyed."

"That's part of the problem," Miles said. "She's not devastated by that loss. All she feels is hatred for her father. She is sure he is at fault."

"And you believe what?"

"That it's her newest delusion. Her father puts her sister in an institution and she envisions him killing the baby. A robber burns down the house to cover any clues to himself as a thief and she thinks her father did it."

"Paige was right about you."

"Right?"

"You can't be trusted," Lydia said coolly. "You babble."

Lydia rose abruptly.

"I...I don't..." Greenwood began.

"Good day, Sir," Lydia said as she walked away.

Later, Reggie Barre approached Judge Davis seeking the same information.

"I've already refused to divulge the information, other than to say that Paige told you the truth."

"You don't know what she told me," Reggie quipped.

"I know she quoted me. You told me that."

"Oh, yes," Reggie stumbled. "It's just that I haven't done this before."

"That won't play with me either, Doctor. You're an experienced, highly trained professional. You went up against a sixteen-year-old girl and she kept her secret and her cool. She is a most remarkable young woman, don't you think?"

"Oh, she's clever all right. Too clever. No one gets over fears as fast as she did. The only explanation is that they were a sham, a play to use to draw Hawk into a relationship which will last only as long as it suits her."

"My, you are jaded."

"I'm not a romantic if that's what you mean."

"I would say that was an honest evaluation," Lydia agreed.

"I am going to recommend that her father get custody so that she can get the professional help she needs."

"Is that a threat?" Lydia asked.

"No. I'm telling you my recommendation because you can change my mind if you tell me what happened between her and Hawk that rid her of her fear of wild rides."

"So you do believe she was afraid," Lydia remarked sagely. "If I were you, I would reconsider all she told you. You are not Dr. Miles Greenwood's equal. You are his superior."

"Don't try to play me, Judge. I'm no more susceptible than you are."

"Think about your report carefully. A girl's life depends on it."

"If anything happens to her, it will be your fault, not mine."

"Just consider her words carefully. Believe them. Then your report will be worth something."

"You've been a judge too long," Reggie harrumphed. "You see yourself as right even when you're not."

Lydia sat stunned and watched Reggie storm off. Hubert joined her. He put his arm around her and asked her why she was distressed. She told him.

Chapter 17

When Aleta arrived back at the hospital, Stanley greeted her with a smile. He had multiple folders lying around him on the bed.

"It's not a man," he said. "It's a book."

"Lindsman is a book?"

"The book is 'Man' by G. D. Lind, hence Lind's 'Man'," Stanley explained.

"Why didn't Paige know?"

"Maybe her mother didn't realize how ambiguous her phrasing was."

"Well, whatever the reason, it doesn't matter," Aleta said. "We have the book, that is, Hawk has it in the trunk of his car. Ed can take over."

"Get Hawk's permission. Ed may have to break into his trunk.

"The man who wrote those pages," Stanley said, "He is our client, correct?"

"Dr. Schwartzman, yes."

"What a fantastic lecturer! I'd love to meet him."

"He's here in the hospital," Aleta said. "I can arrange it."

"He suffered a stroke, right?" Stanley said, putting the bits and pieces of memories together. "Can he talk?"

"He's fine. He's due to be discharged soon. He doesn't want to go home."

"Have him come here and keep me company."

Aleta chuckled. "Stanley, be serious!"

"I am. I have so many questions."

"I'm trying to persuade him to teach again."

"Why did he stop?"

"Age, I guess."

"He should never stop."

"Stanley, these are old notes. Decades old!" Aleta claimed.

"Not all of them. The man kept writing as if he were going to lecture again. Or write a book. Or something."

"He kept writing?"

"Didn't you notice?"

"We all took different cabinets. I think I had the oldest ones," Aleta explained.

"His writing is shaky but his thinking isn't."

"He has arthritis in his hands," Aleta said. "I think he needs to meet you."

Aleta left immediately after saying that. Stanley went back to reading. If he was lucky, she'd bring back Dr. Schwartzman. If she came back without him, he'd still have her.

She came back with Dr. Schwartzman who was as eager to meet the man who would take over should anything happen to Aleta. Stanley was obviously delighted. He began asking questions immediately and soon he and the doctor were engaged in a fast-paced exchange of ideas. Aleta slipped away.

As she was on her way home with her police escort, Ed called to tell her that Hawk's car had been broken into. The books were gone. He also told her he had recent photos that might help.

They met and talked at length.

"The problem is," Aleta said, "we have nothing I can present in court. I don't dare ask for a court order for DNA. That would put Van Horne on the alert. Too risky for Paige."

"I figured," Ed said. "I give it lotsa thought."

"What did you get?"

"Her hairbrush," Ed replied. "Beatrice's idea. We give her a set. Real pretty."

"Ed, you're a genius!" Aleta exclaimed.

"How we gonna get Van Horne's DNA?"

"Don't have to. We can have Hawk take DNA samples from the siblings," Aleta said.

"He got a kit?" Ed asked.

"All he needs is some Q-Tips and some plastic sandwich bags," Aleta said. "I'll call Stanley's mother and tell her what we need. I have to tell her about Stanley being in the hospital."

"How quick can they run those tests?"

"Not quick enough for the hearing," Aleta said. "I have to think of some way to protect Paige until we can verify her story."

"You got any ideas?" Ed asked.

"If my two psychologists come through, I can keep her out of the mental institution at least. And I'm hoping Van Horne will ask for a continuance so he can bring in his own expert.

"He's sharp," Ed said. "He won't."

"Why do you say that?"

"He's done lotsa stuff. He don't strike me as patient. He'll accept the findings real polite-like and say how glad he is that she's okay."

"You're right. He wants to get Paige under his control, but how'll he keep her under control?"

"Drugs," Ed said succinctly.

Aleta paled. She knew that's exactly what he would do.

"And eventually she'll die of an overdose," Aleta predicted.

"Are your prophesying?" Ed asked.

"No. I'm just guessing," Aleta said. "But maybe he won't kill her. He can make her an addict."

"That'd ruin her," Ed said sadly.

"As a witness?" Aleta asked.

"As a person," Ed replied.

"Let me call Lydia," Aleta said. "Maybe she'll have an idea."

"Can I listen?"

"Sure, get on that extension. She'll be back in her room getting ready for dinner."

"You know her that good?"

"I'm married to her son," Aleta rejoined.

Aleta was correct in her assessment of the senior Praetzel's habits. She told her mother-in-law about the DNA samples they needed, and then asked her if she had everything she'd requested.

"I have Dr. Chesney's report, but the two doctors you sent to evaluate her are going to recommend therapy," Lydia reported.

"Why?"

"Paige confided in me and I told her not to mention it again. She refused to tell either doctor. They came to me. Aleta, they were a pair of pricks. Where did you dig them up?"

"I called everyone in Stanley's rolodex," Aleta said and then told his mother about his relapse.

When she finished, "That explains Greenwood. I couldn't believe Stanley would use him. How about Barre?"

"Barre?" That's whom Greenwood selected?" Aleta asked.

"Paige didn't like either one. She was polite, but she resented their attitude and vice versa," Lydia reported.

"Mom, I'm in a quandary. The book containing the proof we needed was stolen from the trunk of Hawk's car,"

Aleta said. "It'll take the lab time to run the DNA after you get here. I won't have the results in time for the hearing."

"The children are here," Lydia said. "You'll have it before they get home."

"Scuse me, Mrs. Praetzel," Ed said. "I'm on the extension. He'll go down there and get 'em. He won't wait."

"He knows she'll be a creditable witness," Aleta said.

"That's because she is," Lydia said. "She told me her story. She told me even more."

"I'm guessing that the psychologist would have given Van Horne reason to have Hawk arrested if Paige had been as candid with them as she was with you."

"She was too sharp for them," Lydia said. "Their egos couldn't take it. I know Dr. Barre is a friend of yours, but when I appealed to her professionalism, she left in a huff and told me I shouldn't be on the bench anymore."

"Oh, Mom! I'm so sorry," Aleta commiserated. "Reggie isn't my friend. I was told to help her, so I did."

"Is she right?" Lydia asked.

"Mom, I can't answer that," Aleta said. "I don't want my words to push you either way. Whatever you decide, I will still love you and respect you."

"So I should listen to her?" Lydia queried.

"You should always weight a criticism carefully. If it's bogus, toss it. If it's reflective of a truth, use it to better yourself."

"Aleta, can you be at my court at nine sharp tomorrow morning?"

"I have a preliminary hearing at nine."

"I need Paige's birth certificate and some other form of identification that proves her age. Does she have a baptismal certificate?"

"If she does, it was burned in the fire," Aleta said. "Besides the birth certificates, all I have are insurance policies and mortgage papers."

"How old are the insurance policies?"

"Old enough," Aleta said. "What have you got in mind?"

"Can you get a copy of the mother's death certificate?"

"Got it!" Ed chirped.

"But no custody papers, right?" Lydia asked.

"Why is the father in court fighting for custody?" Aleta asked.

Before anyone could respond she rushed on. "He must know that he was locked out by the custody agreement and he needs the court to grant him custody before that agreement is found."

"But in the absence of any documentation the court will act as if no such document existed," Lydia said. "You need to demand that Van Horne present his copy of the agreement to the court."

"He could doctor it," Aleta suggested.

"Hawk could analyze it."

"That would take time," Aleta said.

"Are the other children in any danger?" Lydia asked.

"I don't think so," Aleta said. "Just Paige."

"We'll bring Hawk and Paige back with us so he can run the DNA analysis himself," Lydia said. "Ed, can you meet us at Willow Glen Airport when we land. Bring the documents I asked for."

"What are you planning to do?" Aleta asked.

"I have a someone in mind who will put them on his calendar first thing Monday morning."

"I'm not available at nine," Aleta said.

"I am."

"You aren't going to hear the case. You can't," Aleta said. "You must recuse yourself."

"I'm going to represent them."

"Can you do that?"

"Yes."

"I'll meet your plane," Ed promised.

Lydia turned to Hubert.

"You heard most of that, didn't you?"

"Enough," her gray-haired husband said.

"And what do you think?"

"That you're one of the finest judges sitting on the bench today."

"That's sweet of you."

Hubert chuckled. "Never in our whole married life have you told me I said something sweet."

His tone turned serious. "It's not a sugar-coated lie, Lydia. All of us lawyers in the family are proud of you."

"I won't let you down."

"I know you won't," Hubert said. "Only, if you can, don't give up too much."

"Take a week. I'm going to need a week," Lydia declared. "We've got to fly back right after they're married."

"There's a one day waiting period...never mind, you're going to take care of that as well," Hubert said.

"I need you behind me on this."

Hubert took his wife into his arms. "I love you, Lydia. Nothing will change that. But if we're retiring, I could use a little notice."

"We're taking a week off so we can decide if we want to retire," Lydia said. "And we need to get Paige and Hawk back here before the custody hearing."

"Why?"

"Because once Van Horne finds out she's married, he'll come after them."

"Tell Aleta to stall telling him as long as possible."

Back in Illinois, the woman Hubert named burst into her husband's hospital room. Her appearance caused Stanley and Herve Schwartzman to halt their discussion at once. Aleta was obviously agitated.

"It's your mother, Stanley. She's going to do something that's going to get her into a lot of trouble."

"My mother?" Stanley gasped. "Never!"

"Yes, she is. She was really upset by what Reggie Barre said to her. She asked me if it were true and I didn't say the right thing."

"Dr. Reggie Barre?" Dr. Schwartzman asked.

"Yes," Aleta responded almost as an aside, her focus on her husband was so intent. "Stanley, you've got to do something!"

"You want me to tell my mother what to do?"

"She'd listen to you!" Aleta exclaimed.

"No, she won't. She loves me and respects me, but she tells me what to do, not vice versa."

"What did Dr. Barre say?" Herve Schwartzman asked.

"Something about it being time Mom stopped being a judge."

"Your mother must have struck a nerve," Herve Schwartzman surmised. "Reggie went for the jugular."

"She really hurt her," Aleta proclaimed.

"Reggie can get mean when pushed," Herve said. "What is your mother going to do?"

Aleta was the one who replied.

"I think Mom is planning to quit judging."

Stanley sat up.

"She wouldn't. She loves being a judge."

"Reggie is very good at uncovering people's deepest fear," Schwartzman said. "What she sometimes lacks is compassion."

"Why did you send me to her?" Aleta asked. "I tried to help her. Mom thought she was a friend."

"Are you making it my fault?" Dr. Schwartzman asked.

Aleta was instantly contrite. "No, of course not. I made the choices. I guess I thought she'd like my family."

"I like your family," Dr. Schwartzman said.

"You've only met Stanley," Aleta pointed out.

"Isn't he your family?"

"He's the center of it."

"He told me about your wild parties. Can I come to one?"

Aleta's response was instantaneous. "Of course, you can. We'd love to have you!"

"It won't interfere with the job you're doing for me?"

"It'll actually be good. You'll get to know my dad. He's third on the list. And we've got friends your age in the group... Don't scowl. We've got friends every age. And I don't do any matchmaking. I just invite people I like."

"And you never drop anyone?"

"Reggie will be the first," Aleta said.

"Why are you dropping her?"

"She came in under the wrong umbrella."

Schwartzman chuckled. "Wrong umbrella?"

"I meant for the party to be therapy. She knew it and she resented being there. My mistake. I won't repeat it."

"And me?"

"I like you and Stanley wants you as a friend. That's how everyone has come to be invited. I think you'll find the group to be eclectic in nature."

"Stanley wondered if you could get me moved up here to this room," Schwartzman said. "He's an apt pupil. If I were to have a few more like him, I'd be ready to teach again."

"I'm sure I can arrange it," Aleta said. "Your kids are against the idea of you returning to work. They were pretty adamant."

Schwartzman nodded. That reaction he expected.

"Oh, Hell! I forgot. Tonight is David's night," Dr. Schwartzman cried.

"Do you want to be moved after his visit?" Aleta asked.

"And miss supper? No way. Stanley says we're being treated to homemade lasagna tonight."

"I'll go arrange the transfer," Aleta said heading for the door.

"What about David's visit?" the doctor worried.

"Stanley's good at understanding what makes children tick."

"David's a grown man," Dr. Schwartzman protested.

"I think that's the problem," Aleta said. "He's not."

When she left, Dr. Schwartzman asked, "What are you going to do about your mother?"

"Absolutely nothing," Stanley said. "She's like Aleta. Don't stand in front of her when she's moving. She's apt to run you over."

"Your wife seemed upset."

"She was."

"She got over it pretty fast."

"She felt as if she should do something, but we agreed from the start that we would each leave the final decision about what to do up to the person whose parent it was. She told me. That lets her off the hook."

"Have you ever told her to do anything about her parents?"

"I've never had to. She was always way ahead of me."

"Does she use good judgment?"

"The best. You've no need to worry on that score."

"I'm not worried. She's already given me a new lease on life."

At six when Willow Glen Police Chief Tom Milani showed up with the lasagna, he was greeted by not only Aleta and Stanley, but by Arborville's chief, Lyle West, Dr. Cook, Dr. Hughes and a stranger settled into the other bed in the room.

"Hey, I was planning on lots of leftovers!" Tom complained. "You guys won't leave me any!"

"Hope you brought dessert too," Dr. Cook said. "If I'm going to be limited to one serving of lasagna, I need dessert!"

"Lauren made a chocolate pudding cake," Lyle said. "Tom and I are celebrating. Today was the biggest bust of our careers. Peets will be here in a minute."

Tom groaned. "He's so big."

"Is Tom worrying about his stomach again," came a voice from the doorway. "Who's our new friend?"

"Dr. Schwartzman," Stanley said. "He's a psychiatrist."

"Stanley needs a shrink?" Peets asked. "I thought it was his leg that was shot up. Why am I always the last to know?"

"Because you're black," Aleta quipped. "Now be nice. Dr. Schwartzman is a new friend and he'll be at our next party. And he knows all about you."

"That story is old," Peets huffed.

"You did a magnificent job today, by the way. You really are the best interrogator in the area."

"Hey, I taught him all he knows," Milani put in.

"So it's a case of the pupil exceeding the teacher," Dr. Schwartzman said. "It's the best compliment one can get."

Milani smiled at the wizened oldster. "You do know how to turn a phrase. You fit right into this group."

"I'm glad I made it on lasagna night."

"Me too," Dr. Hughes put in.

"Dr. Schwartzman is thinking of going back to teaching," Aleta said. "Stanley is his first student."

"You wouldn't consider dipping into clinical work again, would you?" Dr. Cook asked. "We could use a man of your expertise around here."

"You mean see patients?"

"Careful," Hughes warned. "With Cook everything is free, that is you give your services for free."

"He's in charge of the Free Clinic," Aleta said. "What few rich patients he has he soaks. That's his way of discouraging them."

"He's got more patients in the clinic than one man can handle," Dr. Hughes added, "even with four interns."

"You've got interns, Dr. Cook?" Schwartzman said. "I've always wanted to teach interns some useful clinical psychology."

"You take a couple of my patients and you've got yourself a class of interns," Dr. Cook said.

"Do you know what you're asking? It seems I'm trading my services for my services, Doctor. How'd you do that?"

"I took two of your classes."

"So, I'm to blame?"

"I give credit where credit is due."

"You've got a deal, but Dr. Hughes has to keep me healthy."

"I can see where this is heading," Dr. Hughes said. "I'll be the first one called if you and Dr. Cook think there's a neurological problem causing the symptoms."

Dr. Schwartzman grinned. "You wouldn't want me to stress out. I get strokes, you know."

"Leave me out of this plan, I beg you!" Dr. Hughes said.

"So we just send you the usual number?" Cook asked.

"I'm already getting half, aren't I?" Dr. Hughes queried.

"You're the best neurologist on the staff," Wayne Cook said. "My patients deserve the best."

"I'm sure there are others equally talented," Dr. Hughes said.

"I could send your partner more."

"It's a partnership. You do know what that means. We share the income," Dr. Hughes said, slightly exasperated. "Or in the case of your patients, the lack thereof."

"So you want me to send any extra directly to you?"

"How did that idea emerge?" Dr. Hughes asked, frustrated. "Just send me my usual half and I won't complain anymore."

Herve Schwartzman laughed at the repartee. He'd forgotten how much fun such an exchange could be. He didn't need to be holed up in his room reflecting upon past accomplishments. He needed to move forward as long as his mind would let him.

When did he lose his direction? No wonder his children were squabbling. Their leader was confused. He'd thought his life was done. They were panicking at the thought of his death. They were acting like children.

He began to think about David. What was it his second son wanted most? That wasn't hard to discern. David had voiced his desire many times. David wanted to be the eldest son. Herve had always shoved that aside as an inconsequential goal, but now he thought about it. Aleta said David hadn't grown up.

He wanted something Jacob got my virtue of being eldest. It wasn't love. Herve loved all his children. When everyone had left including Aleta, Dr., Herve Schwartzman turned to Stanley.

"What do eldest sons gets that second sons don't?" Stanley smiled.

"I was an only child."

"But, you're a child advocate. Surely, you must have a clue."

"Better than a psychiatrist?" Stanley asked.

"I seem to have a blind spot," Herve said. "David has been saying all his life that he wished he were the eldest."

"The eldest is usually the leader," Stanley said. "What he says carries more weight."

"He's older. He has more experience. Why doesn't David accept that?"

"Maybe when your sons were children," Stanley said. "But when they're adults does it matter whether one had had twenty-three years of experience and another twenty-one?"

"I have not let him grow out from his brother's shadow," Herve realized aloud. "But what do I do?"

"You haven't told anyone about your plan to return to teaching. Why not discuss it with him first?"

"Aleta told Jacob and Deborah. He won't be the first to know."

"But he will be the first you tell, the first you consult."

"Where did you learn this stuff? It makes sense."

"I've been reading your notes all day."

"I'm not obsolete?"

"Far from it," Stanley said. "Old men are never obsolete."

At a few minutes past eight, David arrived incensed that his father's accommodation had been downgraded from a private room to a double.

He flew into the room, past Stanley's bed and yanked the curtain between the two beds out and around his father's bed.

"She had no right to do this," he yelled. "Where is she?"

"She's downstairs with another family."

"I'm going to see to this right now!" David stormed.

"Before you leave," Stanley said coolly, "open the curtain please. Your father and I were having a conversation about you that we'd like to continue."

David turned on Stanley. "I don't want him talking to you about me. Who are you anyway?"

"Mrs. Praetzel's law partner and husband," Stanley said. "Also, when my wife is unavailable, I have your father's power of attorney."

"What did my father say about me?" David charged. "That I'm the family hot-head? The one that will cause you the most grief? The one not afraid to speak his mind?"

"Actually, those traits are obvious," Stanley responded. "He was telling me you had a quick mind and great perception and that you could see dangers others couldn't. He was looking forward to discussing his future plans with you."

"I heard about his plans," David charged.

"No one has heard about his plans. Your brother and sister heard about Aleta's plan."

David turned. "Is that true, Dad?"

"Please, David, I need your help on this. I think you understand best how little Jacob listens to anyone whose opinion differs from his own."

David pulled a chair close to the bed and the discussion began with Herve telling his second eldest son about the offer made to him by Dr. Cook only an hour before.

"I hate to let my mind lay idle just because arthritis has stiffened my joints," Herve said. "But what problems do you see?"

"You could have a stroke."

"I'd be lecturing to doctors," Herve chuckled. "They'd all be interested in reviving me so I could go on with my fascinating lecture."

"That's true," David said calmly. "But won't preparing lectures be too taxing?"

"Look at Stanley's bed. I have a year's worth right there," Herve said. "He finds them fascinating. I thought maybe I'd like to write a book but..." he held up his gnarled fingers.

"You could get a secretary," David suggested.

"I wrote and revised my lecture notes over and over. A secretary would get disgusted."

"Tell them that's the job, to do what you can't–edit, correct, retype," David said. "Let me find one for you."

"Would you do that?"

"Sure, Dad," David replied evenly.

"She can't smoke."

"Does she have to be pretty?" David joshed.

"Wouldn't hurt," his father returned.

They were still talking when Aleta returned.

"They have my permission," Stanley said. "David would like to come tomorrow when Rebecca is here and help his father get her on board with his plans."

Aleta went over to Herve Schwartzman's bedside. His whole face was smiling from the parting of his lips to the crinkling of the smile lines next to his eyes.

"We'll give it a shot," she said. "But for now, only David can stay longer and only this once. If it goes well, Stanley will give permission for that to change. I'm going to be in court all day."

"Yes. Thank you," Dr. Schwartzman said.

"You picked a good law firm, Dad," David said. "See you tomorrow. You know, Dad, you could write a text for doctors and try it out on those interns. Base it on their questions. Something practical, you know, everyday stuff."

"Now that idea excites me," his father replied. "Let's talk some more tomorrow."

"Becca might have some ideas too," David said.

When David left, Aleta asked, "How did that miracle come about?"

"Stanley is great with kids," Herve grinned. "I don't know how he picked up on David's strengths, but he did. He doesn't need me to teach him anything."

"You already have," Stanley said, "and when you talked about David I got a glimpse of what you liked in him. I think his blustery attitude never let you say it. He was so afraid of being hurt he had this giant wall erected around his heart. I could say those things because I was a stranger and he could brush me off."

"So, Stanley, did you call your mother?" Aleta asked.

Dr. Schwartzman laughed.

"You just deflated my ego," he shot back.

"I know," she said, kissing him on the forehead. "Now be a good boy and go to sleep. Your mother's a grown woman. She makes up her own mind and she always has good reasons for her actions."

"I'm glad you see it my way," Stanley said, and immediately knew he'd said the wrong thing.

"Your way? You didn't say that! All you said was that she wouldn't listen to you." Aleta recalled.

"Well, then, you read my mind."

"I'm not a mind reader. I'm a prophet."

"Then you know me well enough to know my thoughts."

"You aren't going to give me any credit are you?" Aleta charged.

"Not for my thoughts," Stanley declared.

"Here I was letting you off the hook with a good deal of grace and..." Aleta began.

"You held to our agreement is all," Stanley countered.

"That agreement was made before I made her my mother too," Aleta declared.

"You didn't tell me about the change," Stanley protested.

"You didn't ask."

"That's because I didn't know there was one," Stanley said, exasperated. "How can I ask about a change when I have no idea there was one? Besides you started the whole discussion with 'Stanley, your mother...'"

"I did, didn't I?" Aleta said. "Then I forgive you."

"For what?"

"For being contentious when gratitude was called for."

"I guess we'd better have six children. One child would never be able to argue with you."

"What do you plan to do, teach them group dynamics?"

"Something like that."

Suddenly, Aleta took his head in her hands. "You are the most wonderful man in the world," she said and kissed him. It was not the kiss one gives a small child.

"I can't wait to have six children just like you!"

When she left, Stanley looked at the old man in the next bed. "Did I win or lose that argument?"

"She's not angry with you, so you won," he replied. "Of course, she rendered the verdict and it had nothing to do with reason."

"That was my take."

"You are a lucky man."

"Yes, I am."

Chapter 18

Bertha tiptoed into the girls' room at four thirty and woke Paige.

"Today is your wedding day," she said softly.

"Are you sure?" she asked sleepily.

"I know Judge Davis. She will make it happen."

Paige sat up. "I don't have the right dress. The only dress I have is the one we bought yesterday."

"It's perfect," Bertha said. "I packed it in your suitcase. You can change at Lydia's house."

"It has a bare midriff," Paige pointed out.

"You look lovely in it. The pale cream color sets off the rich brown of your hair. It is long enough to be demur and the blouse isn't too brief. It shows just a hint of your waist."

"It has spaghetti straps."

"So you don't wear a bra," Bertha said. "Men like that."

"He won't think I'm a slut?"

"He'll think you love him," Bertha said. "Hawk is a shy man. And he loves you too much to hurt you. And after yesterday, that will be his biggest worry. He needs to know you want him to make love to you."

"And not wearing a bra will tell him that?"

"It told Robert."

A voice blurted out from the next bed. "Dad liked that?"

"Jocelyn, go to sleep. When the time comes, I'm going to wrap you like a mummy."

"I don't know how to make love," Paige said quietly.

"He'll do the making," Bertha said. "It's wired into his genes. All you need to do is enjoy his touch. Remember that a husband is allowed to touch you anywhere. There are no wrong places."

"What do I wear to bed?"

Again Jocelyn blurted out. "Doesn't matter. He'll take it off you!"

"Ignore her," Bertha said. "Young maidens should be still when a woman is talking."

"I don't want to disappoint him," Paige said.

"Wear whatever makes you feel comfortable," Bertha advised. "He won't care. You are beautiful and he's in love."

"I don't think I can undress in front of him."

"Then don't. Change in the bathroom. Or don't change at all. There are no rules."

"I don't have to have..."

"You don't have to do anything you don't want to. Just relax and enjoy being kissed and he will be a happy man."

"That's all?"

"That's all."

"I can do that," Paige said with renewed enthusiasm.

When they climbed into the cab to go to the airport, Hawk asked Paige why she was so happy.

"Bertha told me everything.

"What did she tell you?" he asked, wondering if he could do whatever it was the older woman had devised.

"How to make you happy."

"Just being with you makes me happy," Hawk put in, wondering if Paige had received a lecture on wifely duties.

"That's pretty much what she said," Paige replied gaily. "She said you'd be happy just kissing me."

"That's a good start," Hawk agreed.

"And that you are a shy man."

"That's true," Hawk agreed.

"And that if I encourage you, that won't mean I'm a slut."

"I won't think that ever," Hawk said.

"And that I can say no to anything."

"Yes, you can," Hawk agreed. "You are young. You get to decide. We go at your pace."

Paige smiled and nodded.

"And she told me the old rules don't apply to husbands. They are for children."

Hawk grew apprehensive, and then he realized Paige was happy, so he decided to just draw her out.

"What rules are those?"

"You are allowed to touch anywhere."

"But you can always say no," Hawk reminded her.

"I want to do it right," she proclaimed.

"Do what right?"

"Be a wife. I want to do that right."

"Paige, however you do it will be perfect for me," Hawk murmured. "There are no rules."

Suddenly, Paige drew back and asked pointedly.

"You didn't forget our rings, did you?"

"No, I didn't forget them."

"We're getting married today."

Hawk took a deep breath. Bertha had jumped the gun.

He spoke cautiously because Paige was so happy. He hated to break the bubble.

"That's not been decided. And even if we get permission, the law says we have to wait for a day after we get our license. So, I'm sorry, Paige, we aren't getting married today."

"Bertha was so sure," Paige said thoughtfully.

"I'm glad you and she talked," Hawk said. "She gave good advice."

Paige snuggled down into his arms. "If not today, then tomorrow."

Aleta has got to get a continuance, Hawk resolved silently. He needed the day to run the DNA. If he sat on it, he could have the results by tomorrow.

Paige handled the plane ride better than previously. Hawk wondered if it was because it wasn't yet fully light when they took off or because she was excited at the prospect of getting married.

He couldn't blame her. He was filled with the same kind of excitement he knew as a child on Christmas morning when he first saw the gifts scattered under the tree.

That memory made him think about what his parents would say when they found out he'd married a sixteen-year-old girl. He gave her a bit of a squeeze and she looked over at him.

"You're troubled. What's wrong?"

"My parents are going to be surprised," Hawk said. "They don't like such surprises."

"You're worried because I'm so young, right?"

"I'm afraid so."

"Tell them as soon as we're married," Paige said. "It's best not to hide things."

"Why afterward?"

"Because then two judges will have passed on our marriage and that's an important fact."

Hawk gave her another squeeze. "They will like that."

"They don't visit you much, do they?"

"My grandmother lives with them. She has Alzheimer's. They can't leave her. We will go visit them, maybe for Thanksgiving."

"I've never spent Thanksgiving away from my brother and sister," Paige said. "I never thought about that."

Hawk saw her distress building. Quickly, he said, "We can go after Thanksgiving. My mom's birthday is the first of December. Why not go then?"

Paige's brow cleared.

"Oh, yes. That would be great! Mothers like to have their birthdays remembered."

"In fact," Hawk said. "It would even be more special in her eyes."

"What kind of present would she like?"

"It's pretty early to be thinking about that."

"It should be something special. We may need to look for a long time."

"Okay, let's talk about my mother's birthday present," Hawk chuckled.

And so they did.

In the pilot and co-pilot seats, Hubert and Lydia exchanged glances. He gave her a single nod.

For Lydia, it was enough.

When the plane landed, after a brief conversation with Lydia Praetzel, Ed collected Hawk and they left the plane. Ed drove Hawk to his lab with the DNA swabs from Florida and Penny's hairbrush. Ed elected himself best man and told Hawk he'd pick up his suit and then pick him up in time for his nine o'clock court date. Ed drove to Aleta's house, gave her Dr. Chesney's report and asked for Paige's birth certificate and insurance policy for Lydia.

"I have a nine o'clock preliminary hearing," she told him. "I can't be there to plead their case. Lydia is going to have to resign to do this."

Ed didn't explain.

"I'm watching Paige," he said. "No one knows she's here. That's how its gotta be."

"Will you keep me informed?"

"No," Ed said. "Someone's sure to be watching you. Forget about me. Forget about Paige. Forget about Lydia."

"How'll I know if the marriage is approved?"

"You won't," Ed said, "but you gotta get us more time. Hawk is doing the DNA. Dean is checking on a glitch he found in Penny's arrival at the home."

"Still no custody agreement?"

"Like I said, Van Horne's lawyer don't remember the details. He's got no copy. Took a lotta dough to erase that part from the court record. Mary's lawyer don't exist far as we can tell."

"So I've got to go with argument."

"Make it a good one," Ed said. "You got reports from the shrinks yet?"

"Lydia said both will be bad for our side."

"Put 'em on the stand," Ed said. "Do your magic."

"Why do you say that?"

"Because if them two nutty shrinks say she ain't right in the head, you're screwed."

"You're right," Aleta said. "Don't contact me unless you got something I can use in court."

In an estate in a northern Chicago suburb, Kurt Van Horne ushered Tully Machi into his den.

"So, what's happening?"

"The senior Praetzels arrived this morning. They were met by Ed Ornstein. The forensic man, Hawkins Monroe, climbed in Ed's car. I followed them. They went straight to the lab. The doors were locked so I couldn't nose around.

"I went back to Aleta Praetzel's place. Ornstein's car was there. He spotted me, so I couldn't follow him when he left.

"Only got the last piece of their conversation," Machi said, "but it was important."

"It better be! You insisted on talking to me before I've read the morning paper over breakfast."

"They got no copy of the custody agreement. And they sent two shrinks down to Florida to talk to Paige and Mrs. Praetzel was told that their report was bad."

"She won't put them on the stand," Van Horne said. "Find out who they are. We'll call them as witnesses."

"I know who they are. Dr. Miles Greenwood. He's a psychologist. Not too sharp, I'm told."

"Mrs. Praetzel must have been desperate," Van Horne said. "Who else did she send?"

"That shrink that quit the Rape Clinic cold turkey, Dr. Reggie Barre."

"Any scandal connected with her departure?"

"None that the paper found," Machi replied.

"When are they coming back?"

"This morning sometime."

"You know them by sight?"

"Don't have to. The server can have them paged after every flight arrives from Florida."

"You go back and stick to Aleta Praetzel like glue."

"She's got a guard. I'll be spotted."

"Make sure you aren't," Van Horne ordered. "If Paige is here, I want to know it."

At Hubert and Lydia Praetzel's house, Hubert holed up in his study for thirty minutes and when he emerged he smiled at his wife and announced that he'd taken the week off.

"I thought you were due in court."

"My commitment to you is greater than any other."

"I can handle this," Lydia said.

"I know that, but anything important enough for you to risk your career deserves my full attention."

"I have nothing for you to do."

"I have," Hubert said. "Ed is going to get Hawk to the court on time. I'm going to sit with Paige while you take care of business."

"Paige," Lydia said, reminding herself that the young girl was alone. "I need to see to her needs."

"Her needs?"

"She is going to be married this morning. She needs, you know–something old, something blue. Hubert have the maid cut a bouquet of flowers from the garden. A bride needs a bouquet.

Lydia rushed down the hall and knocked on the guest room door. The door was opened. Paige picked up a sweater.

"Should I wear this?"

"Not to get married in."

"Aren't we going to court first?"

"I'm signing the documents that will waive the parental consent requirement and also waive the one day waiting period. You're getting married at nine thirty this morning."

Paige's eyes widened.

"You can do that?"

"It's a bit of a stretch but I believe the situation warrants this kind of action."

Paige eyed the older woman thoughtfully.

"Are you going to get into trouble?"

"Perhaps."

Her protest was immediate.

"I don't want that. Hawk wouldn't want that either."

"My decision. My responsibility," Lydia stated. "But what I'm doing is not illegal or even immoral. I wouldn't do it if it was."

"But it's not the regular way, is it?"

"No, but it's the way it has to be done to protect you and Hawk."

"Okay, then. You're older and wiser and I trust you. And I don't want Hawk hurt."

"Hubert is going to stay with you. Ed is going to fetch Hawk from the lab."

"Hawk will be upset if he's not dressed right."

"Ed is taking care of that," Lydia said. "The County Clerk will marry you."

"I'd like you to do that," Paige said. "Would you, please?"

"It would be an honor," Lydia replied.

While Paige and Hubert sat in the last row of Lydia's courtroom and Lydia was in her office hunting for the consent forms she needed, someone rattled the locked door.

"It's Hawk," Paige said rising.

"Sshh," Hubert whispered. "It's not Hawk."

"Who then?"

"I don't know," Hubert said. "We can't be seen, so just stay put."

"How do you know it's not Hawk?"

"Ed is meeting us at the County Clerk's office. We'll be less noticeable going there separately."

"Are we being watched?"

"Yes."

"Then we can't leave," Paige fretted.

"You look like a young lady," Hubert said. "Lydia's shoes make you look older."

"They're old lady's shoes."

"That's why," Hubert said. "They do go nicely with the dress."

"I look like a grown-up."

"Paige, we need you to look that way."

"The clerk is going to look at my birth certificate not my shoes."

"Whoever is following us will look at your shoes."

"Oh.

Tully Machi didn't dare hover around the outside of the courtroom Aleta was scheduled to appear in which is why he was checking out Judge Davis' courtroom. Afterward he checked every judge's docket. The names of the cases and times were posted outside the door of each courtroom.

He'd told Van Horne about the engagement of Hawk and Paige. Van Horne had told him to watch for any cases involving consent for marriage.

Tully didn't like the fact that Hawk had come back without Paige.   Now he realized he hadn't waited long enough. He wasn't absolutely sure she wasn't on the plane.

He was sure Aleta Praetzel had enough pull to insert a case into someone's docket.   Her mother-in-law was the obvious choice.   He decided he'd go into the courtroom where Aleta Praetzel was representing a client and wait. He'd get a feel for how long that case would take and go from there.

Shortly after nine, Tully Machi had a change of heart. He returned to the corridor outside Judge Davis' courtroom.

Downstairs Aleta's case was first on the docket. She would be busy for a while. Better if he not show up right away. He could slip in more easily later.

Judge Davis meanwhile, entered her courtroom and postponed her first case for an hour.   Disgruntled, the litigants filed out. Hubert and Paige slipped out with them.

Tully Machi thought Paige looked familiar. He stared at her for several minutes before he decided she was older than the girl he was looking for.

Sure does look like her though, he thought.

He shook his head. She wasn't with anyone he would have expected her to be with.

Case of mistaken identity, he told himself.

He stopped one of the men exiting the courtroom and asked if Judge Davis had heard any cases at all that morning.

"No," came the response. "Just came in and told us the case was postponed."

"Did she hand out any orders, send out any papers, anything?"

"Nothing," the man responded.

Judge Davis exited as they were speaking and Tully broke away and followed her. She headed straight for the office of another judge. He hung around outside until one of the guards asked him where he was headed.

He asked directions to the courtroom Aleta was in and left the area just before Judge Davis left the office of her superior.

He snuck into the back of the courtroom where a preliminary hearing was just getting underway.

His gut told him he was missing something. Judge Davis' exit was out of the ordinary. Experience had taught him that one unusual happening was usually accompanied by others.

He only half-listened to what was happening in front of him. His mind was on that girl. Suppose it was Paige Van Horne. Had she snagged another man? The custody hearing was only hours away.

Suddenly, the gavel banged and the hearing was over. People began to crowd around Aleta and her client.

"What happened?" he asked the person sitting beside him.

"The case was dismissed with prejudice. She can't be arrested on these charges again."

Tully Machi was torn between following Aleta Praetzel and trying to locate Judge Davis. As he was pondering the decision, the vision of the girl in the corridor reappeared in his memory. Why was it still there? She was a woman carrying a bunch of flowers.

Aleta seemed in no hurry to leave. It didn't appear as if she had another date to keep.

Flowers, he mused. Who carries a bunch of flowers into a courthouse? Then it hit him. A bride. A bride in a hurry.

He hurried back to Judge Davis' courtroom. The clerk would know where she'd gone.

Meanwhile, Judge Davis had presented her credentials to the County Clerk, Paige had presented her birth certificate and an insurance policy verifying her age and Hawk had dug out the thirty dollars cash required for the fee.

Judge Davis signed the waiver of parental consent in the clerk's presence. She presented a signed form that waived the one-day waiting period, Paige and Hawk signed the application, and the marriage license was issued.

"Do you want me to perform the ceremony?" the clerk asked the couple.

"Yes," Hawk said.

"I asked Judge Davis to do it," Paige said turning toward Lydia.

"Just a minute," Lydia said. "I have an emergency call from my clerk."

She answered her phone. "I'll be right there."

"Please have the clerk marry you. Time is critical. Hubert, Ed, take care of them."

Hubert followed her part way out. "What is it?"

"I don't know, but I think it's Van Horne's PI. I'll keep him busy. You get them married and back to the house."

Hubert turned back to the group. "Judges have emergencies too. It'll take a while for her to handle it and she only recessed court for an hour.

A few minutes later, Hawk and Paige exchanged vows and rings in a brief civil ceremony. Their kiss was longer lasting than the ceremony almost. The marriage certificate was signed and the marriage recorded before the group left.

"Take them to my house," Hubert told Ed. "Guard them. I need to see what's happening with Lydia."

He turned to Hawk. "If the marriage is consummated, it's harder to get it annulled."

"Paige isn't ready," Hawk whispered in response.

"What did he say?" Paige asked.

"That we can use the guest room if we want to."

"Do we have to?"

"I'd like to really kiss you," Hawk said.

Ed overheard them. "What'd we just see?"

Hawk stuttered. "I mean...I'd like to kiss her some more."

"Let's go then!"

In the courtroom, Judge Davis had begun to hear the case she'd postponed. Hubert was shocked, but he settled down in the back row.

He looked around the courtroom and saw a man who didn't belong sitting near the front. Something was going on. He didn't know what so he sent his wife a text message.

"Should I stay?"

Her response was one letter: 'Y' for yes.

"Are you in danger?" he asked via the messaging system.

The reply was the letter 'N'.

He started to ask if it was necessary that she conduct this trial, but he decided that her doing it told him it was.

He settled back to watch her. He smiled at her. The newlyweds were safe.

Back at the house, Paige said, "Tell me what Mr. Praetzel told you."

"I don't want to pressure you."

"Just tell me. Then we can decide what to do."

"He suggested we consummate the marriage."

"Does that mean have intercourse?"

"Yes."

"Why?"

"He said it would be harder for someone to get the marriage annulled."

"My father is closing in, isn't he?"

"I think he is," Hawk said.

"Let's do it then," Paige said. "What do I do?"

"Oh, Paige, I do love you, but I won't make our first union a nightmarish experience for you."

"Then just hold me and kiss me."

Hawk tilted her head up and kissed her. His arms embraced her.

Paige felt herself come alive inside his arms and she let her desire take over. She pressed her body against his and put her arms around his neck.

His hands rubbed her back as they embraced. His hands slipped up onto her bare back. Then he stepped back withdrawing his hands as he did so. She stopped his withdrawal, and captured his hands in hers as they moved forward under her blouse.

"May I?" he asked.

"Yes," she whispered, not knowing what he wanted. Slowly, he lifted her blouse.

"You are so beautiful," he said softly.

He touched a breast lightly and Paige felt a shiver cascade down her body to a place she'd never felt anything before.

"Do that again," she whispered.

When he did, she shivered slightly.

"Are you afraid?" he asked gently withdrawing his hand.

"I don't think so," she replied. "Please don't stop."

He led her over to the bed and folded back the spread. Then he removed his coat and tie.

"Are we going to sleep?" she asked.

"We are going to play around on the bed a bit and find out what you like."

"Should I take off my clothes?"

"Not unless you want to."

"Maybe my shoes and these panty hose. I hate them."

"Take them off then," Hawk said. "I'll take off my shoes too."

When she was done, she lay back on the bed.

"Now we consummate?"

Hawk lay down beside her.

"Not yet," he said, touching her gently.

She shivered and his lips found hers. Their kiss was long and passionate. His hands slowly pushed her skirt down her hips and she wound her arms around his neck and kissed him fervently.

His hands stroked her waist and came up over her breasts to her shoulders and her mouth never left his.

He pulled away gently. "If you like what I'm going to do next, take off your clothes. If you leave them on I'll stop."

He lowered his head and kissed her lightly on the shoulder. He then kissed her upper breast. He lifted her blouse and kissed one nipple. The shiver was unmistakable. She took the ends of her blouse and pulled it over her head. He continued kissing her. His hands moved down her body. When they reached her skirt band, she whispered for him to keep going.

She kicked the last remnant of her clothes onto the floor and Hawk found himself in a quandary. He was still dressed. He didn't have any condoms with him. He never dreamed that they would get beyond kissing.

He felt her hands unbuckling his belt. He whispered, "We have no protection."

"I can't get pregnant, remember?"

He remembered that the two doctors agreed that surgery would probably be necessary for her to become pregnant.

"Are you sure?"

"All I know is that I want you not to stop."

Hawk made short work of his pants and bent over to kiss her again on the lips. Her response was so passionate he felt himself almost at his peak.

"Now," she pleaded. "Do it now."

As he positioned himself he found himself surprised at how quickly she had responded. Then his mind stopped thinking and his body took over.

In the back of his mind he remembered the admonition that such an action might cause her pain.

Her response, however, told him that it didn't. When he lay on top of her, spent, she said, "That was great! Can we do it again?"

Hawk chuckled. "Men have to rest a little, but yes, we can do it again."

"So we are consummated?"

"Yes, our marriage has been consummated," Hawk said. "What a trip that was!"

He kissed her lightly. "You were perfect!"

She beamed when he said that.

"What do I do now?" she asked.

"You lie there and let me look at you," Hawk said as he pushed himself up.

He saw her discomfiture and rushed to ease it. "A lot of couples take showers together. Do you want to try that?"

And she did.

The shower proved magical and they consummated their marriage a second time.

Afterward, they lay naked beside each other in bed and fell asleep.

A loud knock on the door woke them.

"We need to go now!" Hubert said.

"Give us a couple minutes to dress," Hawk called. Instantly he wished he hadn't mentioned that they needed to dress.

Paige was already pulling on her skirt. She slipped her feet into her sandals and called to Hawk, "Where's my blouse?"

"On the bed somewhere," he said.

Outside the door, Hubert chuckled. He walked downstairs.

"It'll take them a few minutes, Lydia," he said. "They need to get dressed."

"That was fast," she said. "I hope it wasn't too fast for her."

Lydia's worry vanished when she saw the look on Paige's face as she came down the staircase. Hawk followed her carrying their suitcases.

"Did you have a good nap?" she asked the couple.

"Did you know sex makes you sleepy?" Paige asked innocently.

Lydia smiled. "Yes, that's been my experience."

"It's nice," Paige said. "We consummated twice. Now we won't get annulled, will we?"

"Hubert!" Lydia said sharply. "What did you say to these two?"

"It's okay," Paige said. "Your husband was telling us we could do it here in your house. That got us over the fear hump. We were both pretty anxious."

Lydia turned and eyed her husband suspiciously.

"It's what she said," he replied.

"Then you're forgiven," Lydia said, suspicion lingering in her eyes.

"We left the room a mess. We thought we should hurry. We can go back and fix it if there's time."

Ed Ornstein stepped forward.

"You guys is coming with me," he said. "Out the back way. We gotta hurry."

"Aren't you coming?" Paige asked Lydia.

"You need to be on the plane when we get there," Lydia said. "We're being followed. He mustn't see you."

Paige and Hawk followed Ed out the back, through the rose garden, past the high hedge bordering the property and into the woods separating the house of Stanley's parents from his seventy-two acres. Hubbs waved at them as they passed the barn and Paige held up her ring finger.

"We're married," she said, smiling happily.

"That your wedding dress?" he asked.

She twirled around for him.

"It's pretty," he said.

Neither of the two men with her hurried her. It was, after all, her wedding day.

"Gotcha something," he said. "Wait a sec."

Ed whispered to Hawk, "I'll get the car."

Hubbs came out with a braided piece of leather knotted at each end with streamers of leather past the knot.

"A belt," Hubbs said.

Paige took it and fingered the leather. It was lightweight and soft, a pale tan in color.

"It's beautiful," she said, putting it around her waist and tying it. She spun around. "How does it look?"

Hubbs smiled. "You make it look good."

Impulsively, she went over and hugged him. "It's my first wedding present. Thank you."

She kissed him on the cheek. "Gotta go. My father's sent a bad guy after us. Don't tell anyone you saw me, okay?"

Hubbs nodded.

Ed met his police escort half a mile later and, with the help of its siren and flashing lights, made it to the airport well in advance of the Praetzels who managed to find items to return to the house for.

Earlier Tully had pressured the clerk into forcing Judge Davis to return to her courtroom. Judge Davis had merely given him a withering look. Were court in session she could have cited him for contempt. Instead she ordered him to sit.

"I'll be right back," she said and disappeared into her office.

A bit confused, he'd waited.

People began to pour into the courtroom. The entrance of the judge was announced and court was in session.

Tully waited for a while, trying to figure out what to do. Was she going to talk to him afterward? Or not?

Then he'd seen a man slip into the courtroom and sit in back. He recognized him as the man who'd escorted the girl with the bouquet.

They knew where she was. He decided to wait.

It came as no surprise to him that the judge brushed past him after she recessed for lunch. He followed her and the man to the parking lot. He didn't follow closely. He knew where they lived.

He'd parked his car on a rise in the road as it curved. It wasn't visible. He left the car, took his binoculars and stood in the bushes where he had a clear view of the front driveway, the front door and the car. He watched them park the car.

He smiled to himself. He was right. They were leaving town. Somehow Paige fit into this fast flight. His call had scared them into action.

When they left, he decided they were picking up Paige from wherever she was hiding.

He decided to head straight for the airport.

Ed Ornstein was standing at the gate to the airfield when Tully Machi arrived. The area around the airstrip consisted of flat fields. There was no hiding one's presence. Boldly, Machi left his car and strolled up to his rival.

"Waiting for someone?"

"Yep," Ed said.

"Me too."

"You're Kurt Van Horne's man?" Ed asked.

"That's confidential," Tully responded stiffly.

"You torch the Roach house?"

"I'm strictly legit!" Tully protested a bit heatedly.

"I don't guess you hired out. Too risky," Ed went on.

Tully began to sweat. "You hear something?"

"That a pro done the job. Weren't no accident."

"Gasoline was used," Tully said. "The papers said that."

"Still a pro. Only a pro knows to leave nothing."

"So they have no clues?" Tully responded happy to know he'd covered his tracks well.

"One problem with the job."

"What's that?"

"Van Horne. He ain't one to trust."

A car was seen approaching the airport and the conversation stopped.

Ed helped Hubert transfer the luggage from the car to the plane. He told Hawk and Paige, who were sitting on the floor far back in the tiny plane, not to move to the seats until the plane had been in the air twenty minutes.

Hawk nodded and held Paige close as the luggage was placed in the holding straps on either side. She snuggled back against his chest and lifted her head for a kiss. He obliged her.

He knew when their lips met that he'd never let her go. Nothing was worth more to him, he realized, then she was.

Lydia laid Paige's bridal bouquet on a passenger seat and sat in the co-pilot's seat.

Chapter 19

Aleta received the faxed report from Dr. Miles Greenwood at noon. Dr. Barre's report was delivered by messenger fifteen minutes later. She read them both at once, and then called in her two associates.

"We need to split up the children," she said. "Chin, I want you to represent Tyler. You talked with him at the Barbecue, didn't you?"

"Some," Chin said. "I know he wants to study computer science and he's worried he may never even get to college.

Aleta went on. "Jackson, you represent Molly. Her biggest worry is being separated from Tyler and Paige. She has no animosity toward her father. Play that up."

"Why? Won't that hand Van Horne custody outright?" Jackson asked.

"Not with this judge," Aleta said. "She's into rebuilding relationships. You could mention that there's been no contact, but emphasize that Molly doesn't hate her father."

"And Tyler?" Chin asked.

"He's wary, but he doesn't know why," Aleta said. "We are not going to tell either of these children what we suspect their father has done. It would be far too dangerous."

"Why are you taking Paige?" Chin asked. "Isn't she getting married?"

"We don't know if that happened."

Chin picked up the phone. "I can call the County Clerk."

"No," Aleta said sternly. "We must go in on the assumption that Paige isn't married. I need to argue against custody on her behalf. Van Horne expects me to. Separating out the other children is the only way to protect them in the event Van Horne wins."

"Won't Van Horne's attorney want them there?"

"I'm going to ask Van Horne's attorney to agree that the younger children should not be present because hearing Paige's allegations might hurt their future relationship with their father."

"So what do you want each of us to do?" Jackson asked.

"I'm calling both doctors to the stand and submitting their reports."

"That's risky," Chin said.

"We'll lose before the first bell," Jackson added. "Psychologists do a lot of double talk if you try to nail them."

"What you're going to do is study every word in each report dealing with your client. I want you to paint a picture of two healthy normal children who don't know their father personally so have no animosity toward him. At the same time I want you to indicate that the children have bonded with the Chesneys."

"You want us to present them as an alternative?" Jackson asked.

"Not directly. I want you to present Molly and Tyler's ability to relate to warm, loving people as one of their attributes and at this time in their life one of their primary needs. It is the reason not to split them up. They've lost three people they loved–be sure to include the grandmother–and their house was deliberately destroyed and with it the few treasures they had left. Fight for them to get a warm, loving home."

"We don't know what kind of home the father will provide," Chin said.

Aleta dug out her folder on Tyler Van Horne and handed it to Chin. "Inside is Tyler Van Horne's acceptance letter to a military prep school. He is to be removed from his friends and sisters and sent away.

"What about Molly?" Jackson asked.

He was handed a folder.

"She's enrolled in a boarding school beginning the end of August," Aleta said. "Now, don't think you've got him. This is normal for children in Van Horne's socio-economic bracket. His lawyer will argue that if the children are normal and psychologically healthy, this won't hurt them, that they will make new friends who will be their socio-economic peers, that the trauma caused by their mother and brother's death will be addressed by the school psychologists and that Mr. Van Horne's belief is that their trauma is so serious they really need professional help. It will be pictured as a wise decision."

"You make a stunning case for Van Horne," Chin said. "You've practically won me over."

"How'd you do that?" Jackson said. "You were so convincing."

"Just remember, this man murdered a baby and cleverly hid the evidence. He burned down his children's home on the off chance that it might contain some clue as to his dastardly deed a decade ago. He plans to bury his eldest daughter in a mental institution. Now do you want him to control the lives of two loving children?"

"You can go either way, can't you?" Chin commented.

"Can't we just lose the reports from the psychologists?" Jackson asked. "Van Horne could insist Paige's marriage be annulled."

"That we submit them will catch his attorney off guard. It'll only be temporary, but it'll make her edgy."

"You can't break Dr. Barre on the stand," Chin said. "She's is too experienced."

"Greenwood is so wishy-washy that he'll hedge his way out of any attack," Jackson inserted.

"You two are going to prep them for me."

"Prep them?" the two chorused.

"Soften them. I want pleasant, positive queries that will make the doctors relax," Aleta said. "Go to work."

At two o'clock sharp, Aleta Praetzel, her two associates, Roland Chin and Andrew Jackson, waited outside Judge Norma Jacobi's courtroom. Standing a few yards away were Kurt Van Horne and his attorney, Stephanie Nash.

Stanley had told Aleta that Stephanie was a sharp divorce attorney who frequently handled the battle over custody of the children for her clients. Aleta sized her opponent up with a single glance: poised, self-assured, and well dressed in an Armani suit and matching shoes with a medium heel. She was a full-figured woman nearing forty. Stanley had told his wife to be careful when Stephanie wore the curly wig. Today was one of those days.

Aleta felt her stomach knot up. She told herself she was not going to dash to the bathroom, but after five minutes, she excused herself.

Stephanie Nash walked in as Aleta finished giving up her light lunch. Stephanie asked if she could help. Aleta splashed water on her face, took out a small bottle of mouthwash and rinsed out her mouth.

"I see you came prepared," Stephanie said with mock friendliness.

"My morning sickness doesn't always keep proper hours," Aleta said coolly.

"You're pregnant?" Stephanie queried obviously surprised.

"It's a continual state," Aleta said wryly, "At least so far."

"I thought you just had a baby."

"Two months ago," Aleta said as she exited. "And I'm two months pregnant."

Shortly afterward, when the preliminaries had been taken care of, the judge asked if the children were in the courthouse.

The Social Worker, Dede Briggs, rose. "They are under police protection Your Honor, Stanley Praetzel, their attorney arranged a trip to Disney World with our approval. Two deputies are with them. The police have asked that they not be brought back until the danger is passed."

"They are still in danger?"

"Yes, Your Honor," Dede Briggs stated firmly. "Just before they left the police deputy guarding their temporary foster home was involved in a gunfight. That same night their house was burned to the ground."

Aleta was granted permission to speak next. "We petition the court to excuse the children from appearing during the first days of this hearing when some things might be discussed that two of the children are not currently privy to and which would hurt their future relationship with their father were they to be told while the allegations are unproven."

Stephanie Nash stood up. "We concur, Your Honor. We intend to call two psychologists who will testify to a delusion that one of the three has and we don't want the other children to hear that testimony."

"I want them in the state," Judge Jacobi declared.

"At Your Honor's discretion," Aleta agreed smoothly, and then added, "However, tomorrow Tyler was promised a trip to Epcot Center. The next day Molly was planning to go to the Water Park. She has a new bathing suit. Thursday both were promised a trip to MGM Studio. The Witherspoon child, Kitty, is in the group. Kitty is spending Tuesday and

Wednesday in the Animal Kingdom and Thursday she's going to MGM Studio with the rest. All have to return together as Kitty is too weak to sit in a seat and the deputies who are protecting the Van Horne children are the pilots of Kitty Witherspoons plane. If Your Honor would permit, all can return on Friday. By then the custody will be resolved and the children can go straight to their new home."

"We concur, Your Honor," Stephanie Nash said. "We would prefer that the children be turned over in a happy frame of mind."

Aleta smiled inwardly. Stephanie was laying a good foundation for her case that Van Horne was a caring father, but she was agreeing covertly with Aleta that this case wasn't going to be resolved before Friday.

"They can return on Friday," Judge Jacobi decided. It was apparent both counsels were in agreement that this case was going to take time. The police had been stretched to the breaking point with all the drug arrests over the weekend. The children were safe and happy. What more did she want?

She wanted Aleta Praetzel not to control her courtroom. That's what she wanted. Norma Jacobi wanted to do all the directing.

Aleta recognized at once that she'd won the first two rounds. She'd gotten her associates recognized as attorneys of record for two of the children and she'd postponed the return trip by several days. But while she'd won, she'd lost. The judge was upset.

She was paralyzed by the judge's animosity. She had to present something the judge could knock down.

"Your Honor, I'd like to ask for a continence," Aleta said politely.

"Denied!" Judge Jacobi said without even asking the reason.

"Your Honor, Mrs. Nash is calling two experts whose reports I have not had a chance to consider thoroughly."

"That is not your bailiwick, Counselor. It is mine."

"I apologize, Your Honor," Aleta said sincerely. "I did not mean to encroach upon your authority."

"Even though we are more informal in juvenile court, Mrs. Praetzel, the lines are the same."

"Yes, Your Honor. I am sorry."

Chin and Jackson were confused by the exchange. Aleta's apology was too outsized for the infraction. There was a communication of sorts that was at an entirely different level.

The next exchange told them Aleta had balanced the scales again.

"Your Honor, may we request that Mr. Kurt Van Horne turn over to the court the custody agreement he and his wife made at the time of their divorce."

"There is a legal contract?"

"Yes, Your Honor. Mrs. Van Horne's copy was destroyed when the house was burned. She had placed a copy in a book that was stolen from the trunk of the car of Mr. Hawkins Monroe, the county's forensic expert. The only remaining copy is in Mr. Van Horne's possession."

"I know of no such document," Kurt Van Horne said.

"Let your lawyer speak for you," Judge Jacobi admonished the thin-faced man.

"Mr. Van Horne says he knows of no such document," Stephanie Nash said.

The judge turned to Aleta and asked her what proof she could offer as to its existence.

"Reason," Aleta said. "If there were no such document, why did Mr. Van Horne not visit his children even once in the decade after the divorce? I propose that in the document, he agreed not to. This is not a document that ever came before a judge because a judge would not have sanctioned such an arrangement."

"I need more than that," the judge declared.

"If there were no document, then why did Mr. Van Horne not take custody of the children upon his ex-wife's death, but continued to pay child support. I suggest that the agreement named his son, David, as successor custodian and he didn't argue with David because David had a copy of the agreement."

"Mr. Van Horne, can you explain your actions?"

He whispered into his attorney's ear.

"Mr. Van Horne will look among his papers to see if he has a copy of such an agreement. He does not remember one."

"He has until tomorrow morning," Judge Jacobi ordered.

"Thank you, Your Honor," Aleta said and sat down. They had the continuation everyone needed.

Stephanie Nash called Dr. Reggie Barre to testify.

Judge Jacobi looked at Aleta Praetzel.

"Your Honor, we sent Dr. Barre to interview the children. Obviously, we believe she is an expert. With the Court's permission my colleagues would like to question Dr. Barre before Miss Nash."

Andrew Jackson was first.

"Did you find Molly Van Horne to be a normal, well-adjusted twelve-year-old?"

"Yes, I did," Dr. Barre replied.

"Based on your observation of her interaction with Mrs. Chesney, did you conclude that Molly would be able to relate to a new parental figure easily?"

"Yes, I did."

"Did you find any animosity between her and the male members of the group?"

"No. She related well with all of them."

"Did she like one better than the others?"

"She appeared to prefer Dr. Chesney."

"Of the group, did he not come closest to resembling her biological father?"

Dr. Barre thought for a moment. "You are correct. I didn't note that in my report because I'd never met Mr. Van Horne."

"Wouldn't you say that would bode well for her transferring that preference to Mr. Van Horne?"

Dr. Barre looked slightly bewildered. "Yes, it would."

"Thank you, Dr. Barre," Jackson said.

Roland Chin rose. "Dr. Barre, did Tyler Van Horne like Dr. Chesney as well?"

"Yes, he did.

"Who else did Tyler like?"

"Tiffany, another sixteen-year-old."

Chin smiled.

"Did Tyler impress you as a serious young man or a mischievous one?"

"I would say mischievous."

"Yet, he took on the responsibility for the family after David died, did he not?"

"Mischievous doesn't imply irresponsible."

"Does Tyler strike you as a normal sixteen-year-old boy?"

"Yes."

"Has he the aptitude for college?"

"I believe so."

"Is he handling the death of his mother and brother as well as could be expected?"

"He's handling it well."

"What about the burning of his home?"

"He is aware that it has happened, but he doesn't dwell on it."

"Is this normal?"

"It's a way of coping some choose," Dr. Barre said. "A little grief counseling might help."

"Thank you Dr. Barre," Roland Chin said.

Judge Jacobi nodded approvingly. Short, direct and positive. This wasn't going to last until Friday. She planned to suggest that Mr. Van Horne join his children at Disney World. It would be a good place to get acquainted. This was going to work out splendidly.

Stephanie Nash rose. Aleta's cohorts had done half her job. She began to question Dr. Barre about Paige.

Aleta only half listened. Her mind was searching for a hook to nail Greenwood on.

"So you consider her an intelligent child?" Stephanie suggested.

"Very bright. Well above average. Clever enough to fool anyone with her story," Dr. Barre replied.

And suddenly, Aleta had her hook.

She relaxed and listened aa Stephanie Nash led Dr. Barre down the road she knew she would take.

"Do you believe that she was made aware of the penalty that would be imposed upon Hawkins Monroe were she to admit he and she had consensual sex," Stephanie Nash charged.

"I believe he told her, yes."

"And she wanted to get married."

"Yes," Dr. Barre said. "She saw it as a way to escape the role she was in. I believe she was desperate to get out of her situation and yet she couldn't morally leave her brother to care for her sister alone. If she got married, then she could."

"Did you believe her tale about her father killing her baby sister?"

"No," Dr. Barre stated firmly.

"Why not?"

"If it had happened, her mother would have reported it."

"You're sure?"

"She was a woman of principle. On top of that, she would have wanted to properly bury her baby and grieve."

"Any other reason?"

"Penny Van Horne is alive and living in a long-term care facility for retarded children."

"Who told you this?"

"Mrs. Aleta Praetzel."

Judge Jacobi's face registered her surprise

Stephanie Nash sat down after extracting Dr. Barre's suggestion that Paige needed professional help.

Aleta stood.

"Dr. Barre, is it not true that I told you that a child named Penny Van Horne, purported to be the daughter of Kurt Van Horne, was living in such a facility?"

"That's what I said," Dr. Barre retorted.

"Not exactly," Aleta responded calmly. "Did I not use the word 'purported'?"

"Yes," she said. "But I checked which you could have done."

"Dr. Barre, here is a photo of Penny Van Horne at two months. Here is the age enhanced rendition."

"I don't know anything about age-enhancement."

"Here is a photo of the child in the home. And here is the computer's reversal of the age enhancement procedure giving us a picture of that child at two months."

"They look a lot alike," Dr. Barre smiled.

"Do children with Down's Syndrome look more like one another than like their biological parents?"

"Frequently that's the case."

"So it would not be difficult, hypothetically speaking, of course, to substitute one Down's baby for another?"

"Why would one want to do that?"

"Please answer the question, Dr. Barre," Aleta said coldly.

"Yes," Reggie Bare snapped.

"Did you look at the photos closely, Doctor?"

"Close enough to know they don't prove a thing."

"Is it true that certain characteristics one are born with do not disappear over time?"

"Birthmarks can fade," Dr. Barre said in anticipation of the direction Aleta was heading.

"What about a cleft chin or a dimple?"

"Neither baby has a cleft chin," Dr. Barre noted.

"But Penny Van Horne had a dimple."

"It's just a shadow," Dr. Barre said.

"I have testimony that she had a dimple."

"Except for David, the other siblings were too young to remember."

"Dr. Schwartzman wasn't too young a decade ago," Aleta said coolly. "He told me the baby had a dimple in one cheek. Let's move on."

"But he never saw her, did he? It's hearsay," Dr. Barre accused. "He doesn't know first-hand."

"I never said he saw her. I said he told me," Aleta rejoined calmly.

Dr. Barre harrumphed. "Just as long as we're straight about that not being proof."

"Oh, we're straight about that," Aleta said. "I only mentioned it because it raised some doubts in my mind."

"Not in mine."

"Let's move back to the report. Did you find that Paige was truthful?"

"She's delusional."

"In two specific areas, correct?"

"Yes."

"One was about the incident in the house just prior to the baby disappearing from the house, correct?"

"Yes."

"Please explain the basis of which you believe she is delusional," Aleta said.

Roland Chin glanced at his partner. Aleta was not following the first rule in questioning a witness. Never ask a question to which you don't know the answer.

"Her baby sister was there one day and gone the next. She was told she'd gone to a home. Paige was at that age where one has not yet fully grasped the idea of death. She equated 'home' with 'heaven' and believed the baby had died. She remembered seeing her father with the baby the night before. She had probably seen a television show where someone was smothered with a pillow and she manufactured a scary explanation as to how her sister had died. She couldn't just accept that she had died because that would mean that she might die suddenly herself. The baby was gone, therefore, the baby had died, therefore the baby had been killed, and therefore her father had killed the baby."

"A plausible explanation, Dr. Barre," Aleta said. "Or could it be that she saw her father smother the baby?"

"No. It's a delusion. She is very clever," Dr. Barre said. "She can convince anyone of anything."

Aleta smiled.

"Well, I admit she did convince me. But let's move to the reason you are so angry with Paige."

"I'm not angry with her!" Dr. Barre shot back. "You asked for a professional evaluation and that's what you got. Just because you don't like it doesn't mean it's invalid."

"Is it true you headed the Rape Crisis Center for eight years?"

"Yes."

"So you are familiar with how rape victims deal with the trauma of rape?"

"Yes."

"You've dealt with many teenagers over the years, true?"

"Yes."

Dr. Barre began to relax. She was back on familiar ground.

"I imagine many of your patients are in denial, true?"

"Yes."

"So you would be quick to spot that syndrome, correct?"

"Yes, and Paige..."

Aleta interrupted. "Please answer the questions asked."

"Yes, I am familiar with that syndrome."

"These patients have all displayed physical signs of rape, true?"

"Yes."

"If someone claimed to be raped and there were no physical signs, you would assume she was lying, correct?"

"Yes."

"In your experience, there are three scenarios connected with rape victims. Women either deny being raped when there is evidence they have been or they claim they have been raped and there is physical evidence to back their claim or they claim they have been raped but the evidence proves their story is a lie. These are the three options, simply put, correct?"

"Pretty much."

"Which category is Paige in, in your opinion and please explain your reasoning."

Dr. Barre sat up and leaned forward. She was eager to expound on her theory.

"Paige is in the first. She doesn't think of it as rape however. She believes she engaged in consensual sex, but she is underage. She knows this so she isn't going to say anything to anyone. She wants to get married. It will never happen if her boyfriend is sent to prison for statutory rape."

"Did Paige tell you any of this during your interview?"

"No. She refused to speak about her relationship with Hawkins Monroe except to say she loved him."

"Did she give you a reason for her refusal?"

"She said since I wasn't her doctor, that there was no confidentiality in place and she didn't trust me."

"She knew you were there to make a report for the court, correct?"

"Yes."

"She told you about the incident with her father, yet refused to discuss her relationship with her fiancé, is that correct?"

"Yes, I have an explanation."

"Later, Doctor," Aleta said smoothly. "Did she give any other reason not to confide in you other than that she was aware that you were hired to report your interview at this hearing?"

"She said Judge Davis told her not to."

"Did you check with Judge Davis?"

"Yes."

"And what did Judge Davis say?"

"That Paige told the truth. That is what she advised."

"Nothing else."

"No."

"You do know that a sitting judge must report a felony, don't you?"

"Yes."

"To your knowledge, did Judge Davis make such a report?"

"No, but..."

Aleta interrupted harshly.

"Your Honor, I will not have a sitting judge disparaged without any proof. Please so advise the witness."

Judge Jacobi had welcomed Aleta nipping the derogatory generality in the bud.

"Dr. Barre," she said. "You will assume that Judge Davis acted correctly unless you can prove otherwise."

"Unfortunately, Judge," Dr. Barre said, "the child was never examined near the time the rape occurred, so I cannot prove what I believe to be true."

"Can't the examination be done now?" Aleta charged.

"It's too late. To prove rape, the examination needs to be done soon after the incident."

"You were present when Paige and Hawkins Monroe met, correct?"

"Yes."

"I assume you don't think the sexual act took place at the party, correct?"

"Yes."

"Too many people, right?"

"They met again on the airplane. Not then either. So when? The night before you arrived?"

"Yes."

"So she would have had to have been examined sometime the next day?"

"Yes."

Aleta went back to her table and pulled several sheets from her briefcase. She offered into evidence a signed statement by two gynecologists dated the day after the supposed rape that Paige Van Horne was a virgin and there was no sign of any trauma to the surrounding tissues.

When the judge allowed the document, Aleta handed a copy to Dr. Barre, stumbling slightly so her hand touched Dr. Barre as she was handing her the copy. She apologized.

She then handed a copy to Stephanie Nash.

Aleta waited a moment, then asked, "Is it not possible that Paige did not confide in Judge Davis that she'd had sexual intercourse with anyone?"

Dr. Barre was livid. "He could have performed oral sex. Legally that's rape."

"And you don't believe Judge Davis is aware of all the variations of rape that are considered felonies?"

Dr. Barre glanced at Judge Jacobi. "I'm not saying that."

"Do you have any proof that Paige confided an illegal sexual act to Judge Davis?"

"No, but..."

Aleta was quick.

"Did I molest you?"

"What?" Dr. Barre asked, startled.

"I asked you if I molested you?"

"No."

"I stumbled and my hand brushed against your breast."

"It was an accident."

"Now these two had been on numerous amusement park rides that day and the previous day. Was it not possible that Paige, being as astute a person as she is, felt Hawk's hand brush or bump into her breast and worried about that?"

"People don't worry about such minor things."

"Teenage girls worry about zits all the time," Aleta returned.

"But they don't talk to a judge about them."

"Paige was very aware of the precarious state that Hawk was in. If she wasn't at first, he made her aware. Do you remember the announcement at the Barbecue?"

"Yes."

"Ed said there had been no kissing, right?"

"Yes."

"Hawk said he'd kiss her on her eighteenth birthday and until then they would never meet without a chaperone, correct?"

"Yes."

"So considering how strict a set of guidelines he laid down, do you believe it's possible that Paige could be concerned about an accidental brush and that Judge Davis would advise her not to mention it to anyone."

"Yes, it's possible, but only a person scared to the point of paranoia would do it."

"Isn't that what your report states?" Aleta asked, picking up a copy from the desk and reading a portion.

"Paige is full of fears, almost to the point of paranoia. Some of these have led to delusions."

"I said that," Dr. Barre admitted. "And I recommended therapy to help her get rid of her fears."

"You don't believe she can shake them without professional help, true?"

"That's what I wrote."

"But you also said you witnessed her riding on the scariest ride in the park and that her brother said that she'd never even ridden on a merry-go-round. In fact, isn't that why you wanted to know what Hawk did to bring about this transformation and you are angry because she won't share that?"

"He did something!" Dr. Barre said. "I think the court should know that."

"Evidently, one judge does and she considered it neither illegal nor immoral," Aleta said. "It's apparent that Hawkins Monroe can help Paige overcome her fears, at least the ones that are baseless. In fact, he did in one day what you predict would take months, even years. I submit Dr. Barre that you are dead wrong in your assessment of Paige Van Horne."

Aleta sat down.

Judge Jacobi excused the doctor.

Aleta asked for a short recess and it was granted. She ran to the rest room and entered a stall where she retched several times.

When she emerged, Dr. Barre was at the line of washbasins.

"You are no friend!" Dr. Barre spat out.

"You accepted an assignment you were not ready to take on. You lost your professionalism. Those were forgivable errors. But when you took your rage out on an innocent sixteen-year-old girl and designed a report guaranteed to send her into a life of misery–that was unconscionable! Doctor, you need to review that report and remove the projections of your own despair that you made hers."

"She's using him!" Dr. Barre accused angrily.

"He's an adult," Aleta said. "He can protect himself."

"She's manipulative."

"Who isn't?" Aleta charged. "Is she bad because she's skilled?"

"She's too clever."

"Obviously, she's not or she wouldn't have made an enemy of you."

"I don't know why she did that," Reggie admitted, grudgingly.

"Because the people in my group of friends are honest and non-judgmental. You are neither. You judged her and found her guilty and acted as her executioner all the while pretending you were a dispassionate observer."

"You don't know what you are talking about!" Reggie charged, furious with Aleta's devastating view.

"Dr. Schwartzman is in Tri-Cities Hospital," Aleta said. "You've testified. Now heal yourself. Show him your report. Ask him."

"Screw you!"

Aleta glared at Dr. Barre. "You have already done that!"

Chapter 20

Aleta's two associates were waiting for her outside the rest room. They heard most of the exchange.

"Why didn't you nail her in the courtroom?" Chin asked.

"You stopped short," Jackson argued.

"Judge Jacobi is sharp. She can put the puzzle pieces together. All judges can't. Most juries can't. You need to read your audience."

"But opposing council can rescue the testimony," Chin protested.

"She can try," Aleta said, "but she'd be wiser to let it go. After all, she got solid recommendations on Tyler and Molly."

"Do we want that?" Chin asked.

"Right now we do."

"You want to let us in on your thinking?" Jackson asked.

"You're learning more by not knowing. And you're helping me because you are focusing on your clients and not what I'm going to do."

"We don't want to undermine you," Jackson said.

"You won't. You know all the salient facts. What you don't need to know is my personal agenda," Aleta stated. "Let's go back. And don't look so worried. "I won two of the biggest battles and the third was a stand-off. We're ahead."

Her words cheered her associates.

Van Horne's attorney, Stephanie Nash, questioned Dr. Miles Greenwood first. Most of her questions had to do with Paige. Aleta expected this. She wanted Molly and Tyler to appear as normal as possible, so she was pleased at the way it was going.

Jackson rose first and asked pretty much the same questions about Molly as he had asked Dr. Barre. He received close to the same answers. He added one new query, however.

"Considering Molly's four recent traumatic losses–the death of her mother, grandmother and brother and the destruction of her home and belongings–would you recommend that she be placed in a warm, loving environment?"

Dr. Greenwood fidgeted. He'd already been asked if Molly could handle a boarding school environment and responded with an unequivocal yes."

"Yes, but..."

"Don't anticipate my questions, Doctor," Jackson said. "Even I'm not certain what I am going to ask next."

There was a small chuckle from both lawyers' tables. The joke relaxed the atmosphere. Miles sat back.

"What you told us a few moments ago is that Molly could handle boarding school, true?"

"Yes."

"You must consider her an extremely well-adjusted child to be able to handle an environment not noted for being warm and loving following so much trauma. Is that your assessment?"

"Yes, it is. This child is extremely adaptable. She relates well with others. She will make friends easily."

"If you were to choose a situation for her at this stage in her life, which would you choose?"

Again Miles Greenwood squirmed a bit then hedged. "Both are alternatives with positives and negatives. At the boarding school, Molly would have many girls her own age to relate with. At home, she would be alone. While loving parents are important early in life, one's peer group becomes more important for a pre-teen. I believe Mr. Van Horne's choice for his youngest daughter is a good one."

"You did not choose, Doctor," Jackson pointed out. "It was a generic question. At this point in time, which would you recommend for Molly–a loving home or a boarding school?"

"It's a toss-up," Miles Greenwood replied.

"Thank you Dr. Greenwood," Jackson said and sat down.

Roland Chin rose. "Dr. Greenwood, did you like Tyler Van Horne?"

"I wasn't there to make friends, just to evaluate," Miles replied stiffly.

Chin changed his direction suddenly.

"What did you think of Hawkins Monroe's haircut?"

Startled, Greenwood blurted out,

"What haircut? His hair was long, unkempt and fell across his eyes."

"Was Tyler's hairstyle better or worse?"

"Style? He had no style. It was indicative of his personality. Careless, and undisciplined."

"So he would not do well as the head of a family in your estimation?"

"He's seventeen. He has no concept of what a responsibility that is."

"He lived with his brother David as family head for two years. Are you sure he didn't know what was required?"

"Absolutely. He is a flaky, irresponsible teenager. For example, at Disney World, he never checked on either of his younger sisters. He left them to their own devices."

"Didn't Mrs. Chesney take over responsibility for Molly?"

"Well, yes. But he never checked."

"You expected him to check on an adult?"

"If he was head of the family, he would have."

"Whom did he pal around with?"

"He 'partnered', as he called it, with Dr. Chesney. He said it was a father-son arrangement as Paul was 'hanging with his dad'. Every kid went on the bigger rides with an adult."

"Did Tyler talk to you about Paige?"

"Yes. He said that if Hawk got her to go on the Everest Expedition ride, that Hawk had his vote."

"And did he?"

"Yes," Miles Greenwood said. "I know because I was right behind them. She screamed the whole way."

"Was she the only one who screamed?"

"Most of the girls did."

"Where was Tyler at this time?"

"Watching Paige."

"Did you see Tyler go on any rides with Molly?"

"The rafting ride. Mrs. Chesney couldn't handle the rougher rides. Dr. Chesney or Tyler would fill in for her."

"And yet you say he never checked on either sister," Chin said and sat down.

Aleta didn't even look at Chin before she rose, but Jackson slipped a piece of paper in front of him. Two words were scrawled on it: "Well done." He recognized Aleta's handwriting.

"Dr. Greenwood, I am interested in your specific experience with gifted children," Aleta opened.

"I didn't classify any one of the Van Horne children as gifted." Immediately, after saying that, Miles Greenwood bit his lip. Hastily he added, "I did no tests is all I meant by that remark."

"The school records show all three are gifted," Aleta said. "Now, please tell me specifically how much experience you've had with gifted children."

"I've counseled quite a few."

"So you have some ideas as to characteristics common to gifted children. Please tell us your assessment of them as a class."

"They are, as a whole, blatantly disrespectful, condescending, arrogant and supercilious."

"Were the Van Horne children?"

"Paige was."

"Be specific."

"It's all in my report," Miles Greenwood said. "She wanted to know why I chose psychology over psychiatry."

"And that's supercilious?"

"It's not a proper question for a sixteen-year-old."

"Not a proper question for a student considering entering the field? Not the proper question for a teenager whose mother was a sociologist?"

"That's right!" Greenwood insisted. "She knew the difference."

"But she didn't ask you the difference. She asked you why you chose one over the other."

"She knew why," he said. "She was being disrespectful."

"For that you want her to receive in-patient psychological help?"

"She needs treatment for her delusions," Dr. Greenwood replied. "Not for her attitude. I know the difference. Do you?"

"What delusion does she have?" Aleta asked, ignoring the slur.

"She thinks she saw her father kill her baby sister. We all know the child is alive and well and in a home for retards."

"Is that her only delusion?"

"It's the only one she admits to," Dr. Greenwood replied. "When I asked her about Hawkins Monroe, she gave me some bullshit story about Judge Davis telling her not to tell anyone about their relationship. And the judge backed her up."

Aleta showed her honest surprise. "And you think the judge lied to you?"

"Yes."

"Why would she do that?"

Greenwood grinned. Aleta's associates held their breath. He'd laid a trap.

"Because she's your mother-in-law and she did you a favor."

"Really?" Aleta queried. "Why?"

"To give you a leg up the ladder toward being a judge."

Aleta looked a Judge Jacobi. "Please excuse this digression. I want to ask two questions relating to this issue."

"Permission granted."

"First, Dr. Greenwood, are you saying Judge Davis condoned a felony to help me become a judge?"

"She wasn't being a judge at the time. She was being an ordinary person."

"So the answer is yes?"

"Yes."

"Second question. I have a two-month-old baby and another on the way. What makes you think I want to be a judge at this time?"

"You smart ones are all alike. You're so full of driving ambition, you'll ignore home and family to gain success," Greenwood replied acridly.

"Are you saying Paige and her brother, Tyler, will cast aside their responsibilities to better themselves individually?"

"Yes. That's my prediction."

"When Mary Van Horne died, Paige didn't cast aside her responsibilities to her siblings. She stepped into her mother's shoes and according to you filled them well."

"According to me? When did I say that? I never said that. Judge, have the clerk read back the record and see. I never said that!"

"My, we are testy, aren't we?" Aleta quipped and immediately apologized. "I'm sorry, Judge. I withdraw the comment."

"Clerk, strike Mrs. Praetzel's comment from the record."

"Thank you."

"Dr. Greenwood, isn't the main purpose of parenting to raise compassionate, considerate, well-adjusted children?"

"Yes."

"You said that Molly was that kind of child."

"Tyler isn't."

"He's older than Paige. You expected Paige to raise her older brother?"

"She's delusional herself."

"If she is, she had the good sense not to impose her delusion on her younger sister," Aleta said. "Don't you think that calls for exceptional mothering on her part?"

"So, she cooked a bit. So, what? That's no big deal."

"She also cleaned house, shopped, did the laundry, saw to Molly's needs and went to high school in her spare time where she got A's in most courses."

"She could have been a lousy housekeeper."

"Tyler complained that she made sure the house was always picked up. When I visited there were no dishes in the sink. The beds were made. Clothes were hung up. The floors and windows were clean. Now, Dr. Greenwood, don't you agree that the record points to an exceptional young woman?"

"She's almost seventeen. She should know how to do those things."

"Her dying mother taught her to take her place. She was fourteen at the time. Don't you agree she learned her lessons well?"

"So she's smart. I didn't say she wasn't."

"But you still feel she has serious mental health issues because she didn't show you the proper respect. Did you tell her who you were?"

"Oh, I told her."

"Did she understand how important your report was?"

"I told her that I had the power to decide where she would spend her next few years and she still wouldn't confide in me."

"But only on the subject she was ordered by a judge not to discuss, correct?"

"For the most part."

"So, you threatened her and she didn't fold."

"I didn't threaten her. I warned her."

"I see, Dr. Greenwood. I believe we all see."

Aleta sat down, Judge Jacobi adjourned until two the next afternoon.

Stephanie Nash was not surprised. Dr. Greenwood had been a disaster. Aleta Praetzel had eaten him alive.

Stephanie turned to her client and said, "Find that document. We need to show good faith now. If you do, two of the children are yours."

"I want all three," Van Horne snapped.

"Then cooperate. Get me the document."

"I want this wrapped up tomorrow."

"That will happen if Aleta Praetzel doesn't have any surprises up her sleeve."

"What about her associates?"

"Inconsequential. Aleta Praetzel is the one to worry about."

Chapter 21

Meanwhile, down in Florida, the main subject of that afternoon's custody hearing, the newly married Paige Van Horne Monroe was settled with her new husband in what until that morning had been Claude and Harriet's room. The Luthers had moved their belongings to the honeymoon suite which had been reserved for the newlyweds.

Paige and Hawk sat on the bed while the Luthers and the Praetzels told them what precautions were necessary to ensure their safety.

"Why are we in danger?" Paige asked.

"Aleta had to tell the court that you were here," Harriet said.

"Did she tell them Hawk and I were married?"

"She wasn't told," Harriet said.

"Why?" Hawk asked.

"If she knew," Hubert explained, "some of her arguments would have been irrelevant."

"She was able to tell your story about the July fourth incident, Paige," Harriet added. "It was the center of the focus today."

"How did it go?" Hawk asked.

"Aleta said she didn't plan to convince anyone today. She just wanted the story in the record, so she could address it later."

"Once the DNA tests are complete, won't her story be believed?" Hawk asked.

"I imagine Van Horne will claim the wrong child was tested and demand new tests be done," Hubert said. "That'll give him time to get out of the country."

"Or," Lydia suggested, "He will bribe the manager."

"To do what?" Hawk asked.

"Say his baby died and they substituted another baby to keep the money coming in."

"The court will insist on seeing the body," Hawk said.

"My guess is that the baby was buried in a coffin in a cemetery as a Jane Doe and the grave is unmarked," Lydia said.

"That takes paperwork," Harriet put in.

"Which may be the reason Van Horne burned down the house. His wife had the paperwork," Lydia said. "You know it may not have been the custody agreement he was so bent on hiding, but the paperwork showing the location of the grave site."

"Why didn't her mother tell Paige?" Hawk asked.

"She told David," Lydia replied. "What mother thinks their nineteen-year-old son is going to die at twenty-one."

"How did the hearing go?" Hawk asked.

"Aleta won the first two points," Hubert reported. "She put off the decision for a day by demanding Van Horne produce the custody agreement. That gives the lab time to complete the DNA tests."

"She had a tougher fight getting Norma to agree to let the children stay down here. Norma is the kind of person who wants the subjects in a custody hearing in the state. It helped that they were in police custody," Lydia said. "Only Aleta had to tell her our plans."

"Which is why we're going to one of the water parks tomorrow instead of Epcot Center," Harriet put in.

"Tomorrow!" Paige exclaimed distressed.

"What's wrong?" Hawk asked. "You have a new suit."

"Do you have a razor?"

"A straight razor," he replied.

"What's that?" Paige asked.

"It's one you can't shave your legs with," Harriet said. "Paul will buy you a safety razor and shaving cream."

"Have Hawk help you," Lydia added. "It's not something you should do yourself."

Hawk looked puzzled.

"Just do it, Hawk," Harriet ordered. "She's wearing a bikini."

Hawk's face cleared.

Harriet then reminded Paige and Hawk that they were expected at the reception fully outfitted so the photographer could take their wedding pictures.

Later, as Hubert and Lydia came to fetch them for the reception, they found two radiant newlyweds.

"I gather you put the time to good use," Lydia said as the two ladies walked in front of the gentlemen.

"I'm all set for tomorrow," Paige said. "You were right. I needed help."

"He used a straight razor?"

"We had to have sex first to steady his hand, but afterwards he had no problem."

"I can't believe he used a straight razor," Lydia marveled.

"It was what I chose. I wanted him to use a familiar tool."

"You trusted him that much?"

"Yes. I trust him."

"You're going to have a long and happy marriage."

"You don't think my father can get it annulled?"

"That's the reason Aleta is spending her time tackling what your father and the two doctors are calling your delusion."

"Did you tell them it wasn't?"

"I only told them our conversation was privileged and that you told the truth," Lydia said. "I didn't help."

"I'm surprised Mrs. Praetzel picked them."

"That was a mistake. She thought Miles was a friend of Stanley's and therefore good at his job. He isn't either. Miles chose Dr. Barre to go with him."

"She didn't act much like Aleta's friend."

"Aleta said she punched holes in their testimony. I know Norma. She hates a dumb expert."

"So, I really am in danger tonight."

"Your father has to act fast."

"Are Hawk and I safe going to the reception?"

"We figure Van Horne couldn't have sent any one until after the hearing," Lydia said. "It's a three hour flight. Harriet thinks we're all safe until eight. It's only five."

But, Harriet's estimation was off by three hours.

Tully Machi had spotted Lydia entering the plane carrying the same bouquet of flowers he'd seen in the courthouse earlier. He had gotten hold of Van Horne and they had met in a bar outside Willow Glen.

"I need this Aleta Praetzel taken out," Van Horne said. "Do it before the hearing. She's got too big a rep."

"She's got a police guard," Tully Machi informed the dour Dutchman.

Van Horne's eyes had grown hard and cold. "We are a stone's throw from a city replete with guns for hire. Get one."

"No go," Tully had told him. "There's a boss on the South Side who's put the word out. Aleta Praetzel's not to be touched."

"Same hold true for Paige?" Van Horne asked.

"You want to put a hit on your own daughter?"

"I'll have a chartered plane waiting at the Waukegan airport. You put a man on that plane."

"I could go."

"You went face to face with Judge Davis. Send a stranger. Besides you'll be busy."

"Doing what?"

"Taking out Aleta Praetzel."

"I told you I don't do..."

He stopped. Van Horne had removed a locket from his pocket and was swinging it in his face.

"The fire?" he questioned. "You wouldn't."

Van Horne didn't say a word.

"How much?"

"One hundred thousand."

"For each?"

"For both."

"I can't get anyone to fly to Florida for fifty. Too risky. And the man will want half up front."

To his surprise, Kurt Van Horne pulled out two white envelopes and gave Tully both of them. "For you and your man. Half now. Half when the job's done. Don't think I won't hire someone to take you out if you fail."

Tully's hand shook slightly as he took the envelopes. He was more scared now than before. The man had arrived prepared. Tully didn't like being that transparent.

The charter plane took off an hour after their discussion. The hit man, Bob Rivetti, was dressed like a businessman. He carried a briefcase and small suitcase. His gun was in the suitcase. It had a silencer.

When Lydia and Paige were entering the elevator, Bob Rivetti was registering at the front desk.

Bob Rivetti had very little to go on. He took his keys and headed for his room. Tully Machi had promised him more information via computer. His laptop was in his briefcase.

As he headed for the elevator to take him to the fifth floor, a group of four exited. All were dressed up and he guessed they were going out to dine.

The young woman had a bouquet of flowers in her hand, which Rivetti found unusual. They weren't roses. They were ordinary garden flowers—pretty, but ordinary. They weren't arranged like a bridal bouquet. They were just a handful of fresh flowers. Where does one get a bouquet like that?

Because his attention was riveted on the woman and her flowers, the elevator door closed before he got on. He punched the button to call another elevator.

Tully had told him the girl might be dressed in a pale cream-colored two piece dress with a bare midriff. Could he have lucked onto her?

He watched the group enter a door at the far end of the hall. The elevator came. He climbed on and went to his room.

The foursome, meanwhile, traveled to a room at the end of the second corridor and entered. A whoop went up when the bride and groom appeared. Molly rushed up to her sister and threw her arms around her.

"You look so pretty!" she said.

Tyler shook Hawk's hand.

"You've got my vote," he said by way of congratulations.

There was no reception line, but everyone took a turn congratulating the couple. The Witherspoons had been invited. Kitty decided she wanted to be part of the celebration more than she wanted an extra hour at the Magic Kingdom.

Hawk and Paige were led to a table with a multitude of boxes, each prettily wrapped. Almost every one contained a stuffed Disney character and a note.

Kitty was given the stuffed animals to play with.

The cards Paige read aloud and kept. From Molly was the promise of a huge desk. Tyler promised a laptop so Paige wouldn't have to borrow his anymore. Everyone, including Tyler, knew his had been stolen and figured he planned to borrow hers, but that was okay.

Lydia and Hubert gave her the sapphire necklace she was wearing. When Paige read the card, her hand touched the necklace and her eyes filled with tears.

The Chesneys promised the newlyweds a full set of dishes; the Robert Lockes, a cook's kitchen; the Paul Lockes, an original oil; the Luthers, furniture. Tiffany gave them salt and pepper shakers from the gift shop and Kitty gave them bookends.

When Paige saw two boxes left, she wondered who else knew. The first was a promise from Ed and Beatrice for a show puppy along with vet care and training classes and show entries for two years.

"How did they know?" she exclaimed.'

"Ed listens," Lydia said.

"You can buy any kind of dog you like," Harriet explained. "We have all kinds of dogs in our group and we can put you in touch with a good breeder of whatever kind you like."

"I like most dogs."

"Maybe Hawk has a preference," Harriet suggested.

Paige laughed. "If I leave it to him he'll pick a dog with hair over its eyes. But don't worry, I'll pick one we both like."

Stanley and Aleta's gift was last. When Paige opened the envelope, she couldn't believe her eyes. Speechless, she handed it to Hawk.

He turned to Dr. Chesney and asked, "Is there a house going up next door to you?"

"Yes, someone bought the property on spec and is building. The house is almost done. Three bedrooms, two baths upstairs. A den downstairs. Why?"

"Meet your new neighbors. Stanley and Aleta are giving us the down payment on that house as a wedding gift."

Stunned silence greeted the announcement.

It was Hawk who broke the stillness.

"I guess Tyler chose the right lawyer for the family."

Laughter greeted his comment.

"That decides the dog," Paige commented. "It'll have to love the water."

Harriet chuckled, "That's most of the dogs on the planet."

"I mean really like it!" Paige said.

"It has to be big," Hawk put in.

"How big?" Harriet asked.

"Big!" Hawk said. "I've always wanted a really big dog."

"It has to be really big," Paige reiterated, "and be a water dog."

"Chessies are big," Harriet said. "Stoney is close to eighty pounds."

"Bigger," Hawk said.

"You want a Newfie!" Harriet said. "They weigh over a hundred pounds and they were bred to help cod fishermen pull in their nets. They're mostly used now in water rescue work."

"Are they friendly?" Paige asked.

"Yes, and easy to train. They're good with children. Your neighbors like them because they're quiet dogs and they don't chase little dogs so Beatrice's Scotties will be safe. On top of that they're quite handsome."

"What's the other side?" Paige asked. "I've never seen one so they aren't popular."

"They're huge, so they eat a lot," Harriet said. "And they need room. They have a heavy coat so they shed. And they love to rescue people."

Paige was puzzled. "How is that bad?"

"If you're in the lake swimming, they'll rescue you and you can't say no to a Newfie who's bent on saving you."

Paige laughed. "I've got to have me one of those!"

Hawk smiled happily.

Later, that night Hawk was awakened by a light touch on his chest. He didn't open his eyes as the hand was moving and he felt the light touch of a kiss on his cheek. The hand moved slowly down his body. It was a pleasant sensation and he didn't move lest he frighten the hand away.

He wanted to say something encouraging, but his erection told the story.

"I wanted to thank you for marrying me," Paige said softly.

"I feel thanked," Hawk replied enthusiastically.

"Do you want to consummate now?" Paige asked tentatively.

"Yes!" he whispered.

"It'll be our sixth time," Paige mentioned. Hawk could hear the worry in her tone.

"That's not even as many times as Claude and Harriet did it their first day. And he's over twice my age."

"It's just that..." Paige began as he entered her.

At that very moment, two gunshots reverberated through the night's stillness. The two broke apart.

"Aren't Harriet and Claude above us?" Paige whispered frightened.

"I'm not sure."

"Did someone get shot instead of us?"

The phone rang. "Stay in your room," ordered the rough female voice.

"Harriet!" Hawk exclaimed. "You're okay?"

"I winged him, but he got away," Harriet said. "Stay put!"

Hawk turned to Paige. "She winged him, but he got away. She wants us to stay put.

"Shouldn't we tell the others?" Paige asked.

"She said we were to stay put," Hawk repeated.

"You want to finish what we started?"

"Not now. He's still out there."

"What do you plan on doing?" Paige asked.

"Keeping watch."

"We don't have a gun."

"We have our wits."

Clutching his upper arm, Bob Rivetti ran down the hall toward the elevator whose door he'd left propped open. He kicked the book into the elevator as he slipped in and punched the close button. The elevator descended to the fifth floor.

"How could this have happened? They were prepared. Even so, when he'd eased the door open, he'd hear them in the throes of sexual intercourse.

He threw open the door and found himself staring straight at a naked woman, seated on her husband, facing him. He stared at the gray-haired woman. She wasn't the young newlywed he was after. His gun was still aimed at her when her gun came up. She shouted, "Police!"

He stared at the gun barrel aimed at him, more in bewilderment than fear. Shock froze time.

Where had the gun come from he asked himself, his curiosity overriding his apprehension. Had it been a man he would have pulled the trigger immediately. But it was a woman and an old one, at that.

And in the bridal suite!

These thoughts sped through his mind in a few milliseconds. His finger squeezed the trigger.

No witnesses. That was his motto.

Why he thought the sound of her gun discharging was his he puzzled over in the elevator.

He had a silencer on his gun.

The sound had come as his finger was squeezing the trigger. The pain had shot up his arm as his gun discharged. His hand had released it as it was discharging the second bullet. A second shot nicked his ear.

He saw the gun on the floor, but a warning growl from the rough-voiced woman told him she was in control. He turned and ran.

She wouldn't follow.

Back in his room he held a cold wet washcloth to his ear to slow the bleeding.

He knew the bullet had missed any major blood vessels. Lots of pain, but not too much blood. The bullet had hit a muscle, hence the reflexive letting go of the gun.

The damned woman was a cop, he concluded. Wound. Don't kill. That was their motto. Next would come a room search. Probably limited to single men.

He had to leave. But first he had to find his targets.

He tore his bloody shirtsleeve into ribbons and tied one around his head plastering the washcloth to his ear. The other strips he wound around his arm. Using his teeth and free hand he knotted the last strip.

He opened his laptop and punched in the hotel registry.

Tully had said there were two deputies with the group. He'd just met the deputies. They'd switched rooms with the newlyweds.

He looked at the guests in that block of rooms. He eliminated the parents with children. That left three couples: Dr. and Mrs. Chesney, Mr. and Mrs. Praetzel and Mr. and Mrs. Luther. A doctor was an unlikely deputy. Hubert Praetzel was a well-known criminal defense attorney. That ruled him out. That left the Luthers.

Their room was between the rooms with the Van Horne children. They were his deputies. He now knew where his newlyweds were.

He took out his spare gun, loaded it, attached its silencer and picked it up. The weight of it sent shooting pains through his arm. His hand let the gun drop. He picked it up with his left hand. He needed to practice a bit.

He stacked pillows on the bed and using his left hand shot a round into the stack. He backed up and shot again. It took the whole clip before he hit the center from the doorway.

He reloaded the gun and stuck it in his belt on his other hip. He glanced at his watch. The deputies would be busy with the police. The police would be busy trying to persuade the management to allow a room search. No one would expect a second hit.

His ear was the problem. He had to cover it.

Back in the room on the floor above Bob Rivetti, Hawk had fetched his straight razor while Paige remained standing in the center of the room.

When he reentered the bedroom, he stopped and gazed at his bride. "I'm never going to keep my mind on protecting us if you insist on looking so beautiful."

Paige stared at him. "I'm not doing anything."

"You haven't any clothes on," Hawk said.

"I know."

"What's wrong?"

"I don't like your plan. You're going to get shot."

"Do you have a better plan?"

"Yes."

"Spill it."

"We block the door, so he will wake us up if he tries to open it. And we go to bed and make love."

"And when he comes?"

"We call Harriet on her cell and we hide together in the bathroom. It has a door with a lock and by the time he breaks in, help will be here."

Hawk laid his razor back on the bathroom counter.

Together they moved the desk in front of the door, stacked a chair on top so it would fall if the desk were moved.

Then they went back to bed. Hawk put his arms around Paige and held her. Soon she closed her eyes.

Less than an hour passed before Hawk heard the jiggling of the door handle. He kissed Paige on the mouth to wake her up silently. Paige picked up the phone and punched in Harriet's number. While the phone was ringing, the door was pushed hard enough to open it a crack. The chair crashed.

"Go!" Hawk whispered, taking the phone from his wife's hand.

Paige sprang from the bed.   She looked back and waited.

There was still no answer. Hawk put the phone down, but left it off the hook. It would continue to ring. Eventually Harriet would wake up.

He and Paige made it into the bathroom as one final shove moved the desk enough so Bob Rivetti could enter. Hawk locked the bathroom door and Bob Rivetti knew immediately where the couple was.

Rivetti checked the bed anyway, his gun drawn. He heard the phone beeping. He walked over and replaced the receiver back on the cradle. These two had prepared.

What he couldn't figure is why they hadn't simply moved to another room.

While Rivetti checked out the room, inside the bathroom Paige stuffed toothbrushes under the door and set the wastebasket at the side of the opening so whoever came in would either have to step over it, reach down and removed it or kick it out of the way.

Hawk nodded his approval.

Then she climbed up on the counter and indicated that Hawk should do the same. He hopped up and sat, his legs dangling almost to the floor.

Paige leaned over him, put her hand on his shoulder to steady herself and poured out the bottles of shampoo and lotion onto the floor.

A series of soft pops stopped her.

Bullets pierced the door and buried themselves in the opposite wall. The white terry cloth robe handing on the hook let each bullet lift it slightly as is passed through. Each time it fell back, the folds reassembled themselves and covered the new holes.

Paige crouched down in the corner. Hawk opened his razor.

Two more rounds shattered the door lock. The door was pushed open. The toothbrush handles halted its progress but not enough.

A leg stepped over the wastebasket. Hawk realized that striking the leg would cause the man to reach around and shoot him.

Paige moved behind him. She picked up the glasses and threw them at the leg. They were plastic so they bounced off the knee and fell unbroken on the floor.

Bob Rivetti needed to see his target. He had wasted too many shots. He poked his head around the corner and only caught a glimpse of Paige nude before the ice bucket was thrown in his face.

He knew where she was, however. His left hand snaked through the door, twisted and pointed the gun directly as Paige's chest. Before his finger squeezed the trigger, Hawk's razor had finished its journey and it dug deep into the wrist of the hand holding the gun.

Rivetti screamed in agony as he withdrew his half-severed hand. His gun dropped into the wastebasket.

Enraged by the pain, Rivetti reached for the gun with his right hand. The movement caused pain to rip through the arm still carrying the bullet in its muscle. His shriek pierced the silence of the night a second time. Those hurrying toward the room sped up.

Hawk, not knowing that the cry was not related to his first strike, saw the appearance of the other hand as a new threat and again sliced down through the air into the skin, through the tendons to the bone on the back of the hand. The fingers hung limp and Rivetti bellowed his torment as he withdrew that hand as well.

Hawk pulled back the basket with the gun, handed Paige the robe, removed the toothbrushes jammed under the door, and opened it.

Rivetti was bleeding profusely from the first razor cut. He sank to the ground and stared at his half severed hand.

Hawk grabbed the belt from Paige's robe, wrapped it around Rivetti's upper arm and tightened it until the blood flow slowed to a trickle. He stuck two toothbrushes into the knot and tightened it further. The blood flow stopped.

Rivetti's screeching filled Hawk's ears, but Hawk ignored that and kept the tourniquet tight.

As soon as the police arrived and could take over, Hawk gathered Paige in his arms, carried her past the wounded man and set her on the bed. He pulled the blanket off the other bed and wrapped it around both of them and held her close.

She couldn't stop shaking.

Harriet entered the room bearing two cups of hot chocolate. Harriet sat on the other side of Paige and held her cup.

"She's in shock," Harriet said. "She should probably go to the hospital."

Paige stuttered a shaky but definite no.

"I'll get Dr. Chesney," Harriet said.

"D...Don't...wake him," Paige uttered haltingly.

"He's awake. Everyone is awake," Harriet said, giving Paige another sip of cocoa before she left.

"No hospital," Paige begged Hawk.

"I'm not letting you out of my arms until the sun comes up. This is still our wedding night. And you were amazingly brave."

"B... But... I'm... shaking."

"My insides are in knots. That's why I can't shake."

Paige managed a weak smile.

"You saved our lives," she said, her voice a bit steadier.

"We saved each other," Hawk said. "We were a good team."

"I'm so cold," Paige whispered.

Dr. Chesney appeared, bag in hand.

"You two have had quite a wedding night," he said as he stuck a thermometer in her ear, read it and then took her pulse. "You're way too cold."

"No hospital," Hawk said.

"We can take care of it here at the hotel, only not in this room," Dr. Chesney said. "Wrap her up and let's go. Evelyn has prepared a warm bath. And you, Hawk, are getting in the tub with her."

"Let me get my swim trunks."

"No time for trifles."

"Okay, Paige," Hawk said picking her up. "Let's go get puckered like prunes."

It was, however, Bertha, not Evelyn, who met the young couple and helped Paige disrobe while Hawk climbed into the tub. Bertha helped Paige into the warm water with a professional attitude that relaxed both newlyweds. Hawk wrapped his arms around his young wife and held her close.

Bertha kept the water temperature warm and Hawk realized after a while that while the water behind him cooled, the water in front stayed evenly warm. His body kept Paige's back warm.

Bertha checked Paige's temperature regularly and reported it to Dr. Chesney who slept intermittently on his bed. Bertha told Paige that Evelyn took her place, crawling into bed beside Molly.

"They really do want to live with each other," Bertha said. "I hope Aleta can make it happen."

Chapter 22

Back in Willow Glen, Tully Machi came onto the grounds of Stanley Praetzel's house via the woods that separated his acreage from that of his parents. He knew the senior Praetzels were gone. The help generally partied well into the night and would be dead to the world in the wee hours of the morning.

Stanley Praetzel was in the hospital. Aleta was alone in the house with just the baby. There were two guards patrolling the grounds, but Tully had planned a diversion to take care of that situation–a potentially deadly diversion. It would draw them away from the house, but first they would order Aleta to remain inside.

Tully had set the charges in the dead of night. They were all on timers in the field on the other side of the barn from the house. He had had no trouble bypassing the security system. The motion sensors had been set to catch a man, but not a small animal. He'd scraped a small ditch under the lowest electrical wire rather then trying to crawl between it and the middle wire and thus set off the motion detector.

Once through and in the field, he had planted his devices and set the timer on four of them. The other two would be detonated by the remote he had in his pocket. He intended to take out his pursuers personally.

Now he waited near the back of the field that was directly behind the house. He lay in a depression made a bit deeper by removing a few well-placed shovel's full of dirt, and tossing them randomly in several directions. The shovel was slung over the fence to be retrieved upon his departure.

He closed his eyes and slept lightly. The first explosion of noise would wake him.

The string of firecrackers that went off at first light woke not only Tully Machi but the seven horses in the barn. Jezebel, Hubbs' old mare, Sterling, Stanley's rescue Morgan, and Minx, Stanley's saddle horse, whinnied and pranced in their stalls. The three competition jumpers reared as they whinnied. But it was Shadow who not only whinnied and reared but hammered his stall door so hard he broke several boards.

Just prior to the firecrackers exploding, Aleta had been awakened by a vision. She'd thrown on her robe and opened her front door and said to the two men standing there,

"Under no circumstances go into the field on the other side of the barn."

Almost to punctuate her words the firecrackers had started popping.

"It's only firecrackers," Matt said.

"What orders did Chief West give you regarding me?"

"To protect you."

"What else?"

"To obey you if you give an order."

"I'm telling you," Aleta reiterated. "Do not go into the field where the firecrackers went off."

A second string of firecrackers began popping.

"Go help Hubbs," Aleta ordered. "And make sure he doesn't go into the field. There are bombs planted there."

"Sounds like firecrackers," Charlie said.

"Go!" Aleta commanded sternly.

"We aren't supposed to leave you."

"Unless I tell you to. And I'm telling you!" Aleta said. "I've got five dogs in here."

Matt said, "I'm going. Chief West was definite."

"Okay," Charlie agreed. "I heard Milani tell someone that, but I thought he was joking."

Aleta heard Matt tell Charlie as they ran toward the barn, "He wasn't joking. None of the chiefs ever joke about an order."

Aleta turned and went back inside. She went straight to their gun case. It hung on the wall and was kept locked. It had a fancy electronic opening device responsive to several fingerprints–hers, Stanley's, Harriet's, Claude's and Lyle's. The guns inside were unloaded but the shells were in boxes at the bottom of the cabinet.

Aleta took out her rifle, opened the breech and loaded in the shot. She clicked the rifle shut, set it on the mantle and repeated the maneuver with Stanley's rifle.

The Chessies crowded around her eagerly. The Pug was in his pen. Scooby danced behind the Chessies and he was the first to hear the noise at the back door. He left the group barking.

Aleta commanded the Chessies to stay. All three sat, their eyes focused on Aleta. All three turned to face where the gun was pointing.

"Scooby, come here," Aleta called. "We're going out the front door."

Scooby continued to bark at the back door.

Suddenly, Aleta heard a high-pitched squeak. She stopped calling.

She stood still and listened. The footsteps were soft, but she imagined she heard them step over her half-grown Labrador. She refused to let herself think of him as dead. She hadn't heard a shot.

The Pug continued to bark and the noise he made barking and throwing himself against the side of his pen told her the person near in the laundry room. Try as she would, she couldn't hear anything other than Auggie's barking.

The male voice came from behind.

"Drop the gun."

Aleta turned, saying, "One doesn't drop a loaded rifle. Let me lay it down."

"I have your baby," Tully said.

His words were redundant. She had heard her baby's whimper before the man spoke. He'd snatched Gerard from his crib, entered the door from the hall to the master bedroom and now stood at the second door from the master bedroom, the one that led straight to the living room.

As Aleta turned, the dogs turned with her.

She held the rifle pointed up.

Encouraged, Tully said, "Lay it on the floor slowly. Don't spook them dogs. The first one that charges gets it in the head."

"First you put down my baby."

"No way. It's my call," Tully claimed, moving Gerard directly in front of him. "You hit my gun hand, he hits the ground hard."

Aleta stepped over and laid the rifle on the stone hearth.

"On the floor over here," Tully ordered, shifting the baby slightly and pointing near his feet, "then back up!"

Aleta moved the rifle to the floor near his feet and stood up. She put her hands in the air and backed up quickly. She felt the low stone hearth of the fireplace and stopped. "Put down my baby now," she demanded. "Or I'll shoot you."

Tully glanced at the rifle lying at his feet to ascertain it was still there. Aleta's hand plucked the second from the rough stone mantle and had it to her eye by the time Tully looked up.

The first bullet smashed into his knee. It buckled and he and the baby began to fall.

A duck hunter used to shooting moving targets Aleta's second shot hit its mark. The rifle shot split his right hand apart.

Aleta released the dogs and they ran to the man and stood around him. Aleta picked up her baby who was crying lustily. She held him close and tried to soothe him.

Tully heard the deep-throated growl and ceased all movement. The teeth stayed bared but the growls grew quieter.

Aleta, holding her baby in one arm, picked up the loaded rifle and put it on the hearth next to the rocking chair. Then she sat down and rocked her baby. His crying subsided just enough for Tully to be heard.

"Aren't you gonna call for an ambulance?" Tully cried.

"I think I can soothe the baby without help," Aleta replied icily.

"I'm bleeding!" he yelled. A second dog moved in and a second set of teeth was bared.

"I have a good cleaning woman. She'll know how to get the stains out."

"Get these dogs off me or I'll sue!" he screeched.

"Just try!" she growled. Her eyes were hard.

Tully lay back. There were now three large Chessies standing over him growling. He could smell their hot breath on his face.

The door opened and Matt entered his gun drawn. Charlie was right behind him. In the background sirens were approaching.

"Matt, tell the men there are bombs in the field."

"The third set of firecrackers went off when we were in the barn," Charlie said, spotting the injured man surrounded by three large dogs. He swung his gun toward the dogs.

Aleta's gun was in her hand in a split second and the shot fired hit Charlie's gun.

It flew out of his hand. He stared at her astounded and shocked.

"No one shoots my dogs!" Aleta said. "Matt, get him out of here!"

"Damn!" Charlie cursed as Matt pushed him out the door, "What's with her? Is she loco?"

"No, she's not loco."

"I want my gun."

"Not yet. You go help with the horses and make sure no one goes into the field."

"You aren't the boss here. This is Willow Glen, not Arborville."

"I'm surprised Milani put you out here," Matt said. "You're too new."

"He didn't. I traded shifts."

"Well, both of you guys are in trouble!" Matt said. "Just go do what I say and maybe you'll keep your job."

"Look, I didn't do nothing wrong. That woman is crazy, not me. A crazy psychic, that's what."

"Just go take care of the horses," Matt said.

"Hell, that's not my job!" Charlie snapped.

"Yes it is," Matt said. "Aleta ordered it. You go do it!"

Randy Quinn jumped out of the first squad to reach the house, "What's up?"

"Aleta shot a hit man," Matt reported. "He's hurt bad. Better call an ambulance and your chief."

"Is she in there alone with him?"

"She's got those three Chessies of Harriet's guarding him. This idiot almost shot the dogs."

"Charlie, what are you doing here? You're not cleared for this assignment."

Matt cut in. "Aleta told him to help Hubbs with the horses. All the noise has spooked them."

"Hey Man," Randy said. "You better hop to it."

"She's got my gun!" Charlie shouted infuriated. "She shot it outta my hand."

"Boy, I would have liked to have seen that!" Randy said. "I heard she's quite a shot."

"Lightning fast too," Matt said. "I've never seen the like. I bet she can outdraw the chief. By the way, she said there are bombs in the pasture on the other side of the barn and you should call the bomb squad."

"Gotta call the chief on that," Randy said opening his radio. "What are you doing still here, Charlie? Get down to the barn."

"Who're you talking to?" came Milani's voice.

"Chief?" Randy said, "how come I got you so quick?"

"Who were you talking to?"

Charlie leaned in. "Me, Chief. Charlie. Randy wants me to go to the barn to help with the horses, which ain't my job, while he and this joe from Arborville cater to the crazy psychic."

"Randy, post Charlie at the barn. Get him away from Aleta."

"Yes Sir," Randy said. He turned to Charlie. "The chief says you're to guard the barn."

"I ain't got a gun."

"If you see anything suspicious, call one of us that's got a gun."

Charlie walked off, grumbling, "What a bunch of shitheads."

"How long do you give him?" Matt asked.

"An hour."

"That long, huh?"

"Chief Milani will let him jabber a bit. He's trying to work on his temper."

Randy made a second call to his chief. "We need an ambulance. Mrs. Praetzel shot someone. She says there are bombs in the field behind the barn so she wants a bomb squad.

"Who's guarding the perp?" Milani asked.

"Harriet's dogs," Randy said. "And Aleta has a gun on him."

"Why aren't you in there?" Milani charged.

Randy turned to Matt. "Why are we out here?"

Matt leaned over. "Mrs. Praetzel told me to get Charlie out of the house.

"Never mind the rest. ETA five minutes," Milani said. "Check on Mrs. Praetzel."

A lone siren was heard in the distance.

"What the hell!" Chief Milani cried.

Randy heard him. "Let's get inside."

He opened the door as the siren drew closer. It was coming fast.

"Who do you suppose that is? He must be doing a hundred?"

"Not Milani," Randy said.

The two stepped inside the house and moved toward the man on the floor.

"It's about time someone got here," Tully cried. "Get these damn dogs off me and get me outta here!"

"Where's Mrs. Praetzel?"

"She said something about some fool getting killed, grabbed her rifle and took off. She left the damned baby in the house!"

The siren was closing in fast.

The two ran to the door as the patrol car, blue lights flashing, siren wailing appeared over the rise.

"It's West!" Matt shouted.

The chief's car turned up the drive, tires screeching as it cornered. The car tipped slightly and almost went over, but righted itself and tore up the drive taking the corner next to the house so fast its back end dented the side door of the patrol car parked there.

"She's in the field!" Matt shouted racing from the house. Randy ran after him.

Tully thought about the remote in his pocket. She was in the field. He could pay her back for his hand.

She'd cleverly taken out his right knee so when he fell, the baby fell with him and landed on top of him. His right hand, which was his gun hand, she'd taken out as he fell. He lay on his injured side, but the dogs wouldn't let him turn over.

Now, as he lay there he realized that his left hand was on the outside of his pocket with the remote.

The siren scream filled his ears. Tires squealed. Metal crunched and the house trembled as the parked car was thrown against the living room wall.

Tully's hand was jarred out of place. He inched it back to the remote as he heard the screech of the brakes a short distance away.

The dogs didn't take their eyes off him. How could they be so persistent? He hated them for their watchfulness.

His hand finally reached the remote.

As the car screeched to a halt at the edge of the field, Lyle West jumped out, pointed his gun at Aleta and shouted, "Martha told me to shoot you in the leg if you didn't run to me."

"But..." she started and hesitated for a tenth of a second.

Martha?

She threw her rifle on the ground and started running.

The first bomb exploded as she reached Lyle's arms and the blast threw her into them. The two of them fell backwards onto the car.

The blast flattened Charlie. As a result, he was on the ground when the second bomb went off. It was up the field about ten yards.

The horses in the barn went berserk. Hubbs called for help. Lyle reached in and switched off his sirens and lights. Aleta ran over to Shadow and Hubbs calmed Royal. Lyle came in and talked to Yudi.

Charlie picked himself up and stumbled into the barn as Milani drove up and leaped from his car.

"You realize you hit one of my squad cars."

"It was parked in the wrong place. What fool did that?" West shot back.

Milani pointed to Charlie. "What did Aleta try to do—rescue him?"

"I didn't need rescuing!" Charlie protested. "I was out locating the bombs."

Milani eyed him with disdain.

"When I got here, he had passed the first bomb," West said coolly. "Aleta had a gun on him. She was ordering him to stop."

"Did you see the first bomb or did you miss it?" Milani asked.

"I saw it," Charlie claimed. "I didn't miss nothing!"

"Did you warn her to leave the field?"

"Why should I? She said they was here," Charlie said.

Lyle snorted. "Tom, where did you find this loser?"

Offended, Charlie burst out, "What? What'd I say?"

"She told you to send for the bomb squad. Now why would she do that?" Tom said gritting his teeth.

"To show us where they was."

"Then why were you out here looking?"

"To find them."

"According to you, they weren't lost," Milani snapped. "I'd arrest you for stupidity, but that's not allowed."

"How about reckless endangerment?" Lyle suggested.

Milani nodded to Randy, "Arrest him."

"Chief, the paramedics are here," Matt said. "The dogs won't let them anywhere near the injured man.

"I'll take care of it," West said, letting go of Yudi.

"Scooby's down," Aleta said. "I don't know if he's dead or not."

"I'll check," Lyle added. "You just keep working on calming Shadow."

When Lyle entered the house, he walked straight over to the injured man. Looking down at him, he snarled, "Tell me you didn't kill my dog's son."

"What the hell are you talking about?"

"The chocolate Lab. Tell me you didn't kill him."

The anger in the uniformed police chief frightened Tully. He began to sweat.

The dogs' growls deepened and their lips curled back again.

"I jabbed him with a tranquillizer dart. That's all."

"Dog-sized or elephant-sized?" came the question and Tully could see the fury in his eyes hadn't abated.

"I dunno," he replied looking around anxiously.

A whine from the other room calmed the angry chief as no words could have.

Lyle turned and called to the dog.

"Scooby, come here. Come on, Boy."

The chocolate Lab, wavering on his feet, made his way to Lyle who stooped to greet him.

"Chief, the other dogs?" one paramedic inquired.

"Okay Stoney, Babe, Keeper. Let's get a biscuit and then a walk." He turned and went into the kitchen. All the dogs followed him.

The paramedics loaded Tully on the stretcher. Lyle reentered the room. "Have you been arrested yet?"

Tully didn't know what to say.

"Put him down," Lyle ordered. "I need to arrest him."

"We need to take him now, Sir," one paramedic said.

"He's getting arrested first," Lyle determined. He called to the four dogs that were all at the door waiting for it to be opened and told them to sit.

All four sat immediately.

"What's your name?" Lyle asked the man on the stretcher.

"John Doe," came the reply.

"Okay, search him," Lyle ordered.

"Tully," Tully cried. "Tully Machi."

"Tully Machi, you're under arrest for attempted murder," Lyle said. He looked at the paramedics, "Did you guys search him?"

"No, that's not our job," one said.

"Never mind, I'll do it," Lyle said continuing to recite the Miranda spiel.

When he finished, the paramedics stared at the usual pocket contents plus a few not so usual–a knife, a small gun, and a tranquillizer dart.

They were relieved when West assigned Matt to accompany him.

Chapter 23

Early that same morning down in Florida, Paige stirred and Hawk woke.

"Are we alone?" she whispered, not looking around. She was curled up in Hawk's arm under a mound of blankets.

"Yes."

"I need to talk."

"Go ahead."

"You were almost killed."

"So were you."

"I think maybe you'd be better off if I left. In fact, everyone would be."

"Who's going to walk our dog?" Hawk asked.

"What?"

"All my life I've wanted a huge dog, but I need someone to be around to walk him when I can't."

"I'm not walking your dog."

"Okay. Our dog."

"You want me to stay when I bring so much danger?"

"I need someone to hang the curtains in our new house."

"Is that all I'm good for? Walking dogs and hanging curtains?" she asked, annoyed.

"You warm up the bed really nice."

"Hawk, I'm being serious!" she said sharply.

"I'm not making fun of you. But I'm on your father's list too now. Your leaving won't make it safe for me."

"But no one can protect us."

"Oh, really? Then how did we know to be ready?"

"Harriet?"

"They took the first hit."

"When are the Chesney's going to want to use their room?" Paige asked abruptly.

"What do you have in mind?"

"Finishing what we started."

"So we're done talking?"

"I'm dressed for another activity."

"You aren't dressed at all," he noted.

"Only two things to do in such a state. Take a hot bath is one."

"I can't think of the other," Hawk teased. "Give me a hint."

And she did.

Ten minutes later, Harriet found Dr. Chesney standing in the hallway outside his room.

"Why are you standing out here?" Harriet asked as Claude joined them.

"They asked for ten more minutes."

"So Paige is feeling better?" Harriet asked. She didn't expect a reply.

"They're going for our record," Claude remarked.

Harriet eyed him suspiciously. "What record?"

"Paige was worried about breaking him."

"Breaking him?"

"Hurting him."

"With sex?" Harriet said raising both eyebrows.

"So I told him to tell her we did it six times."

Harriet looked at her husband a bit annoyed. "It was seven."

"I knew it was a lot," Claude grinned.

"Whatever you do, don't tell Evelyn," Bernard warned them.

The door opened and Hawk stammered a greeting. Paige was still lying in bed.

"I need my razor," the doctor said.

"I need to update you two," Harriet put in.

"I was wrong," Claude announced, "I guess I lost count after six. It was seven."

Harriet whirled around, "For heaven's sake, Claude! That's not the update I meant!"

"It was seven by her count," Claude said. "She's better with numbers than I am."

"I called Aleta to tell her about last night. She said she'd been attacked."

Paige sat up abruptly. "What?"

Hawk rushed over and handed her a robe. She put it on quickly.

"She's fine, dear," Harriet replied evenly. "She shot the man in the knee and hand. But she should've killed him just as I should've done last night."

"He went after someone else?"

"He planted bombs in the field. Had a remote in his pocket," Harriet said. "Martha sent Lyle over to rescue her. Told him to hit a hundred or he'd never make it. He smashed one of Milani's cars on the way in. Aleta says they're arguing about who's going to pay for that."

"Why didn't West radio?" Hawk asked.

"Aleta would have argued with anyone but Lyle," Harriet explained. "She was following her own vision."

Hawk put his arm around Paige as he spoke, "Paige thinks she should split so the rest of us will be safe."

"That would be a bad move," Harriet said. "Hawk would pine for years. You'd break his heart."

Claude spoke up. "Harriet and I have been dodging bullets ever since we got married. It won't stop if you leave. Aleta..."

Harriet interrupted.

"She's not the only one at fault."

"She's not at fault at all!" Paige declared. "It's me."

"This time," Claude said. "With Aleta it's more continual. But not one of us wants her to leave. Same with you. Please stay."

"And neither of you is at fault," Harriet said. "The problem is in the people doing the attacking not in the ones being attacked. You remove one lamb from a flock and the wolf doesn't go away. He selects another lamb."

"The hotel gave you a new room," Harriet said. "I moved all your things over."

"What about the custody case?" Paige asked. "Will these attacks on us help any?"

"Not unless one of the men talks," Harriet said regretfully.

"DNA?" Hawk asked.

"The Penny in the home is not related to Paige, Tyler or Molly," Harriet reported, "but your father is a clever man. He will have an answer."

"We need to find the body to prove murder," Hawk added. "All we need is time."

"Aleta can get another continuation on the basis of the DNA," Harriet said. "We take one day at a time. I need the group to stay together. Are you two up for the visit to the water park?"

"She has a new bikini," Hawk said and smiled.

Back in Willow Glen, Aleta made an early morning visit to the hospital. Dr. Barre was in the room of Dr. Schwartzman. She scowled when she saw Aleta. Aleta merely nodded politely. She had forgotten that as a medical doctor, Reggie had access anytime she chose.

"I need to talk with you alone, Stanley," Aleta said.

"He can't leave," Dr. Schwartzman said to Reggie Barre, "Why not let me study your report before I comment. Give me an hour."

"Your son is coming this morning," Stanley reminded him.

"Do it now," Reggie demanded. "They can talk softly." Her tone was harsh and strident, her manner, officious.

"If they whisper, I can't hear them," Dr. Schwartzman commented, winking at Stanley who held up his hand, signaling Aleta to wait.

Dr. Schwartzman handed Reggie back the report. "On second thought I don't need to read this. I know you. I can tell by the way you bristled when Aleta walked in that you're really furious with her. I'm guessing you did something and she called you on it."

"There's more to it than that!" Reggie protested. "I want you to read my report."

"It's hogwash and you know it!" Dr. Schwartzman said. "You're a good psychiatrist, Reggie, when you've got your head on straight. You only get like this when you're dead wrong."

"Dr. Greenwood agrees with me," Reggie argued.

"Now I know your report is garbage," Dr. Schwartzman said. "If you can't read your own report objectively, analyze his."

"I came to you for help."

"And that's what I just gave you. Now, go."

"You've changed," Reggie said. "She's changed you."

"Yes, she has," Herve Schwartzman said smiling.

"I don't like the new you," Reggie remarked dourly.

"Less easy to manipulate, right?"

"Screw you!" Reggie said as she stormed out of the room.

"It's her favorite expression," Aleta observed. "I think she thinks it means goodbye."

"Oh, she'll be back," Dr. Schwartzman said. "Unfortunately."

"So what is it you wanted to tell us?" Stanley asked.

"This is privileged," Aleta said.

"He's my new shrink," Stanley responded. "He's going to teach me how to handle you."

"Handle me? Handle me? What did you tell him?"

"That you could get me to do anything you asked anytime you wanted to."

"That's not a trait I want changed."

"Maybe I do."

"Stanley, you have the ultimate authority in this marriage. That's never going to change."

"Lyle called," Stanley said. "He said you almost got killed trying to rescue some idiot who ignored your warning about planted bombs. He had to drive at breakneck speed, crash into one of Milani's squads, which Tom is pretty upset about, by the way, to tell you to get the hell out of the field. And he had to threaten you with a gun."

"All he had to do was say Martha sent him," Aleta said.

"She told him to shoot you to stop you."

"He wouldn't have done it."

"The problem is that he would have," Stanley said. "He apologized to me half a dozen times."

"But, he didn't shoot me."

"If you hadn't obeyed, he would have."

"But I did."

"I don't ever want you to take it upon yourself to rescue anyone again," Stanley said, "And that's an..."

"Before you say 'that's an order', I need you to make it clearer," Aleta countered. "I saved myself. I saved Gerard. You already ordered me to do that."

"Don't try to confuse me," Stanley said. "It won't work. You disobeyed that order and you know it."

"We've talked about directions from God," Aleta reminded him.

"God gave you the vision so you could warn the men. You did. He did not direct you to personally try to save the man who ignored your warning. You were so upset because the cop didn't obey you that you decided to take matters into your own hands and personally stop him."

"That's the method Lyle was going to use to stop me!" she argued.

"I'm not saying you chose a poor method," Stanley said. "I'm saying you ignored my order to protect yourself. Then you let your emotions take over. You got incensed and you acted foolishly. God Himself had to step in and stop you!"

"God knows me. He loves me," Aleta said defensively.

"He gave you me," Stanley countered.

"What's that suppose to mean?"

"I'm to tell you when you leave His will and substitute your will."

"And you'll know when I do that?" she queried with only a hint of derision.

"He gave me this great love for you. He had a reason. I have to believe He wanted me to act on that love."

"So you're going to order me to do what?"

"Not to personally move past what God asks."

"But..."

Stanley interrupted. "Don't 'but' me. You did that today. There was a wiser choice then the one you took."

"Wiser?" Aleta asked doubtfully. "Charlie wasn't listening to me. He was going to get himself killed."

"That's when you let him go and concentrate on ameliorating the damage his foolhardiness was about to cause to others. You don't join the fool in the mine field!"

"What others?" Aleta pressed. She wasn't ready yet to admit that Stanley was right. Hers had been a foolish move. Admitting that to Stanley would be bad enough but in the presence of Dr. Schwartzman made such capitulation abhorrent to every fiber of her being.

"Hubbs, the horses," Stanley said. "Did you even think about Hubbs being in danger?"

Aleta bowed her hand and began to cry.

"Oh, my God! Oh God! Forgive me. Oh please, God, forgive me. I am so sorry. I was being so self-righteous. I am so sorry."

She dropped to a chair beside Stanley's bed and, putting her head on her crossed arms, wept.

Dr. Schwartzman was astounded at the exchange, awed by it. These two dared to fight without once dipping to any of the basest levels, the levels where words are spoken that cut deep, leaving scars that often never heal.

They did honor to each other and even when Stanley won the argument, bitterness and resentment were not his reward. Instead, his wife fully acknowledged the truth he presented. Her regret washed them both clean.

No wonder God used this woman, Schwartzman thought. No wonder He saved her. He smiled at the thought of a police chief racing through two towns at a hundred miles an hour, cornering so violently that he smacked a parked police car and yet not hitting a single other car or person. He smiled at all the stalled cars and flat tires God had to produce to clear the way for the chief's reckless dash to obey one prophet and save another. It was a testament to Lyle West's belief in these prophets that he obeyed without hesitation.

Dr. Schwartzman was glad he sent Dr. Barre away. She would have ruined this.

I'm beginning to make good choices, he thought.

He lay back and waited for the next episode.

Chapter 24

Aleta cried for a quarter of an hour. Stanley didn't try to comfort her. He just waited.

Puzzled, Dr. Schwartzman waited with him. Dr. Barre would have said Stanley was a cold fish, that he didn't love his wife. Dr. Schwartzman had listened to the love embedded in his argument. He loved her. Why then didn't he comfort her?

The answer came almost immediately after he posed the question.

Aleta raised her head.

Tears streaming down her face, she sobbed out her apology to him. "I didn't think. I'm so sorry I disobeyed you. I was so angry, I didn't think. I can't believe I did that. I forgot your order. I can't believe I forgot. I can't believe I broke my promise. Will you ever trust me again?"

That was when Stanley gathered his wife into his arms and held her. She cried on his shoulder for another five minutes.

Finally, as the sobbing subsided, Stanley said. "You cried four times as long when you were asking God's forgiveness."

She choked back a sob and reared back. "Stanley, He's God!"

He looked at her and grinned. "That's a perfect argument."

She pummeled his chest with her fists.

"Don't do that!"

"What?"

"Make jokes."

"That was no joke," he said. "Now, calm down. He forgives you. I forgive you. We start over."

"But I messed up."

"My stars, Aleta! Do you know how staunch you've been in obeying me? How determined you've been? How much you have honored and delighted me each time? Even I didn't see this as your disobeying my order until Lyle called. I saw you as bent on saving the life of a recalcitrant cop. That's what I saw. But the same God who parted the traffic so Lyle could speed to your rescue gave him the words to wake me to what you had done."

"You could've just said, 'that's okay, God. I understand.'"

Stanley raised his eyebrows in mock surprise.

"Alright. You couldn't say that," Aleta acquiesced. "Yes, you were right in taking me to task even when you knew how devastated I would be by the truth...and don't tell me that the truth will set me free. I don't feel free. I'm loaded under more guilt than I've ever felt before."

"So you believe God is a liar?"

"Stanley! How can you say that?"

"And you think I am too?"

"That's not true!"

"But you're clinging to guilt."

"You think I should just forget what I did."

"I'm not going to tell you that what you did was noble. You are already clinging to that thought to assuage the pain you feel. It was a foolish act. You acted recklessly. You acted contrary to my will and God's will. If you had stayed,

Machi would never have set off the bombs. Your so-called act of bravery actually brought about the explosion."

To Herve Schwartzman's surprise, Aleta didn't burst into tears anew.

"Ugh!" she grunted. "Can't even wash my stupidity away with the tiniest noble thought can I?"

"We won't let you," Stanley declared.

"So how do I get over feeling like I betrayed you?"

"You accept my forgiveness and my love," Stanley said.

"That's all?"

"Well, then you accept God's forgiveness, or vice versa."

Aleta was silent for several minutes. Her head was bowed. Both men knew she was praying.

When she looked up again, she said. "Okay we start over. Remind me again of your new order."

"You remember the old one?"

"The new one supersedes it, doesn't it? It's broader in scope, isn't it?"

Stanley thought for a moment. "Yes it is."

"Whatever it is, I'll obey it," Aleta said.

"I don't want you to personally move past what God wants you to do. That's the new order. You check with Him. If He tells you it's dangerous, you listen to Him just as you wanted that cop to listen to you."

Aleta nodded.

"Now, what's bothering you about the case?"

"He's going to get away," Aleta said. "He'll put up some excuse for why the Penny in the home isn't his daughter. And he'll demand an investigation."

"He'll get a continuance," Stanley said, "and he'll split."

"You don't think he'll have an alternative in place? I can't believe he wasn't called when Ed showed up at the Home the first time. He's been one step ahead of me the whole time."

"If that's true," Stanley said, "then he could know about the DNA testing."

"Hawk wouldn't have told him," Aleta objected.

"But the lab guy that works with him, that guy that Hawk says is careless, he might have told him there was a test in progress. He'd know not to tell anyone the results, but Van Horne doesn't need the results."

"So, he'll be waiting for me," Aleta said. "He wants custody of Paige. What would happen if he manages to persuade the judge that he is a victim and he needs the opportunity to convince Paige?"

"Judge Jacobi would give him custody and send him to Florida," Stanley predicted. "Van Horne's lawyer knows that. Judge Jacobi is high on reconciliation."

"I know," Aleta said. "How do I fight that possibility?"

"You think of another approach."

"There's none left," Aleta said. "It's not like he's a deadbeat dad."

"You know," Stanley said. "There's support and then there's support. What did Tyler tell us David said about college?"

"That his father wouldn't send him."

"It's not as if it would be a hardship," Stanley said. "He'd hardly notice the cost."

"Since the custody agreement was secret, what if Van Horne got his wife to accept minimal support or less?" Aleta posed.

"That would explain the modest house and the old car. I wonder what else they did without."

"It's not that," Aleta put in. "It's that children who've lived as children of wealthy parents are suppose to be maintained in that style after a divorce."

"That's all past history," Stanley said. "He's not going to stint on them once they're his again."

"I need to go," Aleta said.

She kissed Stanley lightly.

"I love you," she said. "Take care of Dr. Schwartzman for me."

"What are you going to do with Van Horne?" Stanley asked.

"Outflank him."

Chapter 25

Aleta hurried back to her office and called in both associates.

"We are taking a new tack. As advocates for Tyler and Molly, you will see they get what's due them before Kurt Van Horne slips out of the country."

"You know he's leaving?" Chin asked.

"Ed's checking on that now."

"So what do you want us to do?"

"Research the child support agreements in divorce settlements where the husband is as wealthy as Van Horne," Aleta said. "Stanley will tell you where to look."

"Then what?"

"Write a brief demanding back payment of the amount you figure is due each child," Aleta said. "Work on this as a team. The hearing starts at two."

"Anything else," Jackson asked.

"I need to find Penny's body," Aleta said.

"Look in the cemetery," Jackson returned. "That's where most bodies are buried."

"Are you being factitious?"

"This guy is really smart," Jackson said. "He's counting on you to think he buried it in some clever place. The Purloined Letter scenario."

"Dr. Schwartzman said she loved that baby," Aleta said. "She would have had priorities as a mother."

"Like what?" Chin asked.

"Custody of the children," Aleta said, "and proper burial of her baby."

"Not child support?" Chin asked.

"She traded," Aleta said. "Her life, her children's lives for her silence."

"He would have insisted the child be buried with another name."

"Van Horne wouldn't have let her use his last name or hers," Jackson said.

"What's her mother's maiden name?"

"Tyler," Chin said. "That's where Tyler's name came from."

"It's a place to start," Aleta said.

"You'll need a court order to exhume the body," Chin pointed out.

"But you'll never get that unless you can prove it's Penny Van Horne," Jackson added. "And you need to exhume the body to prove it is Penny Van Horne."

"You just do your jobs," Aleta said. "I'm counting on you two to make your case."

"Yes, Ma'am," the two associates chorused.

Aleta heard them discussing their project enthusiastically.

An hour later Aleta requested a meeting with Chief West. When Lyle got the message, he was shocked.

"Requested?" he asked the dispatcher. "She requested?"

"She said it was important. She desperately needs your advice."

"Tell her I'll see her as soon as she can get here."

"She's here," the dispatcher said.

"Send her up," Lyle said, smiling. "And get hold of French. Tell him I want to see him ASAP."

Aleta breezed in shortly afterward. "I've never been to your office. What a great view of the city!"

"One end of it anyway," West said. "I inherited the window. It is rather grand. Not too many captain's offices have a picture window."

"Let me not waste your time," Aleta said. "I have reason to believe there's been a murder."

"The Van Horne baby?"

"Yes," Aleta said. "She's not in the Home, she's in Oakwood Cemetery."

"Oakwood? Why there? Why not in one north of Chicago, near where the Van Horne estate is?"

"Too close to home," Aleta replied. "I think that's why Mary chose to settle in Arborville."

"So what is your problem?"

"Jurisdiction," Aleta said. "The murder wasn't committed here. The custody hearing is being handled here because this is where the children live."

"The county Van Horne lives in would have jurisdiction," Lyle replied. "That's Lake County."

"Does the fact that the body is here make a difference?"

"It would if the body were found here, but it wasn't."

"So Lake County would have to investigate?"

"Yes. But there are good people over there."

"The Van Hornes are politically influential," Aleta said. "The Sheriff is an elected official."

"Don't assume he's in their pocket," West scolded.

"Sorry," Aleta said. "I did do that, didn't I?"

"Even if it were in my jurisdiction, the exhumation and autopsy would take days even if we rushed it."

The light on West's phone blinked. He pressed a button. "Send French in."

He turned to Aleta, "Remember that drug case of yours?"

"Dr. Matsuki?"

"Remember how angry I got when the DEA arrested Lauren thinking she was you?"

"You arrested everyone you even suspected of drug offenses."

"It turned out to be one huge unplanned raid. No chance of a leak. It was based on my anger only," Lyle recounted. "And it was more fruitful than any staged raid we ever undertook. Here's French. I'll let him fill you in."

"We're almost there," French said. "I have a couple loose ends to tie up."

Aleta looked puzzled.

Lyle smiled. "Remember when you casually mentioned that David's death might not have been an accident."

"You've been working on that?" she asked, taken aback.

"French has been on it full-time ever since the arson," Lyle said. "I figure then that Van Horne had decided to clean up loose ends so I began my own investigation."

"Do you know where the baby is buried?"

"No. I decided since you were paying Ed to search for her," West said with a wry smile, "I'd concentrate on the current crimes in my own town. That reminds me. Did Stanley talk to you yet?"

"Yes, he did. And I apologize for putting you in such... er...trouble with Chief Milani."

"The car?" Lyle chuckled. "We both decided it was your fault so we're charging you for the damage. Didn't Stanley tell you?"

"Stanley never tells me about money matters. He just handles them," Aleta responded. "How close are you to an arrest?"

"A week maybe."

"Can you arrest him on suspicion?" Aleta asked.

"Not yet," French said. "The case is too weak. He'd be out in an hour. And we'd compromise our investigation."

"If you can tell me he's about to flee," West put in, "then we'd chance it."

"Ed's working on that. Van Horne hasn't booked himself on any commercial airlines," Aleta reported.

"Then get us more time," Lyle said. "Work your magic."

"Why does everyone keep telling me to do that?" Aleta retorted. "It's not magic. It's research and there's not enough time."

"Don't try to nail him," Lyle advised. "Go for a continuation. Give us time to do our job."

Aleta went back to the office and called Ed. "Anything?"

"No flight plans to Orlando or out of the country," Ed reported. "I did find something. Van Horne's a real miser. You know who's footing the support bill on the kids? Get this! His mother."

"Out of a trust fund she set up for him?" Aleta asked.

"Nope. Straight from her. His name ain't on the account."

"Does he have any money or does she control all the family monies?"

"You want I should find out?"

"Yes. And any other financial info you can dig up. I want it all," Aleta said. "I'll be working at the house until the hearing. Get me everything you find by one o'clock."

"He's legit–just stingy as hell."

"That's what I'm counting on."

Aleta called Hawk on his cell.

"Are you between rides? Can we talk?"

"We're at Blizzard Beach," Harriet responded. "Hawk and Paige are in line for the Slush Gusher. It's a ride not a drink. I'm holding his phone."

Forty minutes later, Hawk called back.

"Paige with you?"

"What do you want me to ask her?"

"Did her mother's insurance pay for her funeral?" Aleta asked. "Ask her about her brother's funeral expenses too."

"David took out a loan for their mother's funeral. Tyler emptied the bank account and pawned two of their mother's rings and a necklace to pay for David's."

"Thanks," Aleta said. "One more question. This time for you. Tully Machi was arrested for attacking me. MacMurray went over his car. He said it was clean."

"Don't believe him," Hawk said. "Tell Natsumi Genjo to go over it again. Tell her that you and I touched a lot of things in that house."

"Thanks, Hawk."

Chapter 26

Ten minutes before two o'clock, Aleta met her two associates outside Judge Jacobi's courtroom.

"Andrew, you will be first again," Aleta said. "I will probably be handed a copy of the original custody agreement between Van Horne and his ex-wife. You talk while I read."

"And what should I do?" Roland Chin asked.

Aleta handed him a sheet of paper.

"You get Tyler out of debt."

Roland glanced at the paper. "Wow!"

"Andrew is going for an increase in child support retroactive. You, Roland, are going for a reimbursement for monies the children put out when there were insurance policies in place. These are his children, Gentlemen. Today is when he pays financially."

"Do you want me to go all the way for the child support or turn it over to Roland to close?"

"Read the judge," Aleta said. "Go with your gut."

After the lawyers were seated, Stephanie Nash presented the original custody agreement. The judge asked Aleta if she needed time to study it.

"We can proceed, Your Honor. Mr. Jackson has an important matter to bring before the court."

Given permission, Jackson rose. Citing child support settlements awarded to children in Kurt Van Horne's socio-economic bracket Jackson argued that Mr. Van Horne should pay his children the difference between what was paid and what should have been paid. He then presented his calculation for Molly and asked that this amount be placed in a trust fund with the court as trustee.

Stephanie Nash after receiving objection from Van Horne, rose and stated that Mr. Van Horne would make up for any deprivation once he became custodian.

Jackson countered by stating that Mr. Van Horne had circumvented the court's judgment ten years ago. He cannot 'make-up' as he says for the deprivation Molly has suffered. What he can do is show his daughter he loves her enough to put money in a trust fund for her. What he can do is accept the consequences of his penuriousness in her early years. What I want for my twelve-year-old client is to see the court award her what is due 'her plus the cost of my having to demand it."

Aleta was startled by the last phrase, but she had told him to go with his gut. He was asking for a penalty.

Stephanie Nash was arguing furiously with her client. Aleta knew she was telling him he couldn't win on this.

Roland Chin rose. "If Your Honor will allow me, I have another financial request on behalf of Tyler."

He presented and reviewed his calculations for Tyler which were substantially higher than Molly's telling the court that Tyler would have spent four years in the prep school his father planned to send him to. He argued that his delay in going for custody was a parsimonious act on his part if, as he claimed, he wanted custody of his children all along.

"Moreover," Chin said, "even though there were life insurance policies on both Mary Van Horne and David Van Horne, with Mr. Van Horne as the beneficiary, he let his sons carry the full burden of both funerals. Tyler is saddled with debt for both. I'm asking that Tyler be reimbursed for this expense as well as for the child support difference owed him. In addition, as Tyler has proven to be an outstanding scholar and cannot qualify for financial aid with so wealthy a father,

I'm requesting that Mr. Van Horne set aside in a trust fund enough money for Tyler to attend the college of his choice."

Stephanie Nash rose. "Mr. Van Horne would like to be heard at this time. I would like a recess to confer with my client."

Aleta kept a straight face. They had hit a nerve.

"Fifteen minutes," the judge ordered.

She picked up the custody agreement and retired to her chambers.

Stephanie Nash took her client outside.

Aleta shared the agreement with her two associates who read it avidly.

When they finished, she said, "We will study this document further tonight. This afternoon we have two goals. We want retroactive child support and a continuance. Right now his lawyer is telling him to agree to pay and he is thinking of a way out, but I have a little surprise for Mr. Van Horne that will separate him from his money."

When the court was reconvened, Kurt Van Horne took the stand. Stephanie Nash led him carefully through his explanation. The child support payments were what his wife requested. He didn't know there was any insurance policy on his wife's life. The one in which he was beneficiary was meant to pay him back for a loan he had made so she could make a down payment on her house. As for Tyler's college education, he would pay that when the time came.

"And what about David's insurance policy?" Stephanie Nash said.

"I intended to turn that money over to Tyler as soon as he asked for it."

"Why didn't you approach him?"

"I figured that when I got custody, I would, of course, take care of the funeral bills," Kurt Van Horne said.

"So what do you suggest?" Stephanie Nash asked.

"I'm willing to pay fifty thousand dollars into each child's trust fund at the rate of five thousand dollars per year.

It took me ten years to accumulate this debt. I don't think it is unreasonable to ask for ten years to repay it."

"Mrs. Praetzel, Mr. Jackson, Mr. Chin, do you accept Mr. Van Horne's offer?" Judge Jacobi asked.

Aleta rose.

"If Your Honor would permit me to ask a few questions, I believe we can come to an understanding."

"Proceed," Judge Jacobi ordered.

"Mr. Van Horne, who has been paying the child support payments these past ten years?"

"I have."

"Judge Jacobi, please instruct the witness what the penalty is for lying under oath," Aleta said and then waited.

Judge Jacobi explained what perjury was and what the penalties were. Kurt Van Horne was incensed over being treated as if he were unaware of the law. He glared at his attorney who sat listening attentively to every word the judge uttered, hoping her client would take the hint and do the same. It didn't happen.

When she finished, Aleta thanked her politely and repeated the question.

Kurt Van Horne hesitated and then said coolly, "You might say my mother."

"Do you have your own savings account, checking account, money market accounts, stocks, bonds, real estate holdings?"

"Yes."

"Is your mother a co-signer on any promissory note you've executed?"

"I don't need a cosigner," Van Horse huffed.

"Currently, how much money, give or take a thousand dollars, do you have in your checking account?"

"I currently have three hundred fifty-seven thousand dollars."

"And in your savings account?"

"Is this necessary?" he asked his tone laced with derision as if Aleta was asking permission to unzip his fly.

"Answer the question," Aleta responded evenly.

He hesitated, waiting for his lawyer to object. When she didn't he said icily,

"Two hundred thousand."

"Why would you have more in your checking than savings?" Aleta asked, her tone implying neither censure nor suspicion."

"I have upcoming expenses," Kurt Van Horne replied.

"Does the amount in these two accounts represent less than one percent of your holdings?"

"Do I have to answer that?" Van Horne asked, his fury boiling up beneath his cool exterior. He glared at his lawyer.

Aleta kept the floor.

"If Your Honor wishes, I can present the court with a financial statement outlining Mr. Van Horne's known holdings tomorrow."

Van Horne accepted his defeat stoically.

"Yes! That is true," he acceded.

"Is it fair to say part of the reason you are wealthy is because you are skilled in the manipulation of money."

"Yes, it is," he replied readily, his mind wondering why she would leave him an open door to walk through.

"Therefore, what your offer represents requires a capital investment of three hundred thousand which is what we asked for. Properly invested, however, these monies will return you at least fifteen thousand dollars a year and after ten years, you will still have the capital. Is that not so?"

"But I won't have the interest," Van Horne said smugly. "I will be out that money."

"But you will still be ahead," Aleta responded watching his eyes carefully. "You will be ahead because you had the loan of that money, interest free for ten years."

She saw acknowledgement in his eyes while his jaw remained set.

She continued, "What I propose is that you pay not only the three hundred thousand up front, but that you also pay seventy-five thousand in interest for the use of the money for the past ten years. That is a measly five percent per year."

"That's too high. That interest rate is calculated incorrectly. It is outrageously inflated," Kurt Van Horne protested. "This women has no head for numbers, Your Honor. She pulled that figure out of a hat. It should not even be considered!"

"Your Honor, my calculations are correct," Aleta said firmly. "And I hope the court will not be sidetracked in this. Please let me remind the court that Mr. Van Horne has not personally paid one cent in child support of any kind. In addition, he has given no gifts for any occasion in ten years. There is nothing in the custody agreement that precluded him from giving his children gifts, yet he chose not to. He has not offered to pay for music lessons or summers at camp or private schools for any of his children, which he now says, are their due. Because, Mr. Van Horne appears to be reluctant to share his wealth with his children, we wish to take this opportunity to see that a mere six-tenths of one percent of his income be put in a trust fund for his children. Should he die tomorrow, they would not be penniless. This way their future education is guaranteed. In this matter we do, however, have one concern. We do not believe Mr. Van Horne will willingly part with any funds no matter what the ruling."

Aleta sat down, signifying that she was done.

"Have you any more questions for this witness, Counselor?" the judge asked.

Aleta rose. "Yes, Your Honor, but my colleagues do not. This is a matter of utmost importance and they want to be assured that the children they represent will have a financially secure future. I would like to deal with the other custody issues after this is resolved."

Judge Jacobi announced a fifteen-minute recess. She made a single phone call and then painstakingly forged her

         Susan Davis Sandberg

decision. It was simple and brief. It was more difficult to overturn a simple decision.

All were waiting when she returned.

She looked straight at Aleta. "Do you have the trust funds for the children set up?"

Aleta's heart skipped a beat.

"Yes, Your Honor."

Judge Jacobi nodded and then announced her ruling.

"Mr. Van Horne, for ten years you have woefully neglected the financial well-being of your children. When parents divorce, it is not the children's fault.

"They, therefore, should not be made to suffer. They are in fact to be supported in the manner to which they were accustomed. You failed to do this. Consequently, the court orders you to pay the following to each of your three living children known as Tyler, Paige and Molly, the sum of one hundred ninety thousand dollars as past due child support including interest, plus four hundred thousand dollars for future educational expenses."

Van Horne stood up. "I refuse to put aside any money for future expenses. I reserve the right to decide if they go and where they go when the time approaches."

Stephanie tried to hush her client several times, to no avail.

"You're in contempt," Judge Jacobi said. "Sit down. I'm not finished."

Finally, Stephanie prevailed and Kurt Van Horne sat down.

"As for the minor requests, such as, payment of funeral expenses, Mr. Van Horne is not liable for those. The law does not require a spouse to pay for his ex-wife's expenses and he is entitled to keep any insurance monies as named beneficiary. He is not required to share them."

Stephanie was whispering in Van Horne's ear. Aleta could tell he was beginning to relax. That part of the ruling was a giant win in his eyes. She kept her countenance respectful and hoped her associates were following her lead.

Fortunately, both young men were so stunned by the major victory that they didn't react at all to the minor adjustments to the total monies owed by Van Horne. When each of the associates looked over at their boss, they patterned their response after hers.

"Finally," Judge Jacobi stated, "while no mention was made of the debt owed to the eldest son, David, now deceased, the court notes for the record that monies were owed to him as well. Not only was he deprived of proper support, but also, by virtue of Kurt Van Horne's inaction, he was deprived of a college education and forced to take the role of the parent. I therefore award him a sum equal to that of his siblings."

Stephanie Nash was hastily assuring her client that that was a mere gesture. Parents inherited from their children in the absence of a will.

The judge rapped her gavel and Stephanie immediately resumed her attentive posture. The judge continued.

"Because, in the absence of a will, the parents inherit from the children, I am ordering that David's portion be paid to the law firm of Praetzel, Locke and Praetzel as the total fee for their services."

"Thank you, Your Honor," Aleta said politely.

"Mr. Van Horne, are you prepared to comply with the court order?" Judge Jacobi asked.

Kurt Van Horne rose. "I am not. It is an outrageous ruling and I intend to fight it."

"I can hold you in contempt," Judge Jacobi said.

"Then do it!" Kurt Van Horne challenged.

"Bailiff, take Mr. Van Horne into custody."

"Mrs. Praetzel, have the appropriate paperwork submitted to my office by ten o'clock tomorrow morning."

"You can't take my money?" Van Horne asked, shocked.

"Legally, I'm allowed."

"You can't!" he protested. "I'll sue!"

"Bailiff, remove Mr. Van Horne," Judge Jacobi said. "This custody hearing will resume at two o'clock tomorrow afternoon."

As they were leaving the courtroom, Stephanie Nash hissed at Aleta, "It's not over."

Aleta eyed her coolly, "I'm aware of that."

"I will get him back his money," she said. "And we will get custody of those children as well."

"We know that the Penny Van Horne in the Home is not Kurt Van Horne's daughter," Aleta said.

"Everything is not always what it seems," Stephanie warned.

"I can't see him wiggling out of that one," Aleta said. "He committed perjury."

"He is not a liar," Stephanie insisted. "He proved it in court today when he admitted honestly that he would not pay the outrageous sums the judge demanded."

"He is both mean and miserly," Aleta retorted. "And tomorrow I will prove him a liar."

When the two parted, Jackson asked Aleta, "What was that about?"

"It was an exchange of information," Aleta said. "She knows we're going to present the DNA evidence tomorrow and I know she is going to sue to have the award overturned."

"The money will be tied up for years," Roland predicted.

"The money will be transferred at ten tomorrow morning," Aleta said. "It will go into irrevocable trust funds, except for our portion."

"But you are only delivering the paperwork," Chin said.

Aleta smiled, "The president of Signet Bank will accompany me to explain what needs to be done. He will see that the transfer is complete before court reconvenes tomorrow."

"And why will he do this?" Chin asked.

"Because the three trust funds will be handled by his bank," Aleta explained.

"So we won?" Chin asked.

"Can't the court break an irrevocable trust?" Jackson said.

"It can. That's why tomorrow is critical. We won a battle today, but not the war. Tomorrow Stephanie will admit that her client is a skinflint, but even skinflints should be allowed to rear their children. There was never any evidence that when the children lived with him before that they were not properly cared for. Tomorrow will be our most difficult battle."

Chapter 27

A little after five Aleta dropped in on her husband.

"We got five hundred ninety thousand apiece," Aleta announced. "We asked for less. I assured Chin and Jackson that the money was secure. But is it?"

"Have you got it yet?"

"Tomorrow at ten," Aleta replied. "Van Horne's in jail for contempt. Court reconvenes at two."

"You set up irrevocable trusts?"

"Yes, but if the decision is overturned..."

"You know the old adage: Possession is nine-tenths of the law. We have the advantage. We can appeal as well."

"It's not all in irrevocable trusts," Aleta said. "You can't set up a trust for a dead person. Because Van Horne would inherit David's settlement, she is giving it to us as our fee."

"You accepted, I hope," Stanley assumed tentatively.

"Yes. After Chin asked for it in his presentation, I couldn't turn it down."

"Well, I'm giving him a bonus!" Stanley declared.

"Don't you dare leave Jackson out," Aleta scolded.

"Yes, Ma'am!" Stanley quipped.

"So what's our next move?" Aleta asked.

"You're lead counsel."

"Who's been busy all day capturing bad guys, being chewed out by a superior, guiding two associates into a brilliant performance and personally putting on the finishing touches that earned us five hundred and ninety thousand."

"So you've been busy," Stanley acknowledged.

"While you've been lying in bed nursing a sore leg."

"So?"

"So, it's your leg that's been injured, not your brain. I know it's been mulling over our next move, so spit it out."

"I'd rather you told me what you had in mind," Stanley responded.

"Not today. I'm all used up," Aleta groused.

"Your brain is never used up. It's probably in hyper drive right now."

"Don't fuss with a tired, pregnant woman. Give."

"Present a petition from the Chesneys requesting that they be considered as foster parents."

"And Paige?" Aleta asked. "I can't believe Van Horne doesn't know she's married."

"He's waiting for you to bring it up, so he can petition for an annulment, so don't mention it," Stanley said. "Start with the DNA. Let Van Horne waste time explaining that. Get your points in then. Hammer away at why the custody agreement didn't list him. Don't expect a confession or anything damaging. Just buy the police another day. And keep yourself in the ballgame. Stephanie will try to get rid of you."

"I understand. I need to go now."

"So soon?"

"Unlike you I have work to do," Aleta said.

"You are taking care of yourself, aren't you?" Stanley asked.

"I wish you were home. I miss you dreadfully."

"Why are you leaving then?"

"Because I want so much not to."

"Then stay."

"Can't."

"At least kiss me goodbye properly."

Aleta leaned over and took his head in her hands and kissed him with such tenderness, he thought seriously of quitting the bed and forfeiting his leg if that were the consequences of him insisting on going home with her.

She pulled back and said, "You will not come home with me. You will stay put and get well. That, my dearest husband, is an order."

He didn't speak for a long time after she left.

Herve Schwartzman chuckled. "I see she's righted the ship."

"You could say that," Stanley said. "She likes to boss me around and so I let her."

"Yours is a complicated relationship," Herve remarked. "What I just saw tells me she's boss. What I saw this morning tells me you are. So who is?"

Stanley smiled. "As you said, it's complicated."

"She is."

When Aleta arrived home, she smelled something wonderful cooking on the stove. Jamara emerged from the nursery and announced that she had arranged to stay the night.

"I can handle things," Aleta said, "but I appreciate the gesture."

"Mr. Praetzel asked me to stay. Tomorrow be a tough day for you."

"Yes, my toughest," Aleta said. "Let me make one phone call then I'll be ready to eat."

As they sat at the table, the two began to talk.

"Are you staying to watch Gerard for a concussion as well?" Aleta asked abruptly.

"He be bruised," Jamara said. "The doctor says to monitor him."

"For how long?"

"Twenty-four hours."

"Oh," Aleta said in a small voice. "I don't think I had a choice."

"Don't be thinking it be worse than it be."

"You will wake me if you notice anything, won't you?"

"Yes, Ma'am," Jamara promised. "Mr. Praetzel say you be in bed early."

"I need to walk the dogs," Aleta said. "It'll help me sleep."

"He be worried," Jamara told her.

"I won't be long," Aleta promised.

Half an hour later, Aleta was asleep.

When the phone rang, Jamara answered it.

"She be sleeping," Jamara responded when the caller asked to speak to Mrs. Praetzel.

"Well, wake her," the voice demanded. "This is important."

"Who be this?"

"None of your damned business!" the harsh voice sputtered. "Just put her on the phone!"

"I ain't wakin' her for the likes of you," Jamara said and hung up.

The phone rang a few minutes later.

"I need to speak to Mrs. Praetzel. This is Dr. Trattner."

Jamara recognized the voice from the prior call.

"I be sorry, Doctor. She be sleeping," Jamara reiterated.

"This is important," he insisted, an edge to his tone.

"Her sleepin' be more important," Jamara responded firmly.

"Do I have to come over there?" he said his anger breaking through. "If I do, you'll be sorry."

"Be a waste a time," Jamara replied. "You won't be seeing her until tomorrow."

"Don't tell me what I can or can't do!" he spat out.

The phone went dead.

Jamara went out and told the guards an angry man was coming. "He be a doctor. Don't be letting him disturb Mrs. Praetzel."

"No, Ma'am," Gary said.

Jamara smiled. She liked being called ma'am.

In the morning Jamara told Aleta she had a phone call the prior night.

"He be one pissed doctor," she reported. "Dr. Trattner."

"We're suing him, not us personally, our client."

"He come here," Jamara said. "The cops sent him packin'."

"You did the right thing," Aleta said. "Thank you."

"Gerard seem fine this morning," Jamara remarked.

"Do you need to check back home this morning? I can work at home until nine thirty."

Jamara smiled. "I told my daughter 'bout that girl you be representing, how she care for her brother 'n sister for two years."

Aleta smiled. "Next she'll want to get married and go to Disney World."

"I gotta die first."

Aleta chuckled. "I've got a dilemma. Maybe you can help me think it through."

"Sure."

"I know Paige is married, but not really. I'm sure Lydia pulled it off, but I haven't received any official notification yet. It's a technicality, but I've been hiding behind it because I'm afraid if I tell the judge, Stephanie will argue that since I'm Paige's lawyer I should step aside."

"You gots to tell her," Jamara responded. "Judge's be people. People don't like being on the outside when a door be shut."

"You're right," Aleta said. "I guess I'll be going to the office after all. I've got to prep Chin."

But Roland Chin had distressing news. "Dr. Trattner called our client last night. He told Ronda Lunt that he had researched her case and he had a therapy that would help her immediately. He insisted on an arbitration meeting today. She agreed. It's at one o'clock."

"The Van Horne hearing's at two," Aleta said.

"I got hold of Trattner's lawyer," Chin said. "She said Trattner wouldn't budge on the time. She said to tell you its 'quid pro quo'."

"Be sure to thank Dr. Trattner," Aleta said. "Tell him I appreciated his favor."

"What favor?"

"I needed to take your place today representing Tyler. You have a legitimate emergency that takes precedence. Your client is in physical pain and her doctor is withholding medical help ending a resolution of her suit."

"I want to be at the hearing," Roland said.

"I was planning to prep you, but this is better. You aren't really ready to take on Stephanie Nash."

"Dr. Trattner's lawyer is Lorraine Geer. Am I more ready to take her on?" Chin asked. "There's a lot of money on the table. And Ronda Lunt is a friend of Bessie Dobbins and you promised her you'd represent her."

"Geer as in Nash, Geer and Kuchera?"

"The same."

Aleta grimaced. "She planned this. Stephanie wants me pulled off onto another case. She knows that Robert is out of town and Stanley's in the hospital. She knows the Lunt case is a big one."

"What do we do?" Roland asked.

"Are you prepared?" countered Aleta.

"Yes, but I'm not experienced enough," Roland said. "I know, with less experience, you breezed in and won big, but I'm not you. I need help."

"Take all your materials and go over to the hospital. Let Stanley prep you," Aleta said.

"This isn't a child advocacy case," Roland mentioned a bit apprehensively.

"He chooses to be a child advocate but not because he couldn't be as fine a lawyer as his father or his mother but because he believes children need the finest representatives. He is a brilliant lawyer."

"I'm sorry. I didn't mean to disparage his ability," Roland apologized. "I'm suffering from the first stages of panic."

"While I know Dr. Trattner," Aleta said, "guess who knows him better?"

"What's knowing the doctor have to do with the case?" Roland asked.

"Hey, Man," Andrew Jackson butted in. "Why do you suppose we gutted Kurt Van Horne yesterday? We attacked his Achilles heel, not Stephanie Nash's."

"Stanley's roommate in the hospital is a former patient, a client of ours, Dr. Herve Schwartzman," Aleta said.

Roland's face brightened.

"One piece of advice," Aleta said. "Make sure that the medication is administered before any talking begins. Ronda Lunt needs to be pain-free to negotiate."

"I understand," Roland said.

"Just remember that you are the one that got us our fee. Now I need to go to the bank so we will get that fee. I'll be escorting Guy Stevens to Judge Jacobi's office so don't expect me back before noon. Jackson, you prepare an argument to place the children in foster care with the Chesneys. Did the paperwork come from Judge Davis?"

"The faxes were waiting when we arrived," Andrew said.

"Did she send a copy of the marriage license?"

"No."

"Check with both Tom and Lyle and with Ed. See if anyone can give you any basis for foster care at this time.

Get Social Services to pass on the Chesneys. Call Stanley. He has a contact."

"Isn't he supposed to be resting?" Andrew asked.

"Just his leg. His brain works fine," Aleta replied. "We need a break soon or we're going to lose this case."

Chapter 28

At precisely two o'clock, Aleta Praetzel and Andrew Jackson took their seats in Judge Jacobi's courtroom.

Norma Jacobi's eyebrows asked her question for her.

Aleta rose and apologized for Mr. Chin's absence. She announced that she would represent Paige and Tyler at that day's hearing. The judge was noticeably upset and Aleta hastened to assure her that only the most extreme and unchangeable of circumstances prevented Mr. Chin from appearing.

"Your explanation better be a good one," Judge Jacobi said.

"I'm afraid I cannot give you one," Aleta said.

"I could have Mr. Chin arrested on a contempt charge."

"If Your Honor wishes to do that, please arrest me. I ordered Mr. Chin to fulfill our firm's obligations to this other client."

"At the end of today's session, you will be incarcerated. I won't leave the children underrepresented any more than they already are."

"Thank you, Your Honor," Aleta said. "May I inform the court at this time that, while I don't have any formal documentation, it has been affirmed that my client, Paige Roach Van Horne, married Hawkins Monroe the day before yesterday."

"A minor who was in the care of Social Services got married and I wasn't informed?"

"It appears that that happened," Aleta said.

Stephanie rose. "Opposing counsel knew about it. Her mother and father-in-law flew the couple up here."

"That is true, Your Honor," Aleta acknowledged. "Hawkins Monroe, as you know is the area's leading forensic scientist. He came up to personally start the DNA testing on the Penny Van Horne in the Home and compare that DNA with samples from the supposed siblings. Here are the results. The child in the Home is not Penny Van Horne."

Judge Jacobi scanned the sheets, and then scowled at Aleta.

"First tell me you didn't plan this marriage," Judge Jacobi said.

"No, Your Honor, I only suspected that Judge Davis might be bringing that about. She, however, didn't tell me."

"Did you send her down there for that purpose?"

Aleta smiled wryly. "I would never even have considered that. I do not know how this marriage came about."

"Maybe a couple of nights in jail will refresh your memory," Judge Jacobi said.

"May I first ask Mr. Van Horne to answer some questions about the custody agreement?"

"You are not going to ask Mr. Van Horne to explain the DNA results?"

"No, Your Honor. The police are investigating the matter."

"They believe Penny Van Horne is dead?"

"We have located the body, Your Honor. It will take time to get authority to exhume the body and do the autopsy. So far, it appears that one part of Paige's so-called delusion is based in reality. The baby is dead. And according to the burial records, she died on or about July fourth a decade ago."

Stephanie rose abruptly. "We have a witness, Your Honor, who can explain what happened. He's waiting outside."

Aleta noticed that Van Horne seemed upset.

The Director of the Flower Home for Mentally Handicapped Children, Eugene Vider, told his story. Aleta watched him closely and listened carefully. When he finished, she said she had no questions.

Andrew Jackson was startled, but deferred to his lead counsel's decision after a few seconds hesitation. She was in charge of Paige's case, not him. He would have nailed the liar to the wall. He spotted one glaring error. As he considered Aleta's silence, he realized that not only did she spot it, but she knew the judge did as well.

Eugene Vider was excused.

Aleta rose and said she still had questions about the custody agreement. The judge directed Kurt Van Horne to take the stand.

"Why are you not named in the agreement?"

"Mary was vindictive," Van Horne replied calmly. "She wanted me to have to fight to get back my children. She knew how much it would pain me to pay to recover my rights as a father."

Aleta smile and nodded. Van Horne had been well prepped.

"How do you explain that such a vindictive women did not utter a negative word to either Molly or Tyler?"

"She didn't want to wreck their relationship with me. She only wanted to make me pay."

Again Aleta smiled and nodded.

Kurt Van Horne readjusted himself in his seat. He didn't like her smiling at him.

"Why didn't you sue for custody when David took over?"

"I didn't want a court fight. I thought I could talk him into moving back into my house. It didn't happen. He liked being in charge."

For the third time, Aleta smiled and nodded.

"Are we to assume that the burial date Mr. Vider gave us and the one recorded on the headstone differ because the one on the headstone is incorrect?"

"Yes. It is," Van Horne replied, still tense.

"Why would your wife put the wrong date on the headstone?"

"To make trouble. She was a vindictive woman."

"So your wife knew Penny was dead and she didn't tell you?"

"That's right."

Van Horne shifted his weight again. I was as close to a squirm as Aleta figured she would see from him.

Now was the time to switch tactics.

"Why was David not named Kurt Junior?"

"I didn't want a junior," Van Horne said. "What has that to do with anything?"

Aleta saw him tense. An idea struck her but she needed a bit more information before she pursued it. So she chose to take a more predictable path.

"None of the children carry a single family name from your side of the family, do they?" Aleta asked.

"Mary named them," Kurt Van Horne retorted.

"Did you know the last name on Penny's headstone is Tyler, not Van Horne?"

"No. I told you I didn't know the baby had died."

"Now that you do, will you correct the headstone?"

"No. That's in the past."

His voice and manner were cool.

"It would also not be a prudent investment, would it?"

"No, it would not."

"Despite your wealth, you are never careless with how you spend your money, correct?"

"Yes."

"Yet, you paid twice as much to house your retarded daughter as others paid for similar accommodations for their children. Can you explain that?"

"Mary insisted on the best."

"You personally paid for Penny's care, correct?"

"Yes."

"Not your mother?"

"That is correct."

"Did you and Mary fight over whether or not to put the baby in an institution?"

"Yes."

"She didn't want to. Is that correct?"

"Yes."

"Was she so stubbornly opposed that as a result you divorced?"

"Yes."

Again Aleta saw a flicker of apprehension in his eyes. Did he expect her to press the issue? She decided to press ahead with her acceptance of his statement.

"Do you believe her anger with you stemmed from this one act alone?"

"Yes," he replied. His eyes were cold and hard again.

"You are a wealthy man. Why not create separate quarters for the child and hire round-the-clock help to care for Penny and keep your marriage intact?"

"It was more economically feasible to place her in a home."

"You put your marriage and family on a scale and calculated the cost?"

"Mary wouldn't listen to reason. The child would never amount to anything."

"But Mary loved the child," Aleta said. "That makes me wonder. After you and Mary were divorced, why didn't she go get her baby?"

"At the time I thought she didn't because she couldn't afford to care for one more child. Now I think that she did and was told it had died and she became so incensed that she concocted a scheme with Mr. Vider to make me pay."

Aleta raised an eyebrow.

"Am I to believe she played you for a fool?"

"Not exactly. I just put the child out of my mind once I'd made proper arrangements for her."

"That seems to be a pattern with you," Aleta said.

"That's what I believe is best for each of them."

"Your Honor, Mr. Jackson has some questions for Mr. Van Horne."

Andrew rose as if he expected to question Kurt Van Horne when in fact he didn't. Aleta was obviously heading somewhere. He sensed he was to fill in the remaining time.

"Mr. Van Horne, are you interested in what Molly wants?"

It was meant as an opening salvo, not as a real query, but Kurt Van Horne took it seriously.

"No, I am not. She is a child. Children do not always know what is best for them."

Andrew plunged right in.

"Molly wants to stay in close contact with her remaining brother and sister."

"Molly needs to be weaned from an over-dependence on them."

"She sees Paige as her mother."

"My wife will fill that role," Van Horne said coolly.

"Where is your wife? We have not seen her once during this hearing?"

"She has social obligations."

"Molly wants to be a member of a close-knit family."

"She will be," Kurt Van Horne retorted. "I don't expect you to understand how things are done at my level of society, but our methods prepare our children to take their proper place in society. We are very family-oriented."

"Molly will suffer serious emotional consequences if she is deprived of the type of emotional support to which she is accustomed."

"Molly needs to grow up. She needs a reality check."

"Oh, I believe she's had a stomach full of reality the last few years. She is a very well-adjusted child currently. But even the most well-adjusted child can be overwhelmed by too much loss. Do you agree it would be best to reduce further trauma?"

"I suppose that would be a proper goal," Van Horne said, "however, I don't agree that boarding school is deeply traumatic. She is going to have a period of adjustment no matter where she is placed."

"Suppose I told you there is a place where she will not have to undergo that period of adjustment?"

Van Horne let a hint of smug satisfaction cross his countenance.

"Her sister may be married, but she is too young to be her guardian," Van Horne said. "However, as I plan to get her sister's marriage annulled, Molly will be coming with her and Tyler."

"Only to have you tear her sister from her arms and incarcerate her in a mental hospital?"

"Don't make it worse than it is. It's a treatment center for the mentally disturbed."

"For Molly it would be one more loss to cope with," Andrew stated harshly. "Let's not make it to be less traumatic an event then it is. Further, I suggest you have no love to offer this child, just loneliness and deprivation. To place her in your care would violate her right to the best this system has to offer."

As Andrew Jackson turned to address the judge, Roland Chin slipped into the courtroom.

Andrew didn't see him so he continued. "Your Honor, may I present the petition of Dr. and Mrs. Bernard Chesney to become Molly's foster parents? They have taken a week from their busy schedules to acquaint themselves with Molly and her brother Tyler. Unexpectedly, the children formed a close bond with the Chesneys. As a result, Social Services has passed on the Chesneys' application. The Chesneys have a four-bedroom home on a lake in Willow Glen's newest subdivision. Paige and Hawkins Monroe plan to live next door. Molly will be able to be near what is left of the family she knows and loves. She will have siblings who understand the losses she has endured. In addition, she will be able to enjoy the expansion of her family instead of its reduction. Her father, who has absented himself from his children for a decade, who hasn't even been responsible for a modicum of support in all that time has forfeited his right to demand that his wishes be considered above those of his children. I submit that Molly's wishes be considered in this matter."

"I would need to hear from her," Judge Jacobi said.

"She wrote you a letter," Andrew said, handing the judge an envelope. "It was written in private but signed in the presence of a notary. She will return on Friday to respond to any final questions you may have.

The judge excused Kurt Van Horne who hurried back to his lawyer and engaged in a heated whispered argument.

Meanwhile Judge Jacobi pointedly ignored Roland Chin and addressed Aleta. "Do you have similar letters to present?"

"Mr. Chin does, Your Honor. May he be allowed to present Tyler's letter and speak to Tyler's wishes?"

"What about Paige?"

"I didn't get a letter from her."

"Mr. Chin, do you have any comments to add to Mr. Jackson's?"

First Roland Chin apologized profusely for not being present during the hearing.

"Mrs. Praetzel has already agreed to serve your time in jail on the contempt charge your absence earned for you."

Shocked, Roland looked at his fellow team members who nodded their heads.

"It's done," Aleta whispered. "Don't argue."

"Proceed," Judge Jacobi ordered tersely.

Roland Chin straightened up and silently thanked Aleta for insisting he be fully prepared for this case.

"Tyler will be eighteen in October. He was originally hoping to fill his brother's shoes. He planned to consult a lawyer in October when he had legally come of age, but then the car he was driving was broadsided and Molly was hurt. He ran afoul of the hospital admittance policy. He wasn't old enough to sign the paperwork. He heard from another person in the hospital that a really good lawyer was accepting clients. Mrs. Praetzel assessed him as not being twenty-one as he claimed and sent him to her husband who is a child advocate. Mr. Praetzel underwrote Molly's medical care and with the permission of Social Services, secured appropriate temporary shelter for all three children until the court could rule on permanent custody. He assumed that since the father had not taken over the family upon the death of the mother that there was a reason he did not do so. He was given permission by Tyler to search the house for any documentation relating to the custody agreement entered into by both parents. Tyler remembered that the agreement said that after David, further arrangements were to be left to the court.

Judge Jacobi nodded. She knew the background. Roland hurried on.

"As to Tyler's wishes, he has found in Dr. Chesney the father he has wanted. Dr. Chesney has told Tyler that he is welcome to enter their house as a son and they will see to his education. Tyler does not wish to live with Mr. Van Horne. He is angry with him for refusing to send David to college. Tyler says David was the brightest of all of them except maybe for Paige. On top of that, Tyler feels his father should not have cut David's support payments at eighteen. I explained the law to Tyler; however, his feeling is that need, not an arbitrary birth date, should have been a consideration. Tyler was terribly concerned because he was going to lose his own support in October. He wouldn't even be able to finish high school. He was still reeling from David's death and the loss of the income from David's job when Molly got hurt. He found himself accumulating debt faster than he could handle it. He called his father and told him about David's death. His father told him to sell the house, pay off the debts and then all three could move back with him. For reasons of which this court is aware, Paige didn't wish to return. While she didn't tell either Tyler or Molly why, Tyler accepted her decision. He decided against selling the house because they would be homeless and at their father's mercy. He does not see him as a merciful man. He believes his father burned down his home to force him and his sisters to move back in with him. He does not want to live with so compassionless a father. I am not accusing Mr. Van Horne of any criminal act; however, the court should know how Tyler feels."

When he finished, for some reason Roland remained standing. The judge responded to him directly.

"Mr. Chin, thank you for your report. As you may know I believe that biological parents estranged from their children should have a chance to work through their problems. They have a lifelong bond that can never be truly severed. Parents vary in their capacity to love. Adjustments are required. It appears that all Tyler's objections to his father have to do with Mr. Van Horne's parsimonious nature. The trust funds will guarantee Tyler and his sisters financial security, so perhaps it would be wise to let their natural father have a chance to become acquainted with his children."

"Yes, Your Honor," Roland Chin said, his tone conveying his defeat. "Your Honor, it is obvious that I have failed my client and it is perhaps something I could have avoided had I been present during the earlier questioning. Contempt of court is what I am guilty of, not Mrs. Praetzel. May I be allowed to at least serve the time for the offense?"

"So ordered," Judge Jacobi ruled.

Andrew Jackson stood up. "Your Honor, Mrs. Praetzel had a second contempt charge leveled against her. I wish to serve that in her place.

"On what grounds?"

"An attempt was made on Mrs. Praetzel's life this morning. She has a police guard standing outside the courtroom. Last time she was sent to the county jail for contempt, the local police were not allowed to guard her and the guards at the county lock-up failed to protect her. She was attacked while locked in a jail cell."

"I will order police protection," Judge Jacobi said.

Aleta stood up. "That will be acceptable. Thank you."

Andrew sat down.

Aleta leaned over. "Thank you."

Then she leaned over and said to Roland, "Thank you too. You have no idea that you actually saved our case, but you did. And you probably saved my life to boot."

Roland stared at her. "Me? How?"

"You have all the pieces. Now you'll have time to put them together," she smiled.

"Mrs. Praetzel, do you wish to address the court?"

"I have an expert witness I would like to call and then I will be prepared to close."

"Is your witness here?"

"No, Your Honor, until this hearing, I didn't know I'd need her. It will only take about twenty minutes to get her here."

Judge Jacobi looked at her watch. "It's late. We'll finish up tomorrow. Bailiff, take Mr. Chin and Mrs. Praetzel into custody. Mrs. Praetzel's police guards are to accompany her everywhere. Court's adjourned."

The bailiff opened the courtroom door, "Come on, Guys, you're going to jail."

Chapter 29

At two o'clock the following day Aleta Praetzel was ushered into Judge Jacobi's courtroom and her handcuffs were removed. Roland Chin rubbed his wrists after his release.

"How was it?" Andrew whispered.

"You don't want to piss off a judge, believe me," came Roland's response.

"Did you figure out the puzzle?" Aleta asked.

Roland shook his head.

"I perhaps had an advantage."

The judge entered and once she sat down she immediately asked Aleta to call her expert witness.

"If Your Honor would allow me, I believe that if I can ask Mr. Van Horne a few preliminary questions, the need for my witness may not even be necessary."

"Proceed," Judge Jacobi ordered.

Kurt Van Horne, confident from the judge's final statements at the prior session, took the stand readily. His attorney had told him Aleta Praetzel could present nothing that wasn't based in fact. She had no idea who the expert witness was, but she told him she'd ask for a recess to discuss the testimony. Everything was under control.

"Mr. Van Horne," Aleta began, "I hope your night was pleasanter than mine."

He smirked slightly. "It was."

"Your daughter Paige needs an operation," Aleta said.

"A what?" he stammered. "Why?"

"The premarital examination revealed two things. One is that she was a virgin at the time of her marriage. I'm reminding you of a fact, in case you had forgotten and planned to accuse Hawkins Monroe of statutory rape and call for an annulment on that basis."

"To continue, the other thing that was discovered was a physical abnormality that would probably cause infertility. Such abnormalities are frequently inherited. Did your deceased wife have a tipped uterus?"

"Yes, she did."

"Did she have fertility problems?"

"Yes, she did."

"Did you go to a fertility clinic to solve these problems?"

"She went."

"Were you ever examined?"

"Why? There's nothing wrong with me."

"Did your wife take a sample of your sperm to the clinic?"

"Of course not. There was no reason to."

"Is Tyler your biological son?"

"Yes, he is."

"Is Paige your biological daughter?"

"Yes, she is."

"Molly has the same father as Tyler, but not Paige. How do you explain that?"

"Call in MacMurray. He said they were all siblings in his report."

"They are. They all have the same mother," Aleta said. "Tyler and Molly are full brother and sister. Paige is a half-sister. None of them are related to the Penny Van Horne in the Home. Once we exhume the body of the real Penny Van Horne, will we find yet another father? Did you and your wife agree to use donated sperm and artificial insemination to produce children? Is the reason you didn't allow Mary to use your family's names because none of your children are biologically yours?"

"My name is on their birth certificates."

"Legally, they are your children," Aleta conceded. "Now, were they produced by donor sperm and artificial insemination?"

"They are my children."

"Are they your biological children?" Aleta said.

"Yes."

"I am going to ask you that question again," Aleta said. "You have been made aware that the penalty for perjury is serious. I'm asking you again. Are Tyler, Paige and Molly your biological children?"

"The answer is yes," Van Horne stated adamantly. "If Paige's DNA results are different, it's a mistake. We used a fertility clinic and they fixed Mary's problem and she had David.

"The clinic's records are confidential," Aleta said. "It is not the source of our information."

"Your source is mistaken," Kurt Van Horne stated flatly.

Aleta called Natsumi Genjo to the witness stand.

The bailiff opened the door and a diminutive Japanese woman came into the courtroom and strode confidently to the chair beside the judge's bench.

A masters and five years in her field gave the newest member of Hawk's team the assurance she needed to testify.

"We have a DNA report from Mr. MacMurray before us," Aleta said. "Is it accurate?"

"Yes," Natsumi replied in a soft but firm voice.

"You rechecked his work?"

"I was asked to do so."

"Are Tyler, Paige and Molly siblings?"

"Yes."

"What more can you tell us?"

"Tyler and Molly are full siblings. Paige is their half-sister. None of them are the biological children of Kurt Van Horne."

"Your Honor," Aleta said, "may I interrupt this testimony to ask Mr. Van Horne a few more questions?"

"Do you intend to recall this witness?"

"Yes, Your Honor, I do."

"Mr. Van Horne, take the stand. Remember you are still under oath."

"I object!" Stephanie said. "I want to question Miss Genjo."

"The witness will be recalled later. I'm interested in Mr. Van Horne's answers at this time," the judge declared.

This time Kurt Van Horne's spirit was less ebullient, although considering his stoic manner the change was barely perceptible.

"Mr. Van Horne, you and your current wife have no children. Why is that?" Aleta asked.

"We chose not to have any."

The minute he said that, Stephanie frowned and Van Horne amended his statement. "Anymore, that is. I already had five."

"She never asked for a baby of her own?"

"She doesn't like babies. They're too messy and demanding."

Aleta smiled. "They are that. But she likes children, right?"

"She will treat my children well, if that's what you're getting at," Van Horne snapped.

"Does she agree with you that people should be responsible for the children they produce?"

"Yes."

"Is that why you washed your hands of Mary and her children because they were her children and not yours?"

"I didn't wash my hands of them. They were provided for."

"Mary settled for a house in Arborville and meager child support when she could have gotten a much bigger settlement in divorce court with a good attorney. Why would a vindictive woman do that?"

"She wasn't money-oriented."

"She never spoke a bad word to her children about you. Why do you suppose she didn't?"

"It wasn't her way. She said that it hurt children when someone spoke ill of their parents. She was a sociologist, you know. She would have done what was best for the children."

"Still you say she was vindictive. Do you believe a vindictive person could have reared healthy, happy, well-adjusted children?"

"It's possible," Van Horne insisted.

"Let's return to an area in which you are an expert," Aleta said, her disdain for his reply obvious. "I assume you have calculated the cost of future child support payments should Paige or anyone else be given custody of your children, haven't you?"

"Yes, I have," Van Horne countered, obviously happy to be back on the solid ground of financial permutations. "And I can anticipate your next question. The answer is that it will cost me as much to have the children living with me. I will save nothing."

"The house they were living in was destroyed," Aleta said. "Do you know if it was insured?"

"No, I don't."

"Your insurance agent said you called him to see if the policy was in force."

"Yes, I guess I did," Van Horne admitted. "I forgot I did that."

"You said you didn't know that your children were produced from donated sperm. Did you forget you had to sign an agreement at the clinic absolving them of blame should the children be defective?"

Stephanie interrupted with an objection meant to guide her client. "Clinic records are confidential."

"I withdraw the question," Aleta said. "Let's go back to the insurance on the house. To whom would the insurance money be paid?"

"The owner of the house."

"Your wife left the house to her children. All the living children are minors."

"I guess the insurance would be paid to their custodian," Van Horne said.

"Over the last ten years, the house has appreciated in value. It is worth double what was paid for it," Aleta said. "Would you rebuild it?"

"No."

"It would be a good investment for the children," Aleta said. "The money is theirs, not yours, you know."

"I would use it for their benefit.

"Short term or long term?"

"Whichever is prudent."

"How could any short-term investment be prudent for children supposedly being completely supported by you?"

"They might want something I'm not willing to buy them."

"I assume that you are not talking a necessity."

"Correct."

"Wouldn't it be an unwise use of their inheritance to use it on a luxury you deem foolish? Suppose Molly wants a horse? Or Tyler wants a car? Are those examples of the kinds of luxuries you would spend their inheritance on?"

"Yes."

"What if I asked the court to name an outside trustee to oversee their inheritance?"

"That would be foolish," Van Horne decided. "I'm more capable of handling their money than anyone you could suggest. Anyone you get would charge fees that would eat away at the inheritance. I would fight that."

"Ah, Mr. Van Horne, you do not know me well at all if you think I would suggest someone for such a task that would charge a fee or be less skilled in financial matters than you," Aleta said, "but let's go on with our supposing. What if I were to suggest a legal out for you from all future support obligations?"

"You're talking about that couple, aren't you?"

"Yes, I am."

"You don't know much about the law," Van Horne sneered. "I would still have to pay them. That's why they want the children, you know. It means a hefty income both from me and the foster child program."

"Thank you, Mr. Van Horne. That is all the questions I have," Aleta said and turned away.

"You thought you could get away with it, didn't you?" he charged.

Aleta spun around. "What did I try to get away with?"

"Setting your friends up with a healthy income for no real work," Van Horne spat out. "You didn't think I knew the law, did you?"

"I was suggesting adoption as an option. The Chesneys have also petitioned to adopt your children. If you allowed them to adopt them, your financial obligations cease immediately."

"Would I get the trust fund money back?" Van Horne asked before Stephanie could react.

"Possibly some of it," Aleta answered with the rapidity of machine gun fire.

The gavel banged.

"How much of it?" Van Horne shot back, ignoring the judge.

"Are we bargaining?" Aleta returned instantly.

The gavel banged again.

"Yes," he said. "How much?"

Immediately, Aleta turned to the judge.

"Your Honor, may we be allowed to negotiate this matter?"

"Absolutely not!" Judge Jacobi said banging her gavel down hard as she shouted. "Court is recessed for fifteen minutes."

Everyone scrambled to their feet as Norma Jacobi, dark curls bouncing, rushed from the courtroom, every inch of her plump body quivering.

"She's furious!" Roland whispered to Aleta.

Aleta leaned over and whispered to Andrew.

"When the judge returns, you take over questioning Natsumi Genjo. Judge Jacobi needs more than fifteen minutes to calm down."

"Is there anything more in the report?" Andrew asked.

"One big surprise left," Aleta said.

Exactly fourteen minutes later, Judge Jacobi reentered the courtroom. To her satisfaction, no one had moved from his or her assigned places.

She sat down and the courtroom settled into absolute silence in seconds.

"Aleta Praetzel, please stand," the judge said, her voice trembling with indignation.

Aleta rose and stood silently. She had hoped she could finish before being banished. She bowed her head and prayed for the children she was trying to protect.

Help me do the right thing, she asked silently. And then lifted her head to face the judge who was waiting for her to do so.

Norma Jacobi began to speak, her eyes blazing. "Never in all my years on the bench have I been shown the disrespect I was shown a few minutes ago. Do you have any idea what you did, Mrs. Praetzel?"

"Yes, Your Honor," Aleta said. "I usurped your authority.

"Go on," the judge pressed, her anger unabated.

"I almost committed a felony in your courtroom while you were sitting in judgment and I had the gall to ask your permission to do it."

"And?"

"I ignored your attempt to stop the proceeding twice."

"Would you do it again?"

"I'm afraid I would, given the same circumstances," Aleta admitted.

"So you understand why I'm charging you with contempt of court?"

"I do, Your Honor."

"Thirty days!" Judge Jacobi announced. Gasps from both sides told her she'd made her point.

Aleta sat down stunned.

Andrew rose and said he would like to recall Natsumi Genjo to the stand.

Judge Jacobi's brow furrowed. "Mrs. Praetzel, you will complete your examination of the witness. One more step out of line and I will double your sentence. Am I clear?"

"Yes, Your Honor," Aleta managed to say, knowing that a mere nod would only incense the judge further.

"And then you will close," the judge said. "Immediately afterward you will start serving your sentence."

Aleta's heart sank. Judge Jacobi had already decided to ignore the exchange between her and Van Horne except to punish her.

Aleta sensed that somehow the next round of questions would earn her more jail time. She didn't know how, but she could feel the fury still penned up inside the rotund judge. If she could have, she would have ordered her hung. Thank goodness she was a lawyer in this day and age.

"Ms. Genjo," Aleta began, "you were given several samples of DNA of adult men to process, correct?"

Stephanie shot up. "Objection. Irrelevant."

"Sustained," snapped the judge.

Aleta was startled. Suddenly she knew Stephanie would object to every question and if her objections were sustained, Aleta would not be allowed to ask it in a different way without risking a contempt charge.

"Ms. Genjo," Aleta began and threw a hostile glance at Stephanie who smirked in return. "Please report all findings relevant to the principals in this case only."

Natsumi, who had been sitting outside the courtroom to be recalled, had no idea what had happened in the interim but she sensed a profound change. She hesitated saying anything for several seconds. When no objections were uttered, she began her report.

"Genetically, Paige and David are full brother and sister. They are both half-siblings of Tyler and Molly, who are full brother and sister. Mr. Van Horne is not the biological father of any of those four children whose DNA I tested. However, I have identified the biological father of Tyler and Molly. That is my full report."

Having said that, Natsumi stopped dead.

"Who is he?" Judge Jacobi asked.

"I don't know," Natsumi replied.

"You just said you identified him."

"I matched his DNA to the DNA of all four children and he's the father of Tyler and Molly."

"And you don't know who he is?"

"That is correct."

"Objection! Stephanie Nash said. "I move that this report be stricken from the record."

"I object!" Aleta said. "The information is relevant. I know whose DNA was tested as I ordered the tests."

"What difference does it make?" Stephanie argued. "If it came from a donor bank, finding it out has no relevance. Legally, donors are absolved from responsibility for offspring from their donation. It works both ways. They also have no claim on their offspring."

Aleta spoke up. "Mrs. Nash is correct. I withdraw my objection."

The faces of both Stephanie Nash and Judge Jacobi registered surprise.

Judge Jacobi frowned after considering what Aleta had done.

"You did it again," she said. "The ruling was mine to make."

"It might seem that way, Your Honor, but I actually stayed on my side of the fence this time. If, however, giving me another thirty days will allow you to concentrate on the welfare of the children instead of your anger with me, then I will serve the sixty days without objection."

"So ordered!" Judge Jacobi said. "The report given by Ms. Genjo after she was recalled is stricken from the record. Ms. Genjo, you are excused."

"Your Honor, I was objecting to the entire report," Stephanie Nash clarified.

"Your reason only dealt with the identity of the biological father of the children and his possible claim in the matter before this court, Mrs. Nash," Judge Jacobi ruled. "That is the part that I have stricken. That Mr. Van Horne committed perjury is a matter that will be decided at his trial on that charge. Mrs. Praetzel, make your closing statement."

Natsumi walked out of the courtroom. Never had she had a report stricken from the court record. It was a humbling experience.

Witnessing Aleta Praetzel being punished was unnerving. She wished she could talk to someone, but she knew her report was confidential. She had never felt so alone.

Aleta wished she could say something, but she was already looking at more jail time than she thought she could handle.

She stood stoically while Natsumi, head bowed, left the courtroom. Then Aleta began her closing argument.

"Your Honor, you firmly believe that the biological link between parent and child should be nurtured not cast aside as if meaningless. I am not arguing the wisdom of that position; however, between Kurt Van Horne and his three surviving children. no such link is present. In addition, Mr.

Van Horne has not acted in a positive fashion toward his children in a decade. Ignoring a child is a type of abuse by itself. It tells the child he is unimportant. It is one of the subtlest forms of psychological abuse.

"Paige's fear is real. It is not a delusion. Whether she interpreted what she saw correctly is for a court to decide, but she is not mentally deranged because she saw something inexplicable. That her mother never assured her that she interpreted what she saw incorrectly I find compelling. I believe the baby died that night. Paige has developed into a caring and capable young woman who kept what she saw to herself in order to spare her brother and younger sister the pain that the sharing of such a secret might engender.

"She was open and honest with two experts sent to interview her. They were upset because she considered a judge's order to be the ultimate definitive authority, a position that I'm sure I should emulate a bit more closely.

"I have already garnered fifty-two more days of jail time then I can handle easily, but let me risk even more, let me say this: Molly deserves to be placed with her biological father who loves her even though he doesn't know she's his child rather than her legal father who doesn't even want her in the same house with him and who is already figuring how he can dip into the small inheritance she has from her mother."

Having said that Aleta turned to the bailiff. "I'm done. You can take me to jail now."

Judge Jacobi nodded and the bailiff handcuffed Aleta and escorted her out the side door. As she was leaving, Judge Jacobi saw tears streaming down the young lawyer's face.

Stephanie Nash got up and began speaking, but no one heard her. While Stephanie continued to methodically present her arguments, Judge Norma Jacobi's mind remained focused on Aleta's words and her passion.

She wondered how long it would take her to shake off the spell she felt Aleta had cast over her reason.

The last time Aleta had argued before her, she had been persuasive, but Norma had shaken off her arguments enough to protect her sacred cow–the idea that parents and children should be presented with an opportunity to reconcile because, like it or not, one's parents are forever a part of one's self. Her ruling on that occasion had had disastrous results.

As she recalled this, she marveled at the restraint Aleta Praetzel had shown in not even hinting at that error in judgment while arguing a case with many similar attributes.

With nothing but suspicion and an unwavering faith in her client, she had done a brilliant job. Aleta had won a large financial settlement first which even she, as the judge, recognized as fair and just. The man was a prick, but even pricks deserve to have custody of their own children.

As soon as Stephanie Nash finished, Judge Jacobi announced that she would render her decision shortly. Court was recessed for an hour.

Chapter 30

Drained of emotion, Aleta sat hunched on the bench in the holding cell. That she had done her best was not a comfort. She had so angered the judge that she had made it difficult for Judge Jacobi to rule in her favor.

She was too tired to think. In the end she had done the one thing she had vowed not to do. She had revealed that Dr. Chesney was the natural father of Tyler and Molly. She hadn't discovered it by breaking into any confidential sources, however, who would believe how her mind had leaped to that possibility.

She'd had Andrew gather a DNA sample from Stanley as well as a control. The nurse in Dr. Chesney's office had wondered why the young lawyer wanted to take his coffee cup which had been left on his desk half full of coffee.

There had been no question of the samples being mixed. Stanley's sample had been offered on a cotton swab; Chesney's, on a coffee cup; and Van Horne's, on the water glass he'd used at the hearing.

She began to think about Natsumi. She had rushed the DNA work on the extra samples to have them ready in time for court. She'd spent the night at the lab only to have her results disallowed.

When she was granted one phone call, Aleta called Natsumi and told her that her work was not for naught. "I used it in my closing argument," Aleta said. "It was too important not to."

"Thank you for telling me. You are in trouble, yes?"

"Oh, yes. I'm in trouble," Aleta said, "but you did nothing wrong. You did everything right. I am so grateful."

"I have other good news," Natsumi said. "The three sets of fingerprints on the books are yours and Hawk's and Machi's. Hawk told me to look for them."

"Books? What books?"

"Two were found in Tully Machi's car but Mr. MacMurray said they were unimportant. Hawk told me to redo the car and its contents."

"Was one of those books entitled Man by a man named Lind?"

"Yes."

"Hawk and I think that somewhere inside the book is hidden a flash drive with documents stored on it. It is very important that you find it and turn it over to Chief Lyle West."

"Not you?"

"I will be in jail for sixty days," Aleta said. "Contempt of court. At least I think it's no more than sixty days. I hope she didn't add more. I can barely handle thinking about spending the whole summer locked in a cell."

"I will investigate the book immediately."

By the time Judge Norma Jacobi reentered her courtroom to deliver her decision, Aleta was on the first busload of prisoners being taken to the county jail.

Outside the courtroom the two police guards assigned to her waited for the doors to open.

Norma Jacobi's decision was delivered in terse, clipped phrases.

"We have all witnessed a passionate plea by Mrs. Praetzel which was a culmination of various unorthodox approaches the like of which I have not witnessed before. That she inflamed me enough to find her in contempt I have set aside in reaching my decision with regard to the custody of Paige, Tyler and Molly Van Horne.

"First, as to Paige's mental stability. Experts have testified that she suffered from a single delusion but was otherwise a normal, rational person. That delusion was that her baby sister had met an untimely death at the hands of her father. Since the baby did indeed die during that time period, I cannot consider her memory of the event as delusional. She may have mistakenly interpreted the events she witnessed, however, that determination is beyond the purview of this hearing.

"I find Paige Van Horne to be rational enough to have made the decision to marry Hawkins Monroe. Since Hawkins Monroe and Paige Van Horne complied not only with the letter but the spirit of the law since they applied for permission to marry from a sitting judge in the county of residence during a period when Paige Van Horne was temporarily under the auspices of the County Department of Social Services, I therefore deny Mr. Kurt Van Horne's petition to obtain custody of Paige Van Horne, thereby recognizing the legality of Paige Van Horne's marriage to Hawkins Monroe.

"Now, as to the custody of Tyler and Molly Van Horne, the court is not going to decide which of the petitioning couples should have custody and thereby set a legal precedent by choosing the legal father over the biological father or vice versa. I do not wish to go on record as giving weight to Dr. Chesney's position as sperm donor for, in fact, I gave it no weight.

"I am also not basing my decision on Mr. Van Horne's obviously parsimonious bent. There is no parent without flaw. No evidence of physical abuse was presented. That Mr. Van Horne distanced himself from his children following the divorce is regrettable, but should not preclude his being allowed to reestablish his kinship with his children."

At this point Stephanie Nash was allowing a smile of triumph to emerge ever so slowly. On the other side of the room, Stephanie could sense the despair of the two young associates. Did Aleta actually believe her flair for courtroom dramatics would weight into the decision of a juvenile court judge? Emotions always ran high in juvenile cases. The judges had to disregard them and adhere to the law.

She wished Aleta were here to personally taste her defeat. Stephanie needed to win this final battle to balance the scales.

She sensed that the man beside her was distraught over the ruling on Paige. It was not unexpected. One judge rarely ruled against the decision of another except in the appellate process.

She decided that he would know in a few minutes that he had custody of his two remaining children.

Judge Jacobi, who had paused for a brief moment, continued.

"My decision is going to be based rather on the wishes of the mother of these children. I do not know why Mr. Van Horne agreed to the custody arrangement wherein he was excluded from the pre-determined line of guardianship; however, he did sign the agreement. That he did so without submitting the agreement to the court for approval does not invalidate its terms. That he accepted these terms even after his wife's death and that he petitioned the court for custody testifies as to the validity of this document. In keeping with Mr. Van Horne's own compliance with the terms of the agreement with his wife, the court must weigh carefully the spirit as well as the letter of the agreement. That Mary Roach Van Horne established an order of guardianship that included her then eleven-year-old son as third guardian rather than the father must be considered.

"One more fact needs to be addressed at this time. The custody agreement which was dated July 10, 1996 mentioned only four children. No mention of Penny Van Horne is made. This is a critical omission. It suggests that she had already died.

"There is no question that Mary Roach Van Horne did not want Kurt Van Horne to have custody of any of her remaining children. Unfortunately, no documentation has been found to give us her reason. However, she leaves behind three healthy, well-adjusted, friendly children as a testament to her own soundness of mind in reaching this decision.

"Using this document as a guideline, the court names Dr. Bernard Chesney and his wife Evelyn Chesney permanent guardians of Tyler Roach Van Horne and Molly Roach Van Horne.

"Child support payments in the amount directed by this court will continue through the eighteenth birthday of Tyler and Molly Van Horne. Child support payments for Paige Van Horne are no longer required.

"Court adjourned."

The judge banged her gavel and rushed from the courtroom.

Chapter 31

Norma Jacobi had no sooner settled herself in her chair with a warm cup of coffee when the knock on her door was followed immediately by it opening.

Chief Lyle West charged into the room.

"I didn't give you permission to enter," Judge Jacobi said. "I could..."

"Judge Jacobi, you are under arrest."

"I'm what?" she gasped, shock draining the blood from her face.

A second officer entered and took out a pair of handcuffs and in several swift motions had the judge's hands pinned behind her back. The cuffs were tight and she voiced a complaint. The officer ignored her whine and continued reading her rights.

"You're out of your jurisdiction," she said. "I'll have your badge for this."

"Add threatening a police officer," West said coldly.

"I don't even know the first charge," she griped.

"Reckless endangerment."

"Of Mrs. Praetzel? Just because she was attacked in her cell a couple months ago is no reason to believe she is in danger there now."

"She was attacked at her home two days ago. Paige was attacked in Orlando the same night. Both were hired killers. Did you think I was playing a game?"

"You are a friend of hers," Norma Jacobi argued. "And she has a flair for the dramatic."

"Why did you put her in jail?"

"She didn't show me the proper respect."

"Well, Judge Jacobi, that is exactly what you haven't shown the police. And you have put an innocent citizen at risk."

"I get a phone call," the judge said.

"After you're processed," West stated icily. "That's when Aleta got hers."

"And she called you," the judge quipped disdainfully.

"No, she called Natsumi Genjo and assured her that she had done nothing wrong, a common courtesy you did not offer."

West signaled his man and Norma Jacobi found herself escorted through the halls of the courthouse and out to a waiting police car past a score of strangers and colleagues. It was the most embarrassing walk of her life.

Seated in the back of the car, her hands still cuffed behind her, she was driven straight to the county jail for processing.

Norma decided to be stoic. The worse was over. She'd make her call and be out before she even saw a jail cell.

What she envisioned didn't happen. She was placed in an interrogation room, still handcuffed and left there for several hours.

When she was allowed to place her phone call, she got the law office answering machine and waited until it spewed out the emergency number then hung up. She began to redial, but the receiver was removed from her hand and placed back on the cradle.

"You are allowed one call," the officer said. "It's the rule."

Norma found herself placed in a cell adjacent to the one Aleta was in.

"Whom did you piss off?" Aleta asked.

"Chief of police," Norma responded dourly.

"They're as powerful as judges," Aleta said amiably. "Especially Lyle West. When we piss him off, he makes Stanley work eight hour shifts as a deputy."

"Does that happen often?" Norma asked, her curiosity taking over.

"Stanley owes him a month of nights right now," Aleta said.

"So, will he be guarding you tonight," Norma quipped testily.

"He's in the hospital. He would have been able to come home if I were there to wait on him. Most of my family is in Orlando with the Van Horne children. Anyway, Stanley has to stay off that leg for another week at least."

"What happened to his leg?"

"He was shot and then he got an infection."

"A hunting accident?"

"A hit man. Someone I pissed off, but not as nice as you. They came to kill me."

"You won, you know," Norma said a bit of warmth seeping into her tone. It was hard not to like this woman.

"Yes, I know. Thank you."

"I thought I'd see guards posted outside your cell."

"The county won't let West's men guard me without an order from a judge."

"Is that why I'm here?"

"Lyle doesn't play games," Aleta said. "That's not why you're here. He's already taken care of me by warning the guards here. They put an extra man on."

The following morning Andrew and Roland visited Aleta early. Each was carrying an armload of folders.

"I reported your incarceration to your husband," Andrew said. "He was very upset."

"The baby's okay," Roland said. "Jamara took him home with her. Hubbs is taking care of the dogs. They were all in the barn with him when I went over last night."

"Mr. Praetzel said he wasn't going to allow you to go into court again until after the baby is born," Jackson added.

"But just in case," Roland said, "we brought the folders we started before we came."

"But it's only eight thirty."

"They were lined up at the door at six thirty," Andrew said. "Chief Milani called Roland and me and we went in early. We did the interviews like you taught us."

Roland handed her a stack folders. "These are the ones we turned away."

Aleta looked through them. "Good. We don't want divorce cases and no criminals either."

Aleta pulled out one folder.

"I rather liked this one. We'll take her case."

"It's a divorce case," Roland pointed out.

"When you hire her, tell her one of the perks of the job is free legal services. Tell Alice to make up an employment contract. Then send her to me."

Aleta quickly sorted through the rest of the folders. She pulled out six. "I can do these from here."

"But they're grunt work," Andrew said.

"I'm good with contracts," Aleta said. "The rest are good cases. Andrew, here are six for you. Roland, these five are yours. These go to Stanley or Robert whichever one walks through the door first."

"You've got six still in your hand," Roland said.

"These I'm handling," Aleta said.

"How?" Andrew asked. "You're going to be in here for two months."

Aleta waved a folder. "Gentlemen, meet our legal aide, Tim Jordan. He wants us to sue his former employer for discriminating against him because he's gay."

"Which one was he?" Roland asked.

"That tall lean freckle-faced guy that kept organizing everyone," Andrew said. "He shuffled the people around so those who had jobs were moved up in line."

"Yeh, they thought he was working for us," Roland said. "He helped a couple of people fill out the forms."

"So go back and tell him he's hired. We need a person like that," Aleta said.

Roland scowled. "Alice has practically promised a job to someone. She's been interviewing for two weeks."

"We need two new secretaries. We are an office of five lawyers."

"There's a problem with Alice's pick," Andrew said. "She's experienced, but she's a bit...er...fat."

"Why are you hesitating?" Aleta asked.

"She's been turned down a lot. She's very fat," Andrew finally admitted.. "But she's Afro-American. Her name's Cora Jo Hayes."

"Will we need to get new chairs?"

"Possibly one."

"Tell Alice. Also tell her I want her to process these new hires right away and send them over this morning."

"What will Mr. Praetzel say?" Chin asked.

"Andrew can tell him," Aleta said.

"I told him about you. He'll think I didn't tell you how upset he was," Jackson responded.

"Did he bite you?"

Jackson reared back, startled.

"So if he doesn't bite, why are you afraid of him?"

"He's the senior partner," Andrew said.

"Well, be polite when you tell him."

"It's not good to make the senior partner unhappy."

"I do it all the time."

"But he loves you," Andrew argued. "He's not even sure Roland and I are worth paying. He may not be happy that three new employees were added."

"Are you suggesting we let him walk in and see our new staff working?"

Both men shook their heads.

"Okay, Andrew, it's up to you."

"Did I do something to anger you?"

"Roland spent a night in jail because he did what I asked. It's your turn."

"I volunteered," Andrew argued. "I know it was only for one day. But doesn't that count?"

"Roland, does that count?"

"No way!"

Shortly afterward, an officer came to Judge Jacobi's cell. "You can make your phone call now."

The guard handed the phone through the bars. When Norma got the law offices, she gave her name and said she'd been arrested but she didn't want Mr. West to show up before one o'clock.

"Tell him to check out the charges with his son who arrested me," Norma said. "This is no joke. And I don't want to see him until after lunch."

"So you know Lyle?" Aleta asked when Norma was finished.

"Everybody knows Lyle," Norma replied. "But no one really knows Lyle until they've been arrested by him."

"His father can't bend him, you know," Aleta remarked.

"I got that message loud and clear last night. I sat in that interrogation room, handcuffed, for three hours!"

"Unpleasant, isn't it?" Aleta sympathized.

"You know I can't change your sentence."

"Not if you think you'll lose face if you do, but don't worry. I'll adjust."

The guard came down the hall carrying an armload of packages. He opened the door and brought them into Aleta's cell.

"Any chocolates?" she asked the guard.

"West said no to any food."

"He would!" Aleta sighed. "He's so sure someone will poison me."

"Has anyone ever tried that?" Norma asked watching the unloading of packages from the adjoining cell.

"Yes, only I offered the chocolates to Stanley and Lyle and one of them had his stomach pumped before the lab came back with the results. One piece of candy wouldn't hurt you, but half a box would kill you. I think Stanley went first."

"Where did all these gifts come from?"

"Care packages from fellow lawyers," Aleta said.

"Friends?"

"My friends will send food."

"But West won't let you receive food."

"Ah, here he is now. He delivers the food himself," Aleta said. "Are you ready for warm homemade rolls?"

Norma watched Aleta greet Lyle warmly. Then she saw a bag being handed through the bars to her.

"Dad called me," he said to Norma. "He said he wasn't to bail you out until one. What's going on this morning that you want to watch?"

"Aleta has hired three new staff members, sight unseen," Norma Jacobi said. "I want to watch the meetings."

"Stanley won't be happy," Lyle said.

"We need the staff!" Aleta rejoined.

"It's not that exactly. He doesn't want the practice to expand. He's happy with a small office."

"Alice needs help," Aleta said. "She can't keep up with five lawyers by herself."

"More staff means more cases," Lyle said. "You know that."

"We already have the cases."

Susan Davis Sandberg

"Stanley wants you to cut back, not expand."

"Andrew told me that already. Do you have any good news?"

"Everybody is coming home on Friday. Wayne is going to let Stanley go home that afternoon."

"You need to have a party to celebrate the Chesneys' good news and Paige and Hawk's marriage. Next week on Friday, I think."

Lyle drew in a deep breath indicating his astonishment.

"Without you?"

Aleta scowled lightly. "Of course, without me. The group can function without me. Scratch Dr. Barre."

"It won't be the same if you're not there," Lyle said. "We can wait."

"Claude can't wait for two months to use his barbecue stuff again," Aleta remarked. "And we need to celebrate the marriage of Hawk and Paige now! Lauren will agree with me. I know she will. It's time for a celebration."

"You're right," Lyle said. "Lauren will agree that we need to celebrate Paige and Hawk getting married."

"Be sure to tell Lauren Dr. Herve Schwartzman is to be added to the guest list. He's Stanley's new friend–one that doesn't stick him with deputy duty when he should be home in bed making love to his wife!"

"Anything else?" Lyle asked.

"No lunch?" Aleta quipped.

"I'm going to be at an autopsy."

"You dug up the baby?"

"We dug up the baby. Natsumi found the flash drive in the book and it told us where the legal documents were."

"Where were they?"

"Buried," Lyle responded.

"In the coffin?"

"In the yard."

"How close are you to an arrest?"

"After the autopsy, we can pick him up."

"He's in Orlando," Aleta stated unequivocally.

"How do you know this?" Lyle asked.

Aleta paled.

"Oh, my Lord!" she exclaimed. "He's not going to kill Paige. A woman is going to do it. Lyle, get your sketch pad!"

"Stay there!" Lyle said, rushing out.

Aleta exchanged glances with Norma and commented, "He does forget sometimes where we are."

Norma Jacobi watched fascinated as Aleta's words were translated into a recognizable face on Lyle's sketchpad.

You've got to go now," Aleta urged just as he was finishing.

Aleta passed a blanket through the bars to Norma and whispered something to her.

"You're making no sense," Norma said loud enough for Lyle to her.

"Please trust me," Aleta said. "Do it for Jinx and Tigger."

"How'd you know the names of my cats?"

"Aleta knows things when she needs to. Whatever she told you to do, do it," Lyle remarked. "Is this close?"

He held up the sketch.

"Yes," she replied. "You must hurry."

"Can you give me a hint as to when this is going to happen?"

"The gun won't leave her purse. She's going to shoot from the hip."

"Where are they?"

"I don't know," Aleta said. "What I do know is that you have to get this off as quickly as possible."

As he left, Lyle looked around for his driver.

"He's in the john," one of the guards said

"Thanks, Jerry," Lyle said, rushing through the open steel door when Jerry pushed the button. A man came down the hall. Lyle heard the door close behind him, then open again to let the man enter. The man was dressed in a business suit and carried a briefcase. He didn't recognize him and he thought he knew all the criminal lawyers in the county.

Lyle puzzled over this as he took the elevator down. It stopped at the second floor to pick up more passengers and Lyle realized that one of the offices would have a fax machine. He needed to get this off right away.

He radioed French and was given the fax number. Harriet was waiting. As he was writing the additional detail about the killer shooting through her purse, he thought about the stranger with the briefcase.

He handed the sketch to a clerk. She put it and the cover letter into the machine.

While he waited, his mind puzzled over why Aleta would be handing a blanket to Norma Jacobi. The judge wouldn't be spending another night in jail. His father would have her out at one on the dot. Besides, it was summer and she had a blanket. She didn't need two.

Upstairs Aleta was telling Norma Jacobi she had to lay down and cover her head completely.

"You are making no sense," Norma reiterated. "I can't afford to look foolish."

Her comment sparked Aleta's mind to give birth to a more compelling argument. "A reporter is coming. He will sneak a photo of you behind bars," Aleta said. "You don't want to make this afternoon's edition of the Independent Register, do you?"

"How do you know a reporter's coming?"

"Justin keeps tabs on me. He always gets a quote from me before he files any story on me. Besides, I'll bet he knows you're here."

Norma laid down quickly.

"Put your feet on the pillow," Aleta added. "And cover all of you."

"Why?" Norma asked.

"Sshh," Aleta whispered. "He's coming."

Norma decided to do as she was told. She'd be covered, after all.

The Arborville cop, who drove Chief West to the county jail, lay unconscious on the men's room floor.

Jerry looked at his partner as the man passed Lyle West in the hall. "I'm going to check on Drew.'"

He walked over to the restroom door, opened it and shouted, "Hey, Drew, your chief's gone!"

When he didn't get an answer, he stepped inside the door part way. "Hey, Drew, you okay?"

Those were the last words he spoke before dropping unconscious in the doorway. The second guard turned as the man in the business suit set down his briefcase on the rolling belt.

The guard handed him the stun gun, opened the door to the cellblock and turned away. The charge rendered him unconscious immediately.

The man slipped on a mask and strode down between the rows of cells to the last cell in the row on the right. Aleta was standing in the center of the cell. She backed away as he approached, the unconscious guard's gun in one hand, a pillow in the other.

He stopped at the cell before Aleta's and put two bullets in the bump on the pillow. Norma shrieked and jerked her feet when the bullets smashed through her shoe and into her foot. Then she lay still.

Now she knew what was happening. Her reason told her to freeze.

The man stared at the blanket-covered woman for over a minute.

Norma was in too much shock to move let alone breathe. Someone wanted her dead. It had to be Van Horne. He was going after Paige. How had she failed to see the truth? Where had her instinct been? When had she stopped believing the children? Suddenly, she was grateful for

Aleta's outrageous action that had unmasked Kurt Van Horne as a man who would exchange his children for money. She had tried to deny the influence the young lawyer had on her and sought for a legal argument not offered by the lawyers. Fortunately, Aleta had presented her with mounds of evidence from which to choose. She remembered not wanting to hand her the victory. She almost went the other way, but Aleta had satisfactorily proven that Paige's delusion was not a delusion. Still she had not believed the father had killed the baby. And now she realized that the child had witnessed the murder of her sister.

The time between the two shots into her foot and the next shots fired was barely two minutes. It seemed like an hour.

The first shot into the adjacent cell missed its target.

Aleta was standing in the middle of the cell. The man derided himself. How could he miss?

He shot again.

Again he missed. He decided the mask was messing with his aim. He tore it off and took aim.

Aleta backed up a couple steps. It was an automatic movement. One naturally withdraws from danger.

She began to pray. Not aloud, but silently from her heart. She asked God to care for her husband and son.

The words "bow before the Lord your God" flashed into her mind. She dropped to her knees as the trigger was squeezed. The bullet creased the top of her head as she dropped.

It stunned her and she fell to the ground as another round followed. It buried itself in the back wall of her cell as well.

The gunman lowered his gun. His finger tightened on the trigger. He meant to finish the job.

The sound of the bullet that pierced his skull reached him when he could no longer hear. His finger squeezed the trigger and the round buried itself in the floor beside Aleta's prone body.

Lyle West radioed for help as he ran up to the shooter. He kicked the gun away and stood above the man who lay dying at his feet.

The man gargled something, but West didn't stoop over to listen. His gun was trained on the man's head.

Aleta laid still, blood seeping from her head wound. West radioed for two ambulances and told them to alert Dr. Cook. He pushed back his self-recrimination. Time for that when his duty was done.

Norma Jacobi peeked out from under the blanket.

West asked her if she was okay.

"He shot me in the foot," she announced. Then, looking over at Aleta, she cried, "Tell me she's not dead!"

"I can't," he choked, getting on his radio and calling for a third ambulance.

As officers appeared, West began issuing orders.

Aleta's new hires appeared as the ambulance was loading an unconscious Aleta. Chief West told them to see Stanley, and then he climbed aboard the ambulance with her.

Aleta regained consciousness in the ambulance as it was nearing the hospital.

"I'm still alive?" she asked.

"As am I," Lyle replied. "Judge Jacobi was shot in the foot."

"Yes, I know," Aleta said. "I need to go back. I have people coming and I left all my stuff."

"Your people came. I sent them to Stanley."

"You didn't'!" Aleta gasped in dismay.

"When were you going to tell him?"

"Andrew was supposed to do that."

Tim Jordan led the two secretaries to Stanley's room. He looked inside and saw Stanley sitting in a wheelchair in front of the window.

He went to him directly. "We have to hurry, Sir," Tim said.

"Who are you?"

"We're your new staff, that is, we are as soon as one of the partners signs our contracts.

"Cora Jo Hayes and Karyn Bishop are legal secretaries. I'm a law clerk."

"What does a law clerk do?"

"Right now he rushes you to emergency so you can see your wife before they take her back to jail."

"Hurry, Man!" Stanley ordered.

"You aren't surprised?" Cora Jo asked as she hurried after the fast moving wheelchair. Once inside the elevator, she tried to catch her breath, but couldn't.

Stanley got up out of his wheelchair and using Tim as a crutch told Karyn to help Cora Jo into the chair. When the elevator doors opened, he yelled for a nurse. The response was immediate.

"Where's my wife?" Stanley asked.

The nurse pointed while the orderly fetched another wheelchair. Stanley was lowered into it and Tim pushed the chair toward the room.

Cora Jo, who was left behind in the wheelchair, began to cry softly.

Suddenly, Stanley's wheelchair was turned around.

"Are you coming?" Stanley called. "If you're going to work for me, you're going to need to know who the boss is."

The nurse smiled and pushed Cora Jo's chair toward the group. Cora Joe entered only a couple seconds behind the others.

She was in time to hear Stanley said, "You were going back without seeing me?"

"I'm a prisoner, remember," Aleta said. "There are rules."

"The reason you were cited for contempt is because you bent the rules," Stanley said. "Now why are you avoiding me?"

"I hired three people without telling you," Aleta put forth.

Stanley knocked that explanation away. "I agreed to one. That you went over the line doesn't surprise me."

"Now's the time when I tell you I'm gay and you tell me you don't need a law clerk," Tim said

Aleta laughed.

"Stanley knew you were gay the minute he saw you."

"I'm not that obvious," Tim protested.

"No, you aren't," Stanley said. "You presented yourself properly in every way. Now Aleta tell me the real reason you didn't come to see me."

"First, tell these people they're hired," Aleta demanded.

Stanley turned. "You're all hired. I trust Aleta's judgment."

He turned back and looked at his wife.

"Why is it you're so anxious to go back to jail?"

Aleta sighed in defeat. How well he knew her.

"You know how I hate stitches."

"Who says you need stitches?"

"It's an option," Aleta said. "You didn't mind my having a scar the last time."

"But you did."

"It's my head. I should get to choose," Aleta stated defiantly.

"Aleta, it's an order," Stanley countered softly.

Two doctors walked into the room.

Dr. Taekman chuckled. "You win, Wayne. He ordered her.

"Does everyone need to know?" she griped.

"If I could persuade you to do it my way, we'd never have to do it again," Stanley said.

"That would be worse," Aleta said. "It would mean I lost the argument."

Stanley chuckled. "I can see where that would not be palatable."

Lyle walked in while Dr. Taekman was stitching Aleta's head.

Stanley looked up. "When were you going to tell me she was shot?"

"Never," Lyle said. "I didn't want to get yelled at by my best friend."

"I know she sent you away."

"Did she tell you?"

"Hey Guys, I'm conscious," Aleta put in.

"Hold still!" Dr. Taekman ordered.

"I didn't move!" Aleta protested.

"Don't talk then," he responded. "I'm used to my patients being silent and still."

"Dead?" Aleta quipped.

"Sshh," Stanley cautioned.

"What I don't understand is why Martha or Harriet didn't call me," Lyle said.

Aleta wanted to explain, but she remembered the doctor's order not to speak. The two kept discussing her actions as if she weren't there. After a minute she began to enjoy the exchange. They were so astute, these two.

As Dr. Taekman was finishing up, Stanley asked Lyle if she had to go back.

Slowly the tears began to stream from her eyes and disappear in the hair above her ears.

Stanley wiped the tears away from the side of her face. "It's an unusually harsh punishment. It's hard to believe she didn't soften when you apologized. Most judges do."

"Finished," Dr. Taekman announced.

"At least she didn't rule against me," Aleta said. "The kids all have a real home and a bright future. I think about that a lot."

"Couldn't you have gotten it without antagonizing her?"

"She'd set up a wall," Aleta responded. "I think she was upset that we were denying the father his rights. After all, the mother was dead and the father wanted the children. Reggie Barre did us a lot of harm."

"Which reminds me, we've never axed a regular guest before. Are you sure you want to do this?"

"Yes. She betrayed me," Aleta remarked. "She wanted to put Paige in a mental institution. Paige shouldn't have to deal with Dr. Barre at our party where we're celebrating her wedding."

"I agree," Stanley said. "I wish you could be there. I can come and sit with you in jail if you want."

"You would do that?"

"Yes."

Aleta was warmed by his offer. She realized that she wanted to say yes. She didn't want to be the only one missing the party.

"Don't do that. I want you to be there," she decided. "Then you can share it with me on Saturday."

Once back in her cell, Aleta sat on her bed that was little more than a metal bench with a thin mattress pad and told herself that she couldn't dwell on what she was missing.

One by one realizations hit her like slow drum beats. There was a purpose to all this. God had personally saved her. He'd heard the prayer from the deepest part of her being, deeper even than her prayer for her son and her husband. She hadn't wanted to die.

Her gratitude filled her. Her husband would be visiting her in jail, not in a cemetery. Her son would lie in her arms again.

God had not only sent her two visions, but He'd showed her the face of the killer. He hadn't ever done that before.

She smiled. She was still a prophet. Judge Jacobi may be angry with her. God was not.

God wanted her here. He had a purpose. She wasn't happy about it, but He didn't require that she be happy. One can't help the feelings that well up unbidden from the deep recesses of the mind where memories are stored. It is what one does when those feelings arise that matters.

I'm suffering the consequences of my actions. Actions have consequences. What did I think? That God would free me from the natural order of things?

And, unbeknownst to her, the next battle would be decided by that very truism.

Chapter 32

It would happen in Orlando.

Kurt Van Horne knew his wife. She had no affinity for children. She was interested in social position and wealth. Kurt offered both. Paige was a threat to the former.

Heidi did not want her husband to be accused of any crime. The accusation itself would hurt their standing. And such an accusation would give birth to rumors which would live long after both were dead.

On top of that Heidi resented the judge's order that Kurt pay additional child support supposedly owed his children. In Heidi's eyes he owed them nothing.

When she discovered they weren't his biological children, she demanded he sue to recover the money. He told her that such a suit would embarrass them. He prevailed. Social standing came first.

Interestingly, he forgot that in the end.

Heidi had sat at breakfast that Friday morning near the group from Willow Glen. She'd sorted through the people quickly. While nibbling on toast, she'd listened as they openly discussed that day's plans.

The youngest wanted to revisit the Animal Kingdom and she was allowed to choose that day's activity. That galled Heidi. A child should never be allowed to make a decision for a group of adults.

Susan Davis Sandberg

One of the teenage boys objected. He wanted to go the Typhoon Lagoon, whatever that was. Two men volunteered to take the teenagers there.

Heidi was pleased. The group was cut in half with two of the men and the two teenage boys, who could run her down, going to what she soon learned was a second water park.

Paige and Hawk said they'd meet the group for lunch at noon.

"Same place," was all Paige said.

Heidi couldn't figure that out, but Kurt knew the restaurant was in the Animal Kingdom when she reported the conversation to him.

He then told his wife she would lunch in the restaurant nearest the main gate. He didn't explain his decision and Heidi didn't ask.

"Can't you have lunch with me?" she pleaded. "I hate eating alone."

"We can't chance it," Kurt snapped. Her whining annoyed him.

Didn't she understand how important it was that he be elsewhere with a solid alibi? Not that he'd be mistaken for a woman, but it had to seem as if it were an act of a madwoman, a woman out for revenge.

He wasn't even registered in the hotel. She'd registered as a single. She'd arrived on a commercial flight while he was still in court.

He'd flown down in a private aircraft.

He'd thought of everything. Just in case.

Paige and Hawk had celebrated all night after hearing the news about Tyler and Molly. That the judge had declared their marriage valid was a bonus.

They'd spent the night in each other's arms, waking periodically to rejoice in their love and surprising themselves as new layers of passion unfolded.

After breakfast, wanting desperately to do something to please her, Hawk headed for the barbershop.

"Tell the barber how to cut my hair so that it pleases you," he said.

The barber, a plump man with a well-groomed black moustache, looked at the young girl expectantly.

"But I like your hair," Paige said, worried.

"It needs a trim," Hawk said encouragingly. "Go ahead. It'll grow back."

"I want to see his eyes," Paige started. "And then trim the rest so it balances with that."

The barber smiled and asked, "The eyebrows too?"

Paige studied Hawk's face. "No. Just the eyes."

Paige began to bite her nails as she watched.

Hawk admonished her lightly. "If you're going to chew your nails down to the nub every time I get a haircut, I'll have to let it grow down to my knees."

"Don't worry, Miss," the barber said. "He'll look good."

"That's 'Mrs.'," Hawk said. "She's my wife. We're on our honeymoon. And if you make me look good, that'd be a real plus."

"He's kidding," Page remarked. "He knows he's good-looking. I wouldn't marry a man that wasn't after only two days. It'd take at least a week."

The barber laughed. "This one's on me. You two are fun."

"Oh no!" Paige said. "Hawk will pay you. You are giving us good service. Your attitude is all the gift we need."

The barber whispered to the man in the chair, "Where did you find her? She's wonderful."

"You are so right!" Hawk responded.

When the barber finished, Hawk commented, "You did a great job."

"Do you really like it?" Paige asked.

"Yes. I honestly do."

"So do I," Paige said. "It was a nice gift, letting me choose your haircut."

"What do I owe you?" Hawk asked.

"Just stop cutting your own hair. This lady deserves you at your best."

"She said I should pay," Hawk insisted, "and I don't want to underpay you."

Paige intervened. "Do you have a hundred in that wallet of yours?"

"Yes, why?"

"It's your wedding present to me," Paige said.

Hawk handed the barber the hundred. "Thanks, Man."

"No," the barber replied. "Thank you!"

After they left the barbershop, Paige suggested they each buy new shorts.

"I don't wear shorts," Hawk said.

"Why not?" Paige asked. "You've got great legs."

"I just don't."

"It's hot down here. Shorts will feel good. Everyone wears shorts down here or haven't you noticed?"

"I'll go with you to buy shorts for you," he said firmly.

"If I get khaki shorts like yours, it won't look wrong, will it?"

"No, but I'm not wearing shorts," Hawk reiterated.

"We don't have to get matching shirts," Paige said.

"We aren't getting me shorts!" Hawk declared.

"Of course we are. It's hot down here."

"My legs are too long," he complained, but Paige ignored that argument.

"It was your idea to transform yourself."

"Just to cut my hair, that's all."

"You wore swimming trunks yesterday."

"I had to," Hawk said. "We were going to get wet."

"It would please me if you would try them," Paige said softly. "But, the choice is yours."

Hawk wore his new shorts to lunch.

No one could help commenting on Hawk's new look. No one, however, seeing Paige's beaming face could bring himself to tease Hawk.

"I like the haircut," Harriet said.

"You look good, Hawk," Molly added. "Really handsome. My sister did a good job."

"The haircut was Hawk's idea," Paige said.

"I like your hair shorter," Robert said. "More professional."

"I'd like to meet your barber," Claude said. "The man has a gift."

Hawk began to feel positive about the changes. Pleasing Paige had been his main objective, but the positiveness of others sat well in his stomach.

Harriet showed Hawk the sketch she'd received from Chief West.

"Who's this?"

"The woman who's come to kill Paige," Harriet said. "Don't try to shake us today. If you want privacy, we will take you back to your hotel room anytime you ask. But I can't guarantee you'll be safer there. Usually we know where and when. This is the first time we've been shown who."

"This came from which one of the prophets?" Hawk asked.

"Aleta," Harriet said, and then she told him the rest of the story.

"She risked her life to get this sketch to us, didn't she?"

"I think she was trying to save West, but her concern for Paige was a close second."

"Paige wants to go on the trek through the forest first. Will that be okay?"

"Try to keep her off any rides until later," Harriet said. "We're hoping we can spot this woman. She has no idea we're looking for her, so Claude and I can be pretty blatant. Separate from Molly's group. I'll clue Robert and Bertha in. I don't want anyone accidentally shot."

"Do you two have guns?"

"No."

"What do you plan to do?"

"Surprise her," Harriet said. "Disarm her. Arrest her."

The minute she said that Harriet realized how she could do that.

"Trust us," she said. "We love Paige."

Hawk and Paige headed for Africaland and the Pangani Forest Trail. Her buoyant spirit carried them along into the simulated forest and through an African forest of bright green. Paige laughingly referred to them wearing the right colors for the trek.

Hawks lack of response told her something was wrong.

"You're upset," she remarked. "Tell me why."

"It's not you," he hastened to assure her.

"You look really nice," she observed.

"It's not that," he assured her. "I'm actually more comfortable than I thought I would be."

"Tell me what's wrong. Please."

"Harriet and Claude are sticking close to us for a reason."

"Not to chaperone us surely?"

"In a way," Hawk began gently. "They're guarding us."

Paige stopped, color draining from her face. "From whom?"

"A woman," Hawk said, and then briefly described the face he'd seen in West's sketch.

"My stepmother," Paige said. "What is there about me that makes my parents want to kill me?"

"It's not you," Hawk said. "It's what you know."

"I want to have parents too–like Molly and Tyler," Paige cried softly. "I want to be loved again like my mother loved me."

"Your mother's love isn't dead," Hawk said. "It is a part of you. Molly is letting Evelyn mother her. There are people who love you. They are walking behind us."

Paige looked back at Harriet who was checking the people passing them.

"She told you she loved me?"

"Yes," Hawk affirmed. "You take the parental love that's offered and let it fill the void. Don't be afraid to reach out for parent figures. I won't mind."

"Shouldn't I be outgrowing that need?"

"That never happens," Hawk said.

"It would be nice to know my real father."

"Your mother would have selected someone like Dr. Chesney. You have a good father," Hawk declared. "I know it."

He put his arms around her and pulled her to him.

Suddenly Harriet's rough voice said, "You don't want to do that."

"What are you talking about?" another voice challenged.

Hawk didn't see Harriet move between him and the woman but he heard her voice coming from a place closer to him.

"This is the sketch that will make the front page tomorrow," Harriet announced.

"That's me!" gasped the woman, her surprise coating her words. "How did you get that?"

"Chief West faxed it to me," Harriet said.

"But I just bought the earrings yesterday," Heidi Van Horne commented, puzzled. Her hand stayed in her purse, her finger on the trigger of the gun hidden there.

"A prophet described you, complete with earrings," Harriet explained.

"What the hell are you talking about? What prophet?"

"Aleta Praetzel."

"She's in jail!"

"Do you want to know what the headline will be?" Harriet charged abruptly. "Oh yes, you are going to make the front page."

Heidi's fear quickly surfaced as Harriet continued, "Socialite Murders Daughter."

"She's not my daughter!"

"They'll explain that in the article, but it's an eye catcher. It'll sell copies."

Harriet saw the desperate look of a trapped animal. She continued quickly.

"I can offer you a way out. No publicity."

Heidi caught herself succumbing to the raspy voice of the old lady. Her husband's scowl flashed in her mind. One didn't cross Kurt Van Horne.

"You're in my way. If you stay there, I'll shoot you and then her," Heidi threatened, a new determination rife in her voice and manner.

Harriet opened her hand. "Police. You're under arrest for conspiracy to commit murder."

Heidi saw the badge in the open hand. She hesitated.

"The headline will be even worse. 'Mad Socialite Kills Daughter and Cop.' That will sell tons of papers," Harriet predicted. "It'll make the evening newscasts nationwide. Your husband will leave you to your fate."

Suddenly, Heidi knew what this woman was saying was true. Kurt's alibi was solid. He had urged her to come down here alone. They hadn't been seen together even once.

"It was his idea," she said.

She felt the purse being tipped and pulled away from her hand. She released the gun.

"You said there'd be no publicity."

"How much do you know?"

"You mean about him burning down the house?" she asked. "I know Kurt has the lockets."

"That's enough," Harriet said. "We have a deal.

Warrants were issued for Kurt Van Horne's arrest both in Florida and Illinois. He was captured entering the private plane he'd chartered to fly him to South America. He knew at once who had betrayed him.

When he saw her at police headquarters, the look in his eyes told her that her only hope was to hold nothing back. He had to be convicted.

Aleta's prophecy didn't come up. Harriet simply explained that the Illinois police had faxed a photo of Mrs. Van Horne with a warning to be on the lookout for her. The explanation satisfied the Florida police.

Chapter 33

Over the weekend that followed, the entire contingent from Northern Illinois arrived home. Aleta's father and Stanley's father visited Aleta immediately.

They were distressed at the sight of her. She apologized for her uncombed hair.

"Dr. Taekman told me not to touch my head for at least five days," she explained. "I look as if I'm at the end of my tether which I am, but I'm coping. Don't let Stanley worry about me."

"As if we could stop him," her father said.

"Do you want us to fight this contempt charge?" Hubert asked. "It's unusually severe for putting a toe over the line."

"You had to be there," Aleta said. "The air was charged with emotion and I had to break Van Horne and I took Judge Jacobi farther than she was prepared to go. She tried to stop me. You two know how futile that is."

Both men nodded.

"I dread spending my whole summer in jail, but, I could be dead," Aleta rationalized aloud.

"If you were dead, you wouldn't be suffering," her father said. "I'm not sure that's a comforting thought."

Aleta laughed. "You're right. There is no comforting thought for this situation. Just help me keep busy, Dad. The time will go quicker."

Stanley said you took on twelve new cases yourself and hired three new staff," Robert mentioned. "I think you're going to be plenty busy without my help."

"I gave you and Stanley five new cases too. I didn't hog them all."

"Stanley told me. He said to remind you we can get our own cases."

"Why did he say that?" Aleta asked.

"Can't you guess?"

"You're talking about the Van Horne case."

"What else?"

"But we got such a great result!"

Her father smiled at her. "Stanley's idea of a great result is to have you home with him, uninjured."

"I'm for that kind of result too," Aleta admitted. "But I sleep well at night knowing those three kids are happy."

"Paige and Hawk are packing to move into their new house," Robert said.

"Ask them if they want to sublet their apartment furnished," Aleta said. "Karyn needs a place to live with her two daughters. She has no furniture."

"And no money," Robert put in.

"She can make the rent," Aleta said. "We can give her a starting bonus."

"Then we'd have to give them all starting bonuses," Robert pointed out.

"What a great idea!"

"It wasn't mine."

"Sure it was," Aleta insisted.

Hubert spoke up. "Don't worry, Robert. Stanley will know who's spending the firm's money."

When the two men left, Hubert asked Aleta's father if she could handle sixty days.

"She'll handle it," Robert replied. "But it will be hard on her. And she doesn't really deserve such punishment."

"I agree. But I got the feeling she doesn't want us to pressure Judge Jacobi," Hubert said. "She's thinking much farther ahead than I would in her shoes."

"Me too, I'm afraid. I'm not as strong as she is."

"Don't give me that. Where do you think that determination came from?"

"She was born with it. I think she stole some genes from another gene pool."

"She's like your mother."

"It's a sex thing then. Bypassed me completely."

"You just show your determination a bit differently. I was your divorce lawyer, remember?"

"And witness to my first marriage to Bertha," Robert mused. "I was determined to have a private honeymoon."

"I think that one night was it," Hubert said. "This was your fourth attempt. How much privacy did you have?"

"I haven't given up."

"I call that determination."

The week passed swiftly for all but Aleta. Only lawyers were permitted to visit during hours other than visiting hours. On Monday Tim delivered a packet of contract cases and Aleta began working on them.

The loneliness hit her on Tuesday. She had encouraged her friends and family not to worry about her. She was going to be there a while. She told everyone she had plenty to keep her busy.

On Monday she completed two of the contracts. By Tuesday noon she'd completed a rough draft on one more.

When she stopped for lunch, she realized she couldn't dispel the loneliness with work. She had to deal with it another way.

She lay on her bunk after lunch and stared at the ceiling above her. The men were housed on the floor above. When Norma had been in the next cell, her presence had helped dispel the loneliness that crowded in on her now that both of the cells next to her were empty.

Her brave front had been just that–a front. Despair seeped in sapping her determination not to cry out for relief.

She forced herself to pick up the next contract and she worked on it stopping only for supper. She found she'd been given a double portion of meat and realized Dr. Cook had sent over medical orders. A pill was offered to her at supper as well.

She felt better after that. She wasn't forgotten.

Wednesday she finished the fourth contract and immediately began working on the fifth. Tim showed up just before noon with a bag of sweet rolls and two hard-boiled eggs and two case files. He took the four contracts with him.

Thursday Tim returned with a bag of cold chicken and a brownie and three typed contracts for her review. Aleta handed Tim her notes on the cases plus the fifth contract ready for typing.

Tim told her he'd bring enough work on Friday to keep her busy on the weekend.

When Tim said that, Aleta's heart sank. There was no way he could bring enough work for three days. Something always needed checking before she could go on.

After he left, despair set in again. This time it wasn't easily shaken, but she reminded herself that if she didn't finish what she was given, Tim would bring her less. She shook off her disheartenment and set down to work.

One hour at a time, she told herself. One hour at a time. I'll give melancholy its chance after I've finished if I'm not too tired to wallow in sea of despondency.

She worked fast and poured a full measure of concentration into each project, hoping that by so doing the feeling of hopelessness knocking at her heart's door would get discouraged and leave.

By supper she'd consumed the chicken and the brownie and reviewed each contract twice. She was out of work.

She laid back and let depression wash over her. She could feel it working its persuasive magic on her mind distorting reality by resurrecting the bad memories and burying the good ones. She allowed its gloomy outlook to take over her reason.

Fifty-three more days, she mused and the thought overwhelmed what little hope she'd clung to. That was too many days. She didn't care that it was a relatively short jail sentence. It was too long for her.

The tears came soon afterward. She put the pillow over her face to muffle the sound of her weeping.

Prayer came much later.

By the early morning hours she'd long ago stopped crying and slept fitfully afterward. She'd awakened in the still early morning hours and began to talk to God.

"Why am I here?" she asked silently. "I thought maybe I was to help someone but I'm even farther away from the rest of the female jail population than I was this morning."

There were now three cells between her and her nearest neighbor. She felt like a pariah.

"Why am I an outcast?" she murmured. "What did I do?"

Her perception of the events began to fall into place.

"I did something that displeased You, didn't I?"

Her mind raced over the events surrounding the Van Horne trial. She dismissed her high-handedness in Judge Jacobi's courtroom. She was being punished for that.

She'd liked Norma Jacobi. She sensed that the judge had wanted to find a way to reduce her sentence and still save face. The attack had presented her with that opportunity. That she'd been automatically returned to jail she'd chalked up to the judge being under anesthetic at the time.

She had expected to be released as soon as the judge was conscious.

Lyle had told her that his father had presented a good argument to him and the DA and the charges against Judge Jacobi were dropped.

Aleta remembered the telling part of the argument. If the judge had thought that there was danger, she would have protested being jailed next to Aleta.

That she was still in jail had to be God's handiwork, Aleta mused.

"So you've kept me here, God," she said. "And not to help someone else. Even the cases I've been given to work on are not significant. So what did I do?"

Then it came to her.

Her first words were a protest. "She betrayed me."

She recalled Stanley asking her if she was sure. She remembered her response and his cautious acceptance of it. Her guest list had always been exclusively hers.

"But Dr. Barre testified against Paige," Aleta muttered irritably. "Yes, I know she was barely recovered from her own problems."

It was much later before Aleta admitted that she hadn't considered how difficult going to the barbecue would be for Reggie Barre.

"Nothing like rubbing her face in the realization that she had no friends," Aleta murmured.

"So what do You want me to do?"

Aleta began to think about Reggie Barre. Her anger at the psychiatrist came flooding back.

Another thought occurred to Aleta. What if Reggie had connected at the party with a person or two?

I know she and Martha got along, Aleta remembered. She and Evelyn seemed to hit it off. And Reggie's report on Molly and Tyler were positive. She liked them.

"Not inviting her to the party is vengeful? I guess it is. But she won't come..."

Suddenly Aleta chuckled.

"Oh, yes, that's what I'm hoping, but if that's what You want, I need to talk to Lauren. She needs to understand to truly make Reggie feel invited. And yes, I will apologize first chance I get."

Aleta fell asleep immediately after making that promise.

The guard woke her.

"You're new," Aleta said.

"Sorry about the trouble you had," the guard said. "Your doctor's here."

"Dr. Cook?"

"Dr. Barre," the guard replied with a questioning tone.

"I need to see her," Aleta said. "I have several doctors."

"She's not on the list," the tone slightly challenging.

"She's a psychiatrist," Aleta said. "She probably heard I had a head injury. Speaking of which, is my hair worse this morning?"

"I'll bring her right down," the guard said hurrying away.

"It's worse," Aleta murmured. "I wish I knew whether or not it's safe to shower."

Swallowing her pride, Aleta greeted the grim-faced woman with a smile.

"I asked God to send me Lauren, but this is even better," Aleta said warmly.

Dr. Barre eyed her skeptically, "I'm better than your best friend?"

"Lauren was supposed to invite you to my party tonight and to tell you I was ready to apologize. Now I can do it in person."

"Apologize? For what?

"For pressuring you into attending my last party for which you weren't ready and for taking you off my list for this one because I was in a snit."

Reggie sat back. "I don't believe I've ever had a better apology. But, I didn't come here for that. I came to apologize to you and to see if you needed the help of a counselor. I hear Dr. Schwartzman is taking on a few cases and well as some teaching assignments. I was going to recommend him."

"I'm his lawyer," Aleta smiled. "And I have his power of attorney."

"I know that, but I wasn't sure you knew how good he is."

"I know."

"Well, that's it," Reggie said, "except for my apology. I don't know how to go about this. Let me start by saying you were right. I was wrong. I was unprofessional. I was in, what did you call it, a snit because I felt uncomfortable at the party and I felt like you were showing off. And then I watched Paige making friends the way you do and then, when she didn't give me her trust, I wanted to bring her down. I am so glad now that I lost, but it was Dr. Schwartzman who knocked me for a loop. He was disgusted with me. I blamed you for that at first. I talked to my patients who were dying. They listened. They counseled. I eased their physical pain. They eased my psychological pain. It wasn't just one. I got a little bit of guidance from different ones. I really like the work I'm doing now. I guess I came to say thank you."

Aleta smiled. "That was an A+ apology in my book."

"About your party, I can't come. I'd feel awkward."

"You want to bring someone who'll feel more awkward?"

"There is no such person."

"Judge Norma Jacobi is such a person."

"Why do you want her at your party after what she did?"

"She's the reason the children are all happy and settled in good places," Aleta said. "She deserves to see the result of her decision."

"But I didn't help at all," Reggie countered.

"You were wrong about Paige, but even the judge was temporarily fooled by the fake Penny in the Home for the Retarded. Your reports on Molly and Tyler were accurate and important. They bolstered my argument that Paige had been a good mother to her sister. Oh, you helped a lot."

"That's a subtle point."

"I have friends capable of appreciating subtlety," Aleta said. "Please come. You were there when Paige and Hawk were engaged. I hear that married they're extremely happy. You weren't the only one to think it wouldn't work, that she was too young. Bring a little gift. Be a part of the celebration."

"I'm surprised your friends are throwing a party without you."

"Go and find out why," Aleta urged. "Bring Norma Jacobi with you. I'll tell Lauren to expect the both of you."

"What about you?"

"If you and Norma go to the party, I'll have a good evening too."

"Okay, we'll go," Reggie said. "It's crazy, but I think she'd like to see the kids she saved."

Five thirty that evening, Chief Lyle West showed up at the county jail with two of his officers. Aleta was shocked and dismayed.

"What are you doing here?" she charged.

"You're moving. The judge is moving you. She said my jail had better accommodations."

"You'll miss the party."

"Not if you don't change."

"Go like this?" Aleta gasped.

"You're going to another jail, Aleta. And you're going to be transferred like any other prisoner. I'm sorry that that means cuffed. Regulation."

"Lauren will be so upset with me," Aleta groaned. "She depends on you. And with Stanley on crutches...oh, heck, let's just go. Have one of your men pick up my stuff tomorrow."

"It doesn't work that way," Lyle said. "Are you ever going to learn to stay on your side of the fence? I've already told my men to follow us."

When Aleta saw the leg chains she gasped.

"We take extra precautions when transferring prisoners between jails," Lyle explained.

"Lyle, I'm not going to run," Aleta protested.

"It's the night of your party. You just might be tempted."

"Oh, for Heaven's sake!" Aleta exclaimed. "With my hair all matted and me not having had a shower for a week, there's no way I'm going anywhere but to another jail."

"Stand still!" Lyle ordered.

Once the chains were fastened, Lyle told his men to take over.

"Where are you going?" Aleta asked.

"Back to the party," he said. "These men know their job."

"Well, yes, I know they do," Aleta admitted quickly. "I just thought...never mind. Go help Lauren. And thank her for me."

"I'll do that."

The men escorted her to their patrol car and put her in the back. She couldn't take regular steps so it was slow going. It was also humbling.

"I'm learning, God," she prayed silently. "Please, help me."

When they started off, the driver asked his partner, "Do you have the paperwork?"

"No," came the response.

"The chief's got it then. We've got to go get it," the driver determined.

"Why don't we take her to jail first?"

"It's on the way," the driver said. "West will be upset if we don't come get it right away."

"Yeh, you're right," the second man responded.

Aleta slid down in the back seat and began to weep.

"Oh God," she prayed. "Please don't let my friends see me like this," she prayed. She knew, at once, that God didn't like egotistical requests and immediately agreed. "Whatever you ask, I'll do."

The patrol car parked in the shadows near the front door. There were only a few lights on in the house. Aleta sat up. She watched her friends milling around outside on the new stone patio at one end of which was Claude's new barbecue grill. Her heart yearned to be with them. The officer emerged from the house and opened the rear car door.

"Chief West wants you to come inside. He says as long as you're here, you can have a bath," the officer told her.

"Alone?" Aleta asked hopefully.

"Prisoners don't bath unattended," the officer said, helping her out of the car.

The house was quiet when Aleta entered. Lyle West pointed to the master bedroom.

She heard a click. It sounded like a camera but no light flashed.

"My chains?" she asked holding out her hands.

"The female officer will removed them inside the bathroom," Lyle said. "You have ten minutes."

Aleta looked through the window as she shuffled through the bedroom. Her guests were having a good time. At least she got to see that much. They had become friends over the months. The groups of people were mixed. Couples had split up. Men and women were mingling freely.

Aleta opened the bathroom door and stepped inside.

"Grams!" she gasped delightedly as Harriet unfastened her cuffs. "Bertha!"

"Hurry," Bertha said. "We've only got ten minutes. I'm here to check out your head and shampoo your hair."

Aleta cast aside her modesty and let her jumpsuit drop to the floor. She slid into the warm sudsy water. Bertha looked at the scarred section and pronounced it healed. Despite her pronouncement, Aleta noticed that Bertha used a gentle touch in shampooing the matted hair. Aleta hastily washed the rest of her body.

"Time's up," Harriet announced.

Bertha rinsed Aleta's hair quickly. Aleta rose and stepped from the tub. Harriet handed her a towel. After she hurriedly dried herself, Aleta reached for the jumpsuit.

"You can't put that on!" Harriet protested. "It's filthy."

"It's regulation," Aleta replied.

"I laid out clean clothes for you."

"Can't, Grams. Sorry," Aleta said, pulling on the jumpsuit. "The bath was wonderful though. Thanks!"

A knock on the door and Chief West's voice saying that time was up gave Aleta no time for even a quick hug. She immediately held out her hands. Harriet secured the cuffs as Bertha opened the door. Aleta hobbled through the bedroom willing herself not to cry. The tears, however, came unbidden. She couldn't reach her face to brush them away. That would have to wait until she was in the back of the patrol car.

When Aleta entered the dimly lit living room a second person was standing beside Chief West.

"You win," Judge Jacobi said to Lyle West.

Again Aleta heard the click of the camera shutter. This time there was a flash.

Aleta ignored the camera flash. She looked at Lyle quizzically. "What was the bet?"

"Doesn't matter," Lyle responded. "So are you ready to join your party?"

"Oh yes!" Aleta said, hobbling toward the door.

"Harriet, you've got three minutes," Judge Jacobi said. "We'll be outside waiting."

The cameraman left with them.

"What was the bet?" she asked her grandmother as Harriet uncuffed her hands and Bertha yanked the jumpsuit off the top of her body slipped a camisole over her head followed by a soft silk flowered blouse.

Harriet undid the leg cuffs and Aleta stepped into her briefs and then her slacks while Harriet set her shoes in front of her feet.

As the two women were helping her, Aleta again asked what the bet was.

"Lyle bet that you'd obey the rules even when you knew Lyle would forgive you for disobeying them," Harriet said.

"That's why you offered me clean clothes," Aleta mused. "What if I'd put them on?"

"Then we'd be doing the reverse of what we're doing," Harriet said.

"You'd have gone to your party in your jumpsuit and leg irons," Bertha added.

"Lyle gambled on my response?" Aleta asked obviously disturbed.

"Lyle doesn't gamble," Harriet said. "He knows you."

"Am I that predictable?" Aleta asked, vexed.

"You're that honorable," Bertha responded warmly. "Welcome home, Aleta!"

Aleta hugged both women.

"Who knows I'm here?"

"Just the four of us," Harriet said.

"And Stanley?"

"You are tonight's surprise. Even Lauren doesn't know," Harriet replied.

"She will never forgive Lyle."

"Sure she will," Bertha assured her. "She loves surprises the same as the rest of us."

Late that night, lying beside her husband in bed, Aleta began to cry uncontrollably.

"Too much, too fast, too unexpected?" he asked putting his arm around her and drawing her toward him.

"You need to wear your pajamas when I need to cry," she scolded.

He handed her a towel.

"You came prepared?"

"I learned from your last pregnancy that you cry unpredictably."

"Where are your pajamas? I put them on you myself."

"And I removed them myself because sometime during the night we are going to have sex."

"We can't," Aleta objected. "Your leg."

"It's healed enough."

"Who says?"

"I say."

"You aren't a doctor."

"Are we done crying?"

"You weren't crying."

"I've been holding you in my arms in a platonic manner. Do you know how difficult it is for a man to hold a beautiful naked woman in his arms and not think about sex?"

"You're not holding me platonically anymore," Aleta quipped.

"You're done crying."

"How do you know?"

"Because you're arguing."

"Did you know Lyle bet on me tonight? I don't like being predictable."

"Aleta, you are anything but predictable. But we can count on you to be honest and honorable and to treat us with dignity and love."

"Wow, Counselor! Who's been teaching you new skills?"

"I love you. I missed you. I want us to enjoy this last evening alone. After tomorrow Jamara won't be taking Gerard home with her. We'll be parents again."

"So this is a mini honeymoon?"

"Are you game?"

"The night is yours," Aleta said happily.

He started with a kiss.

Two hours later he woke her with another.

"Is this going on all night?" she asked as she relaxed in his arms.

"You tell me," he replied. "You're calling the shots."

"I am not!" she protested. "But as long as I'm awake..."

He kissed her with no less passion and desire than he had the first time.

When they'd finished, he said, "Do you want me to make love to you while you're sleeping?"

"Without waking me up?"

"You seem to want both," he said without even a hint of censure.

"Um," she murmured as she drifted off. "Try it next time."

The dawn had just begun to break when Aleta woke from a delicious dream to find that it wasn't a dream.

"I'm awake," she whispered. "But don't stop."

And he didn't.

When he finished, she whispered, "You are a magnificent man!"

"Does that mean you'll make me breakfast?" he asked.

"Other people cook," she said. "I let you have sex with me anytime you want."

"I told you that you called the shots."

"How could I do that? I was asleep."

"Your hand wasn't."

"It's never done that before, has it?"

"No."

"Let's take a shower."

"Why?"

"It's morning."

"It's only six and it's Saturday and we were up late."

She rose saying, "I'll get the water running."

He watched her lithe body leave the room. He reached for his crutches and hobbled into the bathroom. She was leaning against the open shower door waiting for him.

He couldn't believe the surge of desire that overtook him. She smiled when she saw the evidence of his longing.

"This time it's you," she quipped.

"You are an irresistible woman," he responded. "So, it's really your fault."

"Let's take a shower, dry each other off and then go to sleep. I think we've had enough sex," she said.

"Aleta, you are so wrong," he declared firmly.

"That's what you said on our honeymoon," she whispered. "And in just that tone of voice."

Her words reached deep into his mind.

Was it possible to recapture that moment again, he wondered, to erase the trauma of the rapes and the blackening of what was once pure joy in marital intercourse? Such a trauma couldn't be forgotten. It was buried too deep in the soul. It was a part of her now. But was it possible to wash away the last taint from the act of love that the brutal rapes had left in their wake. Was it possible to recapture the spontaneous wholehearted joy they once knew.

The rapes had robbed them both of that. The couplings earlier that night had been more a matter of satisfying sexual needs denied them the past weeks by his hospitalization and her imprisonment. They had come a long way. He'd even thought they'd come all the way back. Now he sensed that she was asking for something more. They had just risen from the marital bed so it wasn't pure animal desire. She had opened a door to a new level.

Stanley entered the shower with her and they kissed as they had that first night–tenderly. He remembered well how slowly he'd moved after that kiss as tentative now as it had been then.

He set the foot of his injured leg on the floor of the shower. The warm water ran down his leg as he put his weight on it. Surprisingly, it didn't hurt. It wouldn't have mattered if it had. If he were to help Aleta relive that moment, recapture that sense of purity that she felt then, he could not be a cripple.

He kissed her again, just as tenderly, his hands cupping her head. They slid down across her shoulders as he bent to kiss her neck. As he continued to caress her he felt her body tremble slightly. Her hands rested on his head as they had that night as it moved lower and lower.

He didn't rush. This wasn't about satisfying his sexual needs or even hers. This was about telling his wife he considered every part of her pure and holy.

With great care he left no part untouched. It was a testimony of his total acceptance of her now as then. While some men would consider such a violation a permanent desecration, Stanley didn't. In his mind it was in the same category as the breaking of the third commandment–taking the Lord's name in vain. In doing so one profaned what was holy; however, the profanity did not alter the holiness of the name. It was inviolate.

Aleta needed to know he truly felt this way for the final healing to take place. He knew he'd told her before, but she was asking again. She'd dared to go deeper. When he rose to kiss her again, he realized she'd been crying.

"We can't make another baby," he said. "We're already done that. You keep rushing things."

She smiled through her tears, "And you never do."

He kissed her then and he felt the same response he'd felt that first night. Their joining was a joyous one. And he knew without a shadow of a doubt that this wife was his again–totally.

The Prophet Series